D0094517

NEW STORIES
FROM THE SOUTH
The Year's Best, 1996

The editor is grateful to her colleague, Memsy Price, for her good taste, good sense, and good advice in all things literary — and otherwise.

Edited by
Shannon Ravenel

NEW STORIES
FROM THE SOUTH

The Year's Best, 1996

Algonquin Books of Chapel Hill

Published by
Algonquin Books of Chapel Hill
Post Office Box 2225
Chapel Hill, North Carolina 27515-2225
a division of
Workman Publishing
708 Broadway
New York, New York 10003

ISSN 0897-9073
ISBN 1-56512-155-4

CONTENTS

PREFACE

R eviewers of this annual series often debate the degree of Southerness of the stories included each year. What, they have asked, makes a story truly eligible for an anthology that identifies itself regionally? Setting, of course. But what if the story's tone or accent doesn't match the reader's expectation? Isn't there such a thing as a truly Southern theme? Shouldn't the old Southern masters still be influencing contemporary imaginations?

Last year's volume was thoughtfully reviewed for the *St. Petersburg Times* by Peter Meinke, himself a contemporary master of the short story. He pointed out that while one of the stories ("Boy Born With Tattoo of Elvis," by Robert Olen Butler) seemed close "to the old Faulkner/O'Connor tradition," most of the others did not. And he went on to write: "One generality that might hold up is that the main influence behind . . . most of the other writers is not William Faulkner, but James Joyce. For better or for worse, the South has joined the larger community."

That's the kind of criticism an anthology of "regional" fiction thrives on. And I hope reviewers will continue to focus on the importance of imagination versus accent because it serves to keep all of us attentive to what is at the heart of good fiction. But, this year reviewers—and readers—could have fun with the question of the "newness" of all the included stories as well as their "Southerness." The first volume of *New Stories from the South,* published in 1986, was introduced with the following paragraph: "Each of the stories in this book first appeared in an American magazine, review, journal, or quarterly. And all of them appeared there within the year preceding selection for this book. So truly, they are all 'new.' "

The same criteria for "newness" hold true with this volume—the eleventh—even though, in addition to the work of fourteen contemporary short story writers, the 1996 collection includes a story by a Southern writer who died thirty-four years ago. That story's 1995 publication—its first appearance and in magazine form—to our great delight, makes "Rose of Lebanon" by William Faulkner eligible for *New Stories from the South: The Year's Best, 1996.*

Until it appeared in *The Oxford American*'s May/June 1995 issue, "Rose of Lebanon" had never seen print. Faulkner wrote it in 1930, a year after he married Estelle Oldham Franklin and took on the support of her two children from her first marriage. His novels had, at that point, earned him almost no money and he hoped to join the ranks of writers like F. Scott Fitzgerald who were selling stories to *The Saturday Evening Post* and *Colliers* for thousands of dollars. In 1938, he put a new title—"A Return"—on a much revised, simpler, and what he perhaps hoped was a more commercial version of the story. Though Faulkner didn't sell "A Return" to a magazine during his lifetime, Joseph Blotner, Faulkner scholar and biographer, included it in the *Uncollected Stories of William Faulkner* (1979). Blotner omitted "The Rose of Lebanon" he said, because "where two treatments of the same short-story material exist, as in 'Rose of Lebanon' and 'A Return,' the one that seemed the better of the two has been used."

Mark Smirnoff, editor of *The Oxford American*, wondered one day in 1994 "if there were any unpublished Faulkner manuscripts lying about." Since Oxford, Mississippi, Faulkner's hometown, is also Mr. Smirnoff's magazine's hometown, he asked the local experts, who put him on the trail of "Rose of Lebanon." He read it, liked it much better than "A Return," and so arranged to publish it in his magazine. Mr. Smirnoff disagrees with Mr. Blotner not only about which of the two versions is better, but also about whether the two are truly different versions of the same story, saying: "'Rose of Lebanon,' though written eight years before 'A Return,' is not a rough draft. It is instead a completely different, and I think, deeply superior interpretation of how the story should be told. The language in both, except for a few lines of dialogue and a few phrases, is strikingly different. Minor characters in one story are major characters in the other (& vice versa)."

What strikes me as remarkable about "Rose of Lebanon" is its daringly experimental handling of the story's heart. Faulkner's management of the pivotal scene—at an elegantly laden Memphis dining room table—is as "new" in its approach as any fiction being written today. As for the rest of the story, Faulkner dodges the obvious throughout "Rose of Lebanon" and, true to his form, requires very careful reading if we are not to miss the point. And in this story, the point is of special interest, having to do with how reenactment—or artistic reinvention—of the past must do more than simply validate that past. Faulkner sets us down at the Memphis dinner party so that we can see for ourselves how re-creation imbues the past with new romantic vitality, new meaning, new life. How extraordinary to watch it happen in what is indeed—in every respect—a great new story from the South.

No wonder that thirty-four years after his death, fiction writers —and not just Southern ones—are still influenced by William Faulkner (and I believe most of them are, even if *also* by James Joyce). Faulkner's contribution to fiction is as Shakespeare's to drama. "Rose of Lebanon" catches him in the act of refining that contribution.

—*Shannon Ravenel*
Chapel Hill, North Carolina
1996

PUBLISHER'S NOTE

The stories reprinted in *New Stories from the South: The Year's Best, 1996* were selected from American short stories published in magazines issued between January and December 1995. Shannon Ravenel annually consults a list of ninety-five nationally distributed American periodicals and makes her choices for this anthology based on criteria that include original publication first-serially in magazine form and publication as short stories. Direct submissions are not considered.

NEW STORIES
FROM THE SOUTH

The Year's Best, 1996

William Faulkner

ROSE OF LEBANON

(from *The Oxford American*)

I

D r Blount stopped his coupe before a two-acre sprawl of scrolled and gabled house. It had a great amount of plate glass and fanlights, set among neat big trees on a neat, big lawn; the street itself was neat and broad and quiet. The trees on the lawn were mostly oaks and maples, the oaks still bare, though the maples were already swelling into feathery russet against the late February sky. It was a gusty, chilly, thick day across which came as from a great distance, rather of time than space, the faint sound of the city, of Memphis.

The coupe was of a popular make sold on the installment plan, though Blount's widowed grandmother and the maiden sister of his father, with whom he lived in a house a little like the one which he was now approaching, owned two clumsy limousines of esoteric make that used to be advertised by the inch in the magazines twenty-five years ago.

He went up the concrete walk and rang the bell. An old negro man, in a white serving jacket which looked as though he had borrowed it for the emergency when the bell rang, opened the door. "How you, Mr Gavin?" he said.

"I'm fine, Ned," Blount said. The negro had a slick, saddle-colored head fringed with gray hair. "How are you?"

"Aint so good," the negro said. "We thought maybe you wasn't coming this evening." Blount took off his overcoat. He was slight and dapper, in a dark suit that might have cost twenty-five dollars or a hundred and twenty-five. He was dark, with a long, impractical face, thirty-seven years old and a bachelor. He lived in the house in which his grandfather had been born. It was in the country then, though it now sat on a street named after an inferior flower, surrounded by subdivisions of spurious Georgian houses bought and sold among themselves by Main Street and Madison Avenue Jews. He lived there with his grandmother and his aunt and three negro servants. The grandmother was a fat woman who lived in a wheel chair, though she had a good appetite, coming to the table in the wheel chair, where she would unfold her napkin, refold it and smooth it along the table edge and lay neatly upon it her small, plump, soft, ringed, useless hands. "You may commence now, Gavin," she would say.

Blount left the negro in the hall, and mounted the stair. The stair was broad, heavy, and gloomy, the hall broad and heavy and gloomy too, and a little too warm to be healthy. The upper hall was identical, faced with doors of dark and gloomy wood. He entered a room where a woman lay on a day-bed drawn across the hearth, with a small table and one chair drawn up beside it. The woman was wrapped in a steamer rug. Her hair on a white pillow was perfectly white.

"I had begun to think you were not coming today," she said.

"Yessum," Blount said. "I was late. I met Ran Gordon this afternoon at the Battery." He sat down, on the chair beside the table. "And you'll never guess it."

"He's made another million," the woman said.

"Yes," Blount said. He spoke in an eager, oblivious tone, leaning a little forward. "I reckon so. You'll never guess it, not in a year." He talked, rapidly, leaning forward, in that eager, diffuse tone. "It was the men that got whipped in that war; if they'd just got out of the way and let the women, the women like—" The door opened. The negro in the white jacket entered, without knocking, carrying a tray bearing a coffee pot, a cup, a decanter, a flared, heavy wineglass almost as big as a goblet. He set the tray on the table.

"Cherry Bounce done give out," he said. "This here's Yankee's Head, but it'll bounce you, too." He filled the coffee cup at the woman's hand, and the wineglass from the decanter at Blount's, and went and stood beside the fire. "Aint seed your Grammaw in some time," he said to Blount.

"She was here not six weeks ago," the woman said to the negro. "You brought the coffee up, yourself."

"You thinking about Miss Levinia," the negro told her. Miss Levinia was Blount's aunt. She was a thin, indefatigable woman. She was president of the Confédération Française, a woman's club which exchanged volumes of the *Mercure de France*, of Paul Fort and Mallarmé and Henri Becque. They met on stated afternoons at the Country Club (the oldest one, the Country Club; the others all had designations, names or locations) where they drank coffee and talked in English of their sons and daughters, nieces and nephews, of the Junior League and the Nonconnah Guards. "It was Miss Levinia that come to see us," the negro said. "About Christmas time. But you aint seed Mrs Blount outen that house since last summer. And you aint going to see um till summer come again." He watched Blount sip from the glass. "How you like that Yankee's Head?"

"It's fine," Blount said.

"Aint as good as that Bounce was. But Bounce all gone now. We didn't make no more this winter. I told um it was getting low."

"No you didn't," the woman said. "You didn't tell me until about two days ago."

"Just listen at her," the negro said. "I told her long before Christmas. But you cant do nothing with um. I done found that out long time ago." He went toward the door. "I reckon I better get on down and see about them kitchen niggers."

"I wish you would," the woman said. "I wish you would stay out of here."

"Yessum," the negro said. He went out; again he opened the door and looked in. "When you get home, Mr Gavin, you tell your Grammaw I inquired for her kind health and say for um to come and see us."

"I will," Blount said. The door closed again. He turned back to the woman, his mouth already open for speech, but she spoke first.

"How much did Ran Gordon make?"

"Make what?" Blount said. Then he said: "It's better than that. Lewis Randolph is coming back to town."

"Lewis—?" The woman's voice ceased. She looked at him. Her hair quite white, her face waxy, flaccid, shapeless, the eyes like the coals of two cigars which might at a single breath be drawn into life.

"Yessum. She's coming back to town; it's only been sixty-five years." He talked rapidly, the half-empty glass in his hand, leaning a little forward. The woman watched him with that dark, arrested, intent expression about her eyes.

"How much money have you made this year?" she said.

"—what? What did you—"

"How much money did you ever make?"

"I buy my own clothes, and pay for the car."

"Which car? The twenty-one dollars a month on that little one of your own?"

"How did you know it is twenty-one dollars?" They stared at one another. She had seen him within a week of his birth. Her eyes were inscrutable, speculative. She watched the astonishment fade from his face, but before it was gone, he was talking again. "Not since sixty-five years; not since she came up from Mississippi, sixty miles in a muddy carriage in December, to the Guards' Ball in '61."

"I know that," the woman said. "I was there." Her voice was impatient, a little testy. "Those balls used to be full of Mississippi and Arkansas country belles. I've heard they still are."

"Yes," Blount said; "all right." Then he was talking again, leaning a little forward into the firelight, the half-empty glass in his hand.

II

Almost every afternoon he walked North along the levee, from the same point to the same point. He descended the levee, the steep pitch of worn cobbles, at the Beale Street landing, and followed it and mounted the bluff, to the Battery. This was a small park, with tended grass and walks and flower beds, with a low rock revetment along the bluff studded with bronze tablets bearing serried names, and through the apertures of which rusting iron cannons with spiked touch-holes gloomed down upon the river below. Here he would stand for a time, among the quiet and rusting guns and the careful pyramids of ammunition, the austere (yet florid too) bronze tablets, on one of which he could read the name which he now bore. Beneath the bluff lay the railroad tracks, the cobbled slant of the levee, the shabby and infrequent steamboats warped into shabby landings, taking on shabby and meagre cargoes bound for inaccessible destinations which scarcely scarred any landscape, whose names were on no maps. The boats lay along the levee, with scaling and rust-streaked sides, with grandiloquent names in fading four-foot letters across counter and wheel-box, derided by shrieking apparitions of locomotives and pullman cars fleeing back and forth, to Chicago in twenty hours, New Orleans in ten. From the parapet where he would stand, the river was now almost invisible, hidden by what was, thirty years ago, a shoal, and then a scarce-broached sand-bar, and what was now an island bearing a virgin growth of willow trees among which nomad squatters lived in houseboats hauled or floated ashore and in actual houses built on piles above the sand. But almost invisible was the stream itself, up and down which in '62 and '63 the Federal gallipots steamed, firing into the bluff with Parrott howitzers until the city fell; whereupon the Rebels captured the gallipots and steamed up and down in turn and fired in turn with the same Parrotts, into the grim and abiding and oblivious bluff named after a vanished race.

He had inherited his practice, as a lawyer inherits his; a practice which took him on regular and leisurely rounds to smug, well-to-do houses, where old women overtaken at last by indolence and rich food, who had outlived his father and some of whom would outlive him, received him in close bedrooms where the elegant heavy walnut of the seventies gleamed in the pulsing firelight, and where, like another old woman himself, they would talk also of sons and daughters and the Junior League and the Nonconnah Guards. This was a semi-military organization with a skeleton staff of regular army officers and a hierarchate of elective social officers with semi-military designations, the highest of which was that of Flag-Corporal, an office which Blount had held for fourteen years. In 1859 it had been organised by fifty-one young men, bachelors. They gave the first ball that December. In 1860 it had become a National Guard unit; at the ball of that year the men wore blue dress uniforms, with the yellow stripe of cavalry. The membership had grown to 104. In 1861, at the third ball, the men were in gray, their new kits stacked in a dressing-room, a train at the station ready to leave for Virginia at midnight. The armory was filled that night, not only with dancers, but with older guests, parents, and relatives. At the end of the hall, above the band platform, mute nails still shaped the ripped-down Federal flag, while in its place was fixed the new flag which was not quite yet familiar; beneath it the figures, the gray uniforms and the flared crinoline and fans and scarves, formed and turned. At half past eleven the music—three fiddles, two guitars, a clarinet played by negroes—stopped. The major, the late major in the United States Army, cleared the floor. The men fell in in single file against the wall, the major in front, facing across the empty floor the older guests. The major's uniform was no different from the ones of the men, without insignia save for a crimson sash and a cavalry sabre upon which he now leaned. At the far end of the hall the girls, the late partners, had gathered into still another distinct group. The room was high, a little chilly, looming, the walls lined with improvised candelabra and oil lamps. The major began to speak.

"A lot of you all have already gone. I'm not talking to them. A lot of you all will have made your plans to go. I'm not talking to them. But there are some that can go, that believe it will be over by summer. I'm talking to them." His voice was not loud, yet it carried distinct and sonorous in the cavernous room. Outside, it had begun to snow, though as fast as they fell, the flakes died into the deep, churned, icy mud. "You've heard of Virginia, but some of you haven't seen it. Washington. New York. But haven't seen it." In the cavernous silence, the tenseness, the expectancy, his voice had a profound, sonorous, meaningless quality like the sound of a bee trapped in a tin bucket. ". . . empowered by the President of the Confederate States of America. . . ."

They shouted, the guests, the older men, the voices of the women shrill; that same shout without words that was to be gaunted and worn thin and shrill by many battlefields, to outlast the war itself and be carried westward across the Mississippi by veterans and the sons of veterans and of the slain, to rush, punctuated by galloping hooves and pistol shots, across the dusty plazas of frontier towns. Before it had ceased the music was playing again, a shrill tune too fast for dancing, as though composed for highland pipes. The spectators saw the girls, who had been clumped at the end of the room, moving now toward the gray line in a sort of order, looking in their flaring, delicate dresses like a series of inverted vases as they advanced, blotting the gray line from sight, kissing the men in turn, moving on, so that when the gray line began to come into sight again, against each tunic there was a red rose like a pistol wound. For a little while longer there was order, then gray and crinoline became commingled, inextricable, from which came the shrieks of girls, shrieks of terror not so much feigned and not so very feared, and from all parts of the room voices began to sing with the swift fiddles, the guitars, the shrill clarinet:

Wish I was in the land of cotton,
Simmon seed and sandy bottom,
Look awayyyyyyyy,
Look awayyyy
Look awayyy, Dixie Land.

The major had not moved. He leaned on the sabre, looking at the guests, the civilians, the young men in formal black. "Now, boys," he said, "who wants to spit into the Potomac river before Christmas?"

III

"Lewis Randolph was one of the girls there that night," Blount said. "She was one of the girls that kissed a hundred and four men. Coming all the way up from Mississippi in a muddy carriage paved with hot bricks—they'd have to stop now and then and build a fire with the pine wood they brought with them, the niggers, I mean, and heat the bricks again—to kiss a hundred and four men, so she could give a red rose to Charley Gordon. I dont remember Grandfather very well, but I have heard Granny tell about Lewis Randolph. Maybe it's because Granny was a toast of the town herself. Maybe it's because, even when they get to be ninety, they do not realise that a woman fills and empties the objective shape of a toast just as people fill and empty a telephone booth in a busy railroad station, engendering with the same motion the same sound of the same bell. Anyway, when they have been toasts themselves, they are tolerant, almost unselfish about other women. She told me about how Grandfather told about how Charley Gordon would come to town two days before she was due, from down in Mississippi too, bringing with him a negro boy and a mule. On the day the carriage was due, from daylight on, I hope from daylight on; it must have been from daylight on,—that nigger boy squatting and shivering in the December rain, beside the mule at the roadside, with wrapped in an oilcloth cape a bouquet as large as a yard-broom, cut and borrowed and bribed out of private pits; and Charley Gordon himself a little further along the road, beyond a thicket, in the rain too, waiting from maybe daybreak too, to ride out bareheaded when the carriage came up, in sopping linen and a sopping coat."

"I always said that he was a fool," the woman on the bed said.

"Was it to her you said that?" Blount said. The woman watched him, the face on the propped pillows, in the steady firelight, bloated and waxlike. "Would you say it now, to either of them, if he was still alive? You couldn't say it to him or to his kind, anyhow. Maybe because it would be true. But it's too late to tell them that, now. They all galloped bareheaded with brandished sabres when they had them, but anyway galloping, off the stage altogether, into a lot more rain than a December drizzle; maybe into somewhere else where they could bang themselves to pieces again, like puppets banging themselves to pieces against the painted board-and-plaster, the furious illusions of gardens and woods and dells; maybe to meet brighter faces than Lewis Randolph looking out a carriage window halted in a muddy road. Maybe to him she wasn't anything, anyway, but the sound of the words, Lewis Randolph, above the glasses at Gaston's. Had you ever thought of that?"

"I have told her that they were both fools," the woman on the bed said.

Blount ceased. He looked at her, the flaccid face wakened somehow, the eyes intent on his face, her body backthrust a little, as though he had offered to strike her; her eyes, coming alive for the moment like the two cigars drawn into life, not courageous but invincible, not victorious yet undefeated. "Your name might have gone around above those same glasses too. Dont tell me you have ever forgotten that you ever believed that." Her face died while he looked at it, the eyes died; again on the propped pillows was the face of an old woman, tired with overlong looking and seeing. "I know that men and women are different. It's a deliberate provision. Through no fault nor control of their own, women produce men children, who ennoble them. Not the maternity: that's an attribute, both crown and chastisement, of any female. A girl-child is mothered and fathered and grandsired by her contemporary generation; a man-child by all time that preceded him."

"I dont see what this has to do with Lewis Randolph."

Blount finished the drink, set the glass down and reached for the decanter. But he began to talk again before he uncapped the decanter. "You were there, that night. You kissed a hundred and four men that night, too. That night when she and Charley Gordon found they could not live without one another. You were probably at the station and heard the noise when the train moved and she on it, with Charley Gordon's cape above her ball dress, and she went to Knoxville in that day coach full of soldiers and heated by a wood-stove stoked by a negro bodyservant, and the next day they were married by a minister who happened to be a private in a regiment waiting there to entrain, just in time for her to take the next train south, back to Mississippi, with a letter from Charley Gordon to his mother written on the back of a bill-of-fare from the station eating-room."

The eyes of the woman on the bed were closed. "There were other girls at that ball prettier than Lewis Randolph," she said in a tired tone.

"And (I'll say it for you) saw that train leave without them on it, with a soldier's cloak above a hooped ball gown." He was smoking a cigarette now. "She went back to Mississippi, to her new home. It was a big, square house twenty-five miles from any town. It had flower beds, a rose garden. When she got there, with the letter on the bill-of-fare, her father-in-law was organising a regiment. She and her mother-in-law embroidered the colors, with negro girls to pick and iron the bright, fragmentary silk. From the high, quiet room where they worked they could hear thick boots in the hall all day long, and voices from the diningroom around the punch bowl. The lot was full of strange horses; the lawn, the park, spotted with tents and littered with refuse. In the evenings there would be a bonfire on the lawn, its glare red and fierce upon the successive orators; up to the porch where the women sat or stood the voices came, orotund and sonorous and endless. On the shadowy porch the two women would stand then, their arms about one another, in the darkness lighted by the remote glare darkly too, touching but not speaking, not even looking at one another. Then the regiment went away; the talk, the boots in the hall; the rubbish and litter on the lawn was healed by the first November rains, leaving only the scarred earth, the trampled and broken walks and flower beds. Then the house was quiet again with only the two women in it and the voices of the negroes, the mellow shouts, the laughter, the sounds of chopping wood, coming peacefully up from the quarters on the monotonous twilight.

"She was an only child. She was born in a house like the one she now lived in. They might have been interchangeable: the planks, the flower beds, the negroes. Her own father wore the same broadcloth, the same hats and boots. When she was fifteen he took her in the heavy carriage, the one with the removable brick floor, to a seminary for young ladies in Oxford, where she spent three years. When she was eighteen, they took her to Memphis, to her first ball. They stayed at Gaston's Hotel, and on the night of the first Guards' Ball in 1859 she saw Charley Gordon for the first time. Two years later she got off that troop train in Knoxville and was married in the station, surrounded by soldiers in new gray, by bright, not yet familiar regimental flags. She had not slept in thirty hours, yet she stood there in her ball gown, with not a hair turned and not a bow misplaced. She looked like something made in an expensive shop, of lace and bright frosting, and turned upside down in the center of a hollow square of troops all young and none of whom had ever heard a bullet; by strange faces which, for all their youth and inexperience and perhaps foreboding, wore none the less of doubt for that. I imagine she was the only calm one there. Because women have lived so long when they begin to breathe. While men have to be born anew each hour. Each second."

He reached the decanter again. This time he filled the glass. The woman on the pillow had not moved or opened her eyes. The firelight pulsed quietly upon her face. The windows were fading with dusk, the wet, thick February twilight. "So the two of them lived in that big house. In the late fall of '62 a carriage came, the first one to enter the gates in almost six months. She did not recognise it until it reached the house, then she recognised the driver. It was from her old home, three days away. She had not seen her parents since the previous spring, and she would not see her father again. 'Pappy is dead,' she told her mother-in-law. 'I'll have to go home for a while.'

"When she got home, she found her mother in bed. The mother had fever. 'The silver,' the mother said. 'We've got to get it buried.'

"'All right. We will. We will.'

"'They killed your father. Now they'll come down here. We must bury it.' It rained that night. The daughter went to bed in her old room, hearing the rain. After midnight she was wakened by a negro woman.

"'It's Mistis,' the negress said. She found her mother in the kitchen, a cloak over her nightgown, wet and muddy, her hair draggled across her flushed face. She was unconscious. The negroes had found her in the garden, trying to dig a hole, beside her was a silver coffee service wrapped in a quilt. Three nights later she died of pneumonia. The rain had not ceased; they buried her in it, in the family burying-ground.

"It rained all that winter. I remember how Granny used to tell about that winter, with the sound of the guns from the river batteries, a thick slow sound, and then the Yankee troops in the city and the patrols riding the streets at night. Mississippi must have been full of them; that was when she began to carry the derringer in the pocket of her calico dress. She was back with her mother-in-law then. Then it was almost summer again. One evening a riding horse and a spring wagon came in the gates. Her father-in-law was on the horse. Her husband was in the wagon, on a shuck mattress. He was weak, but mending; but it was six months before he left again to join Van Dorn's cavalry. The father-in-law was already gone, into Bragg's army, captured, and was now in the Rock Island prison. Again the two women were alone in the house, with fewer negro voices from the quarters and the kitchen now. The negroes left one by one, stealing away at night, going to the cities; men and women hanging around the Federal army kitchens and the barracks of the troops, the men waiting for the forty acres and the mule; the women, their desires and needs more simple and more immediate, not having to wait.

"The next year, Ran was born. There was no doctor, but they got along without one, only that night the mother-in-law fell down the stairs while on her way to the kitchen to heat water, and from that night till her death she did not leave her bed. There was still one old negro man and two women. The father-in-law was still in the Rock Island prison, as far as they knew, but one night in the meantime Van Dorn rode into Holly Springs and burned Grant's stores, and Charley Gordon was killed. Shot off his horse. Something about a chicken roost. Ran told me. Anyway, it was dark and close and hurried, with the red sky behind them and a close yard full of surging, excited horses and hurried men; I reckon they were robbing the chicken roost. Then someone fired point blank into them with a shot gun.

"Ran was big enough to remark things, to remember things. Or so he claims. But they are probably things the negroes told him afterward. He said that his mother didn't tell him any of them. He said he didn't talk to her much, because he was afraid of her, afraid to ask her. Like the negroes were afraid of her, the three negroes who were still there when he was big enough to remember. It was them, not his mother, who told him about his grandfather, the Rock Island prisoner. It was almost a year after the surrender, and almost a year since the grandmother had died in the room which she had not left since she fell down the stairs on the night Ran was born. One day his grandfather came home. He came on foot. The negroes said he looked like a hant, wasted, with no hair and no teeth, and he wouldn't talk at all, and the negroes would have to clean the floors and rugs after him like a puppy or a kitten or a child. He stayed there two years, not talking to anyone, not telling anyone where he had been during that year after the war stopped, refusing to take off his clothes to go to bed. One morning one of the negroes came into the kitchen, where Ran's mother was preparing some infant mess for him out of whatever it was they had to make it with. 'Marster's gone,' the negress said.

"'You mean, dead?' his mother said; the negroes told him she did not even stop stirring the dish.

"'Nome. Just gone. Unk Awce been looking for him since early. But cant nobody find him.'

"That was the sort of thing that Ran meant by remembering. Like when he told me of lying in the shady corner of a fence while his mother, in the calico dress with the pocket where the derringer stayed, and a calico sunbonnet, stood with folded arms, not touching the fence, watching a negro plow. 'And he plowed fast, too, while she was there,' Ran said. Or, about lying, wrapped in a quilt on the frozen ground on the lee side of a boiling iron kettle, his mother stirring the kettle while the three negroes flayed and dressed a hog. Then one day—he could have taken no cognizance of war or peace, or of any actual and definite date—he knew that, not only was the derringer missing from his mother's pocket, but that it had been missing for some time. 'It was just gone,' he told me. 'Like there wasn't any further use for it. I knew that Yankees had been there once, but even the negroes would not tell me what had happened. "Ask her to tell you herself when you man enough to hear it," they told me. But they knew that I knew that I would never be that man. So I dont know what happened. Maybe she shot him or them and the negroes buried them in the pasture. I just knew that the derringer was gone, without knowing when I had missed it. As if the need was gone at last.'

"Which it obviously had," Blount said. He drank. The woman on the bed had not stirred nor opened her eyes. "Though what had happened when the Yankee patrol, or maybe a single scout, came there and found a white woman and an infant and three frightened negroes. . . . I hope she didn't shoot him. Think of it: a Yankee, a *Yankee*, to get shot by Lewis Randolph. By a hand in honor of which men, *men*, had drunk glasses of fine whiskey; that until four years ago, had never laid a stick on a fire.

"When Ran left home he was fifteen. She (she was still thin; hard as nails, probably, and sunburned, in the same calico, with the same eyes which he had rememhered watching the plowing negro across the fence) had taught him to read and to write, and that was all. He left home in a cart made out of the front end of a collapsed buggy, drawn by a mule and driven by a negro woman, the old man having died at last, which carried him to a crossroads store. From there he went on afoot, bumming rides when he could, to the county town and the railroad. He had a homewoven shirt and a black gum toothbrush and a baking powder can of homemade soap tied in a handkerchief. He had never seen a town before, or a railroad. He came to Memphis in a box car, sixteen hours without food, light, anything much; he didn't even dare to ask if the car was going to Memphis. Twelve months later he wrote his mother that he had saved two hundred dollars and that she could now come on to him. She wrote back that she was not coming. Two years after he left he went back home on a visit. He had a thousand dollars then. The place had not changed: the big, scaling house, the faint traces of flower beds on what had been a formal lawn; the two negro women; his mother (she had apparently not aged a day) in the same calico, watching a negro boy plowing the same mule beyond a fence, the plow moving at a good pace, too. He did not see her again for seven years. He was married then, cashier in the bank, owned his own house. He found her as he had left her. Again she refused to come to Memphis, even on a visit. 'I dont like cities,' she said. After that he saw her perhaps each two or three years, because he was getting to be president of the bank and such, with a son and a daughter and his wife with her eye already on the Junior League and maybe the Guards. She changed very little when he would see her: the same calico, though the house was falling down. She let him repair it a little, though not much, even when he was a millionaire.

"One day (he was fifty himself, with a grown family) he got a letter. It was written on a jagged piece of wrapping paper, in pencil, in a crabbed, terrific hand like a palsied schoolboy's. He went home (he went home by car then) and found the neighbor in the house and his mother in bed. She had had a mild stroke, yet on the pillow her face was still indomitable, cold, a little coldly outraged at the failure of her own flesh. He moved her anyway then, though he could not get her to make the trip in his car. He had to get a carriage for her, had to buy it. And, even though she was still helpless, he could not get her nearer to Memphis than that bungalow out there on the Pigeon Roost road. He bought that, too, the carriage halted in the road in front of it. She has been there twelve years, in that ten acres of orchard and garden and chicken runs. She has never seen Memphis since she left it that night sixty-five years ago on a Rebel troop train.

"So this afternoon I met Ran. 'She's coming in to dinner tomorrow night,' he told me. 'I have persuaded her at last. But early; six o'clock; she insisted on six, because she believes that she must get back home by eight-thirty. But I had a time finding a carriage for her. There is an Italian truck-farmer that owed me a note. He let me have one, but it had to be repaired and painted.' And that's where I have been," Blount said. "I have been with Ran, seeing how the carriage was getting along, watching them stripe the wheels." He held the glass in his hand. He had not touched it since he refilled it. The windows were completely dark. The woman in the bed had not moved. On the pillow her face was still, the eyes closed, the motion of the intermittent firelight giving it more than ever an appearance of immobility. "As it will look when she is dead," Blount said to himself. "Like the faces of women in this country, in the South, have looked and will look after they have died, and will die for a little longer yet but not much longer, for a lot of years." Then he said aloud: "I had believed . . . feared—I was afraid that I would never have sent flowers to Lewis Randolph. Could never have. That's a summing, a totality, of breath."

IV

She sat at her son's right at the long, heavy table lined by two rows of formal black-and-white and gleaming and flashing bosoms, in the long, heavy diningroom: a small woman in black that was not silk, without any ornament, not even a wedding ring. On her head was a frilled cap of coarse, clean white stuff that negro women wear. Her face was not an old face, in the sense of slackened muscles and flesh; it was old in the sense that wood or stone becomes old, as though scoured down upon itself by the sheer impact of long weather, the passing of sheer days and hours of time. Her eyes were dark; her hands a little stiff, with gnarled knuckles; from the instant when she entered the room and took her place beside her big, broad iron-gray son, in the almost furtive gesture with which her hand came out and touched the ranked silver and withdrew again while her covert glance took in the other faces to remark if anyone noticed the action, there was about her that alertness, that watchful, sidelong stiffness of a woman born and bred in a hill cabin.

At first they made much of her, the women especially urgent, smooth, deferent, and she still sitting beside her son, her soup untasted before her, answering now and then in a cold final voice, in a single word when possible. Then her son intervened and they took the cue, the talk becoming general, and presently she began to eat. She took up the soup spoon and looked at it and put it down and took up a teaspoon and began to eat, putting the whole spoon in her mouth. She did it, discarded the proper spoon and took the other, not as though by mistake or indecision, but as though by prompt and deliberate design.

Dr Blount was opposite her across the table. He had been given his choice of places. "I'd rather be where I can see her face," he said. Most of the guests were young people. "She wont want to meet a lot of fogies, be bothered about Yankees and the war," the son said. "Besides, they wouldn't be any novelty, change, for her. Next to her though was a contemporary, a man who remembered the Yankees in the city; presently Blount saw that they were talking, and about the war. "Conditions were different in the country, I suppose," the man said. "Worse than here."

"The trouble is," Blount said. He leaned a little above the table. "The trouble is, we could never keep them in the right proportions. Like a cook with too much material. If we could have just kept the proportion around ten or twenty Yankees to one of us, we could have handled them. It was when they got to be a thousand to one, or ten or twelve Yankees to a woman and maybe a child and a handful of scared niggers—" He leaned a little forward, his soup too untasted yet. From across the table she watched him. She was chewing a piece of bread. She continued to chew with that careful, deliberate motion of the toothless. Gordon looked at Blount, then at his mother. Blount leaned forward, his face eager, diffuse. "When just a few of them came around to houses away back in the country, where the folks should even have been safe from Yankees; slipping around back doors because they knew the men were gone, the scarecrows without shoes and without ammunition charging the other hundred thousand of them without even wanting less odds—"

She was looking at Blount, still chewing. She ceased to chew and glanced swiftly both ways along the table, her face composed, granite-like. She put her hands on the table and thrust her chair back a little. "Mother—" Gordon said, rising a little also. "Here, Blount—You folks—"

But she was not leaving the table. She was talking. "It was just five of them that I ever saw. Mymie said there were some more in front, still on their horses, but it was just five of them that came around the house, walking. They came to the kitchen door and walked in. Walked right into my kitchen, without even knocking. Mymie had just come back through the house, running and hollering, saying the yard was full of Yankees, and I was just turning from the stove, where I was heating some milk for him"— without moving, with a pause in her speech or a change of inflection she indicated her son—"for his bottle. I had just said, 'Hush that yelling and take that child up off the floor,' when those five tramps came into my kitchen, without knocking."

"You, Mother," Gordon said, half risen, leaning forward too.

She was sitting well back from the table now, her hands on the edge of the table. She was looking at Blount, at the face leaning opposite hers across the table, the two of them: the one cold, controlled; the other wild, eager, like something poised that was fine and bright and of no particular value, that when it fell, it would break all to pieces. "The pan of boiling milk was on the stove, like this. I took it up just like this—" She and Blount rose at the same instant, rigid, erect, like on the same wire. She took up her bowl of soup and threw it at Blount's head. "And I said—" They faced one another with that furious rigidity of puppets, oblivious of the very stage, the miniature boards and tinsel wings within which they created their furious illusion; for the moment the whole huge, ugly, rich room was reduced to the dimensions of a Punch and Judy stage. In her hand she now held a fruit knife, not clutched by the handle like a dagger, but buried somehow in her forward-thrust fist so that the small bright blade protruded level and rigid like the barrel of a small pistol. Standing so, facing Blount above a silence too sudden to yet be consternation or even astonishment, she said to him what she had said to the five Yankees sixty-five years ago, in the same language, in the strong, prompt, gross obscenity of a steamboat mate.

V

From a window ten minutes later Blount and Gordon watched the car drive away, taking her back home. She wouldn't stay, even to finish her dinner. For maybe a full minute she stood there beside the table, clutching the fruit knife in her fist, with on her face that expression which people say that sleepwalkers wear when suddenly wakened, facing Dr Blount's still rigid and erect and dripping head and shoulders, while the silence became astonishment and then became a single shout of laughter, hysterical, relieved, and exultant; for maybe another half minute she stood there, looking from one roaring or shrieking face to another, then she turned and left the room. Dr Blount followed along his side of the table, running, but she passed him at the door. Gordon followed her, and found her in the room where they had gathered before dinner. She had sat down on the first chair she came to. She looked up at him, her face unmoved. Her voice was level. "I want to go home."

"Yes," he said. "All right. But Blount—"

"I didn't," she said. "I dont—"

"He knows you didn't mean it. He is to blame. He knows that. He wants to apologise." She was not looking at him now. She sat, quiet and small, in the chair, her face turned aside but not lowered.

"I want to go home," she said again, in the same tone. Then he heard her draw a long breath. "I reckon I might ride in the car."

"Sure," Gordon said. He believed that it was because she was ashamed, as a child is ashamed when it has been tricked by grown people into an unwitting violation of its own sense of dignity. "The car will get you home quicker. You dont want to see Blount? He can come in here; you wont have—"

"I want to go home," she said.

"All right. You wait here. I'll have the car sent up."

He left her. When he returned, she had her hat and coat on, sitting as before, in the same straight, hard chair. "We can go out the side door," he said. "You wont have to meet anybody that way. But I wouldn't worry about that. There are words like that in all the books nowadays. Without half the reason you had. But where you ever—" he stopped, holding his face smooth. But she did not look up.

When the car moved on and he returned to the house, he could hear the voices in the diningroom, the hysterical laughter which was abating slowly in recurrent surges and gusts. Blount met him at the door. "She asked me to—" Gordon said.

"You're lying," Blount said. "She didn't ask you to tell me any such thing. By heaven, I am the same kind of folks she is; you're the one that's an interloper. I'm nearer Charley Gordon's son than you are." Through the window they watched the tail-lamp of the car pass down the drive. "I know why she wanted to go back in the car; you dont know that. I know about that derringer too, now. It wasn't that she found she didn't need it anymore; it was because she found she didn't deserve to be protected by a clean bullet, the clean bullet which Charley Gordon would have approved. She learned that she could be tricked and surprised into language which she didn't know she knew, that Charley Gordon didn't know that she knew, and that niggers and Yankees had heard it. She believed that now the whole Yankee army would pass the house and they would say, 'That's where that hill-billy woman lives that cussed Jim and Joe and them.' By heaven," he said, looking out the dark window, where the ruby light had disappeared. "She kissed a hundred and four men in one night once, and she gave Charley Gordon a son. But, by heaven, it was Gavin Blount she threw a soup plate at."

VI

In the car, she sat in the exact middle of the seat. She had never travelled so fast before, and the swift glimpses of passing lights, the high, half-seen back-sweep of trees against the lighter darkness of sky added to her feeling of exhilaration, of triumph, of speed. "Maybe he rode this fast," she said to herself. "Except for the sound of the horses, the galloping. And with the glare yonder, it might be the fire of the warehouses." The car went steadily, swift, almost noiseless. "And smooth," she said. "Than a horse. And warm. And I aint going to sleep tonight. I know I aint."

When she reached her home and got out of the car and was admitted out of the quiet, chill darkness by the negro girl who lived with her, she would not go to bed, though it was already a good hour after the time when she usually lay down. "I want to sec about the chickens," she said.

"You come on to bed," the girl said. "What you want to wake the chickens up for?"

"Get me a cup of feed," she said.

"At this time of night? You come on to bed, now, Miss Lewis—"

"Let me alone. Get me a cup of feed."

There was an enclosed passage from the back porch to the chicken house. She turned a light switch beside the kitchen door, whereupon a light came on inside the chicken house, the house itself coming into squat, rectilinear view. She carried the cup of cracked corn and entered the chicken house, into stale warmth, a sudden shifting of white huddled shapes on the roosting poles, and cries of raucous protest. She scattered the corn and with a stick she prodded the chickens down from the roosts, where they huddled again with cries disconsolate and cacophonous, pecking now and then at the corn with blundering, half-hearted thrusts. "Go on," she said; "eat." But they wouldn't eat. She stood among them for a while longer, until they turned and began to blunder back onto the poles again, flapping and leaving the corn untouched. She went out and closed [the door] and returned up the passage, to the porch, and turned [off] the light. It was chilly on the porch, and dark save for a light in the kitchen. This also was worked by a switch near the door and she turned it out and stood on the porch again, still in her coat and hat. Then there was no light anywhere; on all sides the countryside lay quiet and dark under the sky. She couldn't even see the hen house. She found the switch again; again the chicken house squatted into pale relief, the flat, neat, white-washed walls, the good windows, the patent doors. "Maybe if there had just been a light in that one, that night in Holly Springs," she said, not loud. "So he could have seen. . . . And I aint going to sleep tonight. I know that." She snapped the switch again; again the darkness came down, like a black blanket coming down for an instant before she began to see a little in the dark, since the sky was a little lighter. It lay thick and close above the dark earth, holding between them the gusty rushing of damp wind among the trees, invisible too. But the sound was there, the long rushing surges dying away like a sudden rush of horsemen, so that, inextricable from the feeling of exultation which she knew was not going to let her sleep, she could almost hear the clash of scabbards and the swift dying thunder of hooves.

———————

William Faulkner (1897–1962) was born in New Albany, Mississippi, and lived most of his life in Oxford, Mississippi. He published nineteen novels, more than eighty short stories, two books of poetry, and numerous essays in a career that spanned more than three decades. He was the recipient of both the Pulitzer Prize for fiction and the Nobel Prize for literature.

Moira Crone

GAUGUIN

(from *The North American Review*)

When people ask him about it, Paul still says it's mysterious to him. He knows he could start back when David Duke was running for governor of Louisiana. But if someone wants to hear the story, he usually begins with a man in limbo, himself—dusk on a Monday, late in August 1992. He was driving downtown to his office for some files he wanted to take with him when he left. He was flying to Wellfleet in forty-odd hours. Meredith would be there. He looked up and saw the overpass: Interstate 10 West a parking lot. He thought, tank-truck turnover, jackknife, petrochemical spill. Bopal. He turned on the local news radio, got the headline, "Coming Up: Mayor Sidney Barthelme on the Evacuation of New Orleans."

He turned around in the road, went back to his little rent house on St. Helena, to wait and see, which would describe his whole life in Baton Rouge at that time.

The year before when David Duke hit, when he got in the runoff for governor, Meredith called him out of the blue. She wanted to know what Paul was going to do. They'd been friends in law school, but involved with other people. Somebody in her new Boston firm told her to call, say, "Stay down there like Nadine Gordimer." But Meredith didn't think so. They went on to other subjects. This developed.

As a matter of fact, that same Duke afternoon, Diana Landry
from across the street came over with her son A.J. She was wearing a "Vote for the Crook, It's Important" t-shirt. "Saw your *No-
Nazis* sticker," she said. Paul assumed he was going to be fired,
however things turned out. Buddy Roemer, the governor, who
hired him through Harvard connections, was out of the mansion
in any case. Paul was a lawyer in the Department of Environmen-
tal Quality. He'd already made some calls—a friend in Princeton
told him about a job in Albany. He was trying.

"Leave, everybody should," Diana Landry said. "If you aren't
from here. I am so ashamed of this place." Then she paused, as if
she were remembering something. "If you want to join the underground I know where to start." Next she was yelling at her son,
who was climbing a delicate crepe myrtle bush. "You can call me.
We'll get that sucker." He did join her. There were some crazy
weeks that fall.

Now, this limbo Monday, in August, almost a year later, things
with Meredith had gotten more interesting. Paul had not been laid
off after Governor Edwards was inaugurated. Nobody understood
this. Paul assumed it was a matter of time; Meredith was handing
his resumé around to institutes on Route 128. It was her cause,
others had taken it up as well: getting him back to New England.
Although Paul was a stoical young man, rather tall, who could be
riled but not easily, he was quietly beginning to panic. He hadn't
actually been with Meredith *in person* in all this time. But one thing
that kept him going was that he and Meredith were closer and
closer, by Internet, he felt.

When he got home, his trip to the office denied him, the phone
rang. Diana across the street. "We've got some 'D' batteries," she said
and he wondered who "we" was, since she told him one morning
when he was jogging that she and her husband Virgil (Cajun, ropey
arms, a sculptor) split up in the early spring. Otherwise, he hadn't
spoken to her for months. "What kind of radio do you have?"

"Huh?" he said. "What's going on in New Orleans?"

"Andrew," she said.

He hadn't been watching TV lately. "Who?"

"After Betsy, we didn't have power for five days."

"I'm going to Wellfleet," he said.

"Where?" Diana said.

"Why are they evacuating New Orleans?"

"Not yet, maybe some early birds," she said. "'The hurricane's got them going." He remembered she was a chatterer. To be nice he suppressed his love of the point.

First thing in the morning, Meredith called. He was thrilled. Raised in Newton, she still dropped her "r's"— he'd almost forgotten. She was at the Cape already, no modem, so they had to use their voices.

"Twenty feet of water in New Orleans," she said.

"There's no water in New Orleans," he said.

"But there will be—"

"No," he said. "This place has a specialty in threatened disasters."

"It's if the locks break, there will be. Do you have them where you are?" she said.

He was interested in her tone. All this time, it had been maybe only chummy. He couldn't tell. The Net is not a hot medium, instead disembodied, like conversations in the afterlife, he thought.

"There's a whole Gulf Coast, a thousand-mile stretch where it could hit," he said.

"How do people stand it?" she said. "Waiting, not knowing?"

He didn't have an answer. Call-waiting beeped.

Because of the time, he decided he'd better take it. It was his boss, Fletcher L'Enfant. Meredith said, "Go ahead, you work for him. I'll call back," before he could tell her L'Enfant could be ignored.

"Son, don't go to work today."

Even if he was waiting for it, it was a creepy feeling, being canned at seven-fifty in the morning. He sat down. L'Enfant called him son. Paul was turning thirty-one. "Non-essential state employees. Just got the call. The hurricane."

He didn't feel relieved. "Will somebody let me in? So I can get that Filtrum Reprocessing File?"

"No," he said in that over-slow voice he used when he thought Paul didn't follow. "Closed up, zippo."

"But I'm on my way out of town!" He suspected L'Enfant was trying to keep him from recommending fines for that plant, and being exquisitely nice about it.

"Fill your bathtub," L'Enfant said. "You be fine." When he hung up, the phone rang almost immediately. Meredith. He summarized his chat with L'Enfant. He asked her, to entertain her, "What good does a bath do in a hurricane?"

"That would never happen in Boston. Your boss would never tell you to fill your tub." She was giggling. Phone was so sensual. "Oh, Albertine is desperate to make a call. Byee."

About nine-thirty that same morning he was in a hardware store on Perkins Road. The atmosphere was snappy. People were out around town, on a mass scavenger hunt. He told himself the best way to make the sun shine in this situation—not that he cared really, since he was on his way out—was to have an ample umbrella. So he was standing in front of a bin full of picked-over supplies—pen lights, busted kerosene lanterns, taped bundles of linty wicks. A woman came up to give him advice—the Radio Shack was having a delivery at 10:30, the 'D' batteries at one chain mart were out of date. And then on to dry ice, how Hurricane Betsy barreled up the Mississippi gaining strength. He couldn't get this woman to stop. He remembered an article he read once, about the Southern urge to explain. It didn't explain.

The first day he went out to the market after Duke was in the run-off, a complete stranger, just like this lady, a frank woman in an all-weather coat, the creased upper lip of a smoker, came up. "Can you believe it? The Saints are going to pull out. We won't get the Olympic trials . . . Used to tell people he was going to burn his mother's bed. She was an alcoholic."

"Who was an alcoholic?" he asked.

"His mamma. And his daddy—don't believe any of that Laotian stuff."

"Laotian stuff?"

"That he was in Laos with his daddy working for the CIA. 'S crazy." She touched his sleeve.

"Who?"

"Who else? The Anti-Christ. I can't sleep. Can you?" She progressed with him to the cash register. "What can we do?"

He told her about the underground Diana had led him to. A bunch of them, meeting down at an office suite on a boulevard in the deep suburbs. They were using this law firm's seventeen telephones, and a set of disks somebody had stolen from the party headquarters, to reach every Republican in the Parish. Over the first week, all kinds of people showed up: little Jewish ladies, professors from everywhere, kids, old ministers, Italian lawyers, arty friends of Diana's, even her brother Danny, a deputy sheriff. They couldn't park at the complex itself—had to use the back of a Circle K across the street. A secretary let them in, by a side door. There was a password. After this got under way, the hard core of the group—somehow Paul was involved—started pressuring politicians and coaches to speak in public, talking rich people into running ads about Duke's past, haranguing the stations every time a reporter let Duke off the hook. Didn't do anything else for three weeks. Paul got so wrapped up in it he never even called that guy in Albany back about the job. He lost weight. Ran a fever. Meredith's message on the Net: "It's existential. You are a partisan." Smiley.

He wrote back, "Get me out of here."

This Tuesday morning, Andrew still pending, he extricated himself from this lady. His booty: two cheap flashlights, sixteen 'C' batteries, a huge expensive cooler.

As he was driving home past massive oaks, palmettos, big banana trees, it occurred to him all he had to do was change his ticket. So he went in and dialed, and waited a million years, feeling like a fool, for the Delta operator. He recognized he was losing his edge, down in Louisiana.

While he floated in the crackling phone noise, he saw Cape Cod, the horizon there, so even and free of business, pines, the simple grays and blues. He thought of Thoreau. How Yankee he was. Finally the operator came on: no seats out of New Orleans or Baton Rouge. No seats going anywhere.

In this north he saw, the laws of cause and effect were well established. Meredith and himself because they'd always liked each other, it made sense. These rules didn't work in Louisiana. Duke, for example, was not entirely a horrible event in the lives of his many enemies. Even specific irony didn't apply often enough in this place. For example, Paul was prepared, in a manner of speaking, for the hurricane by this time, which should have meant it wouldn't come within a thousand miles. This would work anywhere north of Baltimore.

St. Helena was Mexican slang for blondes, he was thinking as he watched Mrs. Diana Landry crossing the street in front of his house. He cringed a little. Then he remembered he'd tell her that David, politically dead, was taking the insurance exam. Her crinkly light hair in the breeze.

"They have dry ice at Party Time," she said. "You want me to pick you up some?" She was wearing tight floral leggings—wisteria growing on her legs. A.J. was behind her, pulling a red wagon loaded with baseball equipment across the lawn. "Virgil came over and boarded up the house—just left," she said, pissed. From the doorway Paul could see her place—the old failing oak in the front yard, the mustard yellow plywood slapped up on all the windows. "I'm sorry to have to ask, but you got a beer?" she said. This was the most personal she'd been in ten months.

He had things called Turbo Dogs, which were beers, in the refrigerator. She had one, he didn't. She went on to say that at Party Time, you had to stand in line. Then she returned to the subject of Virgil. "He wants to see we're okay, okay," she said, biting her lip. "I say like, 'okay 'til you showed up, Virgil,' " one side of her mouth drawn up. He wondered if she knew what that did to her face. "Don't look at me like that," she said, her lips going instantly back to a pout. Her manic skittishness should have bothered him more.

Suddenly she announced, "Mike Graham's on." She pulled a big tracking map she got free at a drugstore out of her jeans pocket. They both thought A.J. was in the dark little back room where Paul hid his television, but when they got there, he wasn't. Diana picked up the remote.

The weatherman said, "Landfall by late Wednesday. Warnings from Pascagoula to Lake Charles—" They heard glass breaking. Running to the front of the house, they found A.J. putting out the small panes along the side of the front door. With his baseball hat. Opening the door to ask A.J. what he was doing, Paul noticed the air, still, and thick. The entire neighborhood—the little cottages, the huge old live oaks, the lamp posts and slate walks—was floating inside a glass of buttermilk. Diana came out and yanked her son inside.

"What's wrong with him?" Paul asked her, sounding more upset than he felt inside—it was this limbo.

She was almost Paul's height, her eyes large. She said, "They don't know. Or won't tell me." He realized this bold, sort of bloated face she had now was the way Diana looked right before she cried.

She went into his bathroom with A.J., who had nicked his finger on a piece of glass. "I didn't mean—" Paul said. She looked at him as if he knew everything. Then he rushed off to his study for cardboard, filmy brown packing tape. He came back to the front saying, "I can fix the panes. Don't worry," but when he got there, his broom was leaning against the foyer wall, and his front door was closed and locked. Diana and A.J. were already bounding across the street. He felt terrible.

At three, Paul dismissed the thought of Andrew entirely. He decided to figure out what dry cleaners would do his things by morning. When he wandered back into the den, the TV was still on, but someone had pressed the mute. There was a computer enhancement of the storm. It covered the Gulf, from Florida on the right side of the screen to the tops of the islands south of New Orleans on the left. For a second it came right up off the map, out of the box. He stared. It startled him. It was like god, or that stuff at the end of "Raiders of the Lost Ark." The next second, he saw a sign on a boarded-up building in New Orleans, "ANDREW TAKE IT OUT ON FERGIE." He laughed, actually very hard, for someone alone. He watched the Baton Rouge commercials, in despair. Monster truck rallies, half-naked Heather who wants you at the Gun and Knife Show. He wondered what was playing at the American Repertory Theatre. He took a snatch of a nap, woke to banging.

Diana was on his front stoop in a plastic poncho. It was late in the afternoon, getting strange. She had a narrow piece of plywood over the place where A.J. put out the window. Hammer and nails. "Hey, I rent, don't worry about it," he said coming out. "And I'm leaving."

"I'm so sorry," she said. "I left A.J. on the Nintendo." She handed him a picnic Thermos, huge. "I brought you hurricanes."

He was grateful. Once before he got drunk with her. The night Duke lost. She recited a ditty to him, the Cajun-consider-the-lilies-of-the-field, "Look at the birds in the yard/who feeds 'em cher." He remembered this right then. A still drizzle, outside. The buttermilk leaving condensation. That big silent swirling thing he saw on TV he thought of telling her about, someone here, who wouldn't think he was crazy, Meredith would, but instead he said, "There's a thousand places it could come in," because he was shy.

"Mike's moved landfall way up," she said. "It's coming in at Vermilion Bay, or Morgan City."

In Morgan City the children had some terrible brain cancer. Statistically significant. A lot of people blamed the toxic waste processor there. He had been on it for seven months. In fact, in June a guy from Hartford told him about an opening at his firm, but he was in Morgan City so much he missed the deadline.

"Winds are still at one-fifty," she said, "The eyewall will be here by midnight."

Eyewall. How fluent she was. He said, "It will fizzle."

"You still going?" she asked.

"Yeah."

"Getting outta here, huh?" jutting her lower chin a little bit as if to mimic some matter-of-factness that was generally Paul's and not hers. Suddenly he wondered if she wanted him to go. If she had an opinion about it. This came up, out of nowhere. For a second those big un-dangerous dunes at the Cape spun out into space, and he was just in the present with Diana, in the middle of this late, odd, afternoon. He felt a little stunned. Maybe she saw this. "Yeah, uh-huh," she said, now nodding to mock him—wasn't he a lucky duck—wasn't he. But he had to do his packing. He had shirts to wash. "Don't you know to fill your tub?" she said—taking off for his bathroom.

"Why's this in here?" she called to him when he got there. "I swear Paul, you got to get square with your TV boy." She handed him his remote, which she'd dropped beside the tub herself, some time ago. In several ways, an unstandable woman, he remembered.

He stood in his front doorway trying to celebrate when she finally left. He noticed breaths, little explosions of rain, under the light on their street, which had come on early. It was an idiosyncratic rain. Usually you could count on rain, to be fairly uniform, he was thinking.

He did a damn good job—toothbrush, Mitchum, Vidal Sassoon, the works. All in a little nylon Lands End bag, zipped up, with room to spare. He finished washing and laid out his outfits, even ironed a few shirts. Lined up his socks. He didn't forget the Eternity cologne, the rugged cotton sweaters he never got a chance to wear because Louisiana was too hot. This took time. At ten he watched the local news, which he hadn't done since the Duke campaign. Back then the news made him sick—the reporters milked the story for all it was worth, at the same time they behaved like cowards, he thought. National news was even worse, completely clueless, missed all the ironies. But tonight the local reporters were standing in outrageously windy spots, their cheeks so wet with violent rain, they seemed to be weeping. He suddenly felt he knew them very well, could go into their hearts if necessary. Some had already been told to evacuate, they said, as they wobbled all over the screen. One guy he called a fascist the year before was standing in the middle of tall, violently swaying cane. The scale was off. He was a grasshopper, reporting to you from an extremely unruly lawn. "Chances are very high it will hit here," he said. A foray into the obvious. Paul felt for this guy, his high eyebrows, syrupy Cajun eyes. He wanted to go into the TV to say, "Pierre, get in the van, it's going to blow."

Thank god he was headed for Wellfleet.

Then there was a live report from the hurricane center in Coral Gables. The director had been up for days. The center itself was hit. Some on his crew were electrocuted. He was disheveled, incoherent. Paul was well into Diana's concoction by then. It tasted like Hawaiian punch plus grain alcohol. He was meditating on the word "here." He called Meredith.

"Oh, Jesus, are you anywhere near La Place?" she asked.

Once again he liked the sound of her voice. It was throaty.

"There was a tornado," she said. "Can you go to a shelter?" just as he saw the red bulletin flash across his screen.

"I'm fine," he said. "That's over near New Orleans."

"I think it's headed right there," she said.

"Hell or high water, really," he said, "the plane's tomorrow, three-thirty."

"We're all worried about you," she said. "Albertine says when she heard you'd gone to Louisiana it was like that painter who went to Tahiti, that's what she thought of."

Albertine was a woman they went to law school with. From Smith. Her eyes were magnified by her glasses. "She and Russell came out, remember Russell?" Meredith said. "We were all so worried. Glued to the Weather Channel," she waited. "Paul? You there?"

"What? Yeah," he said. "I'm not there, I'm here."

"Well, yes. I know where you are."

"Here," he said. "It's different."

"I know," she said, "tell me."

"It's insoluble," he said. "Isn't it?"

"I don't think so," she said. "Here is there for you and there for me is here for you," her deep laugh. "For now."

"Yes, it is, it is, but not really," he said.

Meredith insisted it was. She repeated herself. She was flirting, but Paul couldn't respond. He was serious; he wasn't even sure why.

After they finally said goodnight, he decided to sleep in the back den, which had only one window, and that one shaded by heavy wooden jalousies. He bedded down in front of the TV, under a thin blanket. His flight bag was propped up on his little black couch. He had finished off the jug. And this was all very native, he thought, to be drunk on sweet drinks and be alone, listening to the wind hurling through the banana trees. I really must go, he thought. Really.

At one of the desolate hours, three or four in the morning, he ventured into the kitchen. Cotton mouth. Reaching toward the left, he touched the light switch.

No light. None in the fridge.

In the dark, while he drank all the orange juice from the carton, he thought of the normal size sky they have up there on the Cape. He tried to calm down. He saw himself and Meredith McCartel, a Unitarian, going along the beach, having a thoughtful conversation. He knew peace of mind. He knew exactly what came after that afternoon's walk. He prayed he hadn't upset her.

He staggered back to bed, which was the floor.

When he got up again, the kitchen was filled with a strange pink light. He assumed it was morning. The pecan tree outside his window was waving at the base of its trunk, a big timid hula girl. He put his good French Roast beans into the grinder—no whirr.

For a long time he sat at his little metal table on an old tubular chair, and watched this tree and the others dance. He listened. Around eight his house started to groan. Then all the trees were swaying back and forth, like back-up singers. It was positively choral—the tops in one direction, the bottoms in another. Of course this was terrible, but that didn't keep it from being interesting. Around nine he heard the whistle, like he was on a ship. Andrew going through the lamp that hung from his little porch. His ears were aching by this time. He was surprised when the phone rang.

"I got through!" Meredith said, triumphantly. "How's your airport?" she said. He was thinking about a tree across the street, in Diana's front yard, how heavy it was.

"I don't know," he said. He hadn't called.

"I'll call," she said. "Are you Delta?"

"It's very bad, here," he said. "My ears."

"According to the Weather Channel, it's to your west."

He didn't answer.

"Are you okay?" she said—this irritation, now. "You sounded sort of—"

"I'm fine," he said.

"I don't know, were you drinking last night?"

"Drinking?" This was out of character for him, that he would lie to someone that way.

"I'll call," she said. "Delta." She said it firmly. "How can you stand it? Don't you just wish you knew exactly how this was going to turn out? I'd go crazy."

He agreed he couldn't stand it, of course, but later when he recalled this, he recognized some reservations, which he hadn't uttered. What he said was, "My ears are splitting open." The barometric pressure.

"Last night they said it might fly by and only land in Mobile, how far is that?"

"Mobile?" he asked. "I think it's here."

"I mean your plane," she said.

"I'm too close to the window," he said.

"Oh, Paul, don't," she said. "How bad can it be?"

"It's a hurricane, Meredith," he said. "It really doesn't matter what they say on Cable. I'm so sorry, I really am," and he was, but then he hung up. Next, he was crawling across the floor. As if, if he were to stand up he might be showing the present some disrespect. As if he had seen things, been shown signs. He headed toward the front of the house, though it would have been safer to stop in the little hallway next to the den, away from all the glass. He wanted a view of the whole street. When he got there, he saw several enormous live oaks on St. Helena looked like giants buried in the sand, their heads poking up, straining to get out. The root systems, their shoulders, pulled up more soil with every heavy gust. The trees were heaving. It was amazing. He gazed over at Diana's house, blank, eyeless, the thick plywood patches.

The night Duke lost the race, he could see the candlelight in her windows from his living room. She used little votives for the party. That way she wouldn't have to really clean, she joked. Her home life was not the best right then. For the three weeks of the run-off, they were arguing—Virgil said she was gone too much, and he wanted to know how she could support Edwards no matter who his opponent was. A lot of couples had split over the election. At the party there was a pool, you could pick the point spread. By that time most people figured Edwards was going to win all along— he'd never been in real danger. The underground might have felt used, and bitter. That would have made sense, Paul thought. Instead everybody danced to Neville Brothers, Doctor John, Zydeco, a little Dewey Balfa. There were Creoles there, lawyers and other rich men with paunches. The journalists who listened to some of them had all kinds of stuff they couldn't print—crimes of Duke, rumors about Edwards. There were professors from Southern University, and a tall woman from Sri Lanka, a physicist, with her husband, Buddhists, a man raised in Hungary, who'd been in the Resistance in the war. They had all worked at the phone bank one night or another, but it was sort of amazing to see them there together at once, come from so many different realms, chomping on corn chips. Duke's losing was a certainty, they said they'd never had a question. But at the end of the evening, when it came to how the precincts voted, parish by parish, people from Louisiana went up to the screen, asked for silence. If Duke was defeated in their home precinct, they shouted, "All right!" and held their fists in the air, hugged people. Everybody cried and asked each other personal questions. Where were you from, really, where were you going if Duke had won. When she was in the middle of a long complaint, Paul asked Diana why she ever wanted to marry Virgil. She looked at him—actually very pretty to him just then, another man's wife, and that was okay, that was the mood, no secrets, no status. She said, "Does what you want have much to do with how your life plays out? I think very little." And then she grinned, like it was all right with her, what she'd just said. At the time he thought her remark incredibly strange. He had not forgotten this completely by the day of the hurricane.

Just then the huge oak in her yard succeeded in liberating itself from the soil. A thundering cracking sound. The entire root system toppled out, taking up half the lawn with it. It fell toward her house. In the center of the mass of roots now visible, a black hole ran through. Dead all along. He couldn't see her roof line any more. He crawled to his front door, stood, and opened it up.

Actually, when he unlocked it, it opened itself.

The wind was primary, sovereign. Music, playing at different speeds, different intensities. The rain was being thrown out in gasps, violently, then breathily. As if the wind had to reach inside of itself periodically to find more water to throw forth. Smaller trees, twice as tall as himself, bent down to the ground, then snapped back up, over and over. The street was a river. From his porch he could see that her carport and part of her roof were crushed. He imagined Diana and A.J. trapped inside. Then Paul's nerves were a golden web, lighting him up inside his arms, his thighs, his neck.

He made it across—he was blown, really, that's how it looked, or he was picked up by an invisible hand. He touched down on the little concrete disks that made the path to her front door. He was imagining how he'd break in.

He pounded on the door, stood outside and waited. Never once did he think he was stupid. The door cracked open. There she was. She was fine.

"You crazy? You out of your mind?" She had him in.

It reminded him of a lake at night, inside—so dark with the windows boarded, the light from kerosene lamps. She had shiny oak floors, with puddles here and there. Water was running in underneath the bedroom doors along the hallway on the side of the house where the roof was damaged. There were towels and cotton blankets tossed around, used recently to swab the floors, he supposed, then abandoned. When he looked back to Diana, he saw she was holding a fan of playing cards in her hand, sitting on her skirted, winged old couch in a long cotton nightgown. She looked flushed, younger. Her calves were very white, and smooth, and in placcs dappled pink, and she had big work boots on, her husband's old ones, he guessed. A.J., beside her, was also holding some cards, and eating caramel corn from a pottery bowl, dark blue. From a cooler, dry ice mist furled towards them.

"D'you run across in your bare feet like that?" she said. "That's so wild."

"I saw the tree fall."

A.J. was shuffling the cards. He was excellent at this, very smooth, didn't drop one, Paul noticed.

"Did you hear that?" she asked her son, beaming. A.J. was very calm. The hurricane pacified him. It was odd. For once, the boy looked cherubic and sweet. "It gave us a scare, but we just sat tight." Paul sat on an ottoman, on a damp blanket. They dealt him in. He won a few, but mostly he lost to Diana and A.J. She cheated so her son would win. Generally, Paul would say that was a bad idea, but right then he found it endearing. They ate crawfish salad cold from the dry ice, and delicious. Some boudin. He felt as if he'd been there forever, listening to the storm slowly dying down. More than once it occurred to him the house was going to collapse; this made him enjoy the moment more.

A.J. went into the kitchen at one point. When they were alone,

Diana looked at Paul with her wide-apart eyes, and reached toward his jaw as if to check his shaving, or to bring his face toward her, or to make sure he was real—the place didn't look real at all, stage smoke creeping along the floor. He leaned forward to hear what she was going to say, or maybe to do, attracted by her lovely attention. It was strange, how calm this all made him. But then she said, "Weren't you the one who was going somewhere?"

And when he tells this story he always jumps a little ahead, at this point, to that walk they took. It was about two-thirty, and the winds had died down and he and Diana and A.J. ventured out into her wrecked yard. Paul was carrying his flight bag. The airport was open. Down St. Helena, almost every tree was down or damaged. Things that were hidden before, he noticed, were exposed now by the winds—the flashy white wood inside old branches, the underside of the leaves, all silver. *Immaculate* was the word that came to mind. They passed many women, their neighbors, standing on their porches, their front doors flung open, looking out at the damage—smashed cars, lost roofs, twisted bikes, flooded yards—with a grand and easeful awe, the drizzle blowing in their faces. He felt as if he were in that very late painting of Gauguin's—he always mentions this part—the one with the royal pink sky in the background, and the bare-breasted women in it, who are gazing up mysteriously at something not pictured on the canvas itself. There are tropical vines in the background—for him these are the powerlines, snaking downward. He is supposed to be going to the corner, where Diana's brother Danny the deputy sheriff, out cruising to discourage looters, has agreed to pick him up, take him to the airport. He's planning to dash out onto the runway in the post-hurricane excitement, perhaps holding a sturdy airline umbrella, to board his flight, to escape to New England.

Diana says to him, "Andrew went over Livonia, it missed us by only this much," her papery little fingertips, which he would later learn to care for very much, close together, but not quite touching.

He says, "Did it? Did we miss it?" He finds this hard to believe.

"The eye," she whispers, looking sideways at him, and down, crestfallen when she knows she shouldn't be.

The moment he likes most comes next: he takes her elbow to help her avoid the puddle right beside her—she could be electrocuted. In the same motion, feeling a kind of urgent glory, he picks up A.J. They head back down St. Helena away from where Danny should be waiting, back toward the women on their stoops, Diana's house. What he says to end the story, is "And I just knew then." People here are satisfied with that.

It should have been a great disappointment to go back to the fresh chaos blown in on top of the kinds already in his life in Louisiana. He knew this. But he did and he's still there. He was overcome by a sweet homesickness for the very moment he was living in, just then—not the next, not one somewhere else. And the mysteriousness of it, how nothing ever followed. Such a feeling wouldn't travel to New England, much as he might like to take it. It was indigenous he thought; probably rare other places. He wouldn't be able to translate it. At the same time he was ashamed of himself, the delight he felt. Then he knew.

At a distance, the sirens.

———

Moira Crone grew up in the tobacco country of eastern North Carolina. She was educated at Smith College and at the Writing Seminars at Johns Hopkins University. She has published three works of fiction—*The Winnebago Mysteries and Other Stories*, *A Period of Confinement*, and *Dream State*. She lives in New Orleans and has taught at LSU in Baton Rouge since the eighties.

This story arose out of two specific historic events: the David Duke gubernatorial bid in 1992, and Hurricane Andrew, which came almost exactly a year after. Both events brought with them a communal sense of impending disaster, which in turn inspired many spontaneous gatherings and parties, new friendships . . . strange alliances in South Louisiana. What

I am proud of in the piece is the narrative voice, which is telling the reader how Paul tells the story—I did this to inject a certain omniscience and distance in a polarized situation, either/or. Among Americans, the connotations of South and North are incredibly loaded. You have to be careful or people will get the wrong idea. Until I found the beginning, I couldn't hit the right note. I chose this story to close my collection Dream State, *which is about Louisiana. When Paul walks in Diana's house during the height of the storm—how he finds her—the heart of Louisiana as I know it is somewhere in that scene, I hope.*

Jill McCorkle

PARADISE

(from *The Chattahoochee Review*)

When Adam met Eve they were standing in the champagne line at Missy Malcolm's wedding in Southern Pines. Eve, who wore her thick black hair in a blunt Cleopatra look and had since moving to Atlanta, had grown up with Missy in a small town just twelve miles away. In Atlanta she was Evelyn, an aspiring fashion designer and buyer for Macy's. But here she was Eve. Eve Lyn Wallace, a name selected by her paternal grandmother who had seen the name Evelyn in print and proceeded to misspell and mispronounce it. Here people voiced shock at how dark her hair had gotten since she moved to *the city*. Dark and straight. The woman in the pink knit dress who slipped a business card into the palm of any hand she shook—Gretchel Suzanne Brown, owner and head stylist of Shear Pleasure—stopped and fingered Eve's hair, saying over and over like a mantra, "I don't remember this hair."

Eve finally, in embarrassment, turned and explained all of this to Adam; she explained that when she was in high school she had a perm that made her hair lighter and quite frizzy. "Nobody around here gives a decent perm," she said, traces of the region's accent lingering on the syllables she attempted to clip. "And especially not her." She nodded toward Ms. Gretchel Suzanne Brown, who was working her way down the line to where the bride and groom stood.

Eve's eyes were catlike, almost amber colored in the bright banquet room. It could have been any country club anywhere, any random wedding and Adam was struck by how alike they all were, the tables and flowers and fountains; the little bite-size pieces of food that after awhile began to taste the same, the common ingredients being wooden toothpicks and miniature puff pastry shells. The mothers and grandmothers and aunts all decked out in pastel dinner mint shades of chiffon. Eve was in bridesmaid's garb, a layered gossamer pink number that was identical to those of the other seven attendants, all of them wearing the little pearl earrings that Missy had presented them with at her bridesmaid's luncheon just two days before when wives of the local dermatologists hosted the fete. Adam heard all of this while seated in the church and waiting for the service to begin. The women (who were seated on the left, the *groom's side*, only because they ran out of *good* seats on the right) talked of the scrumptious little delicacies served at the party: cucumber sandwiches, petit fours, and melon balls. They were shocked at how those young women spoke so openly about sexual matters, and wasn't it just so clever of the hostesses to give out little samples of Retin-A like party favors. "If those girls are smart," one whispered, and Adam leaned forward to hear. "They'll use the stuff right now before it's too late. Skin goes fast. Lord, how it goes." Then this same woman turned to the topic of how she had not been awarded Yard-of-the-Month because one of her neighbors had five dead cars up on blocks in his side yard. With that Adam sat back and flipped through the songbook in front of him until the organ swelled and announced that it was time for the show.

The procession was a lengthy one, a great-grandmother with a walker, a great-aunt in a wheelchair, the back of which was decorated with ribbons and flowers, parents, ten groomsmen, ten bridesmaids, a best man (father of the groom), a maid of honor, a matron of honor (pregnant and thought by the women seated in front of Adam to be way out of line for having even participated even if she was the bride's sister). There was a little shiny-faced kid

wearing a mini suit and carrying a satin pillow and there was a little curly-Q looking girl strewing flowers onto the green-carpeted
aisle where the bride then walked, her spike heels piercing petals
along the way. The children looked moronic with their fakey
smiles. The women in front whispered that they were *deliciously
adorable precious precious things*. They said it was so very special that
the bride and groom made children a part of the day. No children
in the oven, thank you, just fully baked.

"I'm Adam," he finally said as the hair stylist floated to the end
of the champagne line, stopping once to lift a strand of the mater-
nal grandmother's hair. "You're Eve?" Several people standing in
line snickered.

"Evelyn," she said. "I go by Evelyn, now."

"But she'll always be Eve to me." The woman behind them—a
woman who oddly resembled Minnie Mouse with her pelvis
thrust forward and big white pumps turned outward—stuck her
head up close. "I taught little Eve piano for years and years."

Adam nodded and the woman momentarily disappeared only
to then pop out again to recall how Eve, at age five, had had a little accident just before playing "Get Aboard the Big Airliner" in
the big recital down at the junior high school auditorium. "Wet
herself a teensy bit," the woman whispered to Adam, her breath
like some kind of denture adhesive, all the while leaning close and
staring at him. "You don't look or sound like you're from around
here. You must be one of the groom's guests."

Of all the people in that lengthy procession to the front of the
church, Adam noticed Eve first thing. In twenty-six years he had
never set foot in a church, and now he had done it for the fifth
time in two years. It was his first time in a Baptist church and he
was surprised to find the stately grand room—plush carpeting and
mahogany molding, red velvet chairs like thrones. He had envi-
sioned snakes slithering up and down rock hard pews and signs
such as *this way to eternal damnation* and *this way to everlasting life*
in the sloppy misspelling of what he had encountered on the roadside: *watermelluns, cantelope, hunnydo*.

Adam and John Jeffers had been fraternity brothers at the University of Maryland, the high point of their relationship being the annual BurnOut bash their fraternity held to commemorate the house fire that left them in need of raising money for repairs. For four years the two of them worked on planning the event: bands, kegs, tee shirts. For four years they blasted their stereos and played pinball in the dank beer-soaked bar near their frat house. For four years John was a part of Adam's life, his face a daily sighting, and now he was marrying a complete stranger, this woman with short blonde hair and a church full of relatives. Marriage plans were incongruous with the lives his fraternity brothers *said* they were living and yet the calls kept coming. He had been in two of the five weddings.

In Adam's experience weddings were either in a temple or some nice gilded banquet room of a hotel where women turned out in black-sequined cocktail dresses that showed cleavage. He had overheard at the first big Southern church wedding that a woman wearing black was absolutely tasteless. That was almost as bad as a woman wearing white. Only the bride wears white. There is only one virgin on that day. At one wedding a man had stepped out in a powder blue dinner jacket with tails and sung "We've Only Just Begun." Adam thought he could have just as easily been in Las Vegas or on *Star Search* and so as not to start laughing spent the entire service (all written by the bride and the groom with a little help from Elizabeth Barrett Browning and Kahlil Gibran) reading and studying the program he'd been handed at the door. He could now quote from *Corinthians* and the *Book of Ruth*.

He was thinking about all of this during the prayer, a very long prayer, glancing around the packed room but always coming back to Eve (who then was simply *the one with the thick black hair*). He was thinking about the grooms who had gone before John Jeffers and how they were now all seated here, looking somehow old and washed out, wimped out. They seemed subdued, professional, lobotomized. Their wives looked fixed and powerful with their tailored linen dresses and little clutch bags. These marriages were walking advertisements for Talbots and Brooks Brothers. They talked about the mortgage and the dining room chairs that were ordered. If they weren't trying to have babies right that minute, they were buying AKC puppies. It was like all these guys had hopped on a ferry and left Adam there at the landing. With each wedding the gap widened.

The preacher's prayer was well into its second minute when Eve's groomsman—cousin of the groom—began looking a little questionable: pale, shaky, perspiring. There had been a big party the night before, a *wild* party designed to mark the passing of John Jeffers from former lacrosse player, part-time history major to MBA graduate and Stepford husband. The cousin passed out cold. He fell face forward, pulling Eve and a small candelabra entwined with gardenias and ivy with them. Adam watched while a roomful of people (hundreds of people) sat with their eyes closed and missed this scene of a lifetime. She fell forward as gracefully as possible, her pink skirt momentarily hiding all but a slender white leg. The preacher was talking about trust and loyalty, the everlasting gift of faithfulness, while Adam raised up out of his seat to get a better view. He watched her emerge from the folds of pink fabric, gracefully ease out from under the dead weight of the groomsman's arm, mouth what looked like "shit," and then stand perfectly still by herself as if she didn't notice this post-adolescent lunk sprawled in front of her. The preacher talked a bit more about the state of the world today and how important it was to have a partner, but by then the whispering had begun and people were peeping, one eye, both, until that final amen. Eve stood with shoulders back and eyebrow raised, daring anyone to link her in any way to the body at her feet, his face pale and slack against the carpet. During the vows someone from the congregation tiptoed up and as inconspicuously as possible checked his pulse and then rolled him under the front pew, his head right near great-grandmother's walker.

Now that same groomsman was standing in the champagne line with a can of beer. *Hair of the dog*, people were saying. Men in Lily Pulitzer suits nodded to the nauseated-looking fellow with great

respect and recalled the wild nights *they* had known at bachelors'
parties. Adam's friends from college winked and grinned, elbowed
him and others knowingly. Their well-rehearsed marriages seemed
to force further exaggeration of male bonding, boys' night out,
their women smirking with what was supposed to be great wis-
dom about these matters, these "boys will be boys" moments; it
was like these women had opened the cage doors and *allowed* their
guys a little recess. Adam imagined the prices they would submit
to their husbands: a diamond tennis bracelet, a trip to Barbados,
a summer home, four babies. The price of freedom was exorbitant
these days. So why was everybody biting the hook? Why were
these reasonably intelligent, likeable guys *choosing* to acquiesce,
their suppressed desires left to blow up at some occasional wedding party.

Adam was relieved not to have been a part of the fiasco known
as the bachelor's party—men too drunk to stand, peeing in a
downtown parking lot—shaving John Jeffer's pubic region, writing *Help Me* on the soles of his shoes, visible to all when he knelt
with the last prayer. "Those boys, those boys," John's mother said
several times.

The bride and her maids were no better it seemed. Rumors cir-
culated (and later were confirmed by Eve) that the bride had been
stamped with butcher's ink "Prime Cut" and "Choice Meat."

"Sally Snow's dad works at Winn Dixie," Eve told Adam when
he asked how they had gotten the ink. It was chitchat, small talk,
right in there with the insufferable North Carolina June weather,
his completion of Duke Law School and recent move to Washington, her aspirations of getting into the fashion world. As a
designer of course, she said, I'm much too short for anything else.
She laughed and handed him a glass. Adam was five nine and she
easily was eight inches shorter, her hand half the size of his as they
both leaned into the stone swan fountain that spit forth pink
champagne.

"They all act so juvenile," she said, throwing down one quick
glass of champagne and then getting a refill before moving over to

the food. "And did you see the guy I was standing with? The cousin from hell?" She raised her eyebrow again, let out a heavy sigh. "I told him not to close his eyes during the prayer. I could tell he had that sick-as-hell look."

"Best part of the service," Adam said and motioned her out into what people kept calling the solarium, a jungle of ferns swaying over white wicker tables and chairs and a big plate glass window that looked out on the pool and the eighteenth hole. "I particularly liked the way you got out of his hold." He kicked one leg out to the side and held it there, shook it; the great aunt was frowning at him from across the room where she sat hunched forward in her chair. He stopped a waiter and grabbed two more glasses of champagne and a handful of diminutive drumsticks. She eagerly accepted the champagne but turned down what she called biddy legs so he went and found a waiter with caviar and another with fruit. He found a bottle of champagne in the kitchen and brought it to their table. Along with not being carnivorous she was not a fan of the tune selections given to the Casio player, all tunes Adam had heard on the accordion at every Bar Mitzvah he had ever attended, songs like "Spinning Wheel" and "Will It Go Round in Circles." They talked for at least a half an hour about the round ring circle theme in songs sung at weddings. During this time he verified that she was not married but also discovered that she was not *single*. An ideal situation for someone who is not *really* in the market. Back in Atlanta she had a person, friend, lover, significant other, current life partner, spousal equivalent. Again they laughed over all of the stupid names and she changed the subject to some local gossip, one of the old men in a Lily Pulitzer suit who had once been picked up by the side of the interstate wearing nothing but his underwear. And? Adam asked, rolling his hand dramatically for the rest of the story to which she shrugged. "That's all that anybody ever heard. Obviously you're not a local," she said. "If you were you'd be used to half stories and numerous speculations."

He realized then that he'd given her very little of himself. "I *was* in a lengthy relationship," he had offered with the news of her significant equivalent so and so. What he hadn't told was that that relationship was when he was a sophomore in college, that he had been a slow healer, that his own parents flipped out in their fifties and after thirty-odd years of marriage split up and went through all of the same arguments you'd expect from a much younger divorce. They fought over who should get *Barbra Streisand's Greatest Hits* and the *West Side Story* soundtrack, until Adam went out and bought an additional copy; of course then they had to fight over who would get the new versions and the CD player that his/her *nice son* had been forced to buy with his hard-earned money and him not even out of school, yet. It was one of those times he caught himself wishing that there was a sibling with whom to divvy up the worries, someone to call just to say, "So, what do you hear from the insane ones?" By then, Alicia was already out of his life, a glimpse of blonde hair and add-a-bead necklace in the under-graduate library or at a basketball game. Where he had once pic-tured her face in the scenarios of his future, there was now a blur with a voice all too similar to that of his mother and Great-Aunt Izzy whose claim to fame was that she had once seen a very famous actor (she never revealed who) buying every kind of laxative that was stocked at her local pharmacy (which of course was *not* HIS local pharmacy). Every family gathering was punctuated by ques-tions such as: "Was it Cary Grant?"

"Oh no, much sexier."

"William Holden?"

"Shorter."

"Frank Sinatra?"

"You think he's sexy? Do you really?" Izzy had the habit of nod-ding while she talked or chewed. Sometimes she did all three. Ali-cia had once guessed Marlon Brando, to which Izzy laughed hys-terically. "I have never found him to be sexy!" Izzy roared, not long after which Alicia broke things off (it was as easy to blame Izzy for the breakup as it was to come up with any other good reason), and when Alicia left, Adam more than ever relied on the eternal brotherhood made available by Pi Kappa Alpha; he drank beer and shot pool, played pinball and threw darts.

Now he realized Eve was sitting there looking at him. She had refilled both of their glasses and was tapping her fingers to the beat of a jazzed-up version of "Mrs. Robinson." People were trying to dance to it but seemed to be failing miserably. One man in the center resembled a paralyzed turkey, all movement taking place in the head and upper torso. "I just moved to DC." Adam was suddenly determined to give something back to the conversation. "I grew up in New York and then when I graduated from high school my parents moved. They're still there." He didn't offer that his parents didn't speak to each other except through him, that they had successfully made his life miserable.

"Atlanta." She lifted her glass for him to refill it. "I moved there right after college." She paused and laughed. "No big deal *now*, but back then I had never been anywhere. You know I lived at home all through college, small school close by." She threw her thumb over her shoulder as if he could look out into the foyer of the country club, the gold flocked wallpaper and chandelier, and see her school. "I did *not* know anything about anything." She used her hands dramatically as she enunciated each word. He imagined her standing in front of a mirror as she clipped the slow-motioned syllables, as she avoided the contractions like "didn't" where her native tongue pronounced *t*'s for *d*'s, ditten like kitten. Then she brought in the hands, graceful nubby-nailed hands that moved with great energy as if she might suddenly burst into applause or grab you by the throat. Like her half-baked stories about the people from her town, Adam had no idea where the conversation was going. He wanted to tell her that he liked the stripped-down version of her: that image of someone about to go somewhere, Little Eve Wallace with the frizzy hair, peeing at the piano recital, growing up to go to what sounded like a community college, growing up to be the first person he had felt any strong interest in since Alicia, but then he remembered that nameless, faceless significant other opening her refrigerator, watching her television, lounging on her bed down in Georgia. What he pictured was the face of Tom Cruise on the body of Arnold Schwarzenegger; as smart as Einstein and as sensitive as Alan Alda.

"Look, it's Adam and Eve," the goofy-looking little ring bearer said and several guffaws and titters followed. It was clear he had been put up to it. Apparently, their socializing had sparked quite a few Adam and Eve jokes, the punch lines all having something to do with a rib or a snake. Apples. Fig leaves. Then there were jokes about the company, Adam and Eve, that manufactured all kinds of sex toys and devices, the kinds of things that John Jeffers was given after they shaved his groin area clean and that Missy Malcolm was given after her thighs and buttocks and breasts had been stamped with purple ink, leaving her body to look bruised and blemished.

"So you grew up here?" he asked. They had moved over to a table near the window to escape all the traffic and now they were watching people walk up from the eighteenth hole. It was like a wide-screen movie, body parts readjusted as men and women pulled themselves up the pool ladder. She continued her commentary on people at the reception: the woman in a purple sarong who had once chained herself (along with her two dachshunds, Oscar and Meyer) to the door of the local veterinary office to protest pet euthanasia (her husband was an anesthesiologist who was at that time being sued for overgassing someone); the couple making out in the corner who had built a relationship and marriage upon dramatic breakups and reconciliations like the time they were caught having sex behind the shower curtain display in Wal-Mart; and the man stuffing chicken livers wrapped in bacon in his mouth who had taught her high school geometry class and was the first person in town to come out of the closet. A few people came over to try to get in on the conversation, to ask her to dance, or (she said) to check up on them, but they eventually left. An hour into the reception and people stopped asking.

"They will be saying all sorts of things about us before long," Eve said. "Here's the half story. We have spent the entire reception all alone drinking champagne: you the out-of-town stranger, me the local yokel who *supposedly* has a man in *the city*." She lowered her voice to simulate danger.

"Supposedly?" Adam asked. "Are you asking me to speculate?"

The pool shimmered off to the side where children screamed and cannonballed, and teenage girls lounged in bikinis. In the main room the champagne swan had gone empty and bottles were being brought from the kitchen and passed around. The young black man on the Casio was singing "Sunshine of My Life." He put on some sunglasses and moved back and forth like Stevie Wonder, which delighted the old people hugging the wall as well as the youngsters who were periodically appearing and then quickly disappearing with shaving cream and soda cans. He sang *you are the apple of my eye* while the parents of the bride twirled and dipped.

Eve talked freely now and with that freedom came the accent, the slow drawl familiar to everyone else in the vicinity. "My dad grew tobacco, not much, but enough." She was home for a long weekend and in the midst of giving her family history (two younger brothers and a mother who teaches fifth grade) she began describing her room there, the tape marks on the pale yellow walls from where she had hung posters in high school. Posters that said things like "Rain is a Freedom Song" and "Up with People." She described her parents: childhood sweethearts who over the years had developed a whole language with eyebrows, winks, and hand gestures. She described the cool soothing feeling of the central air conditioning and how she had spent much of her childhood without it. "My brothers and I used to sleep on the screened porch in our underwear." She laughed, staring out at the pool now as if she could see her young brothers standing there in their briefs. "And my dad would take us out to the little local airport on Sunday afternoons to see if a plane came. You know, little planes, crop-dusting types." She talked faster and faster, her neck and chest flushed. "We'd spread a blanket and count jets which of course did *not* come to our airport. My dad said, 'Look, they've scarred the sky.' I always liked the sound of that, *scarred the sky*. And sometimes we'd stay until dusk and count the bats that flew out from an old barn nearby."

The lazy haze of the sun, the alcohol, her voice were getting to him. The smell of chlorine and the slow whirring motion of the ceiling fans. He was thinking about his room at the Ramada Inn, how dark those heavy lined drapes could make it, like artificial nightfall, the unit on the wall generating artificial coolness. He couldn't help imagining her there with him and once he'd let the forbidden idea in he couldn't shake it.

"Who looks stupid, us or them?" she asked a mere second after ending the airport story with how they always stopped at the Tastee Freeze on the way home and how her youngest brother always asked if you could order a sundae on any day other than Sunday. For the first time he noticed the slight space between her front teeth, the little whistle sound she emitted with each and every s. It made his chest ache just to look at her.

"What do you mean?" He took off his coat and found his arm stretched out behind her, his finger lightly brushing over the spaghetti strap of that hideous dress that looked amazingly good on her. He was now of the belief that anything would. She could grab one of those starched looking old lady dresses and whirl around a few times, and it would look perfect, soft and easy and lived in. She could wear the tablecloth, the ivy trailing around the ceiling. He waited to see if she would move away from his hand but instead she leaned in closer.

"Well, there they are in bathing suits." She lifted her hand with the champagne glass, index finger pointing outward. "And here we are in formal wear." She had kicked off her shoes and now had her legs stretched out, ankles crossed on the chair across from her.

He was about to make a flirtatious suggestion, something that she wouldn't necessarily take seriously but would still consider if only in jest and then there was a plump twelve year old, her spaghetti straps digging creases into her sunburned shoulders, handing out little net sacks of rice. It was clear, having observed all of the bridesmaids at the front of the church, that Missy had chosen that dress with Eve in mind; she was the only woman there who could do it justice.

"Believe it or not," Eve said, shaking her head with a lovely look of pity on her face, "there was a hell of a lot of thought that went into what just happened." At first Adam thought she had read his mind and then he followed her gaze to the kid with the rice. "The girl, that basket with the streamers that match our dresses and the great-aunt's wheelchair," she laughed a little too loudly and then patted her lips as if to reprimand herself. "The net cut the right shape, the Comet rice dyed a pale shade of pink."

"They dye the rice?"

"Of course." She touched his arm, lightly fingered the fabric of his cuff. "What, you've never dyed rice? All these years and you've never dyed rice? It's a big deal, this dyed rice. The only thing hotter is birdseed." Now her hand was curled up on top of his and it was perfectly natural for him to turn his wrist and lock fingers with her. She talked faster as this was happening, all about birdseed for the environment, nobody has to come and sweep it up. She had told Missy all about this, all about how every wedding she had gone to in Atlanta had had birdseed, but Missy was just so traditional she had to have rice. "She even wanted to go to Niagara Falls!" Eve attempted a whisper but failed. "Donna Reed is her idol." Eve held one of the little napkins that said "Missy and John" up to her mouth, shoulders shaking with laughter as she continued the appraisal of her friend. "She knows how to make seven different meat loaves and forty-seven things to do with Jell-O."

"No lie."

"No lie." She squeezed his hand tightly and leaned in close, their foreheads almost touching.

"Sounds a little kinky."

"No shit, Jack." Clearly she was not entirely sober and he caught himself hoping that the glassy-eyed haze would never wear off, that they could just step out into the bright June day and walk off into a perfect world. "You know I meant Donna Reed as she was on TV, of course, with the Jell-O and meat loaf, you know. Donna in real life was really cool, protested Vietnam, thought women were capable of a hell of a lot more than that show made it look like, you know? Donna was okay."

There was a lot of activity outside and they stood and looked out the window just in time to see the groom lifted and hurled into the pool, a herd of children in bright suits and water wings scattering so as not to be hit by the big drunk man and all of his tuxedo-clad groomsmen and two bridesmaids who followed. Eve said that the local rental place was used to this. She had been surprised when attending weddings in Atlanta that every groom didn't *always* get thrown in the pool. It was a ritual around here, had been for years.

"Are we being antisocial?" Eve asked as the groom stood by the pool, wringing out his coat. He pulled wet money from his pocket and fanned it in the air. It seemed many of the people had gone outside to watch. The singer had packed up his keyboard and was getting some food from the sparse table. They had missed the cutting of the cake and now the little plastic bride and groom along with two doves and a big silver heart perched on the upper tier as if reigning over the half-eaten cake.

"Oh," he said and let his other arm drop around her waist, the light pink fabric cool and slick. "Are there other people here?"

It took forever for the bride and groom to come out for the big farewell. Many people had already left the reception. Supposedly, all the bridesmaids were going to help the bride get dressed but Eve said that she thought they could do without her. The result was lots of people whispering "Where is Eve? Where is Eve?" so that someone else could say "Oh, of course, with Adam."

By now the Biblical humor had been reduced to a lot of snake jokes. The mothers and grandmothers and aunts were perspiring and flat looking, eyes dulled by the champagne they pretended not to drink. Missy's parents wept openly as she turned and whirled her bouquet which was caught by a middle-aged man in a bright yellow suit. Adam said that this was unfamiliar to him, these men in fluorescent colors, that they should be required by law to pass out sunglasses.

Everyone cheered when the car drove away and women pretended not to see where someone had written *get some* in shaving
cream. One of the grandmothers pointed out to everyone the
delightful message "come again and again" written she was sure
for the wedding guests watching them depart. Adam and Eve both
said good-byes to the remaining people they knew, both compli-
menting Missy's parents on a lovely wedding, and then they were
left there, the parking lot of the Country Club, the heat weighing
oppressively. Eve was swinging her shoes by her side, her other
hand still clinging to his. "Well," he finally said and looked off into
the pine trees surrounding the tennis courts. "Would you like to
go get something to drink? eat?"

The ride to the Ramada Inn began quietly as he regretfully had
to let go of her hand to shift gears. She talked in great bursts of
speed, much information delivered such as that she would have to
go back and get her car, her parents were expecting her for dinner,
her feet were killing her, and then she fell silent. He was worrying
about what to say next, what to do. It seemed that the force that
had brought them together was dwindling and he didn't want that
to happen. He pulled into a parking space and, once stopped,
reached over and took her hand.

The rest of the afternoon passed slowly in the cool, darkened
room, the volume of the television turned off as the weather channel continued its ceaseless forecast—Washington, Atlanta, Kala-
mazoo. Her dress was crumpled in the corner like some ghost of
the Victorian era had pulled up a chair to watch. Her unlikely
underclothes, a sportsbra and matching briefs in red and green
striped cotton, were looped over the lamp that was bolted to the
bedside table. He lay there watching her, trying to decide where
to go from here. What did this mean? Were their lives irrevocably
altered or would they say good-bye and pretend it never happened.
A long-distance relationship was the last thing he needed, that and
an angry, hulking boyfriend who now stood seven feet tall and had
multiple tattoos and an arsenal. He had no desire to go through
what he had just witnessed, this ceremony that might lead him

right into his parents' life, the ultimate sacrifice, thirty miserable years thrown down the sewer for the sake of *the child's* well being. But then again what *was* he waiting for? His own history offered none of the porch-sleeping comfort she had described; no higher education, no paycheck could erase that childhood hurt his parents felt he was surely old enough to handle.

The last thing Eve had said before dozing off was that he shouldn't let her sleep past four thirty and already it was a quarter 'til five. He shook her gently and was greeted warmly as if some part of her had not expected to see him there and then she was in high gear, clothes retrieved and adjusted, fresh lipstick and mouthwash. He drove her to her car at the Country Club and without meaning to asked if he could see her again. Without breaking his stride or giving her opportunity to respond he continued "and *if* he could see her then *when*?" How much longer did she plan to live with this guy who obviously meant nothing to her?

During the next two months they met six times, once in Atlanta (the only trace of his predecessor being a book about transcendental meditation, a makeshift bong, and one really ugly polyester blend shirt, which enabled him to replace his Mr. Wonderful image with one that made him question her interest in him), once in Washington, and four times in a Days Inn in Greensboro, North Carolina. They talked on the phone every other day. Adam was starting to feel an obligation. Once he even thought the words *future* and *commitment*, he could foresee all the problems on the horizon: *where* would they choose to live? Would she even consider leaving the job that was going so well for her? God, would she have to have three children just as there had been in her own family?

"You know this is never going to work," he finally said, his hand slowly pointing from her chest to his own to make sure his point was understood. She was in his sparse apartment, her hair still dripping from his shower which she had quietly mentioned was a haven for fungus; she was wearing the flip-flops she kept just outside of the bathroom door.

"Why?" She absent-mindedly picked up the magazine she had brought with her, a woman in tweed blazer looking up from the slick page. She angled herself, terry cloth robe tied loosely, so that he was looking at her. "You mean us?" She said the word *us* as if it had been there forever, *us* like life, truth, God, eternity. He nodded slowly and she nervously picked the magazine back up, riffled the pages sending the heady floral fragrance advertised there into the room. "Why?"

"I'm not sure." He went over to his CD collection and began flipping through cases. "I'm just not sure." What he was thinking was it's now or never. Either we're going to call it off or we're going to make a decision. He was thinking that tradition says *she* should be the one initiating all of this and yet there she sat calmly asking all of the questions.

"Is it the North-South thing? I mean I never said I have to always live in Atlanta." She waited, forehead furrowed while he shook his head. He had given up on the argument that DC was not "the North" and in fact was considered by many to be in "the South."

"Well, is it the Jew-gentile thing because I really feel that I could go either way?" She paused, mouth twisted in thought. "I mean I wouldn't exactly *broadcast* it at home."

"No. That's not it." Now he was thoroughly confused. He had no good reason. All of the likely ones were there but they simply weren't good enough. They weren't good enough to overlook that rare match that might never happen again. How many awful weddings would he have to attend just to even come close to such a meeting? Still, he felt like a fool, confused and speechless.

"It's the Adam and Eve thing," he finally said later that night when she was almost asleep. "It drives me absolutely nuts."

"You're not serious?" She fumbled to turn on a light and then turned to face him. She was lying there propped up on her elbow without a stitch on, her thick hair fanned out around her face. "I was going by Evelyn, remember? *You* were the one who started calling me Eve. *Little Eve Lyn Wallace. Little Eve Lyn Wallace.* You said it so often you sounded like a mynah bird." Her eyes watered but she fought all impulse with a deliberate laugh and a forced shake of the head. He waited for her to deliver her biggest piece of ammunition, the fact that she had let him talk her right out of her old life and romance and right into his. He could hear it coming, the blame and insult. The imposed guilt and obligation, when he knew that what he really wanted was for her to tempt him, seduce him, beg him to marry her.

"You are serious." She sat up and pulled her worn-out robe from the floor. She had announced proudly on her first visit that fashion should never forsake comfort. Now she looked lost in the loose folds of terry cloth, the belt pulled tightly around her waist, and he found himself thinking about how she had said that as a child she had to sleep with her hand over her navel for fear that the boogarman would come and touch her there. He realized then that he had already wrapped the blanket around his body like a cocoon. This was not a conversation to have naked. "What if we were Mary and Joseph?"

"They had better results."

"I have no intention of being the person you want to step in and ruin your life, be an excuse for you to be screwed up and feel sorry for yourself." Her voice gave way to that slow twang he adored. "I know that's what you're looking for and that's not why I'm here."

Now he felt entirely stupid. He felt so incredibly stupid that he tried to turn it all around into a joke. She pulled out that big piece of hard Samsonite luggage that her parents proudly surprised her with (it was a story she often told when she had had too much to drink and was feeling homesick) when she moved to Atlanta, and he felt desperate. He begged her never to leave him. He said they should get married then, that weekend. He suggested they pull out the Atlas and look up all of the Edens they could find—Arizona, Maryland, North Carolina, Texas, Wyoming. They could get married in Eden, North Carolina, or Eden, Maryland; maybe they would live there forever. Maybe they would go to Eden, Australia, on a honeymoon, or maybe that was a trip for later, maybe that was for the silver anniversary. He hadn't meant anything that he'd said; it had all been anxiety talking.

She thought it was all hilarious for awhile. She laughed and kissed him, said that he was sweetly weird. She said that there was no reason to rush into anything, that given all that he had been thinking, she felt it best to wait at least a few months and then talk it over again. This made him feel the need all the more; he said he wanted a standard wedding, everything and anything she wanted. She said that she first needed to find an equivalent job; they needed to find an apartment with a clean bathroom.

When they finally got married it was in that same country club on a June day just about as hot. The bridesmaids wore lavender and there was a champagne fountain but no one passed out and Adam did not get thrown into the pool. Gretchel Suzanne Brown did give out quite a few business cards and there were many many Biblical jokes and great philosophical musings such as whether or not Adam and Eve had navels. Adam's fraternity brothers were threatening to strip him naked so as to answer this question as well as count his ribs, and he was praying to the God he wasn't sure existed that this wouldn't happen. If it did people would see that he had been trapped and held down, shaved, first thing that morning. He had not even told Eve. He was also praying that her body would not be covered in blue ink when they returned to that same Ramada Inn to spend their first night.

And one year, six Chippendale dining room chairs and one neurotic AKC registered Irish Setter later while in labor with their first child, Eve made it altogether clear that she preferred to be called Evelyn whether he liked it or not, that she was sick and *goddamned* (she gritted her teeth for emphasis) tired of the jokes, tired of his telling people that they met on the sixth day. It had been his way out, this ridiculous connection, as if by fate he had been forced to marry her. He was always the innocent one. Always the abused one, the neglected, the ruined man. She told him to put blame where he should, on his toilet training, his parents, his obsession with names, and to tell somebody who gave a damn, like a psychiatrist. She was seized by another labor pain and proceeded to say every word she had ever read on bathroom walls, the slow accent exaggerating the harshness of every single syllable.

"What about Cain if it's a boy?" Adam asked, trying to entertain the young nurse who after many bloody attempts finally got an IV in Eve's vein. Eve pointed to the helpless young woman's head and screamed, *Yoo Hoo! Stoooopid. Anybody home?*

"Cain," he said again. "Now, there's a good strong name from the Bible that you don't hear too often."

"You don't hear Judas, too much," the nurse whispered and stifled a laugh. Thank God, Eve had her bare back to them at the moment and missed that exchange; she was saying "shit" through clenched teeth over and over in the rhythm of "Jingle Bells."

"Judas, I like that," he whispered and then went back to his normal voice. "But Cain."

"If I'm alive," Eve screamed in anger. "If I'm *able*, I'll name this little son of a bitch anything I please."

"Able, she said *able.*" The nurse held her hands up to her mouth and fled the room.

"Don't look back," he said two days later as they were leaving the hospital with Sarah Wallace Rosen, nothing marked or murderous about her. "You'll turn to a pillar of salt." They were in the parking lot, Sarah wrapped in a lightweight cotton blanket, the cloth shielding her face from the sun. "Wasn't that Sarah who turned to salt? Wasn't she Lot's wife?"

"I always thought they said *pillow* of salt," Eve said. "I always pictured something entirely different from what they had in mind." She swung around and stopped, stared at the doorway they had just left. "Still here," she said, "I guess we're not worthy of those Biblical names after all," and Adam lifted the camera hung around his neck and focussed: Eve pasted on a background of chain link, red brick, and shimmering black asphalt that stretched into parking lots and one-way streets, highways and runways, subdivisions and cocktail parties, fields, forests, temptations and promises.

Jill McCorkle was born and raised in Lumberton, North Carolina, and educated at the University of North Carolina at Chapel Hill and Hollins College, in Virginia. She is the author of six books of fiction, the most recent of which is *Carolina Moon*, a novel to be published this Fall. McCorkle lives now just outside Boston with her husband and their two young children. She teaches writing at Harvard University and Bennington College.

With the beginning of every school year, the first thing I did was check to see if Jack Floyd was still in my class; if he was then I could prepare myself for another year of "Jack and Jill" jokes. It's the kind of teasing that people try to resist but in the end, can't. I'm relieved I married a "Dan," but as a result I am super sensitive to all of those pairs with famous names: George and Martha, Liz and Richard, Charles and Diana. In my story I simply began with the first sentence: "When Adam met Eve . . ." But instead of a Biblical garden and fig leaves I gave them a Southern country club wedding reception. The only bit of truth in this story (other than the setting) is that I was once a bridesmaid in a friend's wedding and the groomsman I was paired with at the front of the church closed his eyes and locked his knees during a particularly long prayer and as a result fell down and pulled me with him. A pediatrician got up from the congregation and pulled the groomsman out into the vestibule while I stood back up and pretended that nothing out of the ordinary had happened. I knew I wanted to use that incident in a story but beyond that I had no idea what to do with these characters. So I found myself thinking about the real Adam and Eve. I have always felt that Eve really got the short end; I think that if women scribes had been given a bit of clout, then the story would have differed dramatically and women would not have spent eons having to be eternally grateful for that donated rib. I thought I might really follow the story and consciously turn it all around, but then these two got in the champagne line and I became fascinated with what everyone was wearing and saying (just as I would at a real wedding), and the story went its own way from there.

Marcia Guthridge

THE HOST

(from *The Paris Review*)

I've never understood about fishing and buffalo stomachs. I admit it freely. I am no cannibal. But there are connections between me and the world. I'm not a cog. I'm a bolt. People who know me find me reasonable—neither gluttonous nor profligate. It is only my wife who thinks I devour without permission and eschew what I should eat.

Only yesterday, for example, just back from vacation, I was driving across the city, the water glittering in the lake on one side of me, skyscraping apartment buildings—clean steel Mies—glittering on the other side, Bach's "Air on the G String" on the radio. I soared. The road was newly paved and the high places were long, the dips so smooth and quick the nose of my little car never turned down, just fell for a second vertically and rose again, me with it. Two birds pumped upward in the distance and then a perfectly proportioned curve in the road—a classical Grecian curve—turned me to see an airplane, barely moving, opposite the birds but on the same slant, heading down for the airport I had just left. The plane disappeared behind a building; and when I saw it again, a trick of the sun, I guess, had it sinking straight down now, no slant, falling lazily like a parachute, like me and my little car when the beautiful road dipped. I knew my place.

*   *   *

Even the shells are bleached white here on my seashore. The Gulf of Mexico is so light a gray that the sun above it can blur it nearly to white. Directly across the same Gulf, on the edge of Florida where we went one spring on vacation because he likes color and baseball, the water is altogether different: blue. There are lots of palm trees and sea oats among clumps of long-bladed humid green grass, sea grapes with flat round red leaves, mossy pine trees, and a sky hectic with birds, such birds: blue herons and egrets with necks as slim and wavy as the sea-oat stalks and shockingly yellow beaks, greedy mud-colored pelicans flap-elbowing each other off the crowded fishing piers. The sun is red and sweet, unreal. The shells are striped and glossy. I found one that looked like the hide of a green zebra with one perfect straight orange line up the middle, as if painted on with a fine Japanese brush.

So after we went to Florida that one spring because he wanted to, after I'd spent the whole week comparing where we were to where I'd rather be—the shore of my childhood summers, the resort of my adult dreams—he said he'd see this beach of beaches. "Let's go to Texas. We'll take a few days off at the end of August. I want to see this place." He said it on the plane going home from Florida. Immediately I blanched innerly, like one of my Texas shells, like a brittle white sand dollar with a secret rattling in its closed chambers.

But I said it was a nice idea (indeed it was), and I said to myself that sensing danger would help me to avoid it. I knew he wouldn't like Port Aransas. I knew to him it would seem primitive and brutal. I knew to me it would seem primitive and brutal now, except it was inside me in the way places are inside creatures like creatures are inside places, like mountains are inside mountain goats, like mollusks are inside shells. I knew he was not my brother or my father, or even my cousin (he was my husband), and I knew that would be a problem. Blood bonds to places, and everything there is is layered and surrounded.

I thought I was ready. He would be my guest. But I did not

foresee the argument about murdering fish. How could anyone foresee such a thing?

We flew into Corpus Christi and drove the short distance to the tip of Padre Island in a rented Buick. Already this was wrong. When I was a child, my family strapped plastic buckets and rubber floats and beer coolers atop the car and drove down from Central Texas, where we lived. We crossed from the mainland on the car ferry, so the water snuck right up under us, car and all, first thing. Every year we took the same vacation, my uncle's family too; all eleven of us stayed in one cabin. One pair of grown-ups slept in the bedroom and the other pair in the sitting room, which was the same as the kitchen. Until my little sister and my youngest cousin grew up a little, they slept in the sitting room too, on a pallet made of beach towels on the sandy floor. The older kids got to sleep on the screened porch, on salt-smelling mattresses that felt as if they were stuffed with ancient oyster shells. We tossed and twitched on our crunchy beds gingerly, because of our sunburns. We giggled softly late into the night, and listened to the roar of trucks on the main island road a hundred yards away, and sometimes, as the trucks glided onto the Corpus Christi highway, we imagined we heard the Gulf waves whispering among the tall wheels.

Every morning we packed the two cars full of food and Coca-Cola and beer, and drove to the beach about a mile away. Sometimes the cars were so full of stuff we older kids were allowed to ride sitting on the doors, our legs inside and the rest of us out. You drive—still do—your car right up to the water, and then you could sit on top of it, stare at the Gulf, and pretend to be a pirate or a renowned fisherperson scouting schools. The car glinted in the sun and heated up like a roasting pan with you on it. We made sand animals. We buried each other: we'd dig a deep hole and put somebody in it, then smooth a mound of sand around his shoulders till it was a perfect dune with a head on it, and finally the buried kid's muscles went crampy, and he'd burst from the white earth like a white-hot rock from a volcano. We floated for hours at a time in the steamy salt water, to boil for a while instead of roast. The grown-ups fished in the surf.

We recognized the end of the day by how red our skin was, not by the color or position of the sun, which stayed high and strong till dusk, when it changed momentarily from white to yellow and popped suddenly into the water while no one was watching. When we were red enough we packed the cars and drove back to our cabin. My mother and aunt cleaned vegetables; my father and uncle cleaned fish. It was the children's job to take the laundry to the laundromat without dragging the towels through the sticker burrs in the pale lawn, and to fetch eggs or fruit or pickle relish from the Island Food Store which smelled of hot wood and bread. One afternoon we resolved to help with supper by trapping crabs. It took us hours to catch a dozen from the pier, none bigger than my youngest cousin's tiny fist, with legs like hairs, fleshless. By the time we got them back to the cabin they were dead in our dry creel. My father and uncle came home from fishing and found the bodies where we dumped them in the grass burrs by the back door. They made us boil them and (though my mother fought them on this—she said they'd already started to smell off) eat them. There was no more than a teaspoonful of meat in each crab. We scraped smidgens from crevices in the enameled labyrinths of inner shell, sucked the juice from spider legs, and then my uncle re-boiled the shards and strained the liquid for broth. My father thought it was necessary to eat what you kill. "It's not magic," I heard him say forcefully to someone later in the house, while I lay with the other children on the screened porch thinking of sleep. "It's common consideration. It's keeping things right between us and the fish."

The condo my husband had booked for us this time had a view of the Gulf and a Weber grill. When I saw the modern kitchen with its butcher-block island, I remembered how my mother and aunt laughed as they moved between the sink and the little table in our kitchen–sitting room, working with shoulders touching. I told him about that, and when he looked at me as if there must be more to the story, I added: "My mother didn't laugh when she cooked supper at home."

Immediately I went hunting the thermostat, turned off the air-conditioning and began tugging at the window over the carport. "Don't you think we'll be hot without air-conditioning?" he asked. "It must be a hundred and ten out there."

"This is urgent. There's got to be a crowbar here somewhere," I said. "I need a window open. I need a window open now." The windows were all painted shut. I pulled barbecue tools out of kitchen drawers until I found a hammer and a sturdy spatula. On my way back to the bedroom I saw his face. It looked all flattened out, pulled tight by the ears, so I smiled affectionately. "We're lucky to have the Gulf so close, you know." I didn't want him to be afraid.

I went to work furiously on the window. From well behind me, he peered toward outside. "There are cars right up on the beach," he called out, plainly astonished. "Would you look at that? People are driving their cars right up to the water!" Wood cracked, the sash zinged, and the window rolled open. I stepped back, sweating. Dead white paint chips littered the sill.

"I know. That's what you do here."

"Don't kids get run over?"

"Every once in a while. Not very often, I don't think."

We spent four days going to the beach. The wind was high the whole week. He sat on a towel decorated with the Coca-Cola logo and weighted on the corners by two Top-Siders, a Pat Conroy novel, and a bottle of SPF 30 sunscreen. He squinted at me through eyelashes studded with sand. He didn't wear sunglasses because he didn't want to tan like a raccoon. "Why are there so few birds here?" he asked. "No pelicans or herons like in Florida."

"There are gulls," I said, pointing to a homely line of them gazing with us at the water and staggering in the hot wind.

"Maybe for the same reason there are so few people," he answered himself. It was a Friday morning, and only a pickup and a sun-silvered Camaro were beached near us, pulled up to the high tide mark in line with the gulls.

I made peanut-butter sandwiches with jalapeño peppers on flour tortillas every noon, and carried mine down from the condo to eat them sitting in the breakers. Bits of tar swirled in the water around me. When one hit me it stuck like a leech. Sand blew into my mouth with every bite. Grit silted among my teeth after I swallowed. He usually stayed in the kitchen to eat his lunch, and then took a nap. He never wanted to go back to the beach after that because he'd already cleaned himself up once. It took quite a while to scrub, with mayonnaise, the tar from our skin. He wondered if it would ever come off his new trunks.

Evenings, we walked on the fishing pier to see what people were catching. We dodged flying hooks cast inexpertly by children off the windy rock jetty a mile or so down from the pier. "Sometimes you can catch crabs around here," I informed him.

Tuesday night we brought some shrimp back from Aransas Pass. I told him we might find a good restaurant over there on the mainland, but what I really wanted to do was ride the ferry. So we did, and we saw one restaurant that looked all right to him—a steak house built with stones on the bottom, logs on top, and a concrete Indian tepee on the roof like a chimney. We got as far as the crowded parking lot (it was the crowd that soothed and attracted him), and he stopped the rental car halfway nosed into a space. He left his hands on the wheel and turned to me. His eyes moved from my feet up to my neck. "You know," he began, still not looking at my face. "I don't want to embarrass you."

I can't say I wasn't surprised. The betrayal was too soon and too overt. "Yes?" was all I said.

"Well, it just occurred to me—I just noticed what you're wearing."

"I never knew you to pay much attention to my clothes." I had on a polyester muumuu I had bought at the Island Food Store and rubber flip-flop thong sandals.

"I never saw you looking like this before. You don't wear this outfit at home, do you?"

"No."

"Anyway, I don't think we ought to go in this place. These people look pretty dressed up." There was a group of women getting out of a car near ours. They had on high heels and carried patent-leather purses.

"Okay, forget it then." I didn't care about eating at a crowded steak house with a tepee on top anyway. I wanted to get back on the ferry. "Let's go back."

A couple of miles before the ferry landing, we stopped at an open-backed van by the side of the road and bought some shrimp in a plastic bag. "We'll take them home and boil them," I said. "You won't believe how fresh they'll taste." The fat woman who sold us the shrimp had three fat children playing in the front seat of the van, no front teeth, and flip-flops the same color as mine.

On the ferry I got out of the car, as usual, to feel the wind and look for porpoises as we chugged across the gassy little strip of water from the mainland. I considered the shrimp. I was fascinated by them, and had taken the plastic bag out with me to the ferry's front rail. They were dead, of course, but still perfect: their feelers and legs unbroken, black eye-beads, pale pink stripes. Their last meals were still visible through their fragile shells in their alimentary veins.

"I'd like to eat them with their skins still on," I said to him after we'd boiled them. "Eyes and all." They were pinker, done being cooked but each one still intact. They drained in a colander. Two of them embraced a limp half-lemon, their legs twined about it on either side. They were like mythological figures balancing a symbolic orb over an antique door. Steam rose from the colander: the absolute last of their pale pink spirits.

I relented and did not eat the eyes and shells; but I refused to let him de-vein my portion. Happily, I ate what the shrimp had eaten. I tried not to chew too many times, as if they were holy things, and so I could imagine them coming to life and swimming in my gut, eating what I ate, pink parasites in a gracious host.

It got hotter and hotter. We lay in bed one night at the end of the week listening to the hungry gulls calling for help. Pools of sweat rose in the hollows between my breasts and ribs when I lay on my back. I felt him sighing beside me, awake.

After a time, he got up. He flopped once, disentangled his long feet from the top sheet and popped out of the bed. He fumbled through a drawer and found his blousy seersucker trousers. He hopped on one leg around the room, fighting for his balance as he put them on. "I'm going for a walk, but I don't have much hope of cooling off. Even the goddamn wind is hot."

Now I sighed, answering his sleepless breathing. "Watch out for the snakes as you're crossing the dunes. They come out onto the paths at night."

He changed his mind, refolded his trousers carefully into the drawer, and returned to the sticky bed. Finally, I felt the springs soften and I could tell he was asleep. As I drifted off myself I remembered, too late, that we could have turned on the air conditioner.

When there was only one more day left, I decided we should go out on one of the party boats to fish. I had thought of it a few other times, earlier, but we hadn't gotten to it. I don't think he much cared what we did, and I had been happy floating in the waves, baking in the sand, and eating peanut-butter and jalapeño sandwiches. Now, I thought, it was time to go fishing.

And what caused the trouble was not the fishing, nor even my putting it off until it was so late. It was my real self, which had been flexing inside of me for the whole trip, and which burst out, wide awake, well grown, and ready to kick ass the minute I stepped onto that boat.

Every married person has a real self, I guess (as well as people who live with their mothers and with roommates), which over the years of being only in common places is slowly bludgeoned unconscious by a gathering of small blows with very blunt instruments: dishrags, bedsheets, dandelion roots, now and then a snow shovel. The real self hides like a small fish in a grotto, coils to save itself like a snake in the dunes, and sleeps. Around it, cell by cell, grows another more pliant personage to live in the common places: it knows how to avoid unpleasantness, Mexican food, excessive sun, ecstasy. Still the real self wakes sometimes at night to moon-bask on the cool dune paths and to star in dreams of rebellion and courage, or to fish in the Gulf for its darkly swimming buried kin.

It was a rough trip out that day. It always was, as I remember from when my father and uncle used to take me and the other kids out on these big boats designed for groups of inexperienced fishermen. One side of the boat is designated for being seasick and the other for fishing. I have never been among the seasick. In fact, the happiest I have ever been, I think, is when standing with my hips fitted snug into the point of the bow riding up a swell and crashing down, shrieking, salt water soaking me, stinging my sunburn. I did it this day too, now adult and undignified, having ignored the warnings of the old sailor who captained the boat. Still I shriek and sing; again I am the happiest I can be.

As soon as we stopped, the men around us made a shiny pop-top reef around the boat and let out their lines. I baited my double hook with a ribbon fish and wiped my hands on my orange terry-cloth shorts, which I had bought years ago for my father. He had died a few days before his birthday. I had kept them in a box and had finally decided to wear them myself.

"These guys are drinking beer?" he said. "Jesus, it's 8:30 in the morning." He looked queasy. He hadn't enjoyed the ride out. "But it is hot."

The steel deck rail was becoming uncomfortable to the touch. He leaned over the side, then came back upright but swaying. "This water looks like it's about to boil. I think I'll buy a soda. You want something?"

"Beer." He headed for the cabin. I fished. "Maybe you should get yourself some crackers to settle your stomach," I called after him.

He was wrong: this water was not about to boil. It was still, bubbleless, foamless, as secret as frozen soil in winter. We had left the clattering gulls behind with the shore. I saw one lone shrimper at the very edge of sight, its nets hoisted up, head past us and home somewhere. I trusted the leathery old sailor who had brought us here. Indeed, he even had an electronic fish-finder up on the bridge, if the sign by the dock was true. There were fish below us.

But I firmly felt, staring at my slack line, they were asleep at the faraway mud-misted bottom of the Gulf, as soundly asleep as jonquil bulbs in Yankee January.

It was a half-day trip. We were supposed to be ashore again by noon. By eleven, the captain had moved us twice and all that had been caught was one dark-fleshed jack (my father called them liverfish), two puny kingfish off the stern, and a large pitted gray rock by someone's grandson who had been fishing near me and who, in the process of reeling in his rock, managed to tangle my line hopelessly with his. For a rushing moment, I'd thought we'd awakened the fish and we both had bites; but instead, when the rock was decked I had to squat and cramp my fingers unthreading our lines from it. Many people lost bait. Something down there was nibbling in its dreams.

As I re-baited my hook we moved again. In the new place I lowered my line with a benediction; in answer, ten minutes later, ten minutes before we would have turned for shore, there was a flicker of fish fifteen yards from the bow where I stood. It gamboled near the surface, twisting like a puppy, its energy mixing and shining with the sun. "There's my fish," I whispered.

"That's no kingfish! It's a tarpon," yelled the captain from above me on the bridge.

My line zinged taut. With the calm of the prescient, I raised my pole to set the hook, and in an instant that hook was on its way to Florida. "Let her run awhile," the captain told me. He was right behind me now. "Reel in," he ordered everybody else. "This little lady's got a fish on here, big one. Never expected a tarpon today. Don't see them all that much." He sounded as if he doubted whether I deserved such a fish.

"Now you start inching her in," he advised me. My arms ached already just from holding onto the pole while the fish ran. When the fish rested I braced the end of the pole against my stomach and turned and turned the reel. When it jerked and swam sideways the captain pushed me along with it. Up and down either side of the boat I sashayed and sidestepped to fool the fish into thinking it was pulling me; then, when the captain gave the word, I pulled it. My arms went numb early on. "You want me to take over?" he asked.

I shook my head. "My fish," I gasped. The dearth of breath in my lungs gave this the sound of a question.

It was a fish fight from one of my father and uncle's tales. I had caught a fish or two as a kid, dragged it myself off a boat like this to the scale by the fish-cleaning house, hugging it on the way like a dead child. We used to catch small sharks and kingfish, jack, once a big tuna I didn't like the taste of. They fought, but not like this fish, my fish.

Suddenly the line went slack. I thought my fish was lost. But it was only breathing under the boat, trying to trick me. I waited.

The numbness spread to my legs. By the time the fish started running again I had braced myself against the railing in a V shape, the grip of the pole poking my midsection out into a point, my heels on the deck and my toes smashed up against the side of the boat, my arms stretched to the utmost to keep from losing the tackle. I reeled and waited, holding tight. Finally, I could feel where the fish was: less deep and very close. It lolled, enervated by the warm surface water. I reeled some more, and unbraced my legs enough to lean and peep over at the water. My fish flashed at me a silver greeting from an eighth of a mile underwater.

"I saw it," I sighed.

"Damn straight," the captain whispered in my ear. "You want this fish?" I nodded and shrugged to catch some sweat from my chin. "Then reel." I felt blisters rising on my hands with each heart-beat. I knew how the fish felt. I too had surrendered in warm salt water, unable to swim for the lapping of waves in my mouth. I knew how the hook hurt as it pulled, how it jabbed as I gnawed it; so when my fish began its last run and the pole slipped in my chafed and sweaty hands, I considered going with it over the side, letting my fish catch me.

I re-gripped. And when the fish was done running I reeled with the end of my strength. I bore down like a mother for the last push in a birthing, and up came the fish with a splash like a gunshot. It

flipped, looping the line round its tail in the air. It was miracu-
lously silver-blue-and-green, the same colors as the winking hot
Gulf. Blood covered its face. The captain and I were both soaked
by its explosion out of the water. He climbed to a perch on the
deck rail, ready with his gaffing hook, and kept coaching: "*Up.
Keep the tip up!*"

The fish out of water was too heavy for me. I let it drop back
down. It was gone again. But I sat on the end of my pole as if it
were a seesaw and pried it up again. The bones in my crotch ached,
but the fish was caught. The captain and one of his teenaged assis-
tants gaffed it through its middle and levered it onto the boat.

"That is a nice fish," the teenager dryly opined. We were all
flattened against the side of the boat watching it die. Decked, it
flopped and faded from blue-green to gray. Its gills pulsed hugely
and irregularly. I could not see its eye for the blood from around
the hook. I could hardly breathe. Some of us on deck hopped and
slid around to avoid the thrashing fishtail. The grandson who had
caught the rock climbed with me onto the railing and stared envi-
ously at me as I watched my fish. The teenaged assistant reversed
his gaffer and slammed the fish in the head a few times with the
handle. Soon after that it stopped caroming about the deck. It
lifted itself twice from the slimy pinkened boards, its middle rising
first, then up-ended the curve in the air and thudded down. Finally
it died with its gill chamber wide open. Each filament was discrete:
you could have counted them, hung like harpstrings. If you were
small enough and careful you could have walked among them in
the spaces where the breath had been, like a Chinese weaver in an
ancient silk factory with the worms next door.

"I can recommend a taxidermist in Fulton," the captain said to
me. His teenager had started the boat and was turning us around.
Someone had dragged my fish to the cooler astern, where it lay
ignominiously among mackerel. For a moment I didn't understand the word.

"Taxidermist. Oh, I don't want a trophy," I said. "I'm going to
eat it."

"Oh no ma'am," advised the captain, politely laughing. "Most people around here don't like to eat tarpon." The men around me tittered.

"Why not?"

"It's no eatin' fish. My way of thinking, fish like this, you mount it."

"I'll eat it."

He searched for another way to explain, forcefully: "It ain't good eatin'."

"You expect me to hang it on the wall?"

"Hell yes. That is one good-looking fish. Skull's in pretty good shape." All the men on deck began talking and gesturing about trophies. They didn't know anything about eating tarpon. They were just siding with the old sailor. "Here, we'll see what your old man thinks about it." He had come up behind me, and saluted with his beer can. It was close enough to lunch for him to have one now, and I guess he had gotten used to feeling on the border of sick. He still looked yellow.

"Did you see?" I asked him.

"Of course I saw. I was right here the whole time. Look how wet I am." He jiggled his knees so I could hear his shorts sloshing. "That is a big fish. You should be proud."

"I am proud. I caught it. I'm going to eat it."

"I think we should have it mounted."

"This fish is too important to stuff," I said. The captain wheeled and waved a hand at my face as if I were a fool and words were useless. I hated to lose his approval, but my real self was now in control. He headed for the ladder to the bridge.

My husband reasoned: "It's because the fish is so important that I think it should be mounted. We'll find someone in Corpus Christi and have them send it to us when it's done. We'll leave early tomorrow for the plane and drop it off."

"No."

"Well, we don't have time to eat it, even if we wanted to. We're going home tomorrow." He was becoming annoyed. I could see the tightness in his throat as the words passed through. "You should have gone fishing earlier in the week, okay?"

"I don't care. I'll find some dry ice and take it on the plane in coolers. I'll have it cleaned and cut up."

"They won't let you on an airplane with dry ice. My daddy's a pilot," offered the boy who had caught a rock.

"How many coolers do you think we'll need for a forty-pound fish? Or more?" he yelled, waving his arms and spilling his beer.

"I'll give some away."

"Nobody wants to eat this kind of fish. You heard him. He says it's not good."

"It is good. I'll figure it all out."

I had to eat what I caught. Or, at least, what I caught had to be eaten. If there were someone to help me eat it, I could share. I didn't have to eat it all myself, but it couldn't be wasted. I had been taught this as a child. It was part of my family's science. My father's people claimed kinship with the Plains Indians, a tenuous connection, which my mother maintained was no more than fancy dress for an ancestor's sexual indiscretion; still my father loved to talk about buffalo hunting—eating the meat, making spoons from horns, clothing from skins, and toys from blad-ders—wasting nothing. It was important that if you killed some-thing you kept its life going by taking the whole of the dead into yourself. I don't know that he ever said it to me just that way, but I know it to be true.

I've never seen anyone act so crazy and be so convinced she's right. If I pulled the car over by this curb and stopped a hundred people at random and told them the whole story, I bet they'd all side with me. She said her father made her eat dead crabs. She said I had no soul. She said there was nothing real left of me. She said she was descended from Native Americans who used all of the buf-falo. She made no sense.

I came home on the flight we had tickets for. Christ, I had to be back at work—and she stayed so she could find enough dry ice and coolers to pack up her stinking fish. Maybe they won't let her on any plane. Maybe she'll have to eat the whole thing there, frying it up in chunks on a hot plate in that lousy beach house. Maybe she'll stay down there forever eating tarpons. She's gone completely nuts. She'll swallow the eyes and crunch up the tail, eat the liver and turn into a fish. Isn't that what the Indians did? I tried to calm her, smooth her down. She was bristly. "Let's not make this into life and death," I said.

"What the hell else do you think it is?" she screamed back at me, spitting. The back seat of the rental car was piled high with slimy, bloody plastic bags containing bits of fish. She'd wrestled the thing by herself down the dock and had it chopped up at a fish house. She was covered with blood and the car smelled awful. (Oh, my own little car calms me, now I'm home. It smells so good, and it fits so well around me.) "My fish is bleeding, bleaching into me. It is exactly just life and death," she raved.

"You're scaring me," I said. Her left forearm was clean of fish blood. I touched the salty skin there. I remember we passed one of those big spiraling plastic slides that dump kids into pools of water and I thought how the kids on that one, shadeless in this wild place, must be getting their butts burnt off, and I remember thinking I was glad we were going home.

At first she wheedled me. Her voice was low and monotonous, humming. She suggested we take the fish back to that hot little condo and stay another week (a week or so is what she said—"or so": how long?). We'd jam the refrigerator full of fish and start eating. "We'll eat the fish together. You'll help me eat it."

I pictured that cheap Formica table in the kitchen dripping with slippery fish, the butcher-block island twinkling with scales. I saw barrels of tartar sauce, mountains of lemons, fried filets, ceviche, tarpon chowder in a washtub, minced-fish-and-onion cakes the size of basketballs. I saw the little Weber grill smoking up the carport full-time for a week "or so," scarring slabs of fish with charcoal stripes, and I saw her sweating and grinning through the smoke. I glimpsed the edge of lunacy myself. I thought of fish fritters for breakfast, and my stomach quivered. "I don't really care that much for fish, you know."

That was all I said, and then she cut loose and sang her anger at me. She chanted like a TV evangelist or a witch doctor in a Tarzan movie. Her face was bright orange and shining—sunburnt I guess, but it occurred to me that she'd caught fire from sitting in this deadly sun all week and was about to combust spontaneously, right there on the bloody car seat. Her features looked blurred, as if they were starting to melt like the plastic on the baking water slide. To touch her now would burn me. Her hair was mashed flat on the top of her head from this ugly fishing cap she'd been wearing, and it jutted out in stiff salty tufts around her ears.

She said I had no connections with things. She went on and on about the sea and the fish and the plains and the buffalo and life and death and her childhood. She said even the Christian culture knows how to redeem violence: through sacrament. She would take communion, eat her fish. If she didn't, nothing made sense. I don't remember half the things she said. She said Indians ate what they loved. She said it was a kind of cannibalism, so I should understand it: I had swallowed her.

Marcia Guthridge was born in San Antonio, Texas, and grew up there and in New Orleans, Louisiana. She received a PhD in English Language and Literature from the University of Chicago, where she studied with Richard Stern and David Bevington. Her work has appeared recently in *The Paris Review*. She lives in Chicago with her husband and three children.

Years and years ago I caught a large kingfish off a party boat like the one in "The Host." I was so proud that I began to think of myself as a fisherperson, and I kept right on thinking that way through hot fishless days on other boats. At parties I talked as if I knew all about bait and tackle. I read Jimmy Carter's book on fly fishing; I watched the Saturday morning fishing shows on TV while my kids clawed at me, screaming for cartoons. Finally I realized that my kingfish had provided me not with an avocation but with one of those life-defining moments; and since it was beginning to look as if that mackerel was the only real fish I'd ever catch, I figured I'd better write a fish story. When I'd finished, it was just a silly little story about catching a fish: no challenge to Hemingway or Babe Winkelmann. So I decorated it with stuff about the Texas Gulf Coast and being married. I know it's nothing without the decoration, but to me it's a fish story.

Robert Olen Butler

JEALOUS HUSBAND RETURNS IN FORM OF PARROT

(from *The New Yorker*)

Never can quite say as much as I know. I look at other parrots and I wonder if it's the same for them, if somebody is trapped in each of them, paying some kind of price for living their life in a certain way. For instance, "Hello," I say, and I'm sitting on a perch in a pet store in Houston and what I'm really thinking is Holy shit. It's you. And what's happened is I'm looking at my wife.

"Hello," she says, and she comes over to me, and I can't believe how beautiful she is. Those great brown eyes, almost as dark as the center of mine. And her nose—I don't remember her for her nose, but its beauty is clear to me now. Her nose is a little too long, but it's redeemed by the faint hook to it.

She scratches the back of my neck.

Her touch makes my tail flare. I feel the stretch and rustle of me back there. I bend my head to her and she whispers, "Pretty bird."

For a moment, I think she knows it's me. But she doesn't, of course. I say "Hello" again and I will eventually pick up "pretty bird." I can tell that as soon as she says it, but for now I can only give her another "Hello." Her fingertips move through my feathers, and she seems to know about birds. She knows that to pet a bird you don't smooth his feathers down, you ruffle them.

But, of course, she did that in my human life, as well. It's all the same for her. Not that I was complaining, even to myself, at that moment in the pet shop when she found me like I presume she was supposed to. She said it again—"Pretty bird"—and this brain that works the way it does now could feel that tiny little voice of mine ready to shape itself around these sounds. But before I could get them out of my beak, there was this guy at my wife's shoulder, and all my feathers went slick-flat to make me small enough not to be seen, and I backed away. The pupils of my eyes pinned and dilated, and pinned again.

He circled around her. A guy that looked like a meat packer, big in the chest and thick with hair, the kind of guy that I always sensed her eyes moving to when I was alive. I had a bare chest, and I'd look for little black hairs on the sheets when I'd come home on a day with the whiff of somebody else in the air. She was still in the same goddam rut.

A "hello" wouldn't do, and I'd recently learned "good night," but it was the wrong suggestion altogether, so I said nothing and the guy circled her, and he was looking at me with a smug little smile, and I fluffed up all my feathers, made myself about twice as big, so big he'd see he couldn't mess with me. I waited for him to draw close enough for me to take off the tip of his finger.

But she intervened. Those nut-brown eyes were before me, and she said, "I want him."

And that's how I ended up in my own house once again. She bought me a large black wrought-iron cage, very large, convinced by some young guy who clerked in the bird department and who took her aside and made his voice go much too soft when he was doing the selling job. The meat packer didn't like it. I didn't, either. I'd missed a lot of chances to take a bite out of this clerk in my stay at the shop, and I regretted that suddenly.

But I got my giant cage, and I guess I'm happy enough about that. I can pace as much as I want. I can hang upside down. It's full of bird toys. That dangling thing over there with knots and strips of rawhide and a bell at the bottom needs a good thrashing a couple of times a day, and I'm the bird to do it. I look at the very dangle of it, and the thing is rough, the rawhide and the knotted rope, and I get this restlessness back in my tail, a burning, thrashing feeling, and it's like all the times when I was sure there was a man naked with my wife. Then I go to this thing that feels so familiar and I bite and bite, and it's very good.

I could have used the thing the last day I went out of this house as a man. I'd found the address of the new guy at my wife's office. He'd been there a month, in the shipping department, and three times she'd mentioned him. She didn't even have to work with him, and three times I heard about him, just dropped into the conversation. "Oh," she'd say when a car commercial came on the television, "that car there is like the one the new man in shipping owns. Just like it." Hey, I'm not stupid. She said another thing about him and then another, and right after the third one I locked myself in the bathroom, because I couldn't rage about this anymore. I felt like a damn fool whenever I actually said anything about this kind of feeling and she looked at me as though she could start hating me real easy, and so I was working on saying nothing, even if it meant locking myself up. My goal was to hold my tongue about half the time. That would be a good start.

But this guy from shipping. I found out his name and his address, and it was one of her typical Saturday afternoons of vague shopping. So I went to his house, and his car that was just like the commercial was outside. Nobody was around in the neighborhood, and there was this big tree in back of the house going up to a second-floor window that was making funny little sounds. I went up. The shade was drawn but not quite all the way. I was holding on to a limb with my arms and legs wrapped around it like it was her in those times when I could forget the others for a little while. But the crack in the shade was just out of view, and I crawled on till there was no limb left, and I fell on my head. When I think about that now, my wings flap and I feel myself lift up, and it all seems so avoidable. Though I know I'm different now. I'm a bird.

Except I'm not. That's what's confusing. It's like those times when she would tell me she loved me and I actually believed her and maybe it was true and we clung to each other in bed and at times like that I was different. I was the man in her life. I was whole with her. Except even at that moment, as I held her sweetly, there was this other creature inside me who knew a lot more about it and couldn't quite put all the evidence together to speak.

My cage sits in the den. My pool table is gone, and the cage is sitting in that space, and if I come all the way down to one end of my perch I can see through the door and down the back hallway to the master bedroom. When she keeps the bedroom door open, I can see the space at the foot of the bed but not the bed itself. I can sense it to the left, just out of sight. I watch the men go in and I hear the sounds, but I can't quite see. And they drive me crazy.

I flap my wings and I squawk and I fluff up and I slick down and I throw seed and I attack that dangly toy as if it was the guy's balls, but it does no good. It never did any good in the other life, either, the thrashing around I did by myself. In that other life I'd have given anything to be standing in this den with her doing this thing with some other guy just down the hall, and all I had to do was walk down there and turn the corner and she couldn't deny it anymore.

But now all I can do is try to let it go. I sidestep down to the opposite end of the cage and I look out the big sliding glass doors to the back yard. It's a pretty yard. There are great, placid live oaks with good places to roost. There's a blue sky that plucks at the feathers on my chest. There are clouds. Other birds. Fly away. I could just fly away.

I tried once, and I learned a lesson. She forgot and left the door to my cage open, and I climbed beak and foot, beak and foot, along the bars and curled around to stretch sideways out the door, and the vast scene of peace was there, at the other end of the room. I flew.

And a pain flared through my head, and I fell straight down, and the room whirled around, and the only good thing was that she held me. She put her hands under my wings and lifted me and clutched me to her breast, and I wish there hadn't been bees in my head at the time, so I could have enjoyed that, but she put me back in the cage and wept awhile. That touched me, her tears. And I looked back to the wall of sky and trees. There was something invisible there between me and that dream of peace. I remembered, eventually, about glass, and I knew I'd been lucky; I knew that for the little, fragile-boned skull I was doing all this thinking in, it meant death.

She wept that day, but by the night she had another man. A guy with a thick Georgia-truck-stop accent and pale white skin and an Adam's apple big as my seed ball. This guy has been around for a few weeks, and he makes a whooping sound down the hallway, just out of my sight. At times like that, I want to fly against the bars of the cage, but I don't. I have to remember how the world has changed.

She's single now, of course. Her husband, the man that I was, is dead to her. She does not understand all that is behind my "hello." I know many words, for a parrot. I am a yellow-nape Amazon, a handsome bird, I think, green with a splash of yellow at the back of my neck. I talk pretty well, but none of my words are adequate. I can't make her understand.

And what would I say if I could? I was jealous in life. I admit it. I would admit it to her. But it was because of my connection to her. I would explain that. When we held each other, I had no past at all, no present but her body, no future but to lie there and not let her go. I was an egg hatched beneath her crouching body, I entered as a chick into her wet sky of a body, and all that I wished was to sit on her shoulder and fluff my feathers and lay my head against her cheek, with my neck exposed to her hand. And so the glances that I could see in her troubled me deeply: the movement of her eyes in public to other men, the laughs sent across a room, the tracking of her mind behind her blank eyes, pursuing images of others, her distraction even in our bed, the ghosts that were there of men who'd touched her, perhaps even that very day. I was not part of all those other men who were part of her. I didn't want to connect to all that. It was only her that I would fluff for, but these others were there also, and I couldn't put them aside. I sensed them inside her, and so they were inside me. If I had the words, these are the things I would say.

But half an hour ago, there was a moment that thrilled me. A word, a word we all knew in the pet shop, was just the right word after all. This guy with his cowboy belt buckle and rattlesnake boots and his pasty face and his twanging words of love trailed after my wife through the den, past my cage, and I said, "Cracker." He even flipped his head back a little at this in surprise. He'd been called that before to his face, I realized. I said it again, "Cracker." But to him I was a bird, and he let it pass. "Cracker," I said. "Hello, cracker." That was even better. They were out of sight through the hall doorway, and I hustled along the perch and I caught a glimpse of them before they made the turn to the bed and I said, "Hello, cracker," and he shot me one last glance.

It made me hopeful. I eased away from that end of the cage, moved toward the scene of peace beyond the far wall. The sky is chalky-blue today, blue like the brow of the blue-front Amazon who was on the perch next to me for about a week at the store. She was very sweet, but I watched her carefully for a day or two when she first came in. And it wasn't long before she nuzzled up to a cockatoo named Willy, and I knew she'd break my heart. But her color now, in the sky, is sweet, really. I left all those feelings behind me when my wife showed up. I am a faithful man, for all my suspicions. Too faithful, maybe. I am ready to give too much, and maybe that's the problem.

The whooping began down the hall, and I focussed on a tree out there. A crow flapped down, his mouth open, his throat throbbing, though I could not hear his sound. I was feeling very odd. At least I'd made my point to the guy in the other room. "Pretty bird," I said, referring to myself. She called me "pretty bird," and I believed her and I told myself again, "Pretty bird."

But then something new happened, something very difficult for me. She appeared in the den naked. I have not seen her naked since

I fell from the tree and had no wings to fly. She always had a certain tidiness in things. She was naked in the bedroom, clothed in the den. But now she appears from the hallway, and I look at her, and she is still slim and she is beautiful, I think—at least I clearly remember that as her husband I found her beautiful in this state. Now, though, she seems too naked. Plucked. I find that a sad thing. I am sorry for her, and she goes by me and she disappears into the kitchen. I want to pluck some of my own feathers, the feathers from my chest, and give them to her. I love her more in that moment, seeing her terrible nakedness, than I ever have before.

And since I've had success in the last few minutes with words, when she comes back I am moved to speak. "Hello," I say, meaning, You are still connected to me, I still want only you. "Hello," I say again. Please listen to this tiny heart that beats fast at all times for you.

And she does indeed stop, and she comes to me and bends to me. "Pretty bird," I say, and I am saying, You are beautiful, my wife, and your beauty cries out for protection. "Pretty." I want to cover you with my own nakedness. "Bad bird," I say. If there are others in your life, even in your mind, then there is nothing I can do. "Bad." Your nakedness is touched from inside by the others. "Open," I say. How can we be whole together if you are not empty in the place that I am to fill?

She smiles at this, and she opens the door to my cage. "Up," I say, meaning, Is there no place for me in this world where I can be free of this terrible sense of others?

She reaches in now and offers her hand, and I climb onto it and I tremble and she says, "Poor baby."

"Poor baby," I say. You have yearned for wholeness, too, and somehow I failed you. I was not enough. "Bad bird," I say. I'm sorry.

And then the cracker comes around the corner. He wears only his rattlesnake boots. I take one look at his miserable, featherless body and shake my head. We keep our sexual parts hidden, we parrots, and this man is a pitiful sight. "Peanut," I say. I presume that my wife simply has not noticed. But that's foolish, of course. This is, in fact, what she wants. Not me. And she scrapes me off her hand onto the open cage door and she turns her naked back to me and embraces this man, and they laugh and stagger in their embrace around the corner.

For a moment, I still think I've been eloquent. What I've said only needs repeating for it to have its transforming effect. "Hello," I say. "Hello. Pretty bird. Pretty. Bad bird. Bad. Open. Up. Poor baby. Bad bird." And I am beginning to hear myself as I really sound to her. "Peanut." I can never say what is in my heart to her. Never.

I stand on my cage door now, and my wings stir. I look at the corner to the hallway, and down at the end the whooping has begun again. I can fly there and think of things to do about all this.

But I do not. I turn instead, and I look at the trees moving just beyond the other end of the room. I look at the sky the color of the brow of a blue-front Amazon. A shadow of birds spanks across the lawn. And I spread my wings. I will fly now. Even though I know there is something between me and that place where I can be free of all these feelings, I will fly. I will throw myself there again and again. Pretty bird. Bad bird. Good night.

Robert Olen Butler has published eight books—seven novels and a volume of short fiction (*A Good Scent from a Strange Mountain*), which won the 1993 Pulitzer Prize for Fiction. His stories have appeared in many magazines including *The New Yorker*, *Harper's*, *The Hudson Review*, *The Sewanee Review*, and the *Virginia Quarterly Review*, and have been chosen for inclusion in *The Best American Short Stories* and *New Stories from the South*. His forthcoming book, *Tabloid Dreams*, a collection of short stories that includes "Jealous Husband Returns in Form of Parrot," is being produced as a Home

Box Office series. He lives in Lake Charles, Louisiana, with his wife, the novelist and playwright Elizabeth Dewberry.

*J*ealous Husband Returns in Form of Parrot" *draws its inspiration from a headline in a supermarket tabloid. It was the second piece written in a recently completed volume of fifteen first-person stories, all based on just such headlines. The book, called* Tabloid Dreams, *tries delicately to balance its range of mixed tones between the comic absurdity of popular culture and the serious, enduring human concerns of art. This headline seemed a natural to me: I have lived with parrots and I have lived with jealousy, and this particular narrator seemed ready to speak from both sides of his beak.*

Susan Perabo

SOME SAY THE WORLD

(from *TriQuarterly*)

T here is fire in my heart. I do what I can.
   I sleep deep sleep. I sit in my bedroom window, bare feet
on the roof, and scratch dry sticks across the slate. In the two
months I've been living here, though, I've spent most of my time
playing board games with Mr. Arnette, my mother's new husband.
He seems to have an unending supply of them in his basement
from when his kids lived at home. My mother isn't around very
often. She works at the makeup counter at Neiman Marcus,
although she really hasn't needed to since she and Mr. Arnette were
married. Mr. Arnette retired a few years ago, at forty, when he sold
the windshield safety-glass company he had started right out of
high school for what my mother described as "a fancy sum, for
something that still shatters." It was right after that that she met
and married him. But she works anyway, only now she calls it a
hobby.

   It's early March; more importantly, Monday night, the night my
mother pretends to be in class at community college. This semester it's poetry, but she's run the gamut. Two summers ago she
thought she had me convinced she'd taken up diving.

   When she comes in the door a little after nine she sets her clearly
untouched poetry book on the end table next to where I am on the
couch.

"How was it?" Mr. Arnette asks, smacking his gum and not looking up from the board.

"Oh my," my mother said. "You wouldn't believe the things those people wrote then."

"Who'd you do tonight?" I ask her. It is a game that I have worked up. Sometimes I suspect that Mr. Arnette is playing it as well, but other times I think he's just being duped by her. You can never tell with Mr. Arnette. Sometimes I imagine he has a secret life, although he rarely leaves the house. He seems the type of guy who might have boxes of knickknacks buried all over the world for no reason.

"What's that?" my mother asks, separating the lashes over one eye, which have been caked with sweat-soaked mascara.

"Who'd you do tonight?" I put a cigarette in my mouth, wait for one of them to light it.

"Oh, Browning," my mother says.

"Which one?" Mr. Arnette asks. He looks up at me, not her, then takes the lighter from his shirt pocket and snaps on the flame in front of my face, so close I could reach out and swallow it.

"Which *one?*" she asks.

"Which Browning," Mr. Arnette says. The lighter disappears back into his shirt.

My mother misses a beat, then says, "All of them."

She hovers over the Parcheesi board, feigning interest in the game, and her mink stole knocks one of my pieces to the floor. Mr. Arnette makes a disgusted sigh, although it was him, I know, who bought her the thing. She likes to wear it to work, along with a lot of expensive jewelry. She does not work *for* her customers, she recently explained to me, she works *with* them.

She pats my head. "About your bedtime," she says, as if I am twelve and have to get up early to catch the school bus, not eighteen and drugged beyond understanding anything much more difficult than Parcheesi and knowing that my mother, at forty, is sneaking around in motel rooms.

*   *   *

My parents were divorced when I was five. I have not seen my father since then, but even so I've been able to keep track of his moods. If my mother is irritable on Monday nights I know that my father is considering calling everything off. If she is sad I know that he has asked for her back. If she is her usual perky self, like tonight, I know that things have gone as planned. They have met every Monday in the same motel since I was in the sixth grade and playing with lighters under my covers after bedtime. I used to find motel receipts, not even torn or wadded up, but just lying in the kitchen wastebasket next to orange peels and soggy cigarettes, with "Mr. and Mrs." and then my father's name following. Still, my mother, through eight years and two more husbands, has never spoken of it to me, and acts as if I could not possibly have figured it out. Thus over the years I have been forced to make up my own story of them: passionate but incompatible, my father a dashing and successful salesman, only through town once a week, only able (willing?) to give my mother three hours. Other times I think it is she who insists on being home each Monday by nine, she that likes doling herself out on her terms, only in small doses. I imagine that they do not talk, that their clothes are strewn around the room before there is time to say anything, and back on by the time they catch their breath. It is easier for me to think of it this way, because I can't imagine what they might possibly say to each other.

At Neiman Marcus, where my mother works, they found me in a dressing room last winter with a can of lighter fluid and my pockets stuffed with old underwear and dishtowels. This incident was especially distressing because everyone finally thought that after nearly eight years I had been cured, that the fire was gone, that I was no longer a threat to society. The police led me out of the store handcuffed, first through women's lingerie and then smack past the makeup counter, where my mother was halfway pretending not to know me, or to know me just well enough to be interested in what was taking place. They put me away for almost a year for that one, my third time in the hospital since the first fire. The length of my stay was caused by pure frustration, I'm convinced, on the part of my doctors. The "we'll teach her" philosophy of psychology. Two months ago they let me out again, into a different world where my mother is married yet again, and I spend my days spitting on dice with her husband and asking politely for matches to light my cigarettes. Either the doctors think I am cured or they have given in, the way I have, the way I did when I was only eleven, when I realized the fire was like blood, water, shelter. Essential.

The thing about fire is this: it is yours for one glorious moment. You bear it, you raise it. The first time, in the record store downtown, I stood over the bathroom trash can, thinking I would not let it grow, that I would love it only to a point, and then kill it. That is the trick with fire. For that thirty seconds, you have a choice: spit on it, step on it, douse it with a can of Coke. But wait one moment too long, get caught up in its beauty, and it has grown beyond your control. And it is that moment that I live for. The relinquishing. The power passes from you to it. The world opens up, and you with it. I cried in the record store when the flame rose above my head: not from fear, but from ecstasy.

I sleep sixteen hours a day, more if it's rainy. Another rationale: enough Xanax and I will be too tired to start fires. I am in bed by ten and don't get up till nearly noon. Usually I take a nap before dinner. The rest of the time is game time. It's a murky haze, more often than not. Me forgetting which color I am, what the rules are. Sometimes Mr. Arnette corrects me; other times he lets it go and it is three turns later by the time I realize I have moved my piece the wrong way on a one-way board.

We are on a Parcheesi kick now. Seven or eight games a day. We don't talk much. Mostly we just talk about the game, about the pieces as if they are real people, with spouses and children waiting in some tiny house for them to return from their endless road trips. "In a slump. You're due," Mr. Arnette will say to his men. Sometimes he whispers to the dice. I suspect this is all to entertain me, because he is always checking my reaction. Usually I smile.

*   *   *

Twice a week Mr. Arnette drives me across town to see my psychiatrist. He reads magazines in the waiting room while I explain to the doctor that I am fine except for the fact that I take so much Xanax I feel my brain has been rewired for a task other than real life. The doctor always nods at this, raising his eyebrows as if I have given him some new information that he will get right on, and then tells me the medication will eventually remedy any "discomfort" I might be feeling. I am used to this, and have learned not to greet with great surprise the fact that no one is going to help me in any way whatsoever.

It's Friday, and on the way home from the doctor's we drive by a Lions Club carnival that has set up in a park near Mr. Arnette's house. It is twilight, and my mother will be waiting for us at home, but for some reason Mr. Arnette follows the waving arms of a fat clown and pulls into the carnival parking lot.

"What do you say?" he says. He takes a piece of gum from his pocket and puts it in his mouth.

I look out the window at the carnival. I don't get out much. Grocery stores are monumental at this point, and the sight of all these people milling around, the rides, the games, frightens me. A Ferris wheel directly in front of me is spinning around and around, and it makes me dizzy just watching it.

"I'm kinda tired," I say.

Mr. Arnette chews louder, manipulates the gum into actually sounding frustrated.

"I think it'd be good for you," he says. He has never said such a thing before, but instead of causing me to feel loved and comforted it makes me nauseous. I've been told everything from shock treatments to making lanyards would be "good for me," and in practically this same tone.

I feel like crying, and know if I do that he will panic and take me home. But I don't have the time. He is out of the car before I can well up any tears, and I continue to sit, my seat belt still on, staring out the window into the gray sky. Mr. Arnette stands in front of the fender, gesturing for me to join him.

The last time I was at a carnival was the Freshman Fair at my high school, five thousand years ago. I went on a Saturday night with a boy named Dave who took pictures for the school paper. He held my hand as we walked through the crowds of people and he was sweaty—greasy, almost. He stuck his tongue in my ear in the Haunted House ride and I barely noticed because they had a burning effigy of our rival school's mascot on the wall. The fire licked along the walls and I realized with absolute glee that they had set up one hell of a fire hazard.

Mr. Arnette gets back into the car with a sigh, but does not drive away.

"You need to get out more," he says, and I wonder what has changed, wonder if he had a fight with my mother, or sex with my mother, or some other unlikely thing.

"Used to take the kids here," he says, spinning the keys around his finger. I don't even know his kids' names. They call occasionally, but he speaks so rarely when he's on the phone with them that I can't pick up very much information. I imagine them jabbering away somewhere about work and weather and the price of ground round while he sits on the kitchen stool, picking his fingernails and nodding into the phone.

"I'm not exactly a kid," I say.

"You don't like carnivals?"

"I just don't feel like it."

"If she doesn't feel like it then she doesn't feel like it," he says, as if there is someone else in the car, another part of him, maybe, who he is arguing with.

We continue our drive home in silence. When we stop at a red light he says, "Why do you take all that shit if it makes you feel so bad?"

I laugh at him. It is a question so logical that it pegs him for a fool, and I can't believe I'm really sitting here with him.

"It's not quite that simple," I say.

He shrugs, gives it up, continues the drive home. He is not a fighter, not a radical. Once I came upon him in my bedroom, looking through a photo album of people he had never met. I stood in the doorway and watched him for nearly ten minutes, as he smiled slightly, turning the pages, and I imagined him making up lives for the people in my life. He is that way. Content not to get the whole picture.

I'm standing in the bathroom, trying to stir up enough nerve to just dump them, the whole bottle. My mother taps lightly on the door. I spend more than two minutes in the bathroom and she gets edgy.

"Honey?"

"Just a second," I say. I'm holding them in my hand, all of them. There must be a million of them, at least, enough to confuse me until I hit menopause.

"Are you sick?"

I close my hand around the pills and open the door just far enough for her to get her foot in it.

"Mother," I say. "I'm fine. I'm just putting on a little makeup."

This gets her, physically sends her back a step. She wants to believe it so much that I can see her talking herself into it.

"But it's almost time for bed," she says.

"Just to see how it looks," I say, giving her a big smile through the crack and inching the door closed again. I hear Mr. Arnette's heavy footsteps come tromping up the stairs.

"What's the fuss?" he asks.

"She's putting on makeup," my mother says in a stage whisper. "Maybe she's trying to look cute for you."

That takes care of my clenched hand. It opens of its own accord at my mother's words, and the pills sink to the bottom of the toilet, falling to pieces as they go.

"I think she's really just feeling up to it, starting to feel better," I hear my mother say. It is a new tone for her, and this time it's really a whisper, really some sentiment she doesn't want me to hear. I put my ear against the door. "I'd do anything to make her happy," she says. It makes my chest hurt, she believes it so much.

* * *

Sunday has come and my eyes can't stay open wide enough. I feel as if I have gotten glasses and a hearing aid over the weekend; colors are brighter and words sharper. No echoes. Words stop when mouths stop. My mother looks at me suspiciously when she comes into the kitchen early in the morning and finds me cooking bacon.

"What's gotten into you?" she asks, pleasantly enough, but with a flicker of panic in her face. Me around the oven means bad news for her. But the heat rising from the burners is only making me warm, and the smell of the bacon is so good that I can't think of much else.

"Just feeling awake," I say.

She smiles, nods, then studies me.

"I'm fine," I tell her.

Mr. Arnette drags into the kitchen, his hair mussed and his robe worn. I have never seen him in the morning.

"Well look who's up," he says. He winks at me.

"Why don't I finish up and you two go in and start a game," my mother says brightly. Mr. Arnette sits down at the table and opens the newspaper.

"I don't feel like it," I say. "Why don't we do something today?"

"We have to go to a party later," my mother says, glancing at Mr. Arnette for support. "I don't think you'd have very much fun there."

I set a plate of eggs and bacon in front of Mr. Arnette.

"Where's mine?" my mother asks.

"You hate eggs," I say.

"We don't *have* to go to the party," Mr. Arnette says.

My mother frowns, looks from him to me.

"Well I do," she says. "And I think it would be right for you to come with me. She can take care of herself."

I see my mother now, like she has been stripped down out of her clothes and her skin and even her bones. Her soul is steamed over and dripping fat droplets.

"You all go on," I say. "I don't mind."

*   *   *

I spend the day with my father. I sit out on the porch with the old photo album. The pictures make sense now, fit into an order I have never seen before. My father as a young man raises a tennis racket over his head. He is swinging at something: a butterfly or a bug, though, not a ball. In another he stares away into the distance while my mother pulls his arm, trying to get him to look at the camera. They are so clear now, my father and his bird nose. In one picture he holds me on his lap. I am crying, screaming, and my father is looking at me perplexed. He is barely twenty, I know, and cannot believe that I am his.

My mother and Mr. Arnette do not come home until late. I've lost track of time, still sitting with the photo album when the headlights swim into the driveway. They get out of the car and my mother takes Mr. Arnette's hand, swings it wildly around.

"Oh, darling!" my mother exclaims. I am not sure if it is to me or Mr. Arnette.

They are both drunk. My mother stumbles going through the door and Mr. Arnette catches her, leads her inside. Then he comes back out, grunts, and sits down on the porch step.

"What have you been doing all night?" he asks.

"Looking through this," I say, holding up the album.

He is quiet for a moment. Then he says: "You ever see your father?" He says it almost as an afterthought, but to something that wasn't said. He says it like we've been on the porch together all night, discussing my father for hours like he was really one of the family.

"Just in here," I say.

"Think he's still a good-looking guy?"

"Dashing, I imagine," I say.

He snorts out a laugh.

"Why'd you marry her?" I hear myself ask.

He leans back, rests his head on the wood inches from my feet.

"Company," he says. He yawns. And I can see him now, too. Safety glass that still shatters. He begins to snore.

"Mr. Arnette?" I say. I reach down and just barely touch the top of his head. He doesn't move.

I go into the house and up the stairs. Their bedroom door is closed, and I imagine my mother is in about the same shape as he is, but that they will sleep it off in different places, with dreams of different people's arms.

When I open my door, my mother is standing in my room, the empty bottle of Xanax in one hand, the other hand palm up, as if she were questioning someone even before I arrived.

"Wait a minute," I say. "Just wait."

"I knew it," she says. "I knew there was something wrong."

"Nothing's wrong," I say. "What are you doing in my room? You scared me, standing there like that."

Her mouth opens. "I scared you?"

"I don't think I need those anymore," I say.

"Forgive me if I find it difficult to trust your judgment," she says.

I want a cigarette bad. I had to go all night without them, and I go to the dresser for my pack.

"A light," I say. "Do you have a light?"

"Not on your life," she says.

"I'm fine," I say. I accidentally break the cigarette between my fingers and reach for another one.

She sits down on the bed. "You hurt people," she says quietly. "Not just me. You think you take those pills because I don't want you to hurt me?"

"I never hurt anybody," I say.

"You are so lucky," she says. "You could have killed both of us five times over. In the dressing room, did you ever think about the woman in the next one?"

"I wasn't trying to hurt anybody," I say. "You don't understand."

"You're right about that," she says. She sets the empty bottle on the bed and stands up. "I'm sorry," she says. "I can only live with this for so long."

She leaves. I hear her bedroom door close. The house is silent. Below me, Mr. Arnette sleeps on the porch.

I sit down on the bed. I am crazy, all right. I have always been crazy. I see my mother standing on the front porch as I get out of my first police car, only fourteen, braces squeezing my teeth. She stares at me in disbelief when the police tell her that I have caused over a thousand dollars in damage at the record store, a thousand dollars with only one match. It is then that she begins to look at me like a stranger.

It's Monday again, and she is in her bedroom preparing. Mr. Arnette sits in the rocking chair watching a basketball game. I am on the couch. Cheers from the crowd.

"She wants you to go back into the hospital," he says. He doesn't look at me. He moves his glasses from hand to hand.

"I know," I say. "It's O.K. It's not so bad there."

"Anybody play Parcheesi?"

A man on the court has lost his contact lens. Players are on their knees, hunting.

"Cards mostly," I say. "Lots of jigsaw puzzles."

He nods. "You take those drugs today?"

"No," I say. "Soon enough. It's funny, being able to see so well. But not great so much."

My mother comes into the room and picks up her purse. "Have a good game," she says. She kisses Mr. Arnette on the top of the head, presses her lips into his hair for a long time, until he moves away.

"What was that for?" he asks. He really wants to know, I can tell.

"It doesn't have to be for anything, does it?" she says. She smiles at me, lingers for a moment as if she has something to add but cannot remember what it could have been, and then she leaves.

Mr. Arnette swings the rocking chair around and faces me. "You don't have to go," he says. "Imagine me here, all by myself."

"You'll do O.K.," I say. "Come visit."

He nods, picks up the poetry book from the coffee table where my mother has left it, absently flips through it.

"She didn't even think to take it along," he says.

"She doesn't try so hard anymore," I say. "To fool anybody."

He stops on a page, squints at it, puts on his glasses. "Here's one you'd like," he says, smiling. "*Some say the world will end in fire, others say in ice.*" He stops, looks up at me and raises his eyebrows.

"I'd like to see them," I say. I hear my mother's car start up in the driveway. "Just one time, see them together. Be a fly on the wall."

"We can be flies together," he says.

It is not a long drive, only a few miles, much too close as far as I'm concerned, for something that seems like it must be another world. Mr. Arnette stays a few cars behind her, then drives past the motel after she pulls into the lot. He drives around the block twice, then three times.

"What are you waiting for?" I ask him.

"A reason not to do this," he says. He presses down the accelerator and we speed past the motel again. We drive around the city, looking at closed-down stores, empty streets. We don't talk, act as if we really have nowhere to go. He finally makes his way back to the motel, and this time he pulls into the lot. We park at the far end and walk along the row of empty spaces, toward my mother's car. The motel is nearly empty, but the room next to her car is occupied. The shade on the window is up a couple of inches. Mr. Arnette squats down, then reaches for me.

I close one eye and look inside. The bathroom light is on, the door open, and I can see my mother gingerly applying her eye shadow in front of the mirror. There is a man in the bed, sitting up, yawning. He stretches his skinny arms. He is nearly bald, but has a small mustache under his pointed nose. It is a stranger, no one I have ever seen before.

"He looks a lot different than the pictures," Mr. Arnette whispers.

"It's not him," I say, but as soon as I say this I know that it is.

Mr. Arnette looks at me. "Sweetheart . . ." he says.

My mother shuts off the bathroom light and I can see her silhouette move to the edge of the bed. She sits down and touches the man on the chest, running her finger from his throat to his waist. He takes her hand and puts the finger in his mouth. It is like watching shadows. She says something I cannot make out. Is it about me? Of course, I realize, it is not.

I shiver in the cold. Mr. Arnette takes off his sweater and sets it around my shoulders.

The man begins to put his clothes on, slowly. Next to me, I hear Mr. Arnette's breath catch.

"What is it?" I whisper. I wonder if he can be jealous, if he cares that much.

He only shakes his head. "Chilling," he whispers.

"What?" I say.

"What happens to people."

They are sitting on the edge of the bed together. My mother fumbles for her purse, takes out a pack of cigarettes, gives one to my father and takes one for herself. She lights them both.

"Where will we go?" Mr. Arnette whispers.

"What?" I say.

They are holding hands on the bed. The shadow of smoke drifts above them, the tiny circles of fire all that light the room.

"Where will we go?" he says again. I lean in against him. He is warm.

Inside the room is quiet. Together the man and the woman raise the cigarettes to their mouths. For a moment, the faces of my parents glow in the darkness. Then Mr. Arnette takes me by the arm and actually lifts me off the ground.

"Wait," I say. "Wait." But I don't fight him. I want him to take me away, finally. I have seen enough.

We are three blocks from the motel before he remembers to turn on his headlights.

"Slow down," I say. "You're gonna kill us both." I take out a cigarette and push the car lighter in.

"Jesus Christ," he says. "What would she do then?" For a moment he is insane, so much more than I ever could have hoped to be.

There are lights up ahead. Music. It is the carnival, its last night, in full swing. The car wildly spits up gravel as Mr. Arnette rumbles across the lot. He jumps out of the car, dashes forward a few feet, then turns and slams his fist into the hood. Then he is perfectly still. He looks straight at me, and I am afraid to move. The cigarette lighter clicks out. A father rushes his children into the back of the station wagon next to us, where they look at us through the big back window, mouths open.

I pull the lighter out, touch my fingers close enough to the middle to feel the raw heat. Then I light my cigarette and blow smoke into the windshield. Mr. Arnette watches me. I know now that he will never go back to my mother, will probably never lay eyes on her again. Something about seeing them, even though he knew. Something about seeing them.

He turns and starts walking toward the ticket booth. I get out of the car and follow him, stand behind him smoking while he buys two tickets.

"Ferris wheel," he says, turning to me. He smiles slightly. "None of those puke rides. Slow. Slow rides tonight."

We get into a car that I'm sure is broken. It swings differently than the others, crooked somehow. I start to say something, but a girl with yellow teeth and matching hair closes the bar over us and we are suddenly moving in a great lurch forward.

"Hey, hey!" Mr. Arnette says, squeezing the bar and looking down onto the park.

"These things are dangerous," I say.

"Bullshit," he says. "We're safer up here than anywhere else in the world."

We screech to a halt near the top, for the loading of passengers into the cars below us. We swing crookedly over the game booths, and I can see us, crashing down into the middle of the ring toss. So many ways to buy it, so few to stay alive.

"I've always liked the looks of Canada," Mr. Arnette says. He is smiling pleasantly, innocent as the dawn.

We start moving again. The motion is hypnotizing, and I no longer feel sick, but only strange, detached.

"Nice night for driving," I hear myself say.

He doesn't answer. He is looking at my hands, which are open, palms up on my lap, as if I am waiting for something on this ride. He reaches into his sweater pocket and takes out his pack of gum. He sets it in my hand, and my fingers close around it.

We swing around again. Below me, I see a circle of teenagers standing around a small bonfire, warming their hands. Sparks pop around them and die in the grass as the flame reaches higher. The Ferris wheel whips us toward it, and then away again, up into the night.

———————

Susan Perabo is a native of St. Louis and holds an MFA from the University of Arkansas, Fayetteville. She has recently worked as the director of the Arkansas Writers-in-the-Schools program and as a World Literature tutor for the University of Arkansas Razorback football team. Her stories have appeared in *The Missouri Review*, *Black Warrior Review*, *Denver Quarterly*, *Indiana Review*, and *TriQuarterly*.

This story began for me with a couple of images: the narrator sitting in her bedroom window, and she and Mr. Arnette squatting on the sidewalk outside the motel room. Once I had those in mind, I filled in the middle. Many of the other elements emerged from the "land of misfit toys" in my head, the place where broken and homeless ideas wait for me to find a spot for them.

Annette Sanford

GOOSE GIRL

(from *New Texas*)

When Rooney's mother died, Uncle Pete Polk put her house up for sale and rented a smaller one back of the Gulf station to put Rooney in.

"This is just right for you, Rooney. You have your washroom here, we'll put your bed in there, and you can do a little cooking here in the back—"

Three rooms, it sounded like, but it wasn't but two: the one bigger room and the closet-sized bathroom he was calling a washroom because that's what they called it over at the Gulf where he hung around all day and where now he would be looking at Rooney over the fence to see what she was doing when what she wanted to be doing was taking care of her geese at her house across town, with her mother well again and home from the hospital.

"I don't like it over here." Rooney was thirty-three and had positive ideas on every subject, which she was entitled to, her mother said. "She' s got her own style, the same as the rest of us."

Pete called it backwardness, especially now that he was in charge of her and bent on settling her in a proper place before it dawned on her good that her mother was gone.

"There's no bathtub," said Rooney. No mirror either. Not that she cared much. She wasn't much of a dresser—pants and shirts she bought at garage sales and her hair cut short like a cap on her head. But she did like a mirror before she went to work, in case toilet paper was stuck to her shoe or something was trailing behind her like the Kick Me signs she used to wear home from school, and one time her telephone number with a picture drawn under it that made her mother so mad she bawled out the principal.

"You put a stop to this, Junkins!" His name was Jenkins. "Those bratty kids, they're making Rooney feel dumb."

"Miss Rhoda," said Jenkins, "nobody around here is smart enough to do that."

"He's right, you know it?" Rhoda told Pete when she thought it over. "Rooney can act sometimes like a sack's been throwed over her, but then again, she sure can surprise you."

"Amen to that," her brother said. Twice Rooney had bitten him, once with her baby teeth to see how he tasted, and later on when he reached for a slice of pineapple on her plate.

"I thought she was done with it!"

Rhoda bound up his hand. "She's partial to pineapple."

Rhoda spoiled Rooney, Opaline said. Opaline, Pete's wife, who had set in motion the sale of Rhoda's house and Rooney's relocation to a less valuable property. "The bungalow by the Gulf," Opaline called it. *Like it sets by the sea*, Rooney said. *More like the sewer plant*, she always added.

Spoiled or not, Rooney paid her own way. She had a long-standing job at the tailor shop and a more recent one, sitting Wednesday evenings with Grandma Polk, who wasn't right anymore and was liable to go out in the street and take off her clothes. Wednesday night was when they played Bingo over at the Hall, which Rooney liked to do, but couldn't anymore on account of Grandma Polk, who on several occasions she had prayed would die. Instead, the message got mixed up and her mother had died.

"You don't need a bathtub," Uncle Pete said. "You got this shower." He pointed it out, a pipe with a head on it, dripping through a hole in the galvanized flooring Rooney would have to stand on when she cleaned herself up.

That was the upmost important thing, her mother said. To keep yourself clean. Your body, your hair, and above all, your teeth. And always have something to wipe off your nose with.

"I don't like a shower," Rooney said. "Besides that, there's not enough room in here to swing a pig."

"You won't have to swing a pig," Pete told her. Or feed chickens either, he prevented himself from saying. He had hauled them all off—the geese too—day before yesterday while Rooney was knocked out from what the doctor gave her. When she came to herself, he said the sheriff had done it. In Rooney's best interest is what he said.

Now Rooney said to him: "If I can't swing pigs what else can I do in this squeezed-up place?"

"This nice secure house," Pete corrected. "You can watch your TV and read your books."

Rooney, somehow, was a first-class reader. Nothing at school had impressed her much, but reading she took to. She read everything from encyclopedias to *National Enquirers*, and everything, of course, written about wrestlers.

She named a dog Pete gave her after one of her favorites, Sweet Sugar Brown. His career took a nosedive when a truck hit his namesake, or so Rooney said, said so often her mother banned wrestling on TV forever.

Rooney went out and bought her own set. Two TV's going full blast on different channels was hard on the neighbors, but they had to put up with it or put up with Rooney interrupting their soap operas with a steady string of calls from the tailor shop.

"I can't read in here," Rooney told Pete. "The walls aren't painted."

"You need painted walls? Why is that, when every wall in your mama's house is bare as a baby's butt!"

"Nuh-uh," Rooney said. She fished gum from her purse and filled her mouth with it. "The dining room's painted."

"One room in fourteen, forty-five years ago."

"My bedroom's papered."

"With magazine pages."

"It' s paper, aint it?" Rooney rubbed her front teeth, a habit she had that drove Opaline crazy.

Something else worried Opaline: Rooney and men. There weren't any yet, but who knew when there might be?

"She has no restraint," Opaline said to Pete. Some of the money from the sale of the house they better set aside in case of an emergency.

"Like what?" Pete asked.

"Like having Rooney's tubes tied if things get rough."

Pete had mentioned tube-tying to Rooney's mother when Rooney came into puberty. "You need to see to it, Rhoda, before some fool boy takes advantage of her."

Rhoda ran Pete off, ran him clear to the highway. "You tend to your business and I'll tend to Rooney's!"

Now she wasn't here to do it.

It gave Pete a sour stomach, thinking what could happen if it got around town that Rooney might have money from her mother's estate, Rooney in Rhoda's house off by the highway where any kind of man could slip right in.

"I'm going to locate a truck," Pete said to Rooney, "and get you moved over here first thing in the morning."

"You're not moving me." She walked around, kicking up splinters off the floor. "I need arm room when I read. I need to be in my chair. My chair won't fit anyplace in this house."

"Don't," Pete said. "Don't start on that chair."

"It' s one of a kind in the U-nited States. Just ask Father Bailey. Father Bailey said—"

"I've heard all that, Rooney."

"He said take it to a mall show, you'll get five hundred dollars!" Rooney grinned at Pete the way she did as a child when he picked her up and said, Give me some sugar. She gave him big smacks and he called her his girl.

"Do you know what, Pete?"

He seemed to be praying. "I don't want to know what."

She got up in his face with her ketone breath the doctor said she might grow out of, but she never did. "I got my chair all covered with old-timey neckties. Got 'em at garage sales, ten cents apiece, sometimes a nickel. I got the arms and the back covered, the seat and the sides. Sewed 'em together without any help. It's beautiful, Pete. Did you ever see it?"

"See it, hell. Who had to go to the dump in ninety-degree weather to drag it out?"

"Wasn't me," Rooney said. "I found it, is all. On my lucky day. Just rode my bike out there and there was my chair. Finders keepers. Did you ever hear that, Pete? Finders keepers?"

"We need to move on to another topic."

"I sewed sixty-nine neckties into that cover." She showed him how, using the tail of her shirt to artificially stitch through.

"I've seen how you did it."

"You can see it again."

"Dammit, Rooney, that's the trouble with you!" A pencil-sized vein sprang up on his temple. "You talk a thing to death, you won't let it rest. You beat everything into the ground."

"Don't you holler at me!"

"You wear folks out with all your jabbering."

Rooney nailed Pete with her zebra stare. *Wild* zebra stare, Opaline called it.

They got a good look at it day before yesterday when Pete and Opaline went over to the house with buckets and sponges and cardboard boxes.

"Put everything you want in these here cartons," Pete said to Rooney, who was out in the backyard feeding lettuce to the geese. "We're putting this house up for sale. We got to get rid of things."

"You're not getting rid of any of my stuff." Rooney called her rooster. "Chick a-chick-chick. You better come here. Better come get your breakfast."

"You come on inside now and help your Aunt Opaline."

Rooney set her hands on her hips. She had on a green nightgown and red rubber boots. "You're not the boss around here."

"I'm the executor. The executor of the estate."

Rooney picked up a bucket and poured wet chicken mash over his head.

"God*dammit*, Rooney! Opaline! Git out here!"

His wife came running, having seen everything from the kitchen window. "I told you not to rile her! Now look what she's done. She's ruint that shirt! You ought not to wore it. I told you the blue one, put the blue one on, I said."

Rooney turned a hard spray of water on Opaline.

They had to call the law, a neighbor did. When the police car rolled up, Rooney was in the henhouse gathering more eggs to throw at her aunt and uncle.

The sheriff stepped in. "Now calm down, Rooney."

She saw his badge. She flung up her nightgown to cover her face and rooted herself in the ground like a concrete piling. It took two grown men and the doctor they had to call, to drag her out. You could hear her yelling downtown before the doctor got her quiet.

It put a sweat on Pete, seeing that look again. He commenced backing off. "Now hold on, Rooney. Think what the doctor said, count to ten—"

"Ten of *what*."

"It don't matter what!"

She was swinging her purse when a sound shook the house that stopped her cold. "What the heck was that?"

"God," panted Pete, "—speaking right on the money!"

"That was something blowing up!"

"A tire," he said. "Over at the station."

"A *tire*! Are you sure?"

He said, still shaken, "They blow up easy, those big old semi tires, when they're pounding the rims off."

Rooney gazed at him, thrilled. "You ever seen one?"

"Seen half a dozen."

"Wow!" Rooney said. "I wish I could see one."

"You can see 'em all the time when you live over here. You can get you some binoculars and see it up close."

Rooney worked her chewing gum. "Over at my house I see

everything close, coons washing their feet in the chicken water. Rabbits and buzzards." She pulled on her lips. "Furthermore, I'm gonna get me a goat."

"A goat! What for?"

"The sheriff ran off my chickens. And my geese too."

"What you need is a cat. This is a nice cozy place a cat would like."

"I'd rather have a snake than a mangy old cat, always licking theirselves and coughing up hair balls. I might get me a snake. A bore constrictor. They don't have eyelids. I bet you didn't know that."

"Listen, Rooney, I'm older than you and you need to listen to what I'm telling you. That house of your mother's is way too big for a woman by herself up by the highway. You stay around there and one of these nights a hitchhiker is gonna slip in and hide in one of those rooms you don't ever use and do you some harm."

"I got locks, don't I?"

"Busters like that, they don't stop at locks."

"I bet they stop at ball bats. A hitchhiker fool with me, I'll crack his head open. I got my bat right where I sleep."

Rooney picked up her purse again, heavy as a suitcase from all she had in it, packs of letters from her pen pals all over the country, paperback books poking out the top, and a big ring of keys that didn't open anything, but came from the dump, the same as her chair.

She said over her shoulder, "I'm going home."

Pete hurried after her. "I asked you not to do that, not to go over there while we're showing the house. I asked you to stay away and you said you would."

"I changed my mind." She went down the steps and got on her bicycle. The bumper sticker on the back fender said EAT MORE RICE. The one pasted under it said JOIN THE NAVY. (She covered it up when they turned her down.)

She looked back at Pete, standing glumly on the porch. "You like this bungahole, move in it yourself."

"I can't move anywhere. I got Grandma Polk."

"And you can keep her too, especially Wednesday nights. There's smells in that room, and noises even donkeys couldn't come close to."

Rooney rode off. She rode around a tree and came back again. "I might move in here if you get somebody to paint everything green."

"Rooney, I can't do that! I can't paint a house I don't even own."

"You're fixing to own it."

"Who told you that?" The way she gathered information was worse than a vacuum cleaner. People talking in front of her, thinking nothing would register.

"You're gonna use my money to buy this house and charge me rent."

"That's a big damn lie! We would never charge you rent."

"Green," Rooney said and rode off toward town.

"There's twenty-nine hundred greens!" Pete said to Opaline. "Send Billy Buckley over there. Let her tell him which one."

Billy Buckley the painter had showed up in town to paint the old bank they were turning into a post office. He hung around afterward, painting all kinds of things, and ended up living at the county barn where he was kind of a nightwatchman and got a room free, a partitioned-off place next to the office. A big restroom really. The county men came and went, using the toilet.

Billy was hoping to move, but he had a gambling habit that kept him choosing all the time between cards and food. Finding money for rent was just as unlikely as buying a TV, which he dreamed of nightly.

When he arrived at Rooney's she was sitting in the porch swing giving a ride to a hen that had come out of the bushes after Uncle Pete' s purge.

"I'm the painter," he said. "Name of Billy Buckley." He wasn't bad looking except he let himself go, hair and everything, let his clothes get dirty.

"I know who you are," Rooney said.

"I know you, too. I was painting the firehouse the day they vaccinated the dogs."

"They ran mine over. Sweet Sugar Brown. The Schwann man did it."

"I seen it," said Billy. "I seen you run out there and kick his tires. I asked one of those fire guys, Who is that? 'That's Rooney,' he said. 'Rooney Polk.' "

Rooney gazed off in the direction of the Gulf station. "Tires blow up."

"Up?" said Billy. "I thought they blew out."

Rooney laughed. "That' s car tires, dummy."

"Oh," Billy said. "Well, I got a pickup." He pointed it out, an old blue truck with the door hanging open. "I brung you some paint samples." He set a little packet down in the swing. "Trouble is, all of 'ems green."

"You don't like green?"

"I can take it or leave it." He wiped his nose on his sleeve.

"Use your handkerchief," Rooney said.

"I don't normally carry one."

She stopped the swing. "You don't carry a handkerchief? My mother told me, Always have something to blow your nose on."

"Mine told me, Don't blow out the candle till it's time for bed."

"What'd she mean?"

"I was hoping you'd tell me."

Rooney studied his grin. "You want to sit down?"

"Can you move that chicken?"

"Shoo!" Rooney said and tossed the hen in the air.

"Is she gonna go on off?"

"Look for yourself." Rooney made room for him. "Green," she said, "is nature's color. I read all about it in a science book."

"I don't read much."

"I read all the time."

"I watch TV. Except I don't have one."

"I got two," Rooney said.

"You got two TV's? Billy sat up straight. What do you want to read for?"

"'Cause I do it good." Rooney leaned over and read his cap. "Blue Star Ointment." Then the writing on his shirt. "Grand Gateway to New Orl*ee*ns."

Billy tapped his chest. "This right here is the Huey Long Bridge."

"You ever crossed it?"

"Crossed it all the time. Painted it twice. Painted most of New Orlins and half a Louisiana before I left out of there." He watched Rooney rub her teeth. "Say, what are you doing?"

"Doing what I want to. I could paint if I wanted to, but I got a job already."

"At the tailor shop."

"How did you know?"

"I seen you through the windows when I was painting the frames."

"I'm the presser that's been there the longest of anybody."

"How long is that?"

"Ever since school. I press pants and shirts. And tablecloths. Well, I used to press tablecloths till people stopped using 'em."

"Two TV's," Billy said. "Do you ever watch talk shows?"

Rooney halted the swing. "I'm talking about tablecloths."

"I thought you was through." He broke off suddenly and leaped to his feet. "Git outta here, chicken!"

Rooney laughed. "Git outta here, Joyce, this man is scared of you." She went after Billy. "I guess you're scared of snakes too. I'm gonna git me one. A bore constrictor."

Billy turned around. "Are you cooking stew?"

"Cooking chili," said Rooney. "As soon as you leave I'm gonna eat me some."

"Why don't you eat it now and give me a bowlful?"

"Why should I?" said Rooney.

"'Cause it's the best smelling stuff I ever smelled."

"You'll like it better when you taste it. Come in the house. I'll show you my chair. But you have to take a bath before you can sit in it."

A little after nine Pete's telephone rang. He came running back like a mad dog had bit him.

"Git up, Opaline!" She was soaking her feet. "There's a terrible commotion over at Rooney's."

"Has her geese come back? I told you they would. I told you to take 'em across the river or they'd be back home before you turned around."

"It's worse than geese. It's Billy Buckley!"

"Billy Buckley's over there?"

"You told me to send him."

"Not in the dark!"

"He went in the daylight. They swang in the swing till the sun went down. Then they went in the house and now they're in there, yelling and screaming."

"Call the police!"

"Not twice in one week. We've got to squash it ourselves."

"I'm not going over there with Rooney riled up."

"You're going if I'm going. Put on your shoes!"

They took awhile getting there. Grandma Polk had lathered all over with shaving cream. They had to stop and rinse her off and give her a sleeping pill and then wait around to see if it worked.

Rooney' s house was dark when they stepped on the porch.

"I bet she's pregnant already," Opaline said.

Pete banged on the door. "Open up in there!"

Rooney's voice boomed back. "If you're one of those hitchhikers I got a ball bat waiting for you."

"I'm your Uncle Pete Polk with your Aunt Opaline!"

A light came on. Rooney came down the hall in boxer shorts and a long draggy sweater. "What are y'all doing, waking up people?"

Opaline said, "Do you sleep in that?"

"Do you sleep in those pink sausages pinned to your head?"

"All right, girls! Now you straighten up, Rooney, and tell me the truth. Is that painter in there?"

"No, he aint. He's gone on home where y'all oughta be, tending to Grandma. I bet she's out in the street, catching a cold."

"You pay attention to your uncle," Opaline said. "We were woken up by neighbors to come and quell a disturbance between you and that Buckley man."

"Yelling and screaming," Pete said.

"Oh that," said Rooney. "We was watching TV and a chicken flew on him."

"You don't have a chicken."

"I got one old hen that's smarter than the sheriff. I left a crack in the door and she waltzed right in. Buckley don't like feathers and she lit on his head." Rooney laughed. "You should have seen him run! In and out of these rooms. I had to tear off his collar before I could stop him."

"A chicken?" said Pete. "That's all there was to it?"

"Yup." Rooney yawned. "Until he started up again when I asked him later on would he like to get married."

Opaline shrieked. "You hear that, Pete? An absolute stranger and she's ready to marry him!"

"I didn't say marry *me*. I'd marry a pig before Billy Buckley. He don't read. He don't even know what a handkerchief is."

"Then what did you ask him for?"

"I asked him, Pete, would he like to get married, meaning to any somebody, because if that was in the picture I wasn't going to ask him to move in with me."

"Unlatch this screen and let me sit down."

Rooney led them to the kitchen where the chili was eaten and the bowls still stood, and the crumbled up crackers.

"You've got to understand one thing," Pete said to Rooney. "There has never been a Polk woman that lived with a man that wasn't her husband."

"The heck there hasn't! What about Aunt Lena? Four men all the time, and quick as one left, she got her another one."

"Aunt Lena kept roomers!"

"So am I keeping roomers! I got Buckley cooled off and tomorrow he's coming over here and paint Mama's room foam green and move himself in."

"No, he is not!" Opaline said. "We are selling this house and you are moving to the bungalow by the Gulf."

"I'm staying right here. You said I needed protection and now I got it."

"You won't have it long," Pete told her. "Buckley's got debts all over town."

"He won't owe me nothing. I'm giving him Mama's TV for painting her room and the first month free for doing up mine in sagebrush green. Then he's gonna paint me a big sign to put up by the highway says ROOMS FOR RENT. All of 'em green. Leaf green, apple green." Rooney grinned at her relatives. "When I make enough money, I'm gonna buy me a gas station."

Opaline said, "You can't do anything without our permission."

Rooney gave her the zebra stare. "I got it, don't I?"

Annette Sanford is a native Texan who was born in Cuero, but has lived most of her life in Ganado. She taught high school English for twenty-five years and then wrote twenty-five romance novels under five pseudonyms so that she could afford to write the stories that have been appearing under her own name in magazines and quarterlies since 1968. She published a collection of stories, *Lasting Attachments*, in 1989, and is completing a new one now.

"Goose Girl" evolved out of the pleasures I have found in friendships with unusual people, one in particular, a student from my early days of teaching who still calls me by my maiden name, though I haven't used it for forty-two years—a fact she knows well but prefers to ignore.

Recently, for her fifty-ninth birthday, I sent her a copy of the journal containing the first printing of "Goose Girl." A little uneasily I included a note: "You have often asked me when I am going to write a story about you. I don't write stories about anyone, only about people in my imagination. Sometimes, however, I borrow things from friends' lives and use them in stories. In "Goose Girl" I borrowed some things from your life: your geese, your bicycle, your love of reading and wrestling, and a few other things. I hope you will understand that Rooney is not you and you are not Rooney, and that you will enjoy Rooney's victory in leading her life independently."

A nervous day passed after the birthday and then my friend appeared, smiling, with cake. Yes, her birthday was fun. Yes, she got lots of gifts. The best one, she said, was a Rockets shirt a Houston cousin sent her. Black letters on white, and gold all over it.

She was going down the sidewalk when she turned around to say, "They loved your story."

"How did you like it?"

"Too mushy," she said. "I like Ray Bradbury. And Venusian invaders and extraterrestrials."

Unusual people do not deal in flattery.

Lee Smith

THE HAPPY MEMORIES CLUB

(from *The Atlantic Monthly*)

I may be old, but I'm not dead.
   Perhaps you are surprised to hear this. You may be surprised to learn that people like me are still capable of original ideas, intelligent insights, and intense feelings. Passionate love affairs, for example, are not uncommon here. Pacemakers cannot regulate the wild, unbridled yearnings of the heart. You do not wish to know this, I imagine. This knowledge is probably upsetting to you, as it is upsetting to my sons, who do not want to hear, for instance, about my relationship with Dr. Solomon Marx, the historian. "Please, Mom," my son Alex said, rolling his eyes. "Come on, Mama," my son Johnny said. "Can't you maintain a little dignity here?" *Dignity*, said Johnny, who runs a chain of miniature-golf courses! "I have had enough dignity to last me for the rest of my life, thank you," I told Johnny.

I've always done exactly what I was supposed to do—now I intend to do what I want.

"Besides, Dr. Solomon Marx is the joy of my life," I told them. This remained true even when my second surgery was less than successful, obliging me to take to this chair. It remained true until Solomon's most recent stroke, five weeks ago, which has paralyzed him below the waist and caused his thoughts to become disordered, so that he cannot always remember things, or the words for things. A survivor himself, Solomon is an expert on the Holocaust. He has numbers tattooed on his arm. He used to travel the world, speaking about the Holocaust. Now he can't remember what to call it.

"Well, I think it's a blessing," said one of the nurses—that young Miss Rogers. "The Holocaust was just awful."

"It is not a blessing, you ignorant bitch," I told her. "It is the end; our memories are all we've got." I put myself in reverse and sped off before she could reply. I could feel her staring at me as I motored down the hall. I am sure she wrote something in her ever-present notebook. "Inappropriate" and "unmanageable" are among the words they use, unpleasant and inaccurate adjectives all.

The words Solomon can't recall are always nouns.

"My dear," he said to me one day recently, when they had wheeled him out into the Residence Center lobby, "what did you say your name was?" He knew it, of course, deep in his heart's core, as well as he knew his own.

"Alice Scully," I said.

"Ah. Alice Scully," he said. "And what is it that we used to do together, Alice Scully, which brought me such intense—oh, so big—" His eyes were like bright little beads in his pinched face. "It was of the greatest, ah—"

"Sex," I told him. "You loved it."

He grinned at me. "Oh, yes," he said. "Sex. It was sex, indeed."

"Mrs. Scully!" his nurse snapped.

Now I have devised a little game to help Solomon remember nouns. It works like this. Whenever they bring him out, I go over to him and clasp my hands together as if I were hiding something in them. "If you can guess what I've got here," I say, "I'll give you a kiss."

He squints in concentration, fishing for nouns. If he gets one, I give him a kiss.

Some days are better than others.

This is true for us all, of course. We can't be expected to remember everything we know.

In my life I was a teacher, and a good one. I taught English in the days when it was English, not "language arts." I taught for forty years at the Sandy Point School, in Sandy Point, Virginia, where I lived with my husband, Harold Scully, and raised four sons, three of them Harold's. Harold owned and ran the Trent Riverside Pharmacy until the day he dropped dead in his drugstore counting out antibiotics for a Methodist preacher. His mouth and his eyes were wide open, as if whatever he found on the other side surprised him mightily. I was sorry to see this, since Harold was not a man who liked surprises.

I must say I gave him none. I was a good wife to Harold, though I was at first dismayed to learn that this role entailed taking care of his parents from the day of our marriage until their deaths. They both lived long lives, and his mother went blind at the end. But we lived in their house, the largest house in Sandy Point, right on the old tidal river, and their wealth enabled us to send our own sons off to the finest schools and even, in Robert's case, to medical school.

Harold's parents never got over Harold's failure to get into medical school himself. In fact, he barely made it through pharmacy school. As far as I know, however, he was a good pharmacist, never poisoning anybody or mixing up prescriptions. He loved to look at the orderly rows of bottles on his shelves. He loved labeling. Often he dispensed medical advice to his customers: which cough medicine worked best, what to put on a boil. People trusted him. Harold got a great deal of pleasure from his job and from his standing in the community.

I taught school at first because I was trained to do it and because I wanted to. I was never one to plan a menu or clip a recipe out of a magazine. I left all that to Harold's mother and to the family housekeeper, Lucille.

Anyway, I loved teaching. I loved to diagram sentences on the board, precisely separating the subject from the predicate with a vertical line, the linking verb from the predicate adjective with a slanted line, and so forth. The children used to try to stump me by making up long sentences they thought I couldn't diagram, sentences so complex that my final diagram on the board looked like a blueprint for a cathedral, with flying buttresses everywhere, all the lines connecting.

I loved geography, as well—tracing roads, tracing rivers. I loved to trace the route of the pony express, of the Underground Railroad, of De Soto's search for gold. I told them the story of that bumbling fool Zebulon Pike, who set out in 1805 to find the source of the Mississippi River and ended up a year later at the glorious peak they named for him, Pike's Peak, which my sister, Rose, and I visited in 1926 on our cross-country odyssey with my brother John and his wife. In the photograph taken at Pike's Peak, I am seated astride a donkey, wearing a polka-dot dress and a floppy hat, while the western sky goes on and on endlessly behind me.

I taught my students these things: the first flight in a power-driven airplane was made by Wilbur and Orville Wright at Kitty Hawk, North Carolina, on December 17, 1903; Wisconsin is the "Badger State"; the Dutch bought Manhattan Island from the Indians for twenty-four dollars in 1626; you can't sink in the Great Salt Lake. Now these facts ricochet in my head like pinballs, and I do not intend, thank you very much, to enter the Health Center for "better care."

I never tired of telling my students the story of the Mississippi River—how a scarlet oak leaf falling into Lake Itasca, in Minnesota, travels first north and then east through a wild, lonely landscape of lakes and rapids as if it were heading for Lake Superior, over the Falls of St. Anthony, down through Minneapolis and St. Paul, past bluffs and prairies and islands, to be joined by the Missouri River just above St. Louis, and then by the Ohio, where the water grows more than a mile wide—you can't see across it. My scarlet leaf meanders with eccentric loops and horseshoe curves down, down, down the great continent, through the delta, to New Orleans and beyond, past the great fertile mud plain shaped like a giant goose's foot, and into the Gulf of Mexico.

"And what happens to the leaf *then*, Mrs. Scully?" some student would never fail to ask.

"Ah," I would say, "then our little leaf becomes a part of the universe"—leaving them to ponder *that*!

I was known as a hard teacher but a fair one, and many of my students came back in later years to tell me how much they had learned.

Here at Marshwood, a "total" retirement community, they want us to become children again, forgoing intelligence. This is why I was so pleased when the announcement went up on the bulletin board about a month ago:

WRITING GROUP TO MEET
WEDNESDAY, 3:00 P.M.

Ah, I thought, that promising infinitive "to meet." For, like many former English teachers, I had thought that someday I might like "to write."

At the appointed day and hour I motored over to the library (a euphemism, since the room contains mostly well-worn paperbacks by Jacqueline Susann and Louis L'Amour). I was dismayed to find Martha Louise Clapton already in charge. The idea had been hers, I learned; I should have known. She's the type who tries to run everything. Martha Louise Clapton has never liked me, having had her eye on Solomon, to no avail, for years before my arrival. She inclined her frizzy blue head ever so slightly to acknowledge my entrance.

"As I was just saying, Alice, several of us have discovered in mealtime conversation that in fact we've been writing for years, in our journals and letters and whatnot, and so I said to myself, 'Martha Louise, why not form a writing group?' and *voilà*."

"*Voilà*," I said, edging into the circle.

So it began.

Besides Martha Louise and myself, the writing group included Joy Richter, a minister's widow with a preference for poetry; Miss

Elena Grier, who taught Shakespeare for years and years at a girls' preparatory school in Nashville, Tennessee; Frances Mason, whose husband lay in a coma over at the Health Center (another euphemism—you never leave the Health Center); Shirley Lassiter, who had buried three husbands and still thought of herself as a belle; and Sam Hofstetter, a retired lawyer, deaf as a post. We agreed to meet again in the library one week later. Each of us should bring some writing to share with the others.

"What's that?" Sam Hofstetter said. We wrote the time and place down on a little piece of paper and gave it to him. He folded the paper carefully, placing it in his pocket. "Could you make copies of the writing, please?" he asked. He inclined his silver head and tapped his ear significantly. We all agreed. Of course we agreed—we outnumber the men four to one, poor old things. In a place like this they get more attention than you would believe.

Then Joy Richter said that she probably couldn't afford to make copies. She said she was on a limited budget.

I said I felt sure we could use the Xerox machine in the manager's office, especially since we needed it for the writing group.

"Oh, I don't know." Frances Mason started wringing her hands. "They might not let us."

"I'll take care of it," Martha Louise said majestically. "Thank you, Alice, for your suggestion. Thank you, everyone, for joining the group."

I had wondered if I might suffer initially from writer's block, but nothing of that sort occurred. In fact I was flooded by memories— overwhelmed, engulfed, as I sat in my chair by the picture window, writing on my lap board. I was not even aware of the world outside, my head was so full of the people and places of the past, rising up in my mind as they were then, in all the fullness of life, and myself as I was then, that headstrong girl longing to leave her home in east Virginia and walk in the world at large.

I wrote and wrote. I wrote for three days. I wrote until I felt satisfied, and then I stopped. I felt better than I had in years, full of new life and freedom (a paradox, since I am more and more confined to this chair).

During that week Solomon guessed "candy," "ring," and "Anacin." He was getting better. I was not. I ignored certain symptoms in order to attend the Wednesday meeting of the writing group.

Martha Louise led off. Her blue eyes looked huge, like lakes, behind her glasses. "They just don't make families like they used to," she began, and continued with an account of growing up on a farm in Ohio, how her parents struggled to make ends meet, how the children strung popcorn and cut out paper ornaments to trim the tree when they had no money for Christmas, how they pulled taffy and laid it out on a marble slab, and how each older child had a little one to take care of. "We were poor but we were happy," Martha Louise concluded. "It was an ideal childhood."

"Oh, Martha Louise," Frances Mason said tremulously, "that was just beautiful."

Everyone agreed.

Too many adjectives, I thought, but I held my tongue.

Next Joy Richter read a poem about seeing God in everything: "the stuff of day" was a phrase I rather liked. Joy Richter apparently saw God in a shiny red apple, in a dewy rose, in her husband's kind blue eyes, in photographs of her grandchildren. The poem was pretty good, but it would have been better if she hadn't tried so hard to rhyme it.

Miss Elena then presented a sonnet comparing life to a merry-go-round. The final couplet went

> Lost children, though you're old, remember well
> The joy and music of life's carousel.

This was not bad, and I said so. Frances Mason read a reminiscence about her husband's return from the Second World War, which featured the young Frances "hovering upon the future" in a porch swing as she "listened for the tread of his beloved boot." The military theme was continued by Sam Hofstetter, who read (loudly) an account of Army life titled "Somewhere in France."

Shirley Lassiter was the only one whose story was not about her-self. Instead it was fiction evidently modeled on a romance novel, for it involved a voluptuous debutante who had to choose between two men. Both of them were rich, and both of them loved her, but one had a fatal disease, and for some reason this young woman didn't know which one.

"Why not?" boomed the literal Sam.

"It's a mystery, silly," Shirley Lassiter said. "That's the plot." Shirley Lassiter had a way of resting her jeweled hands on her enormous bosom as if it were a shelf. "I don't want to give the plot away," she said. Clearly, she did not have a brain in her head.

Then came my turn.

I began to read the story of my childhood. I had grown up in the tiny coastal town of Waterville, Maryland. I was the fourth child in a family of five, with three older brothers and a baby sister. My father, who was in the oyster business, killed himself when I was six and Rose was only three. He went out into the Chesapeake Bay in an old rowboat, chopped a hole in the bottom of it with an ax, and then shot himself in the head with a revolver. He meant to finish the job. He did not sink as planned, however, because a fisherman witnessed the act, and hauled his body to shore.

This left Mama with five children to raise and no means of sup-port. She was forced to turn our home into a boardinghouse, keeping mostly teachers from Goucher College and salesmen passing through, although two old widows, Mrs. Flora Lewis and Mrs. Virginia Prince, stayed with us for years. Miss Flora, as we called her, had to have a cup of warm milk every night at bedtime; I will never forget it. It could be neither too hot nor too cold. I was the one who took it up to her, stepping so carefully up the dark back stair.

Nor will I forget young Miss Day from Richmond, a teacher, who played the piano beautifully. She used to play "Clair de Lune" and "Für Elise" on the old upright in the parlor. I would already have been sent to bed, and so I'd lie there trembling in the dark, seized by feelings I couldn't name, as the notes floated up to me and Rose in our little room, in our white iron bed wrought with roses and figures of nymphs. Miss Day was jilted some years later, we heard, her virtue lost and her reputation ruined.

Every Sunday, Mama presided over the big tureen at breakfast, when we'd have boiled fish and crisp little johnnycakes. To this day I have never tasted anything as good as those johnnycakes. Mama's face was flushed, and her hair escaped its bun to curl in damp tendrils as she dished up the breakfast plates. I thought she was beautiful. I'm sure she could have married again had she chosen to do so, but her heart was full of bitterness at the way her life had turned out, and she never forgave our father, or looked at another man.

Daddy had been a charmer, by all accounts. He carried a silver-handled cane and allowed me to play with his gold pocket watch when I was especially good. He took me to harness races, where we cheered for a horse he owned, a big roan named Joe Cord. On these excursions I wore a white dress and stockings and patent-leather shoes. And how Daddy could sing! He had a lovely baritone voice. I remember him on bended knee singing "Daisy, Daisy, give me your answer, do" to Mama, who pretended to be embarrassed but was not. I remember his bouncing Rose up and down on his lap and singing, "This is the way the lady rides."

After his death the boys went off to sea as soon as they could, and I was obliged to work in the kitchen and take care of Rose. Kitchen work in a boardinghouse is never finished. This is why I have never liked to cook since, though I know how to do it, I can assure you.

We had a summer kitchen outside, so that it wouldn't heat up the whole house when we were cooking or canning. It had a kerosene stove. I remember one time when we were putting up blackberry jam, and one of those jars simply blew up. We had blackberry jam all over the place. Glass cut the Negro girl, Ocie, who was helping out, and I was surprised to see that her blood was as red as mine.

As time went on, Mama grew sadder and withdrew from us, sometimes barely speaking for days on end. My great joy was

Rose, a lively child with golden curls and skin so fair you could see the blue veins beneath it. I slept with Rose every night and played with her every day. Since Mama was indisposed, we could do whatever we wanted, and we had the run of the town, just like boys. We'd go clamming in the bay with an inner tube floating out behind us, tied to my waist by a rope. We'd feel the clams with our feet and rake them up, flipping them into a net attached to the inner tube. Once, we went on a sailing trip with a cousin of ours, Bud Ned Black, up the Chickahominy River for a load of brick. But the wind failed and we got stuck there. We just *sat* on that river, for what seemed like days and days. Rose fussed and fumed while Cap'n Bud Ned drank whiskey and chewed tobacco and did not appear to mind the situation, so long as his supplies held out. But Rose was impatient—always, always so impatient.

"Alice," she said dramatically, as we sat staring out at the shining water, the green trees at its edge, the wheeling gulls, "I will *die* if we don't move. I will die here," Rose said, though Bud Ned and I laughed at her.

But Rose meant it. As she grew older, she had to go here, go there, do this, do that, have this, have that—she hated being poor and living in the boardinghouse, and could not wait to grow up and go away.

We both developed a serious taste for distance when our brother John and his wife took us motoring across the country. I was sixteen. I loved that trip, from the first stage of planning our route on the map to finally viewing the great mountains, which sprang straight up from the desert like apparitions. Of course, we had never seen such mountains; they took my breath away. I remember how Rose flung her arms out wide to the world as we stood in the cold wind on Pike's Peak. I believe we could have gone on driving and driving forever. But we had to return, and I had to resume my duties, letting go the girl John had hired so that Mama would permit my absence. John was our sweetest brother, but they are all dead now, all my brothers, and Rose, too.

I have outlived everyone.

Only yesterday Rose and I were little girls, playing a game we loved so well, a game that strikes me now as terribly dangerous. This memory is more vivid than any other in my life.

It is late night, summertime. Rose and I have sneaked out of the boardinghouse, down the tiny back stair past the gently sighing widows' rooms; past Mama's room, door open, moonlight ghostly on the mosquito netting draped from the canopy over her bed; past the snoring salesmen's rooms, stepping tiptoe across the wide-plank kitchen floor, wincing at each squeak; and out the kitchen door into moonlight so bright that it leaves shadows. Darting from tree to tree, we cross the yard and attain the sidewalk, moving rapidly past the big sleeping houses with their shutters yawning open to the cool night air, down the sidewalk to the edge of town where the sidewalk ends and the road goes on forever through miles and miles of peanut fields and other towns and other fields, toward Baltimore.

Rose and I lie down flat in the middle of the road, which still retains the heat of the day, and let it warm us head to toe as we dream aloud of what the future holds. At different times Rose planned to be an aviator, a doctor, and a film actress living in California, with an orange tree in her yard. Even her most domestic dreams were grand. "I'll have a big house and lots of servants and a husband who loves me *so much*," Rose would say, "and a yellow convertible touring car, and six children, and we will be rich and they will never have to work, and I will put a silk scarf on my head and we will all go out riding on Sunday."

Even then I said I would be a teacher, because I was always good in school, but I would be a missionary teacher, enlightening natives in some far-off corner of the world. Even as I said it, though, I believe I knew it would not come to pass, for I was bound to stay at home, as Rose was bound to go.

But we'd lie there looking up at the sky, and dream our dreams, and wait for the thrill of an oncoming vehicle, which we could hear coming a long time away, and could feel throughout the length of our bodies as it neared us. We would roll off the pavement and into the peanut field just as the car approached, our hearts pounding. Sometimes we nearly dozed on that warm road—and once we were almost killed by a potato truck.

Gradually, as Mama retreated to her room, I took over the running of the boardinghouse, and Mama's care as well. At eighteen Rose ran away with a fast-talking furniture salesman who had been boarding with us. They settled finally in Ohio, and had three children, and her life was not glamorous in the least, though better than some, and we wrote to each other every week until her death, of ovarian cancer, at thirty-nine.

This was as far as I'd gotten.

I quit reading aloud and looked around the room. Joy Richter was ashen, Miss Elena Grier was mumbling to herself, and Shirley Lassiter was breathing heavily and fluttering her fingers at her throat. Sam Hofstetter stared fixedly at me with the oddest expression on his face, and Frances Mason wept openly, shaking with sobs.

"Alice! Now just look at what you've done!" Martha Louise said to me severely. "Meeting adjourned!"

I had to miss the third meeting of the writing group, because Dr. Culbertson sent me to the Health Center for treatment and further tests (euphemisms both). Dr. Culbertson then went so far as to consult with my son Robert, also a doctor, about what to do with me next. Dr. Culbertson believed that I ought to move to the Health Center, for "better care." Of course I called Robert immediately and gave him a piece of my mind.

That was yesterday.

I know they are discussing me by telephone—Robert, Alex, Johnny, and Carl. Lines are buzzing up and down the East Coast.

I came here when I had to, because I did not want any of their wives to get stuck with me, as I had gotten stuck with Harold's mother and father. Now I expect some common decency and respect. At times like this I wish for daughters, who often, I feel, have more compassion and understanding than sons.

Even Carl, the child of my heart, says I had "better listen to the doctor."

Instead I have been listening to this voice too long silent inside me, the voice of myself, as I write page after page propped up in bed in the Health Center.

Today is Wednesday. I have skipped certain of my afternoon medications. At 2:15 I buzz for Sheila, my favorite, a tall young nurse's aide with the grace of a gazelle. "Sheila," I say, "I need for you to help me dress, dear, and then roll my chair over here, if you will. My own chair, I mean. I have to go to a meeting."

Sheila looks at my chart and then back at me, her eyes wide. "It doesn't say . . ." she begins.

"Dr. Culbertson said it would be perfectly all right," I assure her. I pull a $20.00 bill from my purse, which I keep right beside me in bed, and hand it to her. "I know it's a lot of trouble, but it's very important," I say. "I think I'll just slip on the red sweater and the black wraparound skirt—that's so easy to get on. They're both in the drawer, dear."

"Okay, honey," Sheila says, and she gets me dressed and sets me in my chair. I put on lipstick and have Sheila fluff up my hair in the back where it's gotten so flat from lying in bed. Sheila hands me my purse and my notebook, and then I'm off, waving to the girls at the nurses' station as I purr past them. They wave back. I feel fine now. I take the elevator down to the first floor and then motor through the lobby, speaking to acquaintances. I pass the gift shop, the newspaper stand, and all the waiting rooms.

It's chilly outside. I head up the walkway past the par three golf course, where I spy Parker Howard, ludicrous in those bright-green pants they sell to old men, putting on the third hole. "Hi, Parker!" I cry.

"Hello, Alice," he calls. "Nice to see you out!" He sinks the putt.

I enter the Multipurpose Building and head for the library, where the writers' group is already in progress. Driving over from the Health Center took longer than I'd expected.

Miss Elena is reading, but she stops and looks up when I come in, her mouth a perfect O. Everybody looks at Martha Louise.

"Why, Alice," Martha Louise says. She clears her throat. "We didn't expect that you would be joining us today. We heard that you were in the Health Center."

"I was," I say. "But I'm out now."

"Evidently," Martha Louise says.

I ride up to the circular table, set my brake, get out my notebook, and ask Miss Elena for a copy of whatever she's reading. Wordless, she slides one over. But she still does not resume. They're all looking at me.

"What is it?" I ask.

"Well, Alice, last week, when you were absent, we laid out some ground rules for this writing group." Martha Louise gains composure as she goes along. "We are all in agreement here, Alice, that if this is to be a pleasant and meaningful club for all of us, we need to restrict our subject matter to what everyone enjoys."

"So?" I don't get it.

"We've also adopted an official name for the group." Now Martha Louise is as cheerful as a robin.

"What is it?"

"It's the Happy Memories Club," she announces, and they all nod.

I am beginning to get it.

"You mean to tell me—" I start.

"I mean to tell you that if you wish to be a part of this group, Alice Scully, you will have to calm yourself down, and keep your subject matter in check. We don't come here to be upset," Martha Louise says serenely.

They are all watching me closely now, Sam Hofstetter in particular. I think they expect an outburst.

But I won't give them the satisfaction.

"Fine," I say. This is a lie. "That sounds just fine to me. Good idea!" I smile at everybody.

There is a perceptible relaxation then, an audible settling back into chairs, as Miss Elena resumes her reading. It's a travelogue named "Shakespeare and His Haunts," about a tour she made to England several years ago. But I find myself unable to listen. I simply can't hear Elena, or Joy, who reads next, or even Sam.

"Well, is that it for today? Anybody else?" Martha Louise raps her knuckles against the table. "I brought something," I say, "but I don't have copies."

I look at Sam, who shrugs and smiles and says I should go ahead anyway. Everybody else looks at Martha Louise.

"Well, go on, then," she directs tartly, and I begin.

After Rose's disappearance, my mother took to her bed and turned her face to the wall, leaving me in charge of everything. Oh, how I worked! I worked like a dog, long hours, a cruelly unnatural life for a spirited young woman. Yet I persevered. People in the town, including our minister, complimented me; I was discussed and admired. Our boardinghouse stayed full, and somehow I managed, with Ocie's help, to get the meals on the table. I smiled and chattered at mealtime. Yet inside I was starving, starving for love and life.

Thus it was not surprising, I suppose, that I should fall for the first man who showed any interest in me. He was a schoolteacher who had been educated at the university, in Charlottesville, a thin, dreamy young man from one of the finest families in Virginia. His grandfather had been the governor. He used to sit out by the sound every evening after supper, reading, and one day I joined him there. It was a lovely June evening; the sound was full of sailboats, and the sky above us was as round and blue as a bowl.

"I was reading a poem about a girl with beautiful yellow hair," he said, "and then I look up and what do I see? A real girl with beautiful yellow hair."

For some reason I started to cry, not even caring what my other boarders thought as they sat up on the porch looking out over this landscape in which we figured.

"Come here," he said, and he took my hand and led me behind

the old rose-covered boathouse, where he pulled me to him and kissed me curiously, as if it were an experiment.

His name was Carl Redding Armistead III. He had the reedy look of a poet, but all the assurance of the privileged class. I was older than he, but he was more experienced. He was well educated, and had been to Europe several times.

"You pretty thing," he said, and kissed me again. The scent of the roses was everywhere.

I went that night to his room, and before the summer was out, we had lain together in nearly every room of the boarding house. We were crazy for each other by then, and I didn't care what might happen, or who knew. On Saturday evenings I'd leave a cold supper for the rest, and Carl and I would take the skiff and row out to Sand Island, where the wild ponies were, and take off all our clothes and make love. Sometimes my back would be red and bleeding from the rough black sand and the broken shells on the beach.

"Just a minute! Just a minute here!" Martha Louise is pounding on the table, and Frances Mason is crying, as usual. Sam Hofstetter is staring at me in a manner that indicates that he has heard every word I've said.

"Well, I think that's terrific!" Shirley Lassiter giggles and bats her painted blue eyelids at us all.

Of course this romance did not last. Nothing that intense can be sustained, though the loss of such intensity can scarcely be borne. Quite simply, Carl and I foundered upon the prospect of the future. He had to go on to the world that awaited him; I could not leave Mama. Our final parting was bitter—we were spent, exhausted by the force of what had passed between us. He did not even look back as he sped away in his little red sports car, nor did I cry.

Nor did I ever tell him about the existence of Carl, my son, whom I bore defiantly out of wedlock nine months later, telling no one who the father was. Oh, those were hard, black days! I was ostracized by the very people who had formerly praised me, and

ogled by the men in my boardinghouse, who now considered me
a fallen woman. l wore myself to a frazzle taking care of Mama and
the baby at the same time.

One night, I remember, I was so tired that I felt that I would
actually die, yet little Carl would not stop crying. Nothing would
quiet him—not rocking, not the breast, not walking the room. He
had an oddly unpleasant cry, like a cat mewing. I remember looking out my window at the quiet town where everyone slept—
everyone on this earth, I felt, except me. I held Carl out at arm's
length and looked hard at him in the streetlight, at his red, twisted
little face. I had an awful urge to throw him out the window—

"That's enough!" several of them say at once. Martha Louise is
standing.

But it is Miss Elena who speaks. "I cannot believe," she says
severely, "that out of your entire life, Alice Scully, this is all you can
find to write about. What of your long marriage to Mr. Scully?
Your seven grandchildren? Those of us who have not been blessed
with grandchildren would give—"

Of course I loved Harold Scully. Of course I love my grandchildren. I love Solomon, too. I love them all. Miss Elena is like
my sons, too terrified to admit to herself how many people we can
love, how various we are. She does not want to hear it any more
than they do, any more than you do. You all want us to *never
change, never change.*

I did not throw my baby out the window after all, and my
mother finally died, and I sold the boardinghouse then and was
able, at last, to go to school.

Out of the corner of my eye I see Dr. Culbertson appear at the
library door, accompanied by a man I do not know. Martha Louise
says, "I simply cannot believe that a former *English teacher*—"

This strikes me as very funny. My mind is filled with enormous
sentences as I back up my chair and then start forward, out the
other door and down the hall and outside into the sweet spring
day, where the sunshine falls on my face as it did in those days on
the beach, my whole body hot and aching and sticky with sweat

and salt and blood, the wild ponies paying us no mind as they ate the tall grass that grew at the edge of the dunes. Sometimes the ponies came so close that we could reach out and touch them. Their coats were shaggy and rough and full of burrs, I remember.

Oh, I remember everything as I cruise forward on the sidewalk that neatly separates the rock garden from the golf course. I turn right at the corner, instead of left toward the Health Center. "Fore!" Parker Howard shouts, waving at me. *A former English teacher*, Martha Louise said. These sidewalks are like diagrams, parallel lines and dividers: oh, I could diagram anything. The semicolon, I used to say, is like a little scale; it must have items of equal rank, I'd warn them. Do not use a semicolon between a clause and a phrase, or a main clause and a subordinate clause. Do not write *I loved Carl Redding Armistead; a rich man's son*. Do not write *If I had really loved Carl Armistead; I would have left with him despite all obstacles*. Do not write *I still feel his touch; which has thrilled me throughout my life*.

I turn at the top of the hill and motor along the sidewalk toward the Residence Center, hoping to see Solomon. The sun is in my eyes. Do not carelessly link two sentences with a comma. Do not write *I want to see Solomon again, he has meant so much to me*. To correct this problem, subordinate one of the parts. *I want to see Solomon, because he has meant so much to me*. Because he has meant. So much. To me. Fragments. Fragments all. I push the button to open the door into the Residence Center, and sure enough, they've brought him out. They've dressed him in his Madras plaid shirt and wheeled him in front of the television, which he hates. I cruise right over.

"Solomon," I say, but at first he doesn't respond when he looks at me. I come even closer. "Solomon!" I say sharply, bumping his wheelchair. He notices me then, and a little light comes into his eyes.

I cup my hands. "Solomon," I say, "I'll give you a kiss if you can guess what I've got in my hands."

He looks at me for a while longer.

"Now, Mrs. Scully," his nurse starts.

"Come on," I say. "What have I got in here?"

"An elephant," Solomon finally says.

"Close enough!" I cry, and lean right over to kiss his sweet old cheek, being unable to reach his mouth.

"Mrs. Scully," his nurse starts again, but I'm gone, I'm history, I'm out the front door and around the parking circle and up the long entrance drive to the highway. It all connects. Everything connects. The sun is bright, the dogwoods are blooming, the state flower of Virginia is the dogwood, I can still see the sun on the Chickahominy River and my own little sons as they sail their own little boats in a tidal pool by the Chesapeake Bay, they were all blond boys once, though their hair would darken later, Annapolis is the capital of Maryland, the first historic words ever transmitted by telegraph came to Maryland: "What hath God wrought?" The sun is still shining. It glares off the snow on Pike's Peak, it gleams through the milky blue glass of the old apothecary jar in the window of Harold Scully's shop, it warms the asphalt on that road where Rose and I lie waiting, waiting, waiting.

Lee Smith was born in southwest Virginia and studied writing at Hollins College. She is a long-time resident of North Carolina, where she teaches in the graduate creative writing program at North Carolina State University in Raleigh. She has published eleven books of fiction, including *Fair and Tender Ladies*, *Oral History*, and the recent *Saving Grace*. *The Christmas Letters*, a novella, is forthcoming this Fall, and she is currently at work on a collection of short stories.

O nce when I had been invited to visit a writing group at a retirement community, I was amazed to learn that they had recently kicked a member out because she wouldn't stick to "happy" topics but chose to write her real memories instead, which had upset everybody. Unfortunately, I never got to meet this determined realist, but she immediately captured my imagination. "The Happy Memories Club" is the result.

Kathy Flann

A HAPPY, SAFE THING

(from *Shenandoah*)

My older sister, Minnie, and her new husband, Sax Smithers, whom she met six months ago, show up half an hour late for their wedding reception at the American Legion. They get held up because all eight guys from the pharmacy, where Sax works sorting boxes of pills, want a ride, right then, in front of Mountainview Lutheran Church, in Grandma Tillie's brand new 1983 Cadillac convertible. Then, Minnie, excited not just about the wedding, but also about her graduation from Smoky Ordinary High School the day before, smuggles me into the passenger seat of the convertible, ignoring what Mom and my stepdad Frank and Grandma Tillie have said over and over about my heart.

"Okay, Sheryl," Minnie tells me, "slouch down in the seat." Minnie's best friend, Gina Potts, is in the driver's seat. On the front steps of the church, Frank is hugging the priest again, and Mom, who's still in the doorway, is too weepy to see us. Minnie, behind me, pinches my cheek and then snuggles up to Sax as if leaning forward from their back seat perch to talk to me has kept her away from him for too long. Sax smiles with his eyes closed.

My heart brought Minnie and Sax together; it's how they met in the first place. My heart is built backwards with a hole in the middle of it. The pharmacy where Sax works and where I pick up my heart medication after school on Wednesdays is next to Cherry

Blossom Jr. High, where I just finished the seventh grade. My stepdad Frank makes Minnie pick up my medication sometimes, when I'm too tired, and that's how Sax recognized her and felt all right talking to her that "destinied" (as Minnie says) Sunday morning at the Flapjack Café on Coover Street where Minnie waits tables. Now, she always says to Grandma Tillie, who wanted Minnie to study court stenography at the community college, "See Grandma T? You can make your future anyplace."

About my heart—it keeps me from riding in airplanes because the air is too thin, and Mom, Frank, and Grandma Tillie keep me from riding in convertibles or pickup trucks or hayrides, too, because Mom says it's not good for me when the air rushes past and makes me catch my breath. My heart also keeps me from running, biking, or swimming, but I can walk far enough and can play badminton in the backyard.

Dr. Brooster, our cardiologist in Lynchburg, says mine is a best case scenario. He says one in five hundred kids have a heart like mine and, so far, at thirteen, I've outlived all the others like me. When we went to see Dr. Brooster in April, I overheard Mom say to him, "How long? Five years? Ten years?" and he said, "She's doing fine." And then I heard Mom say, "Maybe you just don't want me to know."

I was sitting in the hall watching a bright blue fish in the aquarium try to push a smaller yellow fish out of some thick plants—as if the plants were going to hurt him, I thought, as if the blue fish were the mother and the yellow fish the child. Mom came out of Dr. Brooster's office, her mouth tight and worried, but when she looked at me, we both put on happier faces.

Now, as we drive out of our way on the bridge over Crying Indian Lake, Gina Potts honks the horn while Minnie and Sax yell and hoot, holding each other tightly. They had their first kiss in a rowboat on the lake, and now I watch them steal another kiss in the back of the Cadillac, Minnie's veil blowing over both their faces. On the other side of the bridge, the town disappears into Virginia forest, pine and elm trees thick as cotton. Just as it seems we're on our way to Anderson, the next town over, Gina turns us around. Then, as we drive the last eight blocks toward the American Legion, the dark sky, gloomy since the morning rain, makes the town look brighter, especially Pink's Tiny Pink Grocery and the orange Phillips 76 sign and the hands of well-wishers waving in the gray afternoon.

When we pull into the circular driveway and coast to a stop in front of the Legion Hall, which Minnie used to call "the soldier palace," Mom and two of her friends from Tuesday night Apostle Bingo are busy on the big side lawn getting ready for the reception. They have moved almost everything from under the big white and yellow striped tent she rented and into the building because the tent, sagging in the middle, heavy with water from the early morning downpour, is leaking into a family-sized fried chicken bucket.

Minnie says she has pictured her wedding reception on the nicely-mowed Legion lawn ever since Frank started taking all of us to his Vietnam Veterans socials there five years ago. She pictured a pastel tent and herself waltzing in a white dress with a long train. I don't think she counted on the sky being dense and ugly and the lawn swarming with gnats. But she has Sax and the white dress and the train, and she doesn't seem to notice anything else.

Now, though, after we get out of the car and walk up the brick path to the side lawn, she does notice that Mom's hands are shaking after my ride in the convertible, and we stare at Mom together for the few seconds she pretends to ignore us. She bustles under the yellow tent, the sleeves of her pink suit hiked up, revealing arms tender and pale as a baby's.

"I hope that was worth the two years you took off your sister's life," she says to Minnie, angrier and shakier than even the time Minnie lost Grandma Tillie's locket. Mom covers the potato salad quickly, as if it's wild and doesn't want to be touched. Then, she jabs her finger in the middle of the lemon meringue pie and puts a gob of meringue in her mouth. She closes her eyes, her jaw muscles moving. When she opens them, she looks out across the big lawn and across Market Street—all the way, it seems, to the clotheslines in front of Hollywood Apartments, where I can see a housecoat hanging next to a pair of overalls. "Well, never mind," she says finally. "It's a special day and you want to do special things. I know that." She brightens then. She swats at the gnats hovering over the cheese plate and looks at us for the first time. "I know that," she says, and smiles like we all share a secret.

Mom paid a lot for that tent. Two weeks before the wedding, over in Anderson, which is twenty miles east of Smoky Ordinary, Buy or Rent quoted us a price of two hundred dollars. Mom said to me in the car, on the way home, "Two hundred dollars? I only decided to go along with this wedding because, well, they were going to go to the Poconos and do it without us if I didn't. But, as far as I'm concerned, they're too young."

"Sax'll be twenty next month," I'd muttered. Mom popped a Certs in her mouth and stuffed the wrapper in the ashtray. Her eyes were as wide open as she could make them—I imagined them rolling on the floor of the car like brown and white marbles. It's what she does when she gets frustrated, which isn't very often; she's known for being one of the happier people in Smoky Ordinary.

"Mom," I'd said, "I think the wedding theme should be hearts. We'll buy little napkins with hearts on them and have heart-shaped balloons in nets on the ceiling that we make fall down during the first dance. We can have heart cake four layers high and hearts on the tablecloths." Mom's eyes returned to their normal size and she looked over at me. "I can be the expert decorator," I said, and she smiled for real, with teeth showing. She started to say how nice that was, and I pulled from my wallet the card the doctor gave me—a picture of a healthy heart on one side and a picture of a heart like mine on the other. "My card?" I said, handing it to her just as I had seen Frank do with important customers at the hardware store he manages.

"That's in bad taste, honey," she said, looking at me as if I'd become someone else's daughter, only she seemed sadder than she'd be with a stranger.

"I wanted to cheer you up," I told her. "I didn't mean what you think." But she didn't talk to me again the rest of the way home.

Minnie, who has no idea the trouble Mom went to for the tent, now heads toward the building with Sax and Gina on either side like attendants to a big white parade float. Mom mops her forehead with a little heart napkin (they were the only heart thing we ended up getting) and puts her other hand on her hip.

"Well, we're almost done," she says, partly to me and partly to her two Bingo friends, who are making trip after trip into the building. They nod and smile and say, "Thank God" and "Whooey." Mom doesn't like Apostle Bingo, but she goes because Grandma Tillie wants to and Grandma Tillie shouldn't drive at night by herself. Besides that, Mom says, there are a few nice people there who aren't holy rollers.

"Honey," Mom says, "you can handle these, can't you?" and she hands me a bag of Kost Kutter dinner rolls. "And why don't you check on Grandma Tillie while you're inside? She looked dizzy to me. Or maybe like her legs were tired." Mom always says that between Grandma Tillie's hypertension and her blood clots, a stroke won't need a fancy invitation. So, Grandma Tillie only sweeps or pulls up weeds when Mom isn't around because even Grandma doesn't like Mom's wide-eyed look, which she says is like a basset hound in the rain.

"Okay," I say, taking the rolls, "see you inside," and I walk into the building, which is red brick and has white pillars and the words "American Legion" and "With Liberty and Justice for All" attached to the front. The letters are made of stone and there's a bird's nest in the "u" in "Justice." Inside, there is a stage with an American flag backdrop at one end of the long room. The D.J. Frank hired is standing on the stage playing Foreigner's "Urgent" and thumbing through the rest of his records. He's squinting through his reading glasses. The opposite wall is covered with maroon draperies and in front of them there are twenty card tables with chairs. A long buffet table and a small table with the wedding cake on it separate the card table area from the rest of the room, which is empty. Guests chat under the shadows of the antlered heads—deer, elk, moose, caribou—along the side walls. Frank says the animals are arranged so that if they had bodies, they would be standing in formation.

Nobody dances until Grandma Tillie gets Sax to be her partner. The two of them dance right in the middle of the big empty part of the room, and the guests standing under the heads along the side walls either whisper and stare shyly or pretend not to notice. Grandma Tillie is getting funky, waving her index fingers, and she won't stop for anything, not even Frank, who tries to cut in and get Sax back to Minnie.

"This old lady's still got something left," Grandma Tillie says, and Frank waves his hand as if to say, "Okay, you win." Minnie, Gina Potts, and two other girls are sitting in folding chairs around one of the card tables in the back of the room. I hear them worrying in hushed tones that no one else is going to dance.

"It's those heads," Gina says. "They're gross." Minnie keeps peeking at Sax, who's good-naturedly swaying while Grandma Tillie revives the Charleston. Minnie sneaks looks out the corners of her eyes as if no one will notice she's doing it.

"Minnie," one of the girls says when they all notice she has stopped listening. Minnie looks at them and smiles and blushes like she's been caught sucking her thumb. I go over to the buffet table. I open the rolls, put them on a Chinette paper plate and set them next to the cheese.

"That's a lot of food," a voice says behind me. I turn to find Eddie Strubinski, who's the only guest my age. He lives next door to us in a pale green house. Frank calls it "the tall foxhole," because both the house and the sickly grass in front of it are almost the color of camouflage.

"Hope you're hungry," I say to Eddie, because before we left for the church this morning we heard Eddie's mother, Lucille of House of Lucille Beauty-Care Salon, yelling that Eddie would eat his eggs and grits and like it.

Eddie is wearing a blue suit jacket and a tie, but his long brown hair is tucked behind his ears like always and he's still got on the same pants he wears to school every day, brown corduroy with frayed bottoms and a POW-MIA patch on one knee. His father went to Vietnam and disappeared, but Frank says there's no evidence that he disappeared in Vietnam; he probably disappeared in Atlantic City or Miami or who knows where. Frank says that some guys, even one in his own unit, just don't want to go home. Eddie says his dad's probably in a little cage living off bugs and rain water. I point at his pants. "Looks like you washed them."

"My mom made me," he says and looks embarrassed. He usually says "shut up" when people, especially his mother, mention his pants, and I suddenly feel bad. I don't know why I said it unless it's because I'm angry, not at Eddie, but at Mom's happiness being covered up with worries about Grandma Tillie and me, about whether we're dying or whether we're living enough. And I think I was also rude because I knew I could be. Eddie once sent a paper airplane note into my window that said "Sheryl" on it and there were stars around my name.

"Sorry, Eddie," I say, both about his having to wash his pants and about me talking about them.

Standing there next to Eddie, who is now loading up a plate with miniature hot dogs, I watch Minnie, at the card table, whispering to Gina Potts. And right then, maybe because of the light shining from her wedding ring when she cups her hand to Gina's ear, I realize that Minnie will be gone from our house forever. Tonight when I go to bed, I won't hear her over on her side of the bedroom, winding her carousel music box in the dark and listening to it play "Evergreen" with that tiny *plink, plink* sound until she falls asleep.

Just then, the D.J. stops the record and announces that the lovebirds will now cut the cake. Everyone should gather around the cake table. Minnie rushes past us, holding her train with both hands. Eddie and I try to hand out plastic forks to people as they hurry over for a good view. Sax stands behind the cake looking like he might be responsible for the announcement. "I just wanted to get my baby back," I hear him say.

Frank, in front of the cake, begins to make a speech, something he does whenever more than five people gather at the American Legion Hall. Mom likes this trait; she says, "Frank opens up," which is something our father never did. He left before Minnie started school; I was a baby. "Sheryl," Mom says, "if I had a nickel for every time I've missed your father, I'd be a poor woman." Frank clears his throat to get everyone's attention.

"Thank you all for coming," he begins. "What can you say about a day like this? We are lucky to share it with family and friends. Some people don't have what we have—a home, food on the table, four in-tact limbs. But, most importantly, some people don't have love. And what have you got if you don't have that? You've got diddley squat. There's plenty of love in this room tonight. Most of it's coming from right behind me."

Frank turns around and Minnie and Sax push cake into each other's faces and everybody laughs. Several ladies squeal. Then Sax kisses Minnie and, after a minute, dips her and suddenly it's as if they've forgotten the rest of us are here. Sax has one hand around her waist and one in the middle of her back, and she looks like she's not holding herself up at all. Their faces are as peaceful as happy sleepers.

Watching them, I first try to imagine what a real kiss would feel like, and then wonder how they forget that another person's saliva is being rubbed on their mouths, but a second later, I think I know how they forget. I even wish I knew what Sax's lips felt like, and I start to imagine, like I sometimes do, that I'm kissing Cooper Matthews, a boy from my art class who has tan legs and light brown hair and gets paint on his nice face. Then, I quickly look down at the forks in my hand, afraid someone might see what I'm thinking. I stare at the frayed bottoms of Eddie's pants, which are rustling as he rests on one foot and then the other.

"For Pete's sake, do you think this is some kind of peep show?" Grandma Tillie shouts and Minnie and Sax come up for air. Grandma Tillie looks proud of her joke, though a little surprised that it turned out to be one. Lucille pushes through the crowd, making her way toward where Eddie and I stand, and Eddie says quickly, "We're out of here." He takes my arm and rushes me toward the side door that opens onto the lawn and the leaky tent. He flings the door open even though it says, "Use only in emergency." When I look over my shoulder, Lucille is hugging a woman and patting the woman's tall hair as if it's a dog.

"Eddie," I say, "I don't think she's looking for you." But he keeps pushing me along and we go outside.

As the door shuts slowly by itself, I hear Mom, inside, laughing, and I wonder what Minnie or Grandma Tillie or Frank are doing, but Eddie paces under the tent like he might run away any minute. I lean against the building and try to catch my breath.

"Don't you like weddings?" I say.

"I like funerals better," he says and then looks shy all of a sudden and turns his face away. "Like at my grandfather's funeral," he tells the trunk of the dogwood tree next to the tent, "everybody got up and told great stories about him."

"But he was dead. Why is that better?" I say, and Eddie turns and pokes at a red cooler my mother has left on top of the table.

"It's not better exactly. But like with your sister and her husband," he says, pointing at the Legion Hall, "you don't know what's going to happen. You don't know where they'll end up living, or whether they'll have children, or if they'll see the children grow up. You don't even know if they'll be happy."

"But that means their lives could be full of surprises," I say.

"Or not," Eddie says. He stares at the palm of his left hand. "Bad things happen. You just don't know when."

The wind has picked up and blown ripe green leaves onto the table. Eddie and I do not talk for a moment, and the wind whistles under the tent. Eddie's dark brown hair blows into his eyes and he moves it away with his hand; then he opens the red cooler.

"Pay dirt," he says, as he pulls out a bottle of Andre pink champagne.

"Go ahead and drink it," I say. "Mom must have forgotten about it." Eddie pops the bottle open and takes a long drink. His face looks how I feel when I ride on the handlebars of Minnie's bike—like he's a free agent and nobody's going to tell him to eat his eggs and grits.

"Here, you have some," he says. He hands me the bottle and I find myself reaching out to take it. Dr. Brooster has said to me, "As you get older, Sheryl, kids will be drinking. But you can't. Say it with me now, 'I can't drink.'"

"I can't drink," I say to Eddie.

"I knew that. I should have known that. Sorry." Eddie sets the champagne bottle, half empty now, back on the table.

"Let's go back in," I say. When I turn toward the door, Eddie takes my hand and stops me.

"Sheryl?" he says. And as I turn toward him again, he kisses me. He has his eyes closed and his hair spills onto my face. When I close my own eyes, I notice that Eddie's lips don't feel the way I imagined Cooper Matthews's—warm and full and golden tan. Eddie's lips feel like Eddie—thin and pale and trembling. And they touch mine in a way I had never thought of, like he's saying all of the things he couldn't fit on a paper airplane note. When we stop kissing, he puts his hand on the side of my face as if he's wanted to for a long time.

"Are you mad?" he says.

"No. I liked it," I tell him, and I have a strange feeling of dread like maybe I'm telling the truth. Eddie takes his hand away and moves his hair away from his face the same way he always does, with his small, pale hand and thin fingers, his nubby fingernails, but now it almost hurts me to see him do it. Because all of a sudden, it's like his hand holds me inside it. And suddenly, I understand that love isn't the way I thought—it's not a small, happy, safe thing. It's like rain; it keeps falling whether you need it or not.

"We should go back in," I tell him, but I don't move toward the door. I listen to the sound of leaves moving in the wind, and Eddie rocks back and forth on his feet, his hands stuffed deep in his pockets, and his happy face looking up. I look up, too. The sky, almost dark now that night is closer, seems closer, too, with its swirling clouds and its glowing spot where the moon should be rising.

Inside, the lights have dimmed and nearly everyone is dancing. Lucille finds us; she tells Eddie she wants him to see a plaque on the wall that lists his father as a soldier missing in action.

"I'll be right back," Eddie says to me, and as they walk away, I hear Lucille tell Eddie that the plaque had shone out at her like an angel, like a sign from above.

The small disco ball Gina Potts had tacked to the ceiling is making tiny white lights move slowly over the guests like snow. Mom and Frank are doing the twist to Journey's "Separate Ways," Mom's hands hanging limp from the wrist and her hair coming loose in curls around her face.

I see Grandma Tillie standing next to the buffet table, and when I go over to her she puts her arm around me and we watch the dancing. Minnie and Sax, in the middle of the crowd, are the only people slow dancing. Minnie has her arms around Sax's neck, and he has his hands on her waist. They sway slowly, and Sax stops to gather up her train, which has spilled onto the floor. He holds it up for her when they start dancing again. "Do you think they'll always be this happy?" I say to Grandma Tillie.

"Oh, honey," Grandma Tillie says. "Sometimes they'll be much happier than this."

———

Kathy Flann was born in Oxnard, California and grew up in Virginia, near Washington, DC. She studied writing at Virginia Tech and at

Auburn University, where she received an MA with a creative writing concentration. "A Happy, Safe Thing" is from her masters thesis, which consists of two short stories and ten poems. The other story was published in "Crazyhorse" and one of the poems appeared in *Southern Humanities Review*. She is currently a PhD student at the University of North Carolina at Greensboro.

In 1994, at an end-of-the-school-year party, I decided to approach my writing mentor about a story idea. I remember her sitting on a tan couch with a crowd of professors, drinking wine with an air of relief, of summer relaxation. I sat gingerly at the edge of the couch, an empty glass in my hands, and told her about my cousin, Emily, who had been born with a rare heart defect. The doctors never knew how long she would live, but predicted she wouldn't survive adolescence. She did grow up, though. She got married and got the golden retriever she always wanted. But she still, at the age of twenty-three, lived with experimental drugs and surgeries, and with the not knowing, the same not knowing she had always endured with amazing good cheer. My mentor had a look of fascination, and we tuned out the party for a while as we continued the first of what would become a year-long series of conversations about the story. During that year, my dog, a companion of fifteen years, was diagnosed with cancer, and the two of us clung to one another through his chemotherapy and dismaying deterioration. It was during that time that "A Happy, Safe Thing" began to take its present form, as I was living out the not knowing with my dog and identifying more and more with the mother in the story.

The story, finally, reflects much about my own experiences in terms of family, geography, and the painful loss of my dog. But I hope I have captured a small part of the not knowing that Emily lives with every day. She's twenty-five now and doing fine.

Robert Morgan

THE BALM OF GILEAD TREE

(from *Epoch*)

I wouldn't say I noticed a thing unusual at first. There were airplanes coming in and taking off most of the day, and the new road was right under their path. It was the height of tourist season, and the sun was so bright you didn't want to glance up at the sky anyway. I wanted to look into the shade of the trees beyond the highway construction, and forget about the awful heat, and the headache I'd had all day.

"Hey look at that," Roy hollered. He was pulling up surveyor's markers and throwing them into the foreman's pickup. "He's going to hit."

I looked to where he pointed. The airliner was coming in from the south, probably the flight from Atlanta. It was a DC-9 with its flaps down, slowing for landing. I knew what kind of plane it was because I had flown on them when I was in the service. With the sun high in the sky you couldn't see much else about the plane. It was near two o'clock and I still had that heavy feeling from eating my bologna sandwiches too fast. And the headache wouldn't go away. I wished I had some aspirin.

"He's going to do it," Brad said. Brad stopped with a load of dirt in his shovel raised about a foot off the ground. My eyes stung with sweat and the bright light, but I saw it too. It was one of those little private planes—bigger than a Piper Cub, a Cessna—

coming from the west and headed directly toward where the airliner was going.

"My God," Joey, the foreman, said. He was tinkering with his transit beside the pickup. "I don't believe it," he said. I guess everybody on the job was looking up there, except maybe the earthmover and bulldozer drivers who couldn't hear anything and had to keep their eyes on the grading markers.

"I God," I said, sounding like my Uncle Albert without meaning to. It just came out.

"He ain't going to do it," Roy said.

It felt like electric shock jolted through me as the little plane came on. It stretched on and on toward the airliner, seeming to rip the sky in front of it.

"The Lord have mercy," Joey said.

It didn't seem possible. I expected the big plane to turn aside, or the little plane to hank and dive, or suddenly climb. But both pilots must have been blind. It all happened in a second or two, but it seemed to take hours. I couldn't watch. I had flown in planes in the army, all the way to Vietnam and back, and I thought of those people up there, in the clean air conditioning, just having finished lunch and thinking they were about to arrive in the mountains. Women in their fine clothes and perfume and men in business suits and doubleknits in the middle of August, and kids with toys in their laps.

"I God," I said, and raised my shovel like I was trying to push the little plane away. Dirt slid off the blade onto my sweaty arms and chest just as the two planes touched and turned into a fireball bigger than the sun. I don't remember if there was any noise or not. Maybe the sound of the motors continued even after the collision.

The fire just hung there in the sky for a second, and then the two planes pulled apart. The little Cessna went down like somebody had dropped it. It fluttered into pieces that wobbled. I didn't see it hit except out of the corner of my eye because I was watching the DC-9 as it swung away from the impact in a steep curve, carrying the fire on its back, but not spiraling.

"They's people falling," Roy said. And sure enough, we saw the dots and little figures thrown from the burning plane. At first it looked like debris from the explosion, but you could see the tiny arms and legs.

"God-damn," Brad said.

Suddenly the tail of the plane broke off and more people spilled like seeds out of a pod. And the two main sections of the aircraft dropped like somebody had pitched them. They fell among scraps and burning pieces all the way down the sky. I thought at first they were falling right on top of us, but as they descended it was clear they were going to the south, further down the new roadway. As they fell the pieces seemed to get further and further away, and by the time they hit in showers of fire, they looked about two miles down the road, down the river of red clay and machinery.

"God-damn," Brad said again.

"Let's go," Roy said. He jumped into the cab of the foreman's pickup and started the engine. Brad and me threw down our shovels and climbed into the back.

"Hey," Joey called. But Roy ignored him. Roy and Joey had been playing a game of chicken all summer. Roy would see how much he could get away with without being fired. Joey would see if he could act superior to Roy by not losing his temper and not cussing. We had all gone to high school together and played football together. But Joey had stayed out of the draft by taking a course in engineering at the community college, and when we got out of the service he was foreman on the new highway job.

The roadbed was graded dirt, and Roy had to swing the pickup around bulldozers and fuel tanks and piles of crushed rock. Some of the earthmovers were still working and we almost hit one as it lurched across the bed with its belly full of dirt and both front and back engines blasting diesel smoke.

"Watch out," Brad hollered, and beat on the cab with his fist. But what we had to worry about most was other vehicles racing down the soft roadbed. Dozens of people on the job site headed just where we were. And people from town and from the shopping centers had seen the crash and were driving in the same direction.

"People is going crazy," Brad said.

We had to hold on because Roy was hitting rocks and bumps and piles of dirt that hadn't been smoothed. The new road looked like bomb craters in places, a shelled zone. Roy hit a caterpillar track that had been left rusting in the dirt, but he kept going. It was further to the crash than we had thought.

The first body we came to, Roy slammed on the brakes. A farm truck loaded with hampers of polebeans roared past us raising the orange dust. "Damn buzzards," Brad called after it. Nobody but those building the road were supposed to be on the site. The headache pulsed like a strobe light under my hardhat.

Roy got to the body first. It was an elderly woman with blue-looking hair. She was lying on her side with a shoulder drove into the ground. Her glasses lay in the dirt nearby, looking like they had been tossed there. Her dress was thrown up over her thighs and you could see the straps of her garter belt.

Roy rolled her over and felt for her pulse. Her eyes were open and a thin line of blood ran from the corner of her mouth. "She's dead," he said.

"No shit," Brad said. "She just fell a mile out of the sky."

"Excuse me for being so obvious," Roy said. "I forgot to be subtle."

I bent down to look at her, and when I straightened up I felt dizzy from my headache and the blinding sun. Cars and pickups, jeeps and tractors, whined over the rough dirt toward the black smoke of the wreck. I saw another body about a hundred yards ahead, right at the edge of the highway cut, half in the weeds. "Can't do her any good," I said, and started running. I tried to think of what first aid I could remember from the army, in case any of the bodies were still alive. I glanced back at Roy and Brad and they had started going through the old woman's pockets and purse. For the first time it came to me why so many people were running to the crash. We all wanted to get there first, before any authorities arrived and secured the area. I ran up the bank to the edge of the construction.

It was the body of a businessman that lay half in the weeds and half in the graded dirt. There's a sad dry look to dirt and weeds in late summer, and the body had fallen right against some blackberry briars. The berries were ripe and splattered and I couldn't tell at first what was berry juice and what was blood. The man was lying face down in the weeds and I rolled him over. The face was mashed in a little, nose flattened, and the eyes popping out with dirt and trash stuck to them. He was dead as a door bolt. There wasn't a thing I could do for him. A bad smell rose from the body, like it had just farted. His suitcoat had been ripped at the arms, maybe by the explosion or by the wind when he was falling. I lifted his wrist to feel the pulse and his watch was cold as if it had been in a refrigerator. It was still cool from the air conditioning in the plane.

I was really sweating from the heat and running, and from the headache. I reached into his coat pocket to get his wallet. I knew businessmen did not keep wallets in their hip pockets, but in their breast pockets. I thought, I'll just see what his name is. He had this fancy wallet made of madras cloth and rimmed with gold on the corners. I opened it and there was his driver's license and a bunch of credit cards and pictures of kids. The license said "Jeremy Kincaid," and the address was in Aiken, South Carolina. I looked in the bill compartment and there was a sheaf of twenties, and behind them a couple of fifties and a single hundred. I thought, I'll just leave this here for his wife and kids. And then I thought, somebody else will go and take it. Might as well be me.

The whole road was crawling with people far as I could see. More were arriving in trucks and cars, on motorcycles. In the distance I could hear a siren, and then the donkey horn of a firetruck. The bills felt cool and new. Cold cash I thought. A cool million, as they say. It amazes me sometimes how people have already thought of everything. I took out the bills and put the wallet back in the coat. His family will get all the insurance money, I thought. And none of this would ever get back to them anyway. I folded the bills like pages of a little book and slid them in the pocket of my sweaty jeans. Then I thought of the credit cards and reached back into the wallet for the shiny plastic. But I saw they were useless. I'd have to forge Mr. Kincaid's signature on any charges, and I didn't want any of that.

"Hot damn," I said and stood up. The headache crashed down on me. I'd had headaches ever since I got back from the army. I wished I had some cool headache powders, some Stanback or aspirin. People swarmed over every inch of the highway, among the earthmovers and bulldozers, backhoes, between piles of dirt and holes dug for culverts. Somebody had left a tractor running.

I saw there was no way to look further in the highway site. The smoke of the wreck seemed to come from a field or apple orchard to the left, toward the Dana Road. I ran out through the weeds in that direction. The blackberry briars reached out and clawed as I passed. I had to stomp down catbriars and hogweeds, big iron-weeds and the first goldenrods. I could see people ahead running out through the brush and into the trees, like they were racing each other.

Cold cash, I kept saying to myself in the terrible heat. I thought of cool sharp-edged bills that would slice a finger. I thought of a whole plateful of fifty dollar bills served like a feast, and the filling station I would buy to get out of construction work, and the mechanics courses I would take at the community college. Ever since I got out of the army I'd had to work so hard I couldn't make use of the GI Bill. I thought of my girlfriend Diane in her cool lavender shorts and how we could get married and build a beauty shop next to the filling station and she could get out of the hot basement at Woolworth's. Diane was the prettiest woman I'd ever seen, and we had been engaged since last year. I thought of us under the cool sheets at night. She deserved a beauty shop and I deserved a filling station. Enough for a down-payment, and the bank would loan us the rest.

Suddenly I saw somebody bent over in the weeds ahead of me. It looked like an animal pawing carrion, a big dog or a bear. But it

was a man's back rising and falling. I was going to run around him.
I didn't care what he was doing. But he had already heard me and
looked around. He was a big red-faced fellow that was almost
bald, and he was wearing the gray uniform of a delivery man. I
think it was a bread company. He was one of those men who drive
bread trucks.

"Hot dog," he said. He was going through the pockets of a boy
and had found a wallet. He had the boy's watch already and he was
fumbling with bills in the fold of the wallet. "Hot dog," he said.
"What a way to get a case of chiggers."

I ran around him still headed toward the smoke, and he looked
at me like he wanted to stop me, like he didn't want anybody to
get ahead of him. "Hey boy," he hollered. "You ain't trying to hog
it all for yourself are you?" I ignored him and ran on.

There was a fence with a hedgerow in front of me, and I was
looking for an easy way through the barbed wire when I saw the
body in a post-oak tree. The body was caught in the limbs about
twelve feet off the ground. Some of the branches had broke but
the body was stuck there. I thought of climbing the tree. I grabbed
the ends of a limb and tried to shake it loose. But the body had
lodged between the branches and would not slide off.

I looked around for a stick or pole to push it loose. The bald-
headed man in the uniform was running toward me and I figured
if I could just get the body down before he reached the fence it was
mine. There was a dead poplar sapling leaning in the hedgerow
and I jumped on it with both feet. But it didn't break; it was still
rooted in the dirt.

"Hey hog," the bread truck driver hollered. "You can't claim all
of them." He had a look in his eyes, like he didn't hardly care what
he was doing.

"You stay away," I said.

"*You* stay away," he said. He reached up for the oak limb and
tried to shake the body loose. He shook the tree like he was trying
to make acorns fall.

The second time I jumped on the poplar it broke. I snapped off the tip and had a pole about ten feet long. "You stand back, bastard," the bald-headed man said. He took a hawk-bill knife out of his back pocket. It was the kind of knife you use to cut out cardboard or linoleum.

"I'll cut your balls off," he said, holding the knife with one hand and jerking the oak limb with the other. I swung the pole and hit him on the back of the head. He went down like a sandbag in the weeds. "Bastard yourself," I said, but he was out cold.

With the pole I knocked the body in the tree loose and it fell almost beside the bread truck driver. The arms and legs were turned wrong, where they had been broke when they hit the post-oak. The man looked about seventy and was wearing a Hawaiian shirt. There wasn't more than forty dollars in his billfold, but he had a book of traveler's checks in his pocket. I tried to think if you could spend traveler's checks, but they were already signed in one corner and I threw them in the weeds. I was about to run on when I noticed the great bulge in the bald man's uniform pocket. I reached in and pulled out what must have been a wad of a hundred twenty dollar bills. I would leave him his wallet and whatever he had that was his. But I would take the wad because he had threatened me with the knife.

On the other side of the hedgerow was a bunch-bean field. It had been standing in water earlier in the summer and most of the vines had turned yellow. The ground looked painted with baked silt, like the bottom of a dried puddle. There were suitcases and overnight bags fallen among the vines, most of them busted open. I looked through some of them, but they were mostly just shirts and blouses, hairbrushes, women's shoes. I didn't even see any jewelry.

There was a piece of blackened airplane lying in the row, still smoking. It smelled of burnt fuel. It looked like a piece of the DC-9 with a shattered window.

There was a whole lot of sirens now, coming from all directions. And there were voices, and horns honking. I knew the police would arrive any time. I heard a helicopter coming from somewhere. That really reminded me of the army. But at no time in Nam had I seen this many bodies.

There was a woman on her knees in the bean rows near the creek, and I thought she must be picking over a body or a suitcase. I saw her out of the corner of my eye and avoided going in that direction. But after I went through ten or fifteen pieces of luggage and found only one purse with seventy dollars in it I looked her way again. She hadn't moved, and she was leaning in a peculiar way. Her back was twisted.

I ran over there and saw the strangest thing I'd seen all day. She was sunk in the soft dirt by the creek up to her knees. She had fallen out of the sky standing up and drove into the ground like a stake. Her face was stretched from the impact. Her necklace had broke off and was lying in the dirt. It looked like diamonds. I didn't see a pocketbook. It spooked me to look at her face with the eyes pushing out. My headache thundered louder. I grabbed up the necklace and ran on.

To go toward the smoke of the wreck I had to cross the creek. The stream was low from the late summer drought and almost hidden by weeds. Mud from the highway construction lined the banks, and the creek itself seemed one long pool through the level bottomland. It was green stagnant water, a dead pool, like a coma of water poisoned by bean spray and weed killer. There was no easy way to cross. A snake slid down a limb and plopped into the water. A scum like green hair and paint floated on the top.

I didn't see any way to cross except walk right into the creek, so I splashed in. I was halfway across and the water up to my chest when I bumped into something. The body must have been floating just under the surface for when I touched it it turned over and the face shot right up in my face. It was a man whose head had been burnt and his brains had busted out. I pushed the body away and crossed the creek quick as I could.

I climbed up the other bank brushing moss and green scum off my jeans. The water smelled sour but I didn't pay it any mind. When I broke through the tall weeds I was at the edge of a field of apple trees. The wreck was burning still further on, beyond another hedgerow. I could hear people hollering and sirens in that direction. I figured I would stay away from where the crowd was. The orchard seemed to be full of bodies and pieces of the wreck.

It was a young orchard which meant there were wide spaces around trees and you could see a long way between rows. There were dozens of people picking through the rows. I figured if I moved quick through the trees I wouldn't be any more noticeable than the rest. I hoped I didn't see anybody I knew. I hoped I didn't see Roy and Brad again.

The orchard had been plowed once that summer, which meant there was an open break of red dirt around each of the trees. The ground had baked hard and rough. Weeds rose right out of the unplowed ground into the limbs of the trees. The trees were loaded with green apples. The spray looked white and silver on the fruit. I had been raised in an apple orchard down near Saluda and it sickened me to think of the sweat that had gone into that grove. You grafted and fertilized, pruned and waited, sprayed and plowed, and still a late frost or early frost, a beetle or fungus, drought or wet summer, could ruin you. A hailstorm, a flood, a plane crash, a drop in the market price, could wipe you out. You have to fight, I said to myself. I thought of the filling station and the beauty shop I would build.

The sirens were getting closer, and growing in number. It sounded like all the firetrucks and patrol cars and ambulances in the world were screaming and wailing. I was glad I had got off the road, but I had to work fast. The firetruck horns were blasting toward the column of smoke and car horns answered the sirens.

"Clear the area, clear the area," a voice thundered out of the sky. I looked up and saw the chopper. It was the sheriff's chopper, the one they used to look for marijuana fields in the mountain coves.

"Clear the area, clear the area," the voice boomed again, rattled by static on the loudspeaker. I could feel the wind off the blades washing over the apple trees, fluttering leaves, and shaking green apples. For a second I thought they were going to land and try to arrest me. I kept my head down in case they were taking pictures. The heat of the wind and the pulse of my headache made me feel I had slipped through a time warp. If they landed I could try to run for the woods at the other end of the orchard. Then I realized they couldn't land among the apple trees. They were trying to scare people away from the wreck.

The helicopter tilted and swung away ahead of me. I gave it the finger; but there wasn't much time. I ran around a tree and there was this old couple in Bermuda shorts bent over a body. Their straw hats and sunglasses told me they were tourists from Miami. The mountains had been overrun by retirees from south Florida ever since I was a kid. They filled up the streets and highways with their long Cadillacs, driving in the middle of the road. "They come up here with a dollar and one shirt and don't change either," my Uncle Albert liked to say. I God.

They were crouching over the body and the old woman jumped when she heard me coming. She had on thick red lipstick and makeup. "We were just trying to see if we could help," she said.

"You go right ahead," I said.

"Is there nothing anybody can do?" the man said. He was holding his right hand behind his back. He must have taken the wallet from the body and hadn't had time to slip out the bills.

"We're just trying to help," the woman said. "These could be our family. They could be somebody's family."

"You all help yourself," I said. I ran past them and they watched me in horror, expecting to be mugged.

There was a piece of the private plane lying up against an apple tree. It was a part of the cockpit. The fuselage had been sheared like it was cut with a torch. The metal was blackened but not burning. I thought I saw a face behind the window and I ran closer. It was a face, and I lifted the torn section of the plane to free the body. But I instantly wished I had left it alone. It was a little boy about eight years old. The half of his face I had seen through the window was unmarked, but the other half had been sliced off by the impact. The kid never saw what hit him. Nothing I had glimpsed in the infantry was more sickening. I dropped the section of the Cessna and ran.

"You will clear the area," a voice said over a bullhorn. It was from a police car cruising around the perimeter of the orchard. "Looters will be arrested." I crouched down behind an apple tree until the flashing lights were past. It made me think of those preacher's cars with loudspeakers, one horn pointing forward and one backward on top of the car.

Got to fight, I said to myself. You've got to fight. It's what I said to myself for a whole year in the army. It's what I said to myself as a boy working in the orchard, in the heat and mud and stinging spray.

"We're sweeping the area and arresting looters," the loudspeaker crackled.

There were bodies and pieces of bodies all over the orchard. I ran quick as I could from one to the other, avoiding the people like it was a game of hide-and-seek. Flies were finding the torn limbs in the weeds.

There was a beautiful stewardess still in pieces of her uniform, but she didn't have either jewelry or a billfold on her. She had fallen into the lower limbs of a spreading apple tree and looked like she had gone to sleep there.

Some bodies were naked, but I avoided those, not only because I knew there wouldn't be any money on them but because it was embarrassing to get close. I didn't want to be seen looking at naked corpses, and I didn't want to see myself doing it either.

My pockets were stuffed with cash, some of it slightly burnt, some of it bloody, some of it dirty. Some of the money had been soaked in diesel fuel. I found more and more businessmen, but most of them had credit cards and little money. The women carried more cash in their purses. I threw away a lot of traveler's checks. I found bodies that had already been searched.

I was nearing the edge of the orchard and getting closer to the smoke and the gathering sirens. There was another hedgerow, and then a field where the main part of the wreck seemed to have come down.

"Clear the area immediately," the bullhorn blasted. "All looters will be arrested. It is a Federal offense to tamper with an airplane crash."

I dashed out of the orchard and across the haulroad. A pink ladies' purse lay in the brush against the hedgerow. I was about to reach for the handle when a black bullet shot in front of my face. And then I saw the hornet's nest about the size of a peck bucket behind the purse. The falling pocketbook had knocked off a section of the nest and the hornets boiled out of the hole. They hummed and shocked the air like ten thousand volts.

The purse was made of soft pink leather. I just knew it was full of money. But it was dangerous to get near a nest that big, especially if they were all riled up. Ten hornet stings can kill you, can put you to sleep forever. There must have been a thousand in that nest.

"Everybody clear the area," the loudspeaker said. "Only members of the volunteer fire department should be in the area. They will be wearing red armbands. All others will be arrested."

I thought I might have ten minutes before they got to me. The cruiser with flashing lights was circling back on the haulroad. I wiped the sweat out of my eyes and watched the hornets circle. The handbag lay among the weeds and baked late summer dirt.

As I broke a twig off the tree above my head and brought it to my lips I smelled the aroma. It was balm of Gilead. The bright spicy smell woke me up from the heat and reminded me of the tree by the old house down at Saluda. The twig smelled like both medicine and candy.

Somebody was coming. There were voices and it sounded like the volunteer firemen were already sweeping the area. Of course they would take everything they could find for themselves, same as the cops would. Wasn't any reason to leave the money for them, money that would never get to heaven or hell with the owners, or to the rightful heirs.

I had heard boys brag about breaking off a limb with a hornet's nest on it and running down the mountainside so fast the hornets couldn't sting them. But I never believed them. A hornet can fly faster than the eye can see, and these were already boiling. I didn't have any smoke to blow on them, and I couldn't wait till dark. And I didn't have a cloth to throw over them either.

I took the red bandanna off my neck and wrapped it around my left hand and wrist. The hardhat would protect part of my head. I grabbed the handle of the purse and jerked away, but the first hornet popped me on the shoulder and another got me on the elbow. I ran hard as I could through the weeds. A hornet sting always hits you in two stages. First the prick of the stinger, and then the real pain of the poison squirting home. A hornet must release its venom with powerful pressure because it always feels like you've stopped a bullet or had a bone broke and your flesh rings with the pain. I got hit twice more.

I ran along the haulroad like a scalded dog until I didn't hear the hornets circling anymore. There were voices on the other side of the ditch and I dropped down behind a sumac bush. The heat was terrible. It magnified the pain of the stings and speeded the ache of the poison through me. A hornet sting makes your bones and joints feel sick. It makes you feel old with rheumatism.

But my headache didn't seem as bad. I had heard people say you could cure a headache with a bee sting, but I never believed it. Most likely the hurt of the sting makes you forget the headache. But there was no doubt the throb in my head was fading. I thought of the cool frosty powders of aspirin, and looked up at the snowy edge of a cloud far above me.

The voices on the other side of the hedgerow got closer and I hunkered deeper under the sumacs and the balm of Gilead trees. There must have been a whole row of the trees, which is real unusual. I tried to quiet my breathing by chewing a twig. In the shade I could smell myself, the sweat from work in the sun and running, and the raw smell of fear and pain from the stings. My sweat dripped all over the soft leather handbag. It was the most expensive leatherwork I had ever seen. Every seam was rounded and the stitching was concealed. It was leather made for royalty.

At first I didn't see anything inside but a compact and lipstick, some keys to a Mercedes, and a bottle of perfume. There was a wallet with credit cards in the slots but I didn't find but thirty dollars in the bill compartment. I started to throw them all out in the weeds, but that seemed disrespectful, though I couldn't explain why. The woman was dead and wouldn't need her purse again. There was a driver's license that identified her as a resident of Coral Gables, Florida. I pushed aside the little bottle of mouthwash, the cellophane-wrapped peppermint candies, a couple of unmailed letters, and was about to give up when I saw the zipper almost concealed under a flap of shiny lining. I unzipped the pocket and felt inside. I touched edges that seemed stiff and sharp as razor blades. I got my finger around the packet and pulled it out. There was a wad of folded bills, brand-new bills, some twenties, some fifties, and some hundreds. It was the old woman's stash for her vacation in the mountains. The bills were starched with newness, the green and black inks printed in biting freshness, with some serial numbers and seals in blue. What fine cloth money is, I thought. There must have been over three thousand dollars in the folded pages. They were like a new printed book, every page pretty. I stuffed them in my pocket, deep so they wouldn't fall out.

All my pockets were full of bills and jewelry. If I found anything else I'd have to stuff it in my underwear, though that was dangerous for it might fall out. Better to stuff money in my boots. I took the red bandanna off my hand and tied it around my right arm. It probably wouldn't work, but if anybody stopped me I could claim I was a volunteer fireman.

There were shouts from the direction of the crash. The firetrucks wailed and somebody was on the bullhorn again. I could see lights flashing through the hedgerow. "Clear the area, the area must be cleared," the voice echoed across the fields and back from barns. A patrol passed on the other side of the ditch not more than fifteen feet away. They could see me if they looked close. "Whatever we get we will divide up," one of the men was saying.

I had to think fast. If I was stopped by the firemen they would just take everything I had found. There were too many of them, and they would claim I was looting, or resisted arrest or something. If I was caught by the sheriff or one of the troopers, they would either take what I had or beat me up with their clubs, or both.

I chewed on the spicy twig in my nervousness. I used to do that when I was crouched down hiding from my brother, or waiting for the enemy to move or fire. It seemed to help. The medicine smell of the balm of Gilead woke me up a little from my worry. There was something about the smell of the bark that reminded me of soft drinks like root beer or Dr. Pepper. I wished I had a cold drink. If I ever got out of there with my money I would celebrate with a case of cold Pepsi.

"This is the U. S. Marshal," a voice said over a loudspeaker. "All who don't leave the site will be arrested. It is a Federal offense to loot an airplane crash."

There were shouts and more sirens arriving. A truck horn blasted for a full ten seconds. I waited until the firemen had gone on fifty or seventy-five feet on the other side of the ditch, and then I laid the purse down and stood up. The blood must have drained out of my head because it felt like a shadow had passed over everything. I waited for a few seconds to focus my mind. The stings ached worse than ever, but the headache had gone.

There was nobody in sight and I started walking to the east toward the Dana Road. I figured it was safer if I stayed away from the new highway where all the trucks and cars had converged. I would try to get back to the place we had been working before anybody else did. If I got back soon enough I could put my money in my lunchbox and nobody would ever see it. That's what Bishop the bulldozer driver did when he uncovered a mason jar of money on the pasture hill down at the south end of the county. When they first started building the highway, he cut into a bank and a fruit jar rolled out, a quart stuffed full of twenties. He got off the dozer and emptied the jar inside his shirt then threw the jar away. Wouldn't anybody know he got the money except one of the Ward boys saw him. But when the Ward boy told the foreman and they asked Bishop he said he hadn't seen any money, and he showed them his empty shirt. He had already moved the money to his lunchbox and thermos. Wasn't long after that, maybe three months, till he bought a store and fruit stand over near the line and quit driving the bulldozer.

I walked fast as I could without seeming to hurry. A hurry will draw suspicion. I was about a quarter of a mile from the end of the orchard when I saw the red and tan sheriff's car coming down the middle of the grove with all its lights flashing. At the same time I heard the chopper again. I don't know who spotted me first, the patrol car or the helicopter, but the next thing I heard was the bullhorn in the sky, "Hey you there, in the hard-hat, stop."

I kept going for a few steps and the bullhorn blasted again, "Stop there or I'll shoot." I could hear the patrol car whining through the apple trees toward me. The chopper came in closer and its wind hit me like a slap. "Halt there," the voice in the sky said. "You're under arrest."

I wondered if they had seen my bulging pockets. I had to think quick. The haulroad was too narrow for the chopper to land in, but the sheriff's car would run me down in a few seconds. I had to do something or lose everything. The chopper wind smacked at my face.

I dove into the brush and rolled under some sumac bushes. Then I crawled on my elbows through the blackberry briars. The grit cut into my skin. I hadn't crawled like that in years. A moccasin snake plunged into the ditch ahead of me. The water was cloudy with chemicals and moss. I threw down my hardhat and slid in after the snake, and was going to head east, the way I had been running. But I changed my mind and started back the other way, toward the creek. I crawled as fast as I could until the sheriff's car stopped, and then I backed in under some honeysuckle vines and listened.

"Right in front of you," the loudspeaker from the chopper said.

The deputy who got out of the car looked like he had never been out of air conditioning. His shirt was starched and ironed to his back and shoulders. He walked to the brush and peered into the hedgerow. "He went right in there," the voice from the helicopter said.

I wished I had something to darken my face. There was a good chance my skin would shine right through the honeysuckle bushes. I sunk low as I could, almost to my nose in the water. There was green paste thick as pancake batter floating on the surface. I squeezed my lips to keep water out.

"Look right there," the loudspeaker boomed. The wind from the blades shook the leaves of the balm of Gilead trees and trembled the surface of the water. If the chopper came in lower it might blow the vines aside and expose me.

The deputy parted the sumac bushes and looked into the ditch. He looked like he was afraid ticks and chiggers and snakes and spiders would attack him. He never took his sunglasses off, otherwise he would have seen me for sure. He looked at the water and paused, and I was certain he had seen me. I could feel the ditchwater soaking into my pockets among the wadded bills. Luckily money won't melt. The ditchwater was warm as a mud puddle. But the money still felt cool.

"Look to the left," the voice on the bullhorn said.

The deputy peered past the sumac bushes and took out his gun. He must have seen my hardhat. "Come out or I shoot," he said. I pushed back under the vines far as I could. He fired twice and sent the hat skipping into the ditch.

"Look to the left," the voice from the chopper said again. They had seen me running that way and guessed I would continue in that direction. I waited until he had gone forty or fifty feet, and then I slid out of the honeysuckle vines and began crawling on my side through the ditch scum. I didn't have to worry about noise because of the chopper, but if I came out in an open place they would spot me. The chopper hovered just above the deputy.

Another snake slid off a limb, unwinding like a corkscrew, and disappeared into the cloudy water. I'd heard snakes have trouble biting in water because they can't brace themselves to coil and strike. I hoped that was right. The ditch was full of bottles and cans and all kinds of trash. Everything was covered with a slimy coat of silt. Everything felt like mucus. I could have made it out of sight except there was this burlap erosion dam across the ditch, the kind we're required by law to put around construction sites. They don't do any good but they're supposed to catch the dirt washing into ditches. The burlap was almost rotten and covered with leaves and dried mud. But it wouldn't tear. I had no choice but to climb over it.

If I stood up they could see me through the hedgerow. The deputy was about a hundred feet away, and the chopper right above him. I hesitated for a moment, but realized I didn't have much time. If they didn't find me in that direction they would come back looking in the other.

I stood up slowly and bent across the dam, and just as I was swinging over the voice from the chopper blasted, "Look over there, look over there." I had taken my chance and failed. I was going to have to run for it as best I could and hope they didn't shoot. I wheeled myself over the burlap and started running, but out of the corner of my eye I saw these two boys come out of an orchard row lugging a big suitcase between them. They looked like farmboys, maybe fourteen or fifteen, barefoot and without shirts. They started running back into the orchard and the deputy took after them. "No use to run boys, no use to run," the voice from the chopper said.

I knew that was the best chance I would have, so I dropped back into the ditchwater and crawled on my hands and knees for another hundred feet. There were sirens and horns and screams and loudspeakers from the site of the crash to my left. It sounded like hundreds of people had gathered there now. I couldn't go in that direction, and I couldn't go east to the Dana Road. I had no choice but to head toward the creek, and then to the highway construction.

After crawling another hundred yards I climbed out on the bank and started running. I crossed the haulroad dripping on the scorched weeds and darted into the apple trees. My pants were heavy with wetness and the wet bills weighed in my pockets, but I dashed from tree to tree. I didn't know if the helicopter could see me, but I couldn't pause to find out. I ran like I used to as a kid through the orchard, throwing myself forward into every stride, thrusting my chest out and pushing the edge of the world ahead of me.

As I ran I thought how cool my wet pants were in the wind, and how cool the money in my pockets was even where the wet cloth pinched. I passed a sprayer covered with white chemical frost and swung around it.

It was about a mile to the new road, but I could make it in a few minutes. Another half mile and I would be home free.

———————

A native of western North Carolina, Robert Morgan is the author of several volumes of poetry as well as four books of fiction. His most recent novel, *The Truest Pleasure*, was chosen by *Publishers Weekly* as one of the best books of 1995. Since 1971 he has taught at Cornell University.

"The Balm of Gilead Tree" was sparked by an anecdote told to me years ago by a friend. He had been working on a new superhighway when two airplanes collided above and crashed near the site. As he and the construction crew ran to look for survivors, they saw dozens of other people hurrying through the fields and woods, climbing fences and wading through creeks, to steal from the dead even as they pretended to help. I thought about the incident for years before attempting the story.

When I did get around to writing it I saw the story had to be told from the point of view of a participant in the frenzy of looting. But it was only after the narrative was underway that I saw it was a story of triumph, of exhilaration. In the midst of a ghastly tragedy the narrator discovers an exuberance he has never known before as he rifles body after body, racing the competition. He is a struggling, troubled Vietnam vet who sees that his life is going to be changed by this one afternoon. And he feels no guilt, for he is only doing what he must do, since everyone else is grabbing the cash also. He will have his filling station and his girl Diane will have her beauty shop. It is the greatest hour of his life.

If all good stories are about conflicts of loyalty—and I believe they are— then it is his loyalty to opportunity that takes over in "The Balm of Gilead Tree." But we cannot know how he will look back on his actions, on his good fortune, when he is older, say thirty years later. That is another, harder story.

Tim Gautreaux

DIED AND GONE TO VEGAS

(from *The Atlantic Monthly*)

Raynelle Bullfinch told the young oiler that the only sense of mystery in her life was provided by a deck of cards. As she set up the table in the engine room of the *Leo B. Canterbury*, a government steam dredge anchored in a pass at the mouth of the Mississippi River, she lectured him. "Nick, you're just a college boy sitting out a bit until you get money to go back to school, but for me, this is it." She pulled a coppery braid from under her overalls strap, looked around at the steam chests and piping, and sniffed at the smell of heat-proof red enamel. In the glass of a steam gauge she checked her round, bright cheeks for grease and ran a white finger over the blue arcs of her eyebrows. She was the cook on the big boat, which was idle for a couple of days because of high winter winds. "My big adventure is cards. One day I'll save up enough to play with the skill boys in Vegas. Set up those folding chairs," she told him. "Seven in all."

"I don't know how to play bourrée, ma'am." Nick Montalbano ran a hand through long hair shiny with dressing. "I only had one semester of college." He looked sideways at the power straining the bronze buckles of the tall woman's bib and avoided her green eyes, which were deep-set and full of intense judgment.

"Bullshit. A pet rat can play bourrée. Sit down." She pointed to a metal chair, and the oiler, a thin boy wearing an untucked plaid flannel shirt and a baseball cap, obeyed. "Pay attention here. I deal out five cards to everybody, and I turn up the last card. Whatever suit it is, that's trumps. Then you discard all your nontrumps and draw replacements. Remember, trumps beat all other suits, high trumps beat low trumps. Whatever card is led, you follow suit." She ducked her head under the bill of his cap, looking for his eyes. "This ain't too hard for you, is it? Ain't college stuff more complicated than this?"

"Sure, sure. I understand. But what if you can't follow suit?"

"If nontrumps is led, put a trump on it. If you ain't got no more trumps, just throw your lowest card. Trust me—you'll catch on quick."

"How do you win?" The oiler turned his cap around.

"Every hand has five tricks to take. If you take three tricks, you win the pot, unless only two decide to play that hand after the draw. Then you need four tricks. If you got any questions, ask Sidney there."

Sidney, the chief engineer, a little fireplug of a man who would wear a white T-shirt in a blizzard, sat down heavily with a whistle. "Oh, boy. Fresh meat." He squeezed the oiler's neck.

The steel door next to the starboard triple-expansion engine opened, letting in a wash of frigid air around the day fireman, pilot, deckhand, and welder, who came into the big room cursing and clapping the cold out of their clothes. Through the door the angry whitecaps of Southwest Pass raced down the Mississippi, bucking into the tarnished Gulf sky.

"Close that damned pneumonia-hole," Raynelle cried, sailing cards precisely before the seven chairs. "Sit down, worms. Usual game: dollar ante, five-dollar rip if you don't take a trick." After the rain of halves and dollars came discards, more dealing, and then a flurry of cards ending with a rising snowstorm of curses as no one took three tricks and the pot rolled over to the next hand. Three players took no tricks and put up the five-dollar rip.

The engineer unrolled a pack of Camels from his T-shirt sleeve and cursed loudest. "I heard of a bourrée game on a offshore rig where the pot didn't clear for eighty-three passes. By the time somebody won that bitch, it had seventeen hundred dollars in it. The next day the genius what took it got a wrench upside the head in a Morgan City bar and woke up with his pockets inside out and the name Conchita tattooed around his left nipple."

Pig, the day fireman, put up his ante and collected the next hand. "That ain't nothin'." He touched three discards to the top of his bald head and threw them down. "A ol' boy down at the dock told me the other day that he heard about a fellow got hit in the head over in Orange, Texas, and didn't know who he was when he looked at his driver's license. Had amnesia. That sorry-ass seamen's hospital sent him home to his scuzz-bag wife, and he didn't know her from Adam's house cat."

"That mighta been a blessing," Raynelle said, sending him three cards in a flock. She rolled left on her ample bottom.

"No, it wasn't," the day fireman said, unzipping his heavy green field jacket. "That gal told him she was his sister, gave him a remote control and a color TV; he was happy as a fly on a pie. She started bringin' boyfriends in at night, and that fool waved them into the house. Fixed 'em drinks. Figured any old dude good enough for Sis was good enough for him. The neighbors got to lookin' at her like they was smellin' somethin' dead, so she and her old man moved to a better trailer park where nobody knew he'd lost his memory. She started into cocaine, and hookin' for fun on the side. Her husband's settlement money he got from the company what dropped a thirty-six-inch Stillson wrench on his hard hat began to shrink up a bit, but that old boy just sat there dizzy on some cheap pills she told him was a prescription. He'd channel surf all day, greet the johns like one of those old dried-up coots at Wal-Mart, and was the happiest son of a bitch in Orange, Texas." The day fireman spread wide his arms. "Was he glad to see Sis come home every day. He was proud she had more friends than a postman with a bag full of welfare checks. And then his memory came back."

"Ho, ho, the *merde* hit the blower," the engineer said, slamming a queen down and raking in a trick.

"Nope. That poor bastard remembered every giggle in the rear bedroom and started feelin' lower than a snake's nuts. He tried to get his old woman straight, but the dyed-over tramp just laughed in his face and moved out on him. He got so sorry he went to a shrink, but that just cost him more bucks. Finally, you know what that old dude wound up doin'? He looked for someone would hit him in the head again—you know, so he could get back the way he was. He offered a hundred dollars a pop, and in them Orange bars most people will whack on you for free, so you can imagine what kind of service he bought hisself. After nearly gettin' killed four or five times, he give up and spent the rest of his settlement money on a hospital stay for a concussion. After that he held up a Pac-a-Bag for enough money to get himself hypmotized back to like he was after he got hit the first time. Wound up in the pen doin' twenty hard ones."

They played three hands of cards while the day fireman finished the story, and then the deckhand in the game, a thick blond man in a black cotton sweater, threw back his head and laughed, *ha ha*, as if he were only pretending. "If that wadn' so funny, it'd be sad. It reminds me of this dumb-ass peckerwood kid lived next to me in Kentucky, built like a stringbean. He was a few thimbles shy of a quart, but he sort of knew he wadn' no nuclear-power-plant repairman and he got along with everybody. Then he started hangin' with these bad-ass kids—you know, the kind that carry spray paint, wear their hats backward, and stuff live rats in your mailbox. Well, they told the poor bastard he was some kind of Jesse James and got him into stealin' hubcaps and electric drills. He started struttin' around the neighborhood like he was bad news at midnight, and soon the local deputies had him in the back seat for runnin' off with a lawn mower. Dummy stole it in December."

"What's wrong with that?" the day fireman asked, pitching in a dollar.

"Who's gonna buy a used mower in winter, you moron? Anyway, the judge had pity on him, gave him a two-bit fine and sent him to bed with a sugar-tit. Said he was a good boy who ought to be satisfied to be simple and honest. But Stringbean hung out on the street corner crowin'. He was proud now. A real gangster, happy as Al Capone, his head pumped full of swamp gas by these losers he's hangin' around with. Finally one night he breaks into the house of a gun collector. Showin' how smart he is, he chooses only one gun to take from the rack—an engraved Purdy double-barrel, mint condition, with gold and ivory inlays all over, a twenty-thousand-dollar gun. Stringbean took it home and with a two-dollar hacksaw cut the stock off and then most of the barrel. He went out and held up a taco joint and got sixteen dollars and thirteen cents. Was arrested when he walked out the door. This time a hard-nut judge sent him up on a multiple bill and he got two hundred ninety-seven years in Bisley."

"All right," Raynelle sang. "Better than death."

"He did ten years before the weepy-ass parole board noticed the sentence and pulled him in for review. Asked him did he get reha-bilitated and would he go straight if he got out, and he spit on their mahogany table. He told them he wadn' no dummy and would be the richest bank robber in Kentucky if he got half a chance." The deckhand laughed, *ha ha*. "That give everybody an ice-cream headache, and the meetin' came to a vote right quick. Even the American Civil Liberties lesbo lawyers on the parole board wanted to weld the door shut on him. It was somethin'."

The pilot, a tall man wearing a pea jacket and a sock cap, raised a new hand to his sharp blue eyes and winced, keeping one trump and asking for four cards. "Gentlemen, that reminds me of a girl in Kentucky I knew at one time."

"Why? Did she get sent up two hundred ninety-seven years in Bisley?" the deckhand asked.

"No, she was from Kentucky, like that crazy fellow you just lied to us about. By the way, that king won't walk," he said, laying down an ace of diamonds. "This woman was a nurse at the VA hospital in Louisville and fell in love with one of her patients, a good-looking, mild-mannered fellow with a cyst in his brain that popped and gave him amnesia."

"Now, there's something you don't hear every day," the engineer said, trumping the ace with a bang.

"He didn't know what planet he came from," the pilot said stiffly. "A few months later they got married and he went to work in a local iron plant. After a year he began wandering away from work at lunchtime. So they fired him. He spent a couple of weeks walking up and down his street and all over Louisville looking into people's yards and checking passing buses for the faces in the windows. It was like he was looking for someone, but he couldn't remember who. One day he didn't come home at all. For eighteen months this pretty little nurse was beside herself with worry. Then her nephew was at a rock concert downtown and spotted a shaggy guy who looked familiar in the mosh pit, just standing there like he was watching a string quartet. Between songs the nephew asked the shaggy guy if he had amnesia, which is a rather odd question, considering, and the man almost started crying, because he figured he'd been recognized."

"That's a sweet story," the day fireman said, rubbing his eyes with his bear-paw-sized hands. "Sidney, could you loan me your handkerchief? I'm all choked up."

"Choke this," the pilot said, trumping the fireman's jack. "Anyway, the little nurse gets attached to the guy again and is glad to have him back. She refreshes his memory about their marriage and all that and starts over with him. Things are better than ever, as far as she is concerned. Well, about a year of marital bliss goes by, and one evening there's a knock at the door. She gets up off the sofa where the amnesia guy is, opens it, and it's her husband, whose memory came back."

"Wait a minute," the deckhand said. "I thought that was her husband on the sofa."

"I never said it was her husband. She just thought it was her husband. It turns out that the guy on the sofa she's been living with for a year is the identical twin to the guy on the doorstep. Got an identical popped cyst, too."

"Aw, bullshit," the day fireman bellowed.

The engineer leaned back and put his hand on a valve handle. "I better pump this place out."

"Hey," the pilot yelled above the bickering. "I knew this girl. Her family lived across the street from my aunt. Anyway, after all the explanations were made, the guy who surfaced at the rock concert agreed it would be best if he moved on, and the wandering twin started back where he left off with his wife. Got his job back at the iron plant. But the wife wasn't happy anymore."

"Why the hell not?" the engineer asked, dealing the next hand. "She had two for the price of one."

"Yeah, well, even though those guys were identical in every way, something was different. We'll never know what it was, but she couldn't get over the second twin. Got so she would wander around herself, driving all over town looking for him."

"What the hell?" The deckhand threw down his cards. "She had her husband back, didn't she?"

"Oh, it was bad," the pilot continued. "She's driving down the street one day and sees the rock-concert twin, gets out of her car, runs into a park yelling and sobbing, and throws her arms around him, crying, 'I found you at last, I found you at last.' Only it wasn't him."

"Jeez," the engineer said. "Triplets."

"No." The pilot shook his head. "It was worse than that. It was her husband, who was out on delivery for the iron plant, taking a break in the park after shucking his coveralls. Mild-mannered amnesiac or not, he was pretty put out at the way she was carrying on. But he didn't show it. He pretended to be his twin and asked her why she liked him better than her husband. And she told him. Now, don't ask me what it was. The difference was in her mind, way I heard it. But that guy disappeared again the next morning, and that was five years ago. They say you can go down in east Louisville and see her driving around today in a ratty green Torino, looking for one of those twins, this scared look in her eyes like she'll find one and never be sure which one she got hold of."

Raynelle pulled a pecan out of her bib pocket and cracked it between her thumb and forefinger. "That story's sadder'n a armless old man in a room full of skeeters. You sorry sons of bitches tell the depressingest lies I ever heard."

The deckhand lit up an unfiltered cigarette. "Well, sweet thing, why don't you cheer us up with one of your own?"

Raynelle looked up at a brass steam gauge bolted to an I beam. "I did know a fellow worked in an iron foundry, come to think of it. His whole family worked the same place, which is a pain in the butt if you've ever done that, what with your uncle giving you wet willies and your cousin bumming money. This fellow drove a gray Dodge Dart, the kind with the old slant-six engine that'll carry you to hell and back, slow. His relatives made fun of him for it, said he was cheap and wore plastic shoes and ate Spam—that kind of thing." She turned the last card to show trumps, banging up a king. "Sidney, you better not bourrée again. You're in this pot for thirty dollars."

The engineer swept up his hand, pressing it against his T-shirt. "I can count."

"Anyway, this boy thought he'd show his family a thing or two and went out and proposed to the pretty girl who keyed in the invoices in the office. He bought her a diamond ring that would choke an elephant, on time. It was a *nice* ring." Raynelle looked at the six men around the table as if none of them would ever buy such a ring. "He was gonna give it to her on her birthday, right before they got married in three weeks, and meantime he showed it around at the iron foundry figuring it'd make 'em shut up, which basically it did."

"They was probably speechless at how dumb he was," the deckhand said out of the side of his mouth.

"But don't you know that before he got to give it to her, that girl hit her head on the edge of her daddy's swimming pool and drowned. The whole foundry went into mourning, as did those kids' families and the little town in general. She had a big funeral and she was laid out in her wedding dress in a white casket sur-

rounded by every carnation in four counties. Everybody was crying, and the funeral parlor had this lovely music playing. I guess
the boy got caught up in the feeling, because he walked over to the
coffin right before they was gonna screw down the lid and he put
that engagement ring on that girl's finger."

"Naw," the engineer said breathlessly, playing a card without
looking at it.

"Yes, he did. And he felt proud that he done it. At least for a
month or two. Then he began to have eyes for a dental hygienist,
and that little romance took off hot as a bottle rocket. He courted
her for six months and decided to pop the question. But he started
thinking about the monthly payments he was making on that ring
and how they would go on for four and a half more years, keeping him from affording a decent ring for this living girl."

"Oh, no," the pilot said, as the hand split again and the pot
rolled over yet another time.

"That's right. He got some tools and after midnight went down
to Heavenly Oaks Mausoleum and unscrewed the marble door on
her drawer, slid out the coffin, and opened it up. I don't know how
he could stand to rummage around in whatever was left in the box,
but damned if he didn't get that ring and put the grave back
together slick as a whistle. So the next day he give it to the hygienist and everything's okay. A bit later they get married and are doing
the lovebird bit in a trailer down by the foundry." Raynelle cracked
another pecan against the edge of the table, crushing it with the
pressure of her palm in a way that made the welder and the oiler
look at each other. "But there's a big blue blowfly in the ointment.
She was showing off that ring by the minute, and someone recognized the damned thing and told her. Well, she had a thirty-
megaton double-PMS hissy fit and told him straight up that she
won't wear no dead woman's ring, and throws it in his face. Said
the thing gave her the willies. He told her it's that or a King
Edward cigar band, because he won't get out from under the payments until the twenty-first century. It went back and forth like
that for a month, with the neighbors up and down the road,

including my aunt Tammy, calling the police to come get them to shut up. Finally the hygienist told him she'd wear the ring."

"Well, that's a happy ending," the deckhand said.

Raynelle popped half a pecan into her red mouth. "Shut up, Jack, I ain't finished. This hygienist began to wear cowboy blouses and jean miniskirts just like the girl in the foundry office did. The old boy kind of liked it at first, but when she dyed her hair the same color as the first girl, it gave him the shakes. She said she was dreaming of that dead girl at least twice a week and saw her in her dresser mirror when she woke up. Then she began to talk like the foundry girl did, with a snappy Arkansas twang. And the dead girl was a country-music freak—liked the old stuff, too. Damned if in the middle of the night the guy wasn't waked up by his wife singing in her sleep all eleven verses of 'El Paso,' the Marty Robbins tune.

"He figured it was the ring causing all the trouble, so he got his wife drunk and while she was asleep slipped that sucker off and headed to the graveyard to put it back on that bone where he took it. Soon as he popped the lid, the cops was on him asking him what the living hell he was doing. He told them he was putting a diamond ring back in the coffin, and they said, Sure, buddy. Man, he got charged with six or eight nasty things perverts do to dead bodies, and then the dead girl's family filed six or eight civil suits, and believe me, there was mental anguish, pain, and suffering enough to feed the whole county. A local judge who was the dead girl's uncle sent him up for six years, and the hygienist divorced him. Strange thing was that she kept her new hair color and way of dressing, began going to George Jones concerts, and last I heard had quit her job at the dentist and was running the computers down at the iron foundry."

"Raynelle, *chère*, I wish you wouldn't of said that one." Simoneaux, the welder, never spoke much until late in the game. He was a thin Cajun, seldom without a Camel in the corner of his mouth and a high-crowned, polka-dotted welder's cap turned backward on his head. He shrugged off a violent chill. "That story gives me *les frissons* up and down my back." A long stick of beef jerky jutted from the pocket of his flannel shirt. He pulled it out, plucked a lint ball from the bottom, and bit off a small knob of meat. "But that diamond shit reminds me of a old boy I knew down in Grand Crapaud who was workin' on Pancho Oil number six offshore from Point au Fer. The driller was puttin' down the pipe hard one day and my frien' the mud engineer was takin' a dump on the engine-room toilet. All at once they hit them a gas pocket at five t'ousand feet and drill pipe came back up that hole like drinkin' straws, knockin' out the top of the rig, flyin' up in the sky, and breakin' apart at the joints. Well, my frien', he had a magazine spread out across his lap when a six-inch drill pipe hit the roof like a spear and went through-and-through the main diesel engine. About a half second later another one passed between his knees, through the Playmate of the Month and the steel deck both, yeah. He could hear the iron comin' down all over the rig, but he couldn't run because his pants was around his ankles on the other side of the drill column between his legs. He figured he was goin' to glory before he could get some toilet paper, but a worm run in the engine room and cut him loose with a jackknife, and then they both took off over the side and hit the water. My frien' rolled through them breakers holdin' on to a drum of mineral spirits, floppin' around until a bad-ass fish gave him a bite on his giblets, and that was the only injury he had."

"Ouch, man." The deckhand crossed his legs.

"What?" Raynelle looked up while posting her five-dollar bourrée.

The welder threw in yet another ante, riffling the dollar bills in the pot as though figuring how much it weighed. "Well, he was hurt enough to get the company to pay him a lump sum after he got a four-by-four lawyer to sue their two-by-four insurance company. That's for true. My frien', he always said he wanted a fancy car. The first t'ing he did was to drive to Lafayette and buy a sixty-five-t'ousand-dollar Mercedes, yeah. He put new mud-grip tires on that and drove it down to the Church Key Lounge, in Morgan City, where all his mud-pumpin' buddies hung out, and it didn't take long to set off about half a dozen of them hard hats, no." The welder shook his narrow head. "He was braggin' bad, yeah."

The engineer opened his cards on his belly and rolled his eyes. "A new Mercedes in Morgan City? Whew."

"*Mais oui,* you can say that again. About two, t'ree o'clock in the mornin' my frien', he come out and what he saw woulda made a muskrat cry. Somebody took a number two ball-peen hammer and dented everythin' on that car that would take a dent. That t'ing looked like it got caught in a cue-ball tornado storm. Next day he brought it by the insurance people and they told him the policy didn't cover vandalism. Told him he would have to pay to get it fixed or drive it like that.

"But my frien', he had blew most all his money on the car to begin with. When he drove it, everybody looked at him like he was some kind of freak. You know, he wanted people to look at him, that's why he bought the car, but they was lookin' at him the wrong way, like 'You mus' be some prime jerk to have someone mess with you car like that.' So after a week of havin' people run off the road turnin' their necks to look at that new Mercedes, he got drunk, went to the store and bought about twenty cans of Bondo, tape, and cans of spray paint."

"Don't say it," the deckhand cried.

"No, no," the engineer said to his cards.

"What?" Raynelle asked.

"Yeah, the po' bastard couldn't make a snake out of Play-Doh and is gonna try and restore a fine European se-dan. He filed and sanded on that poor car for a week, and then hit it with that dollar-a-can paint. When he finished up, that Mercedes looked like it was battered for fryin'. He drove it around Grand Crapaud, and people just pointed and doubled over. He kept it outside his trailer at night, and people would drive up and park, just to look at it. Phone calls started comin', the hang-up kind that said things like 'You look like your car,' click, or 'What kind of icin' did you use?'"

click. My frien' finally took out his insurance policy and saw what it did cover—theft.

"So he started leavin' the keys in it parked down by the abandoned lumber yard, but nobody in Grand Crapaud would steal it. He drove to Lafayette, rented a motel room, yeah, and parked it outside that bad housin' project with keys in it." The welder threw in another hand and watched the cards fly. "Next night he left the windows down with the keys in it." He pulled off his polka-dotted cap and ran his fingers through his dark hair. "Third night he left the motor runnin' and the lights on with the car blockin' the driveway of a crack house. Next mornin' he found it twenty feet away, idled out of diesel with a dead battery. It was that ugly."

"What happened next?" The pilot trumped an ace as if he were killing a bug.

"My frien', he called me up, you know. Said he wished he had a used standard-shift Ford pickup and the money in the bank. His wife left him, his momma made him take a cab to come see her, and all he could stand to do was drink and stay in his trailer. I didn't know what to tell him. He said he was gonna read his policy some more."

"Split pot again," the deckhand shouted. "I can't get out this game. I feel like my nuts is hung up in a fan belt."

"Shut your trap and deal," Raynelle said, sailing a loose wad of cards in the deckhand's direction. "What happened to the Mercedes guy?"

The welder put his cap back on and pulled up the crown. "Well, his policy said it covered all kinds of accidents, you know, so he parked it in back next to a big longleaf pine and cut that sucker down, only it was a windy day and as soon as he got through that tree with the saw, a gust come up and pushed it the other way from where he wanted it to fall."

"What'd it hit?"

"It mashed his trailer like a cockroach, yeah. The propane stove blew up, and by the time the Grand Crapaud fire truck come around, all they could do was break out coat hangers and mush-

mellas. His wife what lef' ain't paid the insurance on the double-
wide, no, so now he got to get him a camp stove and a picnic table,
so he can shack up in the Mercedes."

"He lived in the car?"

The welder nodded glumly. "Po' bastard wouldn't do nothin'
but drink up the few bucks he had lef' and lie in the back seat. One
night last fall we had that cold snap, you remember? It got so cold
around Grand Crapaud you could hear the sugarcane stalks pop-
pin' out in the fields like firecrackers. They found my frien' froze
to death sittin' up behind the steerin' wheel. T-nook, the para-
medic, said his eyes was open, starin' over the hood like he was
goin' for a drive." The welder pushed his downturned hand out
slowly like a big sedan driving toward the horizon. Everybody's
eyes followed it for a long moment.

"New deck," the engineer cried, throwing in his last trump and
watching it get swallowed by a jack. "Nick, you little dago, give
me that blue deck." The oiler, a quiet, olive-skinned boy from
New Orleans's west bank, pushed the new box over. "New deck,
new luck," the engineer told him. "You know, I used to date this
old fat gal lived in a double-wide north of Biloxi. God, that
woman liked to eat. When I called it off, she asked me why, and
I told her I was afraid she was going to get thirteen inches
around the ankles. That must have got her attention, because she
went on some kind of fat-killer diet and exercise program that
about wore out the floor beams in that trailer. But she got real
slim, I heard. She had a pretty face, I'll admit that. She started
hittin' the bars and soon had her a cow farmer ask her to marry
him, which she did."

"Is a cow farmer like a rancher?" Raynelle asked, her tongue in
her cheek like a jawbreaker.

"It's what I said it was. Who the hell ever heard of a ranch in
Biloxi? Anyway, this old gal developed a fancy for steaks, since her
man got meat reasonable, bein' a cow farmer and all. She started
puttin' away the T-bones and swellin' like a sow on steroids. After

a year she blowed up to her fightin' weight and then some. I heard she'd eat up about half the cows on the farm before he told her he wanted a divorce. She told him she'd sue to get half the farm, and he said go for it—it'd be worth it if someone would just roll her off his half. She hooked up with this greasy little lawyer from Waveland, and sure enough, he got half the husband's place. After the court dealings he took this old gal out to supper to celebrate and one thing led to another and they wound up at her apartment for a little slap-and-tickle. I'll be damned if they didn't fall out of bed together with her on top, and he broke three ribs and ruined a knee on a night table. After a year of treatments he sued her good and got her half of the farm."

The deckhand threw his head back, *ha ha*. "That's a double screwin' if ever there was one."

"Hey, it don't stop there. The little lawyer called up the farmer and said, 'Since we gonna be neighbors, why don't you tell me a good spot to build a house?' They got together and hit it off real good, like old drinkin' buddies. After a couple months the lawyer went into business with the farmer and together they doubled the cattle production, 'specially since they got rid of the critters' worst predator."

Raynelle's eyebrows came together like a small thunderhead. "Well?"

"Well what?" The engineer scratched an armpit.

"What happened to that poor girl?"

All the men looked around uneasily. Raynelle had permanently disabled a boilermaker on the *St. Genevieve* with a cornbread skillet.

"She got back on her diet, I heard. Down to one hundred twenty pounds again."

"That's the scary thing about women," the day fireman volunteered, putting up three fingers to ask for his draw. "Marryin' 'em is just like cuttin' the steel bands on a bale of cotton. First thing you know, you've got a roomful of woman."

Raynelle glowered. "Careful I don't pour salt on you and watch you melt."

The engineer released a sigh. "Okay, Nick, you the only one ain't told a lie yet."

The young oiler ducked his head. "Don't know none."

"Haw," Raynelle said. "A man without bullshit. Check his drawers, Simoneaux, see he ain't Nancy instead of Nicky."

Reddening, the oiler frowned at his hand. "Well, the cows remind me of somethin' I heard while I was playin' the poker machines over in Port Allen the other day," he said, a long strand of black hair falling in his eyes. "There was this Mexican guy named Gonzales who worked with cows in Matamoros."

"Another cow farmer," the deckhand said with a groan.

"Shut up," Raynelle said. "Was that his first name or second name?"

"Well, both."

"What?" She pitched a card at him.

"Aw, Miss Raynelle, you know how those Mexicans are with their names. This guy's name was Gonzales Gonzales, with a bunch of names in between." Raynelle cocked her ear whenever she heard the oiler speak. She had a hard time with his New Orleans accent, which she found to be Bronxlike. "He was a pretty smart fella and got into Texas legal, worked a few years, and became a naturalized citizen, him and his wife both."

"What was his wife's name?" the pilot asked. "Maria Maria?"

"Come on, now, do you want to hear this or don'tcha?" The oiler pushed the hair out of his eyes. "The cattle industry shrunk up where he was at, and he looked around for another place to try and settle. He started to go to Gonzales, Texas, but there ain't no work there, so he gets out a map and spots Gonzales, Louisiana."

"That rough place with all the jitterbug joints?"

"Yep. Lots of blacks and roughnecks, but they ain't no Mexicans. Must have been settled a million years ago by a family of Gonzaleses who probably speak French and eat gumbo nowadays. So Gonzales Gonzales gets him a job for two local lawyers who run a horse farm on the side. He gets an apartment on Gonzales Street down by the train station." The oiler looked at a new hand, fanning the cards out slowly. "You know how hard-nosed the Airline Highway cops are through there? Well, this Gonzales was dark, and his car was a beat-up smoker, so they pulled him one day on his way to Baton Rouge. The cop stands outside his window and says, 'Lemme see your license'; Gonzales says he forgot it at home on the dresser. The cop pulls out a ticket book and says, 'What's your last name?' He says, 'Gonzales.' The cop says, 'What's your first name?' and he tells him. That officer leans in the window and sniffs his breath. 'Okay, Gonzales Gonzales,' he says real nasty, 'where you live?' 'Gonzales,' he says. 'Okay, boy. Get out the car,' the cop says. He throws him against the door, hard. 'And who do you work for?' Gonzales looks him in the eye and says, 'Gonzales and Gonzales.' The cop turns him around and slams his head against the roof and says, 'Yeah, and you probably live on Gonzales Street, huh, you slimy son of a bitch.' 'At one-two-two-six, Apartment E,' Gonzales says."

The deckhand put his cards over his eyes. "The poor bastard."

"Yeah," the oiler said, and sighed. "He got beat up and jailed that time until the Gonzales lawyers went up and sprung him. About once a month some cop would pull him over and give him hell. When he applied for a little loan at the bank, they threw him in the street. When he tried to get a credit card, the company called the feds, who investigated him for fraud. Nobody would cash his checks, and the first year he filed state and federal taxes, three government cars stayed in his driveway for a week. Nobody believed who he was."

"That musta drove him nuts," the welder said, drawing four cards.

"I don't think so, man. He knew who he was. Gonzales Gonzales knew he was in America and you could control what you was, unlike in Mexico. So when the traffic cops beat him up, he sold his car and got a bike. When the banks wouldn't give him no checks, he used cash. When the tax people refused to admit he existed, he stopped payin' taxes. Man, he worked hard and saved every penny. One day it was real hot, and he was walkin' into Gonzales because his bike had a flat. He stopped in the Rat's Nest Lounge to get a root beer, and they was this drunk from west Texas in there makin' life hard for the barmaid. He come over to Gonzales and asked him would he have a drink. He said sure, and the bartender set up a whiskey and a root beer. The cowboy was full of Early Times and pills, and you coulda lit a blowtorch off his eyeballs. He put his arm around Gonzales and asked him what his name was, you know. When he heard it, he got all serious, like he was bein' made fun of or somethin'. He asked a couple more questions and started struttin' and cussin'. He pulled an engraved Colt out from under a cheesy denim jacket and stuck it in Gonzales's mouth. 'You jerkin' me around, man,' that cowboy told him. 'You tellin' me you're Gonzales Gonzales from Gonzales who lives on Gonzales Street and works for Gonzales and Gonzales?' That Mexican looked at the gun, and I don't know what was goin' through his head, but he nodded, and the cowboy pulled back the hammer."

"Damn," the welder said.

"I don't want to hear this." Raynelle clapped the cards to her ears.

"Hey," the oiler said. "Like I told you, he knew who he was. He pointed to the phone book by the register, and after a minute the bartender had it open and held it out to the cowboy. Sure enough, old Ma Bell had come through for the American way, and Gonzales was listed, with the street and all. The cowboy took the gun out Gonzales's mouth and started cryin' like the crazy snail he was. He told Gonzales that he was sorry and gave him the Colt. Said that his girlfriend left him and his dog died, or maybe it was the other way around. Gonzales went down the street and called the cops. In two months he got a six-thousand-dollar reward for turnin' in the guy, who, it turns out, had killed his girlfriend and his dog, too, over in Laredo. He got five hundred for the Colt and moved to Baton Rouge, where he started a postage stamp of a used-car lot. Did well, too. Got a dealership now."

The day fireman snapped his fingers. "G. Gonzales Buick-Olds?"

"That's it, man," the oiler said.

"The smilin' rich dude in the commercials?"

"Like I said," the oiler told the table. "He knew who he was."

"Mary and Joseph, everybody is in this hand," the pilot yelled. "Spades is trumps."

"*Laissez les bons temps rouler*," the welder sang, laying an eight of spades on a pile of diamonds and raking in the trick.

"That's your skinny ass," Raynelle said, playing a ten of spades last, taking the second trick.

"Do I smell the ten millionth rollover pot?" the engineer asked. "There must be six hundred fifty dollars in that pile." He threw down a nine and covered the third trick.

"Coming gitcha." Raynelle raised her hand high, plucked a card, and slammed a jack to win the fourth trick. That was two. She led the king of spades and watched the cards follow.

The pilot put his hands together and prayed. "Please, somebody, have the ace." He played his card and sat up to watch as each man threw his last card in, no one able to beat the king, and then Raynelle jumped in the air liked a hooked marlin, nearly upsetting the table, screaming and waving her meaty arms through the steamy engine-room air. "I never won so much money in my life," she cried, falling from the waist onto the pile of bills and coins and raking it beneath her.

"Whatcha gonna do with all that money?" the welder asked, turning his hat around in disbelief.

She began stuffing the bib pocket on her overalls with half dollars. "I'm gonna buy me a silver lamé dress and one of those cheap tickets to Las Vegas, where I can do some high-class gambling. No more of this penny-ante stuff with old men and worms."

Four of the men got up to relieve their bladders or get cigarettes or grab something to drink. The pilot leaned against a column of insulated pipe. "Hell, we all want to go to Las Vegas. Don't you want to take one of us along to the holy land?"

"Man, I'm gonna gamble with gentlemen. Ranchers, not cow farmers either." She folded a wad of bills into a hip pocket.

Nick, the young oiler, laced his fingers behind his head, leaned back, and closed his eyes. He wondered what Raynelle would do in such a glitzy place as Las Vegas. He imagined her wearing a Sears gown in a casino full of tourists dressed in shorts and sneakers. She would be drinking too much and eating too much, and the gown would look like it was crammed with rising dough. She would get in a fight with a blackjack dealer after she'd lost all her money and would be thrown out on the street. After selling her plane ticket, she would be back at the slot machines until she was completely broke, and then she would be on a neon-infested boulevard, her tiny silver purse hanging from her shoulder on a long spaghetti strap, one heel broken off a silver shoe. He saw her walking at last across the desert through the waves of heat, mountains in front and the angry snarl of cross-country traffic in the rear, until she sobered up and began to hitch, and was picked up by a carload of Jehovah's Witnesses driving to a convention in Baton Rouge in an un-air-conditioned compact stuck in second gear. Every thirty miles the car would overheat and they would all get out, stand among the cactus, and pray. Raynelle would curse them, and they would pray harder for the big sunburned woman sweating in the metallic dress. The desert would spread before her as far as the end of the world, a hot and rocky place empty of mirages and dreams. She might not live to get out of it.

Tim Gautreaux is a native of the oil-patch region of south Louisiana. He received a doctorate in English from the University of South Carolina and teaches creative writing at Southeastern Louisiana University. He has received an NEA fellowship and a National Magazine Award for fiction. A collection of stories, *Same Place, Same Things*, is forthcoming from St. Martin's Press.

I grew up in Morgan City, Louisiana, listening to drillers and cementers tell tall tales about life in the oil fields. I accumulated all these stories, but

I knew I could never write them because nobody would believe a word. While playing bourrée with a pretty noisy group one night, I realized that a card game was the proper stage for semi-believable narrative, the spontaneously generated lie with truth as its seed and group attention as fertilizer. As I wrote "Died and Gone to Vegas," I noticed the opportunity for parallel tales, and I searched my memory of barroom conversations, dockside stories, tugboat-galley fabrications, plus I made a couple of the tales up from scratch, using "real" ones as archetypes. A common thread in the stories involved a quest for delusion. The last tale about Mr. Gonzales Gonzales shows what happens when you refuse to be deluded. Working on "Died and Gone to Vegas" taught me the importance of storytelling within a certain group, plus something about how and why stories are born.

David Gilbert

COOL MOSS

(from *Mississippi Review*)

It was the summer of theme parties. The Millers started it in June with line dancing. They found some group from Texas who called themselves "Get in Line!" and we watched and followed these sequined wonders stomp through the Achy Breaky and the Mason-Dixon. Then the Bissels topped them a few weeks later with a psychic named Francine. She read palms, tarot cards, was even able to talk to Lena Bissel's great-grandfather, but like so many spiritualists, she had no sense of humor and no patience and did not appreciate Chuck Hubert's zombie walk. Soon after that the Makendricks transformed their annual July Fourth pool party into what would have been a spectacular kite party had there been any wind. Laura Makendrick broke into very public tears. And eventually Zoe and I made a stab at it. We concocted a "Foods of the World" party which quickly turned into a "Drinks of the World" party. Once again Chuck Hubert performed his zombie walk—a few people always seem to egg him on—and a table was broken, certainly no antique. I don't know if it was because we were all bored that summer and needed something new. Normal costume parties felt passé, decadent, like Marie Antoinette in a tiered, moth-eaten wig. Instead, there had to be something learned even if it was simply that borscht does in fact taste like shit and a healthy supply of rum can save almost any party.

Tonight belonged to the Greers, Bill and Tammy. In the circle of our acquaintants they dwell in the third ring: the friends of friends with money. Lots of money. I sat downstairs on the couch and waited for Zoe to get ready. We were running late but I didn't care. An awful rumor had spread that there would be no alcohol served, something about false courage and a numbing of the brain. Yes, I thought, it'll do that to you. Thank God. So I was having a drink which quickly turned into a series of drinks, all lit with gin. That summer I was drinking gin. But I wasn't smoking.

The television was on and my five-year-old son was propped a few feet from the screen. Static raised his fine blond hair. The beginning of *Chitty Chitty Bang Bang* was playing on the VCR. Ray loved it. I knew because he had his hands jammed down his elastic pants and he mumbled something about cars—"Vroom, Vroom"—and squeezed his groin like a toy horn. It had happened in May that he discovered the first joy of the pleasure principle. We tried to thwart him by continually slapping him on the wrist and looking angry and pointing a finger to the ever-watchful sky, but he still carried on, our little boner boy. And nowhere was off-limits. Restaurants. Birthday parties. He could pin the tail on the donkey with one hand. For a while we considered building a cardboard skirt, like the kind that prevents dogs from scratching their recently pinned ears, but instead we used it as a gag around shocked friends. It seemed to put them at ease.

"He'll grow into it," I told the nervous baby-sitter. She was sitting on the edge of a chair, her knapsack still hugging her shoulders. Her name was Gwen, and she had a large head and a large nose and I wondered if the kids at school were merciless towards her. Sombrero face.

She giggled. I thought of following up with a joke about Dick Van Dyke, but I didn't know if she'd even know who Dick Van Dyke was, and I didn't want her to just hear the words *dick* and *dyke*. So I offered her a soft drink instead.

"No, thanks. I'm fine." She also had a bad complexion. I figured baby-sitting was a relief to her on Saturday nights.

"We won't be late," I told her.

"That's fine. I mean, it doesn't matter." She shrugged her knapsack. "I have lots of work." And she smiled without showing her teeth. I thought the worst: braces and receding gums.

"And he's easy," I said, gesturing towards Ray. "After this, another video, and if he's still awake after that, pop in another." I went over to the folding table that acts as our bar and made myself another drink. "He's seen them all a hundred times, but still . . ."

There was silence except for the TV and Truly Scrumptious singing her eponymous song. It seemed to fill the entire room. I sat back down and waited. I could hear Zoe's steps on the floor above. I didn't want to rush her. She was always feeling rushed. With the awkward teenager, the child, the drink in my hand, I had that familiar feeling that I was waiting at an airport lounge for a late plane, and the more I waited the more I became convinced that the plane would crash over Ohio or skid into the ocean and that this drink would be my last drink and that this moment would be my last memory of the things that littered the ground. I knew it was just the gin. Over my son's shoulders Truly swung back and forth, her gossamer veil fluttering behind her, and as she smiled and sang, and sang and smiled, I waited for a large bird to swoop down with razor-sharp claws.

Soon Zoe came downstairs and I was relieved to see her. She gave me an expression of exasperation. "Sorry I'm late."

"No problem," I said. I lifted my glass to show her that I was taking advantage of the lag time.

She turned to the baby-sitter. "You must be Gwen."

The baby-sitter stood up. "Yes, hello, Mrs. Scott."

"Well." Zoe's hands dropped lifelessly to her side and she took a deep breath. She was beautiful, tanned from the summer, and her hair had recovered some of its youthful blondness. "Just put him to bed when he gets tired. He's had dinner but if he gets hungry give him a fruit roll-up. They're in the cupboard." I used to love to watch Zoe think. Her eyes have these attractive pouches and when she thinks it seems like she's searching them. "Oh, and the Greers' phone number is by the kitchen phone, along with the emergency numbers."

All during this time the baby-sitter was nodding her huge head. "Got it," she said.

Zoe turned to me. "Okay, we're off." She walked over to Ray and slumped her knees against his back. "Ray, we're going," she said in a louder voice.

"Yep."

"We'll be back in just a little bit." I knew that Zoe wanted a child that would cry at such moments, that would wrap his helpless arms around her and wail terribly, but Ray just sat there, hands down his pants, watching a stupid car that could fly.

I ruffled his hair and said, "Have a good time." As Zoe made her way to the front door, I topped off my drink and took it with me. "Bye now," I said again, a bit awkwardly.

The Greers don't live very far away but they live just far enough away so that we know we don't live in the truly nice neighborhood. "You know they're not serving any booze," I said.

"Yes."

"They've got more money than anyone and they're not serving booze. That just doesn't seem right. There's no heavy machinery involved." Zoe was quiet and looked like a weightlifter before attempting a clean and jerk. I wouldn't have been surprised to see chalk on her hands. "You all right?"

"I'm not in the mood for a party tonight," she said.

"I hear you. Especially a party without booze." The sky had a grenadine glow. A volcano had erupted on some distant island in the Philippines. A whole town was destroyed, fifty-seven people died, but it made every sunset that summer seem straight out of Hollywood.

"They have a surprise in store." Zoe pushed down the visor and checked her makeup in the pop-up vanity mirror. She wiped at the corners of her mouth. "I hate surprises," she said.

"Me too." And while we didn't look at each other as we passed under tree-lined streets, I knew that there were eyes on the two of us and that we were somehow talking to those eyes. A third-party viewer. A witness. "Surprises are for suckers," I said. Salt air filled the car; the ocean was close. The houses and front lawns grew progressively bigger. I rolled down the window so that the rushing wind could blow through the stillness.

"Malachi."

"What?"

She paused for a second. I thought she was going to say something that would force me to pull the car over and face her. At that time there was no melodrama in our life, no affairs, no money problems, no addictions, and we still thought that the people on daytime talk shows were freaks. But we were bored.

"What?" I said again.

Zoe reached over and clicked on the radio. The volume was too high but neither one of us bothered to turn it down. I didn't drive any faster, just a flat thirty-five mph.

The Greers' driveway was filled with cars and edged with standing torches. Mature trees were tastefully lit with spotlights. We had to park on the street along with a few other late arrivals, and then we followed the bending line of torches. The house was large, white with black shutters. During Christmas they placed an electric candle in each window. It was quite dramatic. And during Easter they had a huge Easter egg hunt. They put a hundred bucks in the big egg. Kids would sprint and dive into bushes. But Ray was hopeless. He'd just eat the first chocolate bunny he came across.

"How do I look?" Zoe asked me.

"Fine."

"Really?"

"Yes."

From behind the house a noise sounded. It wasn't a party noise, that mingling of chitchat, music, and laughter. It was more like an angry swarm of mosquitoes. Or worse yet, a solitary two-hundred-and-fifty-pound mosquito. Mosquito-man. My mind tripped onto a late night movie I had recently seen—*The Island of Dr. Moreau*—and I remembered those failed genetic experiments. Boar-man. Weasel-man. Orangutan-man. They terrorized a bare-chested Michael York. And as awful as they were, I wanted them to catch him and rip his body into pretty blond shreds.

"Take my hand," I said to Zoe.

We circled around some bushes, a bit of mulch, a birdbath, and then walked through a gate which opened onto a beautiful back lawn—almost an acre and a half of perfect grass—and off to the side, huddled in a circle, our group of friends hummed a perfect C. Their heads were lowered; their arms were intertwined. Just behind them a fifteen-foot stretch of coals glowed hot. It was a strange pep rally.

"Are we playing State tomorrow?" I whispered to Zoe.

"Maybe it's a barbecue."

We stood still and no one noticed us. No one said, Hey it's the Scotts. No one offered us drinks or cheese puffs. The circle was closed and we didn't want to be one of those pushy couples. Besides, we were late, we had no rights. So we just watched as the hum slowly grew around them. A neighbor's dog howled.

"What is this?" I whispered to Zoe.

"I have no idea."

The hum then reached a breathless pitch, and faces and arms slowly lifted up towards the sky. They looked like chanting refugees waiting for the helicopters to drop down food. I recognized them all. Finally, it ended with a lung-emptying *Ah*, and people cheered and smiled and one man, a tall guy in a shiny suit, said, "Did you feel the power?" Everyone nodded. "Yes?" He looked around the group. "Well, that's the power of positive thinking." He made a point of training his eyes on each and every person. "That's the power you hold trapped within your body." He fisted his hands. "The power you never let out." Raised his finger. "Why?" Paused. "Because of fear."

Still no one noticed us. Attention was focused on this man. He had a manufactured face, smooth and with only a few lines to delineate a mouth, a nose, eyes. His voice was a personal whisper spoken to a crowd. I was sure he had a set of self-help videos in the trunk of his car. Maybe an infomercial in the works. "Fear," he continued, "is what we have to overcome. Most of us are still children. We are afraid of the dark, afraid of the unknown, afraid to succeed. Why? Because if we try to succeed, if we put ourselves on the line, we can fail." I tried to catch the eyes of a few friends by making quick faces, but no eyebrows raised in recognition.

"Maybe these are the Stepford friends," I said to my wife.

"What?"

"You know, robots."

"Shhh."

"Now." The man clapped his hands. It was like a hypnotist breaking a trance. "I see some new guests have arrived." He gestured towards us like a game-show hostess displaying a brand new washer and dryer. "So I think it's a good time for a break. But remember, let's psych each other up. We're part of a team." And then, with surprising quickness, he left the group and came over to us. "Hi," he said. "I'm Robert Porterhouse."

"I'm Zoe Scott, and this is my husband Mal."

We shook hands. He had a pinky ring. A family seal. I hate pinky rings. He also had an expensive gold watch that hung loosely from his wrist.

"Well, are the two of you ready?" he asked.

"For what?" I said.

He grasped our forearms. "To change your life. To become who you want to be."

I smiled. "A baseball player? Sure."

I could tell by the way Zoe looked at me that she wanted to hit me on the arm, but instead she quickly pushed her voice over mine. "Why not," she said. I was a little put-off by her enthusiasm. We used to laugh at our born-again friends.

"Great, Zoe. You have to align your belief system so that you get what you want."

"Even if it's a bigger house? A Porsche," I said.

"Sure, if that's what you want."

"How Eighties," I said.

"No Mal, it's about what you want." He poked the air in front of my chest. "What's in here." He glanced over our shoulders. "Now, I've got to check on things. I'll see you in a few." And he walked away.

I turned to Zoe. "And that night, Malachi Scott learned how to live."

"Don't be such a cynic."

I grabbed Zoe by the arms. "Did they get to you too?" I made a plea to the heavens. "You bastards!"

"Jesus, how drunk are you?"

"Not enough for this crap."

"You're going to make a great bitter old man."

"It's the gin. But thanks anyway."

Zoe used to like this kind of banter, thought it was smart and urbane and so round-table, but now she turned away and made a disparaging sigh. "So clever," she said.

The circle had broken up and smaller groups formed. Bill and Tammy Greer saw us and waved and came over. Nervous enthusiasm creased their athletic faces. He was of Norwegian descent. She was of Finnish descent. They both wore the same shade of blue.

"Hey, you guys," Tammy said.

We apologized for being late, then I gave Tammy a kiss and Zoe gave Bill a kiss and Tammy gave Zoe a kiss and Bill shook my hand. After that, we had little to say.

"So," I said. "What's going on here? A barbecue? A little luau?" I swung my hips.

"No, no," Bill said. He shook his head. "Something a lot more . . . powerful."

"Okay," I said. "Powerful."

"Yep." Bill turned towards the burning coals. A man in asbestos boots was spreading them with a long metal rake. "We're going to walk across those coals." He spoke like a man with a crazy dream.

Tammy curled her arm around Bill and gave him a squeeze.

They were terminally in love: If one died, the other would soon follow. "And we'll never be the same," she said.

"That's what I've gathered," I said.

Bill gave us a spirited thumbs-up sign. "And we can do it. We really can."

"Together," Tammy said. "And with Robert. Isn't he the greatest?"

Zoe nodded. "He seems very motivational."

To show my solidarity in the world of backyard adventure I took Zoe's hand. We were like the suckerfish on the belly of a large predatory shark. "Super," I said.

"He's very well regarded," Bill said. "In his field."

"I'm sure."

Tammy giggled. She was sweating. It wasn't dainty sweat. She needed a towel. "And we can do it. I know we can." I could see the old Wisconsin cheerleader surfacing.

"We can," Bill agreed.

And then Bill and Tammy hugged us. A great big hug. Their skin smelled of apricots and the beach, with a trace of smoke mixed in, and while at first I thought the whole thing absurd and silly, I soon found my head resting on Bill's shoulder and my arm wrapped tightly around Tammy's waist.

Eventually we separated and they left us for another couple that wasn't mixing properly. "Walk on coals?" I said to Zoe.

"We're guests."

"I'll put on a silly hat. I'll run wildly with a hopeless kite. But hot coals. That's beyond the call. I don't remember Martha Stewart mentioning any hot-coal-and-canapé party."

And—thank God—Zoe smiled, and for that moment found me amusing again. "You're the worst."

We decided to separate because we hate couples who cling, so she went off in one direction and I went over to Phil Bissel and Chuck Hubert. They were lingering by the coals. They both looked defeated.

"No drinks, Mal," Chuck said.

"I heard."

"I can't believe they expect me to walk on fire sober. I mean, with a few drinks, maybe." Chuck reached down and ripped up a clump of grass. "I've done worse." From his palm he picked out single blades and dropped them to the ground. "And no food either."

"What?" I said.

"Nope. We can't eat until we've done the firewalk."

"Bribery," Phil said. He was a fat man who milked his baldness for humor. "There's no way I'm doing it."

"They have champagne when we finish. The good stuff." Chuck grinned. "I might make a sprint for it now." He made a cartoon gesture of running—left leg raised, elbow bent. "Hold me back!"

I stared at the coal bed. It had a mesmerizing effect. I pictured a buried city beneath it. Everything laid to waste and eventually covered in ash. "It's a shame to ruin such a nice lawn," I said.

Chuck spat onto the coals. "Oh, you think our man Bill wouldn't think that through. See those stakes?" He pointed. "That's where the pool is going."

"A pool?"

"Yep, Bill's putting in a pool, has the contractor and everything, and these coals are in the deep end."

"That's smart."

Phil threw an ice cube on the coals. "I don't know what he's thinking," he said. "There's just no chance."

Herb Frankel came over and mimed golf swings. "Boys been playing?"

"No."

He patted me on the back. "How're things? Work all right?"

"Fine." They all knew my job wasn't going well, but some people, like Herb, pretended to empathize, while others just pretended everything was fine.

"It's a tough market. No rhyme or reason. Have to sweat it out." The glow from the coals made it look like Herb's face was wrapped in red saran wrap. I imagined him suffocating. "You going to do this shit?"

"I can't imagine."

"How about you, Chuck? A little zombie walk across the coals."

Chuck's face turned sheepish. He always regretted his drunken performances. "I don't think so." Then he lifted his glass of soft drink. "No booze."

I tried to spot Zoe, but I couldn't find her. The sun was down and the night was here and the coals now looked like a very cheap hell that housed very cheap souls. More people came over—the Vollopes and the Burnhams, two couples who always vacationed together; and Leslie Pomeroy, heavily medicated on a new anti-depressant. She threw an espadrille onto the coals. It burned quickly, and we all watched.

The man in the asbestos boots came over and warned people not to disturb his spread. "It's essential that it stays pure."

"Are they just briquettes?" someone asked.

"No. We get this stuff from Hawaii."

People were impressed.

I was drinking 7-Up with three wedges of lime, but it didn't fool me. Nothing fooled me. At that moment I knew the ending to every mystery novel, and all the people around me were stupid. These are moods I get in, most often when I'm in a car. No one knows how to drive except me. But standing next to those coals, their bloom shimmering against faces, I saw each person as an old man and an old woman and I saw them alone and waiting and still cold by the fire. I guess it was the gin. I should never drink on an empty stomach.

Zoe appeared at my side. She was holding a Coke. "It's happening soon," she said.

"What?"

"Tammy wants everyone by the coals. She's ringing a dinner bell."

"I wish Ray was sick," I said suddenly.

"Huh?" She had a look of disgust on her face.

"Not sick sick, not dying sick. God no. Just sick enough so that we had to stay home."

"Please. Don't get this way." Zoe slipped off her shoes. She has tiny feet, and I'm always glad that she never paints her toenails red.

Bill and Tammy Greer walked over with Robert Porterhouse. Bill cleared his throat in a stagy way and everyone hushed. "Well, okay, great. It's great having everyone here, just great. I'm so glad you're all here. Yes. Anyway, it's going to be an exciting night. A bit scary." He chuckled nervously. "But, it could be really special. Now I'm going to turn it over to Robert. So, here's Robert."

Some people applauded.

Robert Porterhouse loosened his tie. He took off his jacket and rolled up his sleeves. He smiled a let's-get-down-to-business smile. I was starving. The coals made me think of the simple cookouts we used to have. He gathered us into a tighter circle—it was like camp—and he told us the story of his life.

"My first memory was of fear. The bogeyman. He was an old man with sharp teeth and long dirty fingernails and he was hungry for children. He used to live under my bed. Whenever I wet the sheets—and I did quite often—I would tell my mother that it was the bogeyman. He made it impossible for me to go to the bathroom. Why? Because he would've grabbed my ankles and dragged me under. As basic as that. It's that fear that stops us from doing what we really want to do."

I looked around the group and wanted to nudge a few people and make loopy gestures at my head.

"So," he continued, "how do we get over this bogeyman that lives inside of us? Do we turn on the lamp and check under the mattress? Does that solve the problem? No, because we all know that the bogeyman can't be seen in the light. Only in darkness. That's when you see his glowing red eyes and you smell his rotten breath. Sure." He put his hands in his pockets and paced. "I know what you're saying: those are kids' fears, and, of course, as adults, we grow out of such fears." He let the word linger in the air. I felt on the verge of being startled, like when you know that the necking couple in a movie is doomed. "Or do we?" he asked.

The silence lasted even longer this time. Robert knelt down and ran his fingers through the grass. Then he started confessing. "I was twenty-three years old. I flunked out of college. I was a hundred and forty pounds overweight. I had no money. No job. I could barely get up out of bed. In fact, sometimes I spent the whole day in bed. Now what kept me there? What brought me so low? It was fear. I still had that bogeyman under my bed. I still thought that if I made one step I'd be finished."

Fireworks would have been so much more fun. We could have leaned against each other and *oohed* and *aahed* at the exploding dandelions and the fluttering snakes.

"How did I break the domination?" He stared at Clare Worden. She was surprised and she smiled and lifted her hands as if she were drying nail polish. "Well, something bigger than me made me take that step," he answered. "It was 1989. And there was an earthquake—a pretty big one—and I'm in bed." He began to act out the scene. It felt very Native American. "Suddenly, my whole apartment collapses, the second floor becomes the first floor. I'm thrown out of bed. I'm in a T-shirt and underwear. And I have to get out. All the windows are broken. There's glass everywhere. A ton of it. I also smell gas. But I still don't move. I'm too scared. And then I hear it, someone crying for help. Then I hear more people crying for help. I know I have to do something. So I concentrate on those cries and I walk and I crawl and I carry those people out of the building. At that moment my mind was completely focused on the task. And I kept on repeating to myself, 'Save lives. Save lives.' That day I took five people out of that building. Most of them were elderly, helpless. And when it was all over, and I was wrapped in a blanket and drinking coffee, I didn't have one cut on either foot."

Some peopled sighed in real wonder. "Is this a miracle?" He shook his head. "Absolutely not. This is the power of the self. At that moment I overcame my fear. I took a step, and with that step the bogeyman disappeared. Now I'm not all that smart. There's nothing 'special' about me. I've just learned a way to align my belief system so that I get what I want. I've empowered myself through positive thinking. Now, I know how this sounds, a whole lot of New Age mumbo jumbo. But I swear to you, and I hope to show you, that with the mind focused, with it directed, there's nothing you can't do. Absolutely nothing."

And for the next hour he tried to convince us that this was all true. He had us doing exercises, meditations; we played games of trust. Everyone reluctantly joined in. We were all gracious guests. Bill and Tammy orchestrated everything like amphetamined cruise directors. But the rest of us were becoming grumpier and grumpier as time wore on. I was dizzy with hunger, and a slight headache had crept in. I watched Zoe fall into the arms of Jasper Cunningham. Then he fell into her arms. They giggled. Jasper brushed aside his too-long hair and tucked it behind his ears. He acted like a tennis pro. And once again I thought I knew how everything would end.

"The heat from these coals is over twenty-five hundred degrees Fahrenheit," Robert Porterhouse told us. "Right now it's hotter than the sun."

"Really?" someone said. I think it was Chuck.

"Yes."

People murmured.

"And we will walk on it without burning ourselves. Right?"

Everyone shouted, "Right!" It was one of the first things we had learned: interjections empowered.

Then Robert slipped off his loafers, slipped off his socks. The man with asbestos boots prepared a discreet little first aid station which no one was meant to notice, but everyone did. Tammy Greer looked like she was ready to cry. Sweat poured down her face. "Okay," Robert said. "Here I go." He stared straight ahead as if his eyes were connected by wire to a distant object. "Cool moss, cool moss," he said.

We all chanted along with him. "Cool moss, cool moss."

He quickly goose-stepped across the red-hot coals. I was ready for his feet to catch fire, for his legs to bubble and melt, but he kept on moving and within seconds, was finished. He let out a whoop. All of us applauded. He came to the group and showed us his feet.

They were dirty, a bit red, but unblistered. "You see, that's the power of positive thinking." He was talking excitedly. "Your mind can do anything."

People smiled. They nodded their heads. There was exhilaration in the air, a sense of the possible. But no one followed his example. Everyone just lingered around the coals. It was like a classroom of kids who don't know the answer to an easy question. Even Bill and Tammy had lost their eagerness. Some excused themselves to go to the bathroom.

Robert Porterhouse walked across the coals again. Once again everyone cheered, once again he showed off his unscathed feet. "That's the power."

The third time he did it people barely noticed. I was standing with Zoe and Jasper. "This is pitiful," Jasper said.

Zoe nodded.

"I mean," he continued, "just pitiful."

Robert was clapping his hands, patting people on the back. His face was desperate. It was like he was seeing the bogey man's red eyes. "We can do it."

Herb Frankel laughed.

Someone said, "No, *you* can do it."

More people laughed.

Then I slipped off my cheap shoes—I wasn't wearing socks—and started across the coals, a glass of flat 7-Up in my hand. There was silence. No one said, "Cool moss, cool moss." A plane flew overhead and I wondered if they could see me. My feet felt the heat in little pricks, like walking across hot gravel, but I just pretended that Bill and Tammy's pool had been put in, and it was a pool party instead of a hot-coal party and I was in the deep end treading towards the floating lounge chair in the shallow end. Before I began I was finished.

Robert ran over and hugged me. "Yes. There it is." His face was all relief.

"And how are your feet?"

"Fine," I said. I lifted them up. They were covered in ash.

Robert turned to the rest of the group. "See. It can be done."

Chuck Hubert shook my hand. "That's the farthest I've ever seen someone go for a drink."

"Well," Zoe said. "That was interesting."

Robert stayed close to me. I was his first convert. "Don't you feel like you could do anything?"

Now that I was his shill, I said a loud "Yes!"

But people weren't convinced. Robert and I both walked across the coals again. Then we did it hand in hand. Soon, we were skipping. By that time Tammy was locked in her bathroom, Bill was apologizing, and everyone was drinking the champagne and eating the caviar, the toothpick-harpooned shrimp, the sliced ham. Robert packed up his motivational devices. "Some people just aren't ready," he told me.

"Yeah," I said.

"But I'm proud of you, Mal."

"Thanks, Dad." I was well into the champagne. "You're not a failure either."

"What?"

"You're not a failure."

"I know that."

When the rum was brought out people cheered. Robert had already left. He drove an El Dorado. Everyone sat by the coals like it was a spent bonfire. Bill brought out hot dogs and metal spits and people started to roast weenies. Chuck Hubert somehow got ahold of the asbestos boots and started to do his zombie walk across the coals. There was laughter and applause. Tammy came back outside. She was smiling. "Oh, that Chuck," she said. Soon everyone was trying on the boots.

After a while the party started to break up, and Zoe and I left. The drive home was quicker than the drive there. "How're your feet?" she asked.

"Fine."

"I still can't believe you did that. Crazy."

I concentrated on the corridor of light and tried to keep the car within it.

"You of all people," she said.

"Did you have a good time?" I said.

"It was ridiculous."

"Yeah." I didn't even try to make her laugh.

When we got home the TV was on and Gwen was lying on the couch watching a late-night movie. She quickly got up. I wanted to help her with that head. "Hi," she said.

"Hey," Zoe said. She leaned against a chair. "Everything go all right?"

"No problem. A little tears in *Chitty Chitty Bang Bang*, but otherwise, fine."

"The Child-catcher, right?"

"Yeah."

I walked over to the bar and made myself a proper drink. "Poor Ray hates that guy. 'Children,'" I said in a shrill voice.

Gwen giggled.

"But he was good?" I asked.

"Just fine."

"Good."

Zoe sighed and then abruptly said, as if she was angry at something, "Well, Mr. Scott will drive you home. I'm bushed. Thanks a lot." She started to make her way upstairs. "Sorry we're so late," she said behind her.

"No problem."

Gwen didn't live very far away.

"Did you have a good time?" she asked me.

"It was all right. Same old stuff."

The sporadic oncoming traffic lit up our faces, Gwen's face a second moon and I was in the mood to talk, my adrenaline still flowing. "My grandmother and grandfather used to live out on this island in Maine," I began telling her. "A beautiful spot. Islands all around. And on one of the islands adolescent children used to get dropped off for three days of survival."

"Take a left," Gwen said.

"Here?"

"Yeah."

The headlights, like searchlights, ran by a corner house. I half expected to see a fleeing convict, his striped prison garb frayed and muddy.

"Anyway, it was some Outward Bound program." I glanced towards her. "They were given something like a hook, some fishing line, five matches, and a knife. That was it. With that they had to make do."

"A right." She was carefully watching the street.

"Right?"

"Uh-huh."

"Well, I used to visit my grandparents during the summer. It was great. Really nice."

"Sounds it," Gwen said.

"And my grandparents had this sailboat, and we used to sail around quite a bit."

"Okay," Gwen sagged forward. I thought something might be wrong. A stomach cramp. "You're going to want to make a right pretty soon. The next right."

"Got it," I said. "And I remember the three of us making sandwiches, a ton of them, all neat in their little bags, and when we got to this survival island my grandfather would honk the fog horn. Right here?"

"Yeah."

I made the turn. I wondered if the people inside could see the lights dash across their walls. I hoped it didn't wake them up or put them into a bad dream. "Well, it was unreal."

"The party?"

"No, no. You see, from the woods these kids would come out, all cut up and covered in bites. They looked miserable. And these kids would wade into the water, and my grandmother, my grandfather, and myself would toss them sandwiches—ham and cheese, turkey, roast beef, chicken salad, egg salad, tomato and cheese."

She turned and looked at me. "Neat," she said.

"Yeah."

We were still a few streets away. Sprinklers were clicking from lawns. It's my favorite sound. I reached over and turned off the headlights. The night sky suddenly appeared.

Gwen didn't say anything. She didn't move. "A left," she said.

"Left?"

"Yeah."

In the darkness, for a moment, things felt present, frozen in presence. My friends were my friends and my wife was my wife and my feet did not burn.

I flipped down the turn indicator. It clicked along with the sprinklers outside.

———————

David Gilbert is a recent graduate of the University of Montana MFA program. He currently lives in New York City.

"*Cool Moss*" *was transmitted to me by television,* TV Guide *my Virgil. I was spending a full weekend merged with my couch, clicker fused to my fat little hand. So I pulled down the shades and accepted the shame of cable. And well into the fourteenth hour of viewing, I came across* Arthur C. Clarke's World of Discovery. *Tonight's episode: Fire-walking. For the next hour I observed a young Tony Robbins (he of infomercial fame) convince a group of middle-aged couples to walk across a bed of hot coals. And you know what? They actually did it, each chanting their mantra of "cool moss, cool moss" before taking the first step. Anyway, I began thinking: there must've been a time when Mr. Robbins wasn't nearly so persuasive. And as I sat there, my eyes dried out from a pixel overdose and my self-esteem at an all-I've-done-is-watch-TV low, I imagined a possible cocktail party—no, no, a theme party—where denial in the abstract multiplied by denial in the concrete equals some kind of acknowledgement (I am obsessed with the basic math rule that two negatives multiplied together equals a positive). For the next couple of days I saw the whole story trace itself against everything on TV.* Chitty Chitty Bang Bang *was on channel seven.* The Island of Dr. Moreau *was on channel three. By the end of the weekend, just as George Michael was shutting down that absurd contraption he calls the Sports Machine, I had it figured out.*

Tom Paine

GENERAL MARKMAN'S LAST STAND

(from *Story*)

T he General's panties were too tight. He clawed at his hip, tried to get his index finger under the biting silk band. "Son of a bitch," whispered General Trevor V. Markman, United States Marine Corps, as the elastic wedged his finger against his flesh. Markman twisted his massive torso; his back cracked. He released his finger and the red panties loosened. He swiveled his hips before the full-length mirror on the back of the wooden door to his Camp Lejeune office. The bra Markman pulled with shaking hands from the mailing envelope was a matching silk, and strapless. He slid the hefty cups around his back and was straining to fasten it in front when the hook snapped off in his hand. Markman grimaced and tossed the new bra across the room. The cups hit the venetian blinds and let two sharp bursts of light into the afternoon shadows.

The hairs on his balls crinkled in their silk pocket. He cocked his hip, threw back his head, and shoved out his jaw. With slit eyes, watching himself in the mirror, Markman ran his fingers down to the panties, back up his scarred chest. He cradled his jaw in his crossed hands, dragged his fingers along his cheeks and the sun-burned ridges of his neck, then groaned. The crunching, rhythmic sounds of a platoon running by at double time wove for a moment in with the drumming of his heart, and then it was over and it was no good.

Markman opened his eyes wide and studied himself in the mirror. He was a huge hairy man in silk panties; nothing more. He shook his head and walked closer to the mirror and scratched the silver bristle on his head until white flakes filled the air. He turned and stared at the backlog of requisition orders on his desk. Captain Loring knocked on the door. Markman held his hands up before the mirror. Another platoon ran by outside. A sergeant barking orders, his voice rasping. The skin on Markman's hands was cracking, ravaged. He balled his fist and winced. Loring knocked on the door again. Markman ran his fingers over his chest. It was muscular, rigid. He looked at the soft cups of the broken bra under the window, at the phone, at the empty mailing envelope, at his watch. He walked to his small fridge, took out a plastic gallon of bottled water, poured the cooling water over his inflamed hands. Markman bent at the waist and cascaded the water on the back of his head. Captain Loring knocked again. Markman straightened and hurled the jug at the door.

Markman slipped into the lingerie department of the post exchange. He didn't expect to find anything worth a shit. A decade of catalog purchases had raised his standards: He knew, and quickly reaffirmed, that the Marine Corps didn't put *beaucoup* imagination into its lingerie. The air-conditioning was off in the PX and the Muzak martial. Markman fingered what looked like a combined bra-straight jacket; the silk was soft and comforting on the back of his burning hand. Markman fell into a trance of touch. A bovine enlisted wife passed by in the aisle, gazed vacantly at him. A couple of recon marines were taking turns punching each other in the gut at the far end of the toy aisle. A child kneeled beside them aiming a plastic bazooka at Markman. He felt faint and grabbed the chrome bar holding up a row of traditional-cut, white rayon panties covered with the faint gold imprint of the Marine Corps' anchor-and-globe insignia.

Markman's life had become a microwave oven, cooking him slowly and invisibly from the inside out. As his retirement approached, his fevers had increased in frequency and intensity. Lingerie cooled him—like parachuting out into a cloud bank. But now, as he stood in the PX, Markman felt the last moisture within him boil off. He saw black dots swirl before his eyes, threw out his left hand to find the bar on the other side of the aisle, and felt something silken under his calloused palm. He twiddled it with his trigger finger, found the spacious cup, and thrust his fingers deep into the forgiving, erogenous interior. He plucked the bra off the rack and with one sudden and smooth motion stuffed it down his green camouflage utility trousers.

After he left the PX and stepped into the North Carolina sun, Markman paused to slip on a pair of aviator shades, silver and straight at the ear. The attack of vertigo had passed; he was again satisfactorily military. A private was weeding with an old bayonet along the side of the concrete walkway. He stabbed the bayonet into the lawn, jumped up, saluted, and said, "Good afternoon, General."

"At ease, marine."

"Aye, aye, sir!"

The marine remained ramrod. Markman closed his eyes and tried to remember his destination. He pictured himself marching naked except for his boots in a rainstorm—arms out, head back, mouth open. The rain sizzled and evaporated when it touched his skin. Markman opened his eyes and discovered anew the frozen young marine, chin tucked violently back into his wattled neck.

"I said . . . at ease, marine," said Markman.

The marine dropped his shoulder a few inches, but stood stiffly. Markman squinted at a vulture circling in a wobble beneath the cobweb of clouds.

"Squared away, marine . . . for the Corps' Birthday Ball tonight?" Markman said, without taking his eyes off the bird.

"Yes, sir," said the private. "Sir?"

"Private?"

"Sir," he said. "I joined the Marine Corps because of you . . . permission to ask . . . is it true the General is retiring today, sir?"

"Private," said Markman. "In my time in this Marine Corps I have tried to impress the men under my command that they are free as Americans to ask me anything . . . and I am free as an American not to answer." Markman reappraised the marine, noted the peach fuzz on his face, and said, "I am retiring because I promised my better half thirty years ago tonight that I would spend no more than three decades serving with you fine men. No lie has ever crossed these lips headed in the direction of Beatrice Markman, and I do not intend to commence at this late date in our hitch. Understood?"

"Yes, sir," said the private.

A Harrier jet streaked low across the base. Markman raised his thumb in a salute, turned to watch as the jet twirled and bent upward into the clouds. When there was nothing left but a fading jet trail, Markman was still watching the sky, the private waiting at attention behind him.

"Carry on," said Markman suddenly, and he continued down the path, across the street to his car, where he was approached by two tall MPs. One raised his hand and said nervously, "General Markman . . . sir. . . ."

Markman stopped, took off his shades, and squinted. The two MPs shifted from foot to foot.

"At ease, marines," said Markman.

One of the MPs said to the air over Markman's head, "Sir, we had a report." The second MP nodded and continued, "Sir, a report from the PX. Is there something down your trousers, sir?"

Markman raised his chin, ground his molars together, and remembered the bra. Beatrice had sent her lingerie to him monthly for the three years he was a young officer in-country. Her bras, panties, and nighties were humped in his rucksack all over Vietnam. He shoved them down his shorts and swaddled his nuts in silk when he had a bad case of crotch rot and fell asleep in the bush with silk clenched in his fist, his wife's smell shoved under his nose, lulling him to sleep. When he was horny he wrapped a bra around his head like a gas mask and beat off into her nightie. Markman put the end of his shades in his mouth, sucked, and recalled grabbing the bra at the PX. He reached down his trousers and took out the bra, sniffed it once, and while handing it to the MP said, "You may not understand, son, but these things saved my life."

As Markman was driven past the depot station by the MPs, a bus full of marines fresh from Parris Island was unloading, their shaved skulls catching the sun. The dispatcher crackled over the radio for a response to a 187 at the Lejeune's B-12 small-arms range.

"Sergeant?" said Markman. "187?"

"A gunshot wound, sir."

"Should you respond?"

"It's a call for the coroner, sir."

"Accident?"

"Negative, sir. Self-inflicted."

Markman rubbed his hands over his head and tried to understand why he had taken the bra. He shook his head.

"Sergeant," said Markman. "You mind if we stop at the Division CP?"

"General?"

"Seventeen hundred. Colors. I never miss it."

"No problem, sir."

Markman leaned forward in the military police car and handed a tape through the slat beneath the cage. He always kept a couple of John Philip Sousa tapes in the side cargo pocket of his utility trousers.

"Would you play this tape for me, Sergeant?"

The MP looked in the rearview mirror at Markman.

"Did you steal the tape, sir? Because if you did, I would have to bag it as evidence."

"No, son, that's my tape. You're Gonzalez?"

"Yes, sir."

"Are you proud to be in the Corps?"

"Yes, sir," said Gonzalez. "Semper Fidelis."

"Good man. Now put in that tape."

Markman was driven back to the CP to "Semper Fidelis" and, after watching the flag lowered to evening colors over the PA, continued on to the Staff Judge Advocate's office on Lejeune Boulevard to "Stars and Stripes." The second MP sat in the passenger seat, refusing to look at Markman. When the trio arrived, General Markman looked out at the low brick building and said softly, "Attack."

Major Rawlings saw the MPs come in on either side of General Markman. Rawlings put Markman on ice in a side room and told Lieutenant Barnwood to take a report, locked the MPs in his office, dropped the bra in a black evidence bag, slid it into his desk under some files, and buzzed General Bowles' office.

Lieutenant Barnwood looked at General Markman sitting before him and said in a southern drawl, "I heard about you when I was a boy, sir. My father was a master sergeant in Vietnam, and he told me some things."

General Markman said, "Your father was a good man, Lieutenant?"

"Yes, sir," said Lieutenant Barnwood. "I believe he always did his duty to his God, to his Country, and to his Corps."

"How'd he treat your mother?"

"General?"

"I said: 'How did he treat his wife?' "

"With due respect, sir."

"Your people Baptist?"

"Yes, sir," said Lieutenant Barnwood. "How'd you know?"

Markman leaned back in the swivel chair. He felt like there was a firefight going on around him and he had been stripped of his weapon.

"Sir?" said Barnwood. "I don't believe. . . ."

"You have some questions for me, Lieutenant? I suggest you get on with it."

"Yes, General. You had some article on your person from the PX?"

Markman sliced the air with his hand and said, "Barnwood, I stole the bra."

". . . Did you say you *stole*, sir?"

Markman stood and said, "I stole the bra, Barnwood."

Lieutenant Barnwood raised his pen and said, "Sir . . . sir . . . you *stole* the article?"

Markman put both hands on the desk and said, "I'm not communicating, Barnwood? I stole the bra, shoved it right down these here camouflage trousers." Markman stood up and exhibited his hand shoved down his trousers. Lieutenant Barnwood fell back in his chair and jumped to attention when he saw General Bowles entering the room. Markman looked over, his hand still down his trousers. Bowles shut the door slowly and pushed out his lower lip with his tongue. He touched the side of his nose tenderly with his finger and said, "Son, if you would excuse us two old warriors, we apparently have a lot of catching up to do."

Lieutenant Barnwood shuffled together his papers, while General Bowles hawked over him. As the lieutenant reached for the handle to the door, Bowles grabbed him by the collar. "Lieutenant, you are to forget you were ever in a room today with General Markman, or I will shoot you myself. Do I make myself clear?"

"Yes, General," said the lieutenant.

General Bowles put his hand on the lieutenant's cheek and turned his face toward him. "What I am saying, son, is that I don't even want you talking to your sweet Jesus about what you think you heard."

General Bowles' face pulled together into a fist.

"Understood, sir," said Lieutenant Barnwood, and Bowles shut the door after him.

General Bowles curled his upper lip, closed his black eyes, and took out a cigar and pushed it between his lips, keeping his back to Markman.

"We're going to take this from ground zero and work our way

along slowly so a simple mind like mine can understand," said Bowles. "Now, am I correct in stating this is your final day as a marine on active duty before retirement?"

"That's right, Bowles."

"And so, on your last day in the Corps, you wander into the PX and perform an act of thievery on an article of women's undergarments? Tell me this is not our present situation."

"I stole the bra," said Markman.

General Bowles fixed his eyes on Markman. "Don't say that."

"It's a fact."

Bowles took two steps toward Markman, then paused and leaned over so their faces were only a few inches apart, and whispered, "Do I want the fucking facts?" Bowles tore the cigar from his lips; he spun and threw it against the wall of the office. The action drained him and Bowles scratched the flaking skin behind his ear and said without turning around, "I never liked you much, Markman." Bowles took the seat at the desk, rested his hands across his gut. "We have a problem here, yes we do."

Markman raised his chin in the air.

"You can't run through this. Not this one. Tomorrow, Rawlings will press formal charges against you. Best we can do is control the collateral damage." Bowles shook his bald head. "Once, we could have swept this shit under the rug. Faggots, dick-hating bitches, and pussy-eaters run this country now."

"I understand," said Markman.

"You understand," repeated Bowles slowly.

"I'll take the flack."

Bowles jumped out of his chair and screamed, "Don't you think I'd love you to choke on your own shit!" Bowles waved his arms wildly, as if trying to clear smoke. "First thing civilians are going to think is a decorated Marine Corps general is a . . . cocksucker!"

"I'm . . . not AC/DC, Bowles."

Bowles pressed out his palms repeatedly as if trying to stop an oncoming car. "Stop right there, Markman, I don't want another fucking word."

Markman heard a howl of wind in his ears, felt shrapnel sear into his chest, saw the room blacken. There were sounds ahead, his men screaming his name, the ambush at Quang Tri. He wanted to press forward, but for the first time Markman was running away, the jungle slapping him in the face. "I took . . . it . . . for myself," he said.

"Say what?" said Bowles.

Markman turned and started running back to the rattling of the M-16s and Kalashnikovs. Sergeant Castillo ahead of him on the trail took a round in the forehead; Markman caught him before he hit the ground. Castillo's eyes greased over as he looked up, his brains falling like worms out the back of his skull. Markman fished in his rucksack and pulled out a pink nightie, tried to stuff the hole in Castillo's skull with the yard of silk.

"I took the bra for myself," repeated Markman.

"Did I hear you correct, Markman?" said Bowles. "Did you say you want to suck my dick?"

Bowles unbuttoned his fly and hung out his gray cock. Markman stood up. Bowles grabbed his service pistol from his side holster, moved closer, and pointed the gun at Markman's temple. "I'd rather shoot you right now than see you dishonor my Corps. I took care of one of you bastards in 'Nam, and I've got nothing against doing it again. If you were a man of honor, you'd do it yourself."

"I didn't want. . . ?" said General Markman.

"You're a faggot, Markman," said Bowles. "I kill faggots."

Bowles pressed the muzzle of the gun hard into Markman's temple.

"Shoot me," said Markman, suddenly reaching up and wrapping his hand around Bowles' gun hand and squeezing. When Bowles felt Markman working his thumb on top of his trigger finger, he cracked his elbow into Markman's face, the nasal bone crunching like a walnut.

Markman slumped into the chair.

Bowles prowled around the edge of the room, put the gun back in the holster at his waist, tucked his dick back and buttoned his fly, adjusted his web belt, kicked the toe of his black boot through the wall. He ran back to Markman, waggled his finger in his face, and said, "I'll promise you one thing right now. No way in hell are you going to hurt my Marine Corps. Do you understand me, you dick-sucking motherfucker? You're going out tonight looking one pussy-loving son of a bitch."

Markman was sitting in the bar in the Officers' Club, eavesdropping on a captain describing the gang bang of a high school girl in Washington. Markman pictured the three naked marines, cocks at attention, sitting on the other bed in the Holiday Inn, waiting their turn to flop on the girl. "The bitch was bleeding and still couldn't get enough dick," said the captain. "We went around a second time."

"General Markman?"

Markman turned slowly from the bar.

"General Markman, what happened to your face?"

"General Bowles broke my nose."

Lieutenant Hardie laughed, showed his fine teeth.

"Sir, General Bowles told me I could find you here at the O Club."

General Markman turned back toward the leather-lined bar and picked up his empty glass of Jim Beam, placed it back on the bar, and waved to the bartender.

"General Bowles told you I was here?"

"Yes, sir," said Hardie. "He told me I was to remind you to leave the O Club at 1800 sharp for your appointment. He said, and General Bowles made me memorize this, sir: 'If you truly love your Corps and are looking forward to your retirement with Beatrice, you won't miss your appointment at 1800 hours in the parking lot outside the O Club.' Don't know what General Bowles means, sir, just passing the word."

Markman rapped his knuckles on the stool next to him.

"Have a drink with me, Hardie."

"I would be honored, General."

Markman stared at his reflection in the mirror behind the bar as his glass was refilled, and then he drained it, pointed for another. The bartender looked at Hardie.

"Double shot of Jim Beam," said Hardie.

Markman took a sip from his glass and said, "You have a woman in your life, Hardie?"

"Yes, sir."

"Is she a keeper?"

"General?"

"Can I advise you, Hardie?"

"Yes, sir. Anytime, sir."

"Marry her, Hardie. The Corps is hard on wives, so be good to her. If it wasn't for Beatrice, I wouldn't have come back from Vietnam."

"General, may I ask you a personal question?"

"I may not answer, Hardie."

"You really dove on a Vietcong grenade?"

Markman looked away.

"You don't have to answer, sir."

"I saw it and fell on it, Hardie," said Markman. "If I'm not under fire, I'm not worth a shit."

"I can't believe that's true, sir."

"It is true, Lieutenant Hardie," said Markman. "I've no brain for staples and paper clips. I could take the objective in a firefight, and I could dive on a grenade. Those are limited talents in the real world."

"You wouldn't be a general if that was all."

"That is all," said Markman. "I'm General Markman because they liked the way my hair went white after the grenade. It was just fucking luck it wasn't live. Woke up the next morning and Blake, my platoon sergeant, said, 'Lieutenant, your hair, it's gone white as snow.' Blake bought it that afternoon, took a chest wound for me. Stepped right in front of me. Couldn't get a medevac. Blake only had sixteen days and a wake-up. He was a good man and a good friend."

"Begging your pardon, sir. You're not a general for your hair."
Markman ran his hand over his head.

"Got more dandruff than hair," said Markman. "But you're right, Hardie. I'm a general because a lot of gooks are dead. My units always had the highest body counts. Wherever I went in 'Nam, gooks got transformed into fertilizer."

Hardie opened his mouth, but Markman raised his hand and said, "Until I shove off, don't say anything."

Markman had always told his men he expected them on time for their own funerals. He swiveled around and examined the wooden doors of the Officers' Club, ripped back the Velcro cover, and checked his watch. Bowles had said to be in the parking lot at 1800. Markman slid off the stool, straightened his camouflage blouse, tugged it downward from his thighs, and brushed the dandruff off his shoulders.

Hardie got off his stool and stood next to Markman.

"I'm heading out, General," said Hardie. "To prep for the ball."

Markman nodded and walked toward the door. From the corner of his eye, he saw Hardie motion to a number of officers standing down the bar. One of the officers had a white rat on his shoulder spray painted with the blood-red letters USMC. Shot glasses in pyramids lined the bar, and the officers were singing:

> *From the Halls of Montezuma,*
> *To the shores of Tripoli;*
> *We fight our country's battles*
> *In the air, on land, and sea;*
>
> *First to fight for right and freedom*
> *And to keep our honor clean;*
> *We are proud to claim the title of*
> *United States Marines.*

Markman put on his aviators as he stepped from the Officers' Club, although the sun had been down for an hour and the trees across the parking lot had fused into a single dark shadow. He stood on the curb clenching and unclenching his hands.

Markman walked slowly to the center of the parking lot, and Hardie followed. General Bowles had ordered him to glue to the General and make sure he was in the parking lot on time but hadn't given him specifics— except to bring along as many young officers as possible. There were more than a dozen watching from under the awning outside the doors of the O Club.

Markman stopped with Hardie a few steps behind him. Markman looked up and down the parking lot, and then his head cocked. Hardie heard it, a rapid clicking, and then from behind a green van emerged a woman, hustling toward Markman, her breath coming in heaving gusts. Her blond hair was a wobbling pyramid, her large gold earrings glittered in the faint light, and her mouth quivered in a red circle of sputtering lips.

"You bastard, Markman!"

She swung her large black purse, caught Markman across the head. Hardie involuntarily stepped backward and saw the General's head snap back, his sunglasses hang off an ear and fall to the ground. She must have a brick in there, Hardie thought. Markman did not raise his arms, and the woman dropped the bag and pummeled him across the face and chest. Markman stepped forward into the blows. "How dare you stand me up on my birthday! You promised me lingerie! Shit on you!" Markman looked down at the unknown woman slapping him.

"Christ," said Lieutenant Hardie.

Hardie took a tentative step toward Markman. From behind came the laughter of the group of officers who had followed them out of the O Club. One officer yelled out, "She's a grenade, General, you should dive on her!"

"General," said Lieutenant Hardie.

Hardie heard the laughing officers moving closer to the scene, heard the door to the O Club open, and the sounds of other officers running toward the General. The woman had now gone limp in Markman's arms and was sobbing against his shoulder. The officers crowded around them in a tightening circle: clapping, whistling, high-fiving, and chanting, "Markman, Markman, Markman. . . ."

Markman walked around his house turning on the humidifiers he had recently placed in every room. He sighed and went to the stairs. Markman stopped on each step and touched the family photos on the wall. Trevor Jr. was at Hampshire College, studying theater; he wore a gold earring in his lower lip. Nicole was in her last year at the Georgetown School of Foreign Service. Blake was a plebe at West Point and had shaved her head to match the male plebes. The children were organizing a surprise retirement party for the weekend. Markman ran his fingers over the wedding photo of his wife Beatrice, the only daughter of Major General Kittridge. After graduation from West Point, Markman had shipped out for his first tour in Vietnam the day after their wedding.

Markman came to the door of their bedroom. Beatrice was in a white gown laced with gold trim, sitting at her dressing table with the back of her dress open to him.

"Hello, Beatrice," Markman said from the doorway.

Beatrice turned her head, but said nothing when she saw her husband's bloody swollen face.

"Beatrice," said Markman.

Beatrice put down her mascara.

"Go on, Trevor."

"I cannot cross this line. . . ." began Markman.

Beatrice remembered the last time she had heard such a formalized beginning: Markman had slept with a prostitute in Saigon after the grenade incident during his second tour in Vietnam. He wrote to Beatrice asking her forgiveness. She wrote Markman back a twenty-page letter that began, "Trevor, I would rather die than have you lie to me. . . ." Beatrice's brief first marriage had been with a sailor who slept with her bridesmaid Pauline Padgett during the wedding reception, took Beatrice's virginity later in the evening, gave her (and Pauline Padgett) gonorrhea, and then shipped out for a twelve-month tour on the USS *Tripoli*.

"Tell me, Trevor," said Beatrice.

"I cannot cross this line without telling you," said Markman. "I have been having an affair. I broke it off this evening outside the Officers' Club. There was a scene, people will be talking tonight at the ball."

Beatrice put out her hand as if to stop a fall. Her dress fell off her shoulders, slipped down her thin arms to her waist. Her breasts were small, sagging, tear-shaped. She closed her eyes. Markman walked into the room, took her by the shoulders.

"It was stupidity."

"But we make love almost every morning."

"We do," said Markman softly.

"And you're home every evening."

"I am."

"We don't even go out on the weekends anymore."

Beatrice shoved Markman away and pulled her dress up over her shoulders.

"I want a divorce, Markman," said Beatrice. "I don't know what's going on, but I know you're lying to me."

Markman went to the cellar and sat in the dark under his house. He listened to the water rushing through the pipes when a toilet flushed above. He unlocked a chest, undressed, and put on a frilly yellow bra and panties he had hidden away since Vietnam. In the dark, running his hands over the bra across his chest, he felt a comfort running through his veins. He put his camouflage uniform back on, went upstairs and carried his dress blues into the bathroom, took off his camouflage uniform, shaved, and slowly, as if in a trance, put on his high-collared dress blues.

Markman held his cock in the head at the O Club, watching the piss splash over the pink deodorant bar at the bottom of the drain. The deodorant looked like pink ice and Markman wanted to hold it against his forehead. He was slapped on the shoulder, and his piss splattered against the porcelain wall of the urinal, sprinkling back on his hand.

"It must be tired," said Colonel Blair, looking over Markman's shoulder. Blair had been a lieutenant with Markman in Vietnam.

"Thought we were getting too old for that stuff," said Blair, waving his drink in the air. "But hell, you're a hero. How many girls you got, Markman? Two, three?" Markman buttoned his fly and Blair saluted and said, "It's too bad you're retiring. You've a cock to respect." Blair bent over and saluted Markman's crotch and dropped his drink. He pushed the broken glass around with his dress shoe, and said, "Fuck it, let those bastards mop it up." Blair left the head and Markman walked over to wash his hands. He opened the faucet, backed away, and listened to the steady rush of water.

Markman walked out of the head, leaving the faucet running. A table of officers called to him, made pumping motions with their fists, and raised their wine glasses to him. Their wives laughed and clapped their hands. One officer stood up and called out, "You're the man, General Markman! More I hear about you, the harder I get!" He repeated it three or four times with escalating emphasis on the word *man*, and then sat down nodding to himself as if he had settled a pressing issue. Markman went back to his seat at the head table, and Beatrice turned her head away when he sat down.

Sally Prescott, wife of Colonel Prescott, leaned over and pressed her dry lips against his ear. She whispered, "Prescott has prostate problems, Markman, can't even get it up anymore." Markman turned his face and Sally Prescott nodded her small head and gave him an eager grin. The white powder on her nose was caked like phosphorous on a used flare cannister. Sitting next to her Colonel Prescott looked blankly at the officers in the dining hall. Prescott was only animated when talking about his military stamp collection. He turned his head and blinked at Markman, the corners of his mouth cracking upward.

"Beatrice," said Markman, slipping his hand onto her thigh. She reached under the table, lifted his hand like a crane; it dropped limp between their bodies.

Major Embrie was applauded when he said, "So with luck we'll get some trigger time in the coming year, grow the hair on the balls of some of you virgin lieutenants. . . ." When he was done, he nodded to Markman as he made his way back to his chair. Someone threw their wine glass against the fireplace, and then there was a cascade of shattering crystal. Markman looked down the table, but none of the other senior officers raised their heads at the sound of breaking glass.

"I wish," said Markman. "I sometimes wish I was a lush."

"What?" said Sally Prescott. "Did you say something?"

"Nothing," said Markman. "Talking to myself."

The civilian waitresses brought in trays of shot glasses, and toasts were made to the Corps, and to the wives, and the shot glasses were hurled against the fireplace. Markman had seen glasses thrown in bars off-base, but never at the Officers' Club, and the Corps' Birthday Ball was particularly formal, at least this early in the evening.

"Beatrice," said Markman, touching her shoulder and wanting to discuss this with her. His wife shivered.

"I want the truth, Markman," said Beatrice, looking straight ahead over the sea of blue gentlemen. "Other than that—cease and desist. That's an order."

The gigantic white, red, and gold birthday cake was wheeled into the room, escorted by six marines, and the band played a slow lugubrious version of "The Marines' Hymn." At first the officers were silent and at attention, and then they broke into cheers, a few of the new lieutenants throwing back their heads and bellowing the Marine Corps seal call of "OOhrah!" One young officer pounded on his table and cried out, "Markman! Markman! Markman!" The call was taken up by the other officers, and the standing chanting soldiers smiled at Markman. The cry changed to "Speech! Speech!"

Another round of shot glasses was brought out, they too were thrown, and a lieutenant stood on his table and made a toast to the memory of General Lewis B. Puller, until his legs were yanked out from under him and he went face down on the floor. When he stood, there was blood on his chest. He grinned and pulled a triangular shard of glass from the front of his dress blues, put it between his teeth, snapped it in half, spit out one half, and balanced the other on the tip of his nose. The officers cheered and made him chug three shots. When the officer on the table had downed the shots, he raised his fists over his head and waggled his knees as if he had just scored a touchdown. The room applauded, and he made another somber toast, little of which was comprehensible.

Colonel Prescott went to the podium, bent his tall frame, and said into the microphone, "General Markman, as we all know, is retiring tonight. I believe all of us have heard how bravely he stood his ground in the face of a recent assault. . . ." The marines hooted and Colonel Prescott smiled broadly. "General Markman, will you please say a few words to these good men!"

Markman had his eyes pressed shut. He was back at Quang Tri; there was a firefight ahead at the edge of the rice patties. The marines screamed out his name.

"General Markman?"

Markman walked toward the firefight. He opened his eyes and took a deep breath. Beatrice stared at her plate, her fading blond hair falling around her face in a curtain. He had dreamed of that hair mopping across his chest when he was humping through 'Nam; the memory of it had often kept his legs in motion long after all else was gone.

"General Markman?"

Markman pushed back his chair, felt it scrape across the wood floor. He stood and the roar in the auditorium rose and a few more glasses shattered in the fireplace. The glass-chewing marine was dancing in front of the head table. Colonel Prescott nodded at two officers and the marine was dragged away laughing maniacally; halfway out of the hall he vomited down the front of his dress blues and the officers applauded when he licked his lips. Prescott beckoned again to Markman, holding the place at the podium.

"Did I say he is the most humble marine in the Corps?" said Prescott, leaning down to the microphone as if it was miles away.

As Markman moved slowly to the podium, he saw a Vietcong grenade rolling toward him, felt his body leap forward and stretch out in the air.

As he stood at the microphone, Markman saw Beatrice headed for the exit between the tables of cheering officers. He watched her retreating from him, reached up, and unclasped the stiff collar of his dress blues.

He saw the grenade under him now, saw it wobbling along the burned ground.

The marines hooted and howled, "Markman!"

Markman landed on the grenade; the breath was knocked from his chest in a broken gasp. He craned his neck to look at his men, who stared back at him in horror from the elephant grass.

At the door to the banquet hall, Beatrice paused and looked back as Markman popped the anodized brass buttons of his jacket. Markman dropped his arms to his side and shook his hairy, shrapnel-scarred shoulders, letting the jacket fall behind him to the floor.

Markman, never taking his eyes from his wife, slipped off his dress shoes and loosened his web belt with the raised Marine Corps insignia and dropped his blue trousers. He raised one bullet-scarred leg and climbed atop the head table in front of Major Learned's hyperventilating wife Agnes, and lowered his arms to his side.

The air in the hall froze; the fat on the plates congealed. There were sounds from the kitchen at first, but then these faded as the silence spread like a nerve agent. The enlisted cooks silently slid from the kitchen and lined the back wall. The wind could be heard in the trees outside the glass doors at the far end of the hall. The candles flickered. There were footsteps across the floor of the room above.

One officer finally walked in front of the head table and without looking at Markman made his way to the exit. Another followed a few seconds later, and a third broke away from the iceberg of officers. Marines and wives silently floated from their tables and out of the hall. Not one looked up at the man on the table.

Markman never took his eyes off Beatrice.

As the marines left the room with their wives in an ebbing flood of blue, as the starched uniformed backs turned on her husband, Beatrice Markman began to clap, gingerly at first, and then with determination.

———————

Tom Paine is a graduate of Princeton University and is the Ellis Fellow in Columbia University's MFA program. His stories have been published in *Story*, *The New Yorker*, *The Oxford American*, and elsewhere. He was recently awarded a fellowship from Yaddo and a grant from The Mellon Foundation.

When I was in Officer Candidate's School in Quantico, Virginia, ten years ago, there was a silver-haired marine who raised and lowered the flag near our parade grounds. I was told the silver-haired marine was a POW in Vietnam who "had never been broke," even under torture. His hair, however, had turned prematurely gray during his years in captivity. I hope I have not done him too great a disservice by putting him in lingerie and changing the scope of his heroism, because my respect for both him and his imaginary double, General Markman, is immense and sincere.

"General Markman's Last Stand" is one of the first stories of which I was proud, but I could paper the road to Quantico with the verbal froth created by the decade or so of learning to tell a story.

J. D. Dolan

MOOD MUSIC

(from *The Antioch Review*)

My sister was sunburned from our trip to the Gulf. In different ways, we all were—my father on his arms and neck, my mother on her arms and face, me on my back, mostly—but my sister, Lucy, had rented an air mattress on the last day of our trip, and floated away the whole afternoon out past the breakers, her skin taking on the color of that last sunset. I swam out with her a little way and told her that she shouldn't go out that far, that with the riptides and the undertows and the Gulf Stream she could end up in someplace like China. And just before I got washed back shoreward by a wave, what I heard Lucy say was, "Fine."

Now, back at home, she said she couldn't even eat, that even her insides were sunburned.

"And music," Lucy said. "Music is im*possible*."

My mother dipped a finger into the mixing bowl and gave the barbecue sauce a taste. You could see from her face that something was missing. "Mr. Leets will be here at six o'clock," she said. Then she said, "Onions—"

There was a flash of light out in the backyard. The curtains on the kitchen window blew gently inward, as if our house had taken a breath. My mother and Lucy and I turned to look. There was smoke, a dark mass of smoke roiling up, and under it, smiling, was

my father. He was holding a can of charcoal starter, and he pointed
it at the barbecue and leaned back. The flames jumped.

"Besides," Lucy said, "I've been thinking that what I really want
to play is violin."

Our mother cut the ends off an onion, peeled away the dry skin
to get to the good part. She cut the onion into slices and then into
squares, her knife making tapping sounds on the cutting board.
"Violin," she said, as if it was that, and not the onion, making the
tears on her face. "To play the violin you have to hold your neck
funny. Why would you want to do that? You have such a pretty
neck." The pieces of the onion got cut smaller and smaller.

Lucy lowered her chin to touch her collarbone and said, "Mr.
Leets is—"

Our mother lifted the cutting board over the mixing bowl and
scraped the onion pieces into it with the knife. "Mr. Leets is what?"
she said, looking around the kitchen for something. She picked up
a dish towel and wiped at the tears on her sunburned face and was
in sudden pain. "Mr. Leets is a *very* good teacher," she said, pointing the hand with the dish towel at Lucy. "You know, we can hear
you getting better every lesson."

Out in the backyard our father said, "Hello, Jack!"

Our mother set the dish towel on the counter, straightened her
dress, touched her hair, then opened the back door and said,
"Why, hello, Mr. Leets."

The family room used to be the garage. Everything inside the
garage had gotten put outside in a permanent temporary pile and
covered with a huge tarp. In the family room my father had put
paneling, a carpet, a piano. He had installed a picture window. He
had plans to do something with the big fluorescent light. He had
plans for an acoustic ceiling, plans for an actual door. With the
garage door pulled up, it looked like a room cut open.

Lucy stood there looking in, holding her sheet music to her
chest. My mother was talking to Mr. Leets, and my father was
working the coals with a broken yardstick. Then Mr. Leets said,

"Well—" and put his hand on Lucy's back. There was a kind of ripple down the cloth of her sundress: her back went stiff but her face stayed the same.

"Can we keep the door open?" Lucy said. "For air?"

Our parents smiled and nodded, as if agreeing on every little thing was something they did all the time, and not just in front of guests.

Mr. Leets smiled and nodded the same way. He said, "Good idea, Luce." Then he looked at the barbecue and said, "Of course, there *is* the smoke."

Our parents smiled and nodded the same way all over again. Then Lucy went into the family room, and Mr. Leets went into the family room and pulled the big wooden garage door shut.

My mother went back into the kitchen humming one of the songs that Lucy usually played during her lessons, and my father went back to working the coals with his stick. The end of his stick kept catching on fire. He picked up the can of charcoal starter again, even though the coals were already white hot, and pointed it at the barbecue. Then he looked at me looking at him.

"Say, you know what I could use?" he said.

I could hear Lucy in the family room playing the piano, or trying to. She was practicing a song she had played about a million times, but now she seemed to keep forgetting it.

"So, how about it?" my father said, tapping his stick against the barbecue in time to the music.

"What?" I said.

My father said something about getting him a wire brush, or a small shovel, or something. I knew it didn't matter what I came back with, as long as I went away to get it. My father liked to be reckless in private.

As I went around the corner of the garage, I could hear the hollow rush of flames roaring up.

It was another world under the tarp, not even just the old things of the garage, but the old things of our life: ancient fishing rods, boxes of clothes that no longer fit, a broken TV set, a standing lamp, a crib that had been mine and, before that, Lucy's, and, over there, most of a broken croquet set. Also there were coffee cans with rusty nails and bolts and nuts; there were used tires, fused metal tools, a lawn mower, a hoe, a broken rake.

The pile hugged the entire side of the garage, covering even the picture window, as if it was something trying to get back inside.

The picture window in the garage was mostly useless now, but then so was the family room, so it didn't matter much—looking in at an almost empty room, or looking out at what used to be in it. As I worked my way closer to the picture window, I could hear Lucy's music getting louder.

Under the tarp, I knew by touch where everything was. This had been my old fort, but the inroads seemed smaller now. I had to duck the jutting pieces of scrap iron. I could feel my old plastic soldiers underfoot in the dirt.

As I got to the picture window, Lucy was on to a new song, and she was having some trouble with it. You couldn't even tell what the song was. Mr. Leets sat beside her on the piano bench, putting his hands on top of hers, as if showing her the notes. But even when his hands weren't on top of hers, his hands kept moving—in the air, on his knees, on the top of the piano, on his face and through his hair, and then on Lucy's back.

Lucy was sitting up very straight, as if Mr. Leets had corrected her posture. His hands were still moving, though—they didn't stop—and sometimes he would touch her back again, even though her posture looked perfect.

There was nothing much to do. I had already looked through all of the old rotting stack of *National Geographics*. I had gone through every box. I thought about putting together one last battle, but the plastic soldiers were buried in the dirt, and games from that many months ago seemed so *juvenile*, as Lucy used to point out.

Mr. Leets got up from the piano bench and started pacing the room, his hands loosening his collar, loosening his tie, and moving in time to the music, which was out of time.

Lucy was playing faster.

Our old crib was near the picture window, and I pulled it a little closer, and lowered the rail on one side, and sat down. In the
dark beneath the damp canvas, the mattress smelled of rat piss. The
plastic cover was cracked and the cotton batting was pushing out.
I thought about doing something funny—maybe tapping on the
window and making a face, or maybe holding up one of my
mother's old Styrofoam wig holders on the end of a stick. But then
I remembered that Mr. Leets taught at the junior high, and that
next week I would be there. I imagined how much taller I would
be next week.

When I looked into the family room again, Mr. Leets was standing behind Lucy. He was touching her back again. He was rubbing
her sunburned neck.

I must have sat up fast, and even just that much moving made
my sunburn hurt. Lucy's sunburn was a hundred times worse than
mine, but she didn't move when he touched her, didn't even flinch.
She kept herself set on the music.

Mr. Leets seemed a little shocked—his face was sort of pinched
—as if he was shocked that she had forgotten something he had
taught her. He was smiling, though, and touching the fine hairs
on the back of her neck.

Lucy kept playing the music. She wasn't making any mistakes
now, but the song still didn't sound right. The notes were too fast,
as if the music had become something that was going somewhere
and Lucy was trying to go there with it.

Mr. Leets moved his hands down Lucy's back. He wasn't looking at Lucy, though, or even at the piano; he was looking up at the
big fluorescent light, as if waiting for some kind of answer. And
then, when his answer came to him, he leaned down and kissed
the back of her neck.

Lucy kept playing the music. When the song ended, she reached
out for a different piece of sheet music. But Mr. Leets reached out
too, and held her hand back, and slid his hand slowly up her arm,
past the vaccination mark, and then inside of her sundress.

J. D. Dolan

There was a space now where the music had been. In it, I could hear the hissing of the steaks on the grill, my father tapping at the barbecue with his stick. I could hear my mother humming out on the lawn, setting the silverware and the plates on the picnic table. I made myself a part of the pile—a box, a tool, a thing that didn't even breathe, that didn't live.

Lucy reached again for the sheet music, as if Mr. Leets didn't have his hand inside of her sundress, on her chest, and another hand pulling down the zipper on the back.

Mr. Leets pulled at the straps on the sundress, but Lucy had started playing the music again and her arms were keeping the straps up, or at least not completely off. Mr. Leets's tongue crossed a thin stripe of white on Lucy's back as he worked his way up her spine, to her neck, to the side of her face. Lucy kept playing the music.

You could see that Lucy was struggling with something, but it looked as if what she was struggling with was the music.

The way Mr. Leets touched Lucy, the way his hands pushed at her chest and then down between her legs—he was touching her all over and very fast, not even as if he *liked* touching Lucy, but as if each part he touched, if he touched enough of them, would help him make a Lucy in his mind.

His hands were still moving as he leaned himself over Lucy and tried to kiss her on the lips.

Lucy seemed to come up for air, and she stopped—just stopped playing the music—and turned her face to one side and breathed deep.

Lucy was staring straight at me. I could see her face full-on, for that moment, as she turned: the dark hair roughed up and the light blue eyes focused hard on something but you couldn't tell what, she was looking at me and beyond me. From the muscles of her face it looked as if she was about to say something—maybe even scream it—but whatever it was got pushed back by his hands, and his tongue, and his lips.

As Mr. Leets pushed Lucy down on the piano bench I could feel the sunburn again on my back: I had a sudden sense of being inside my skin, and I didn't like it. I could feel myself getting hard, and I wasn't supposed to feel like that. Still, I didn't move. The smoke from the barbecue was coming this way, under the tarp, and even though it was burning at my eyes, I couldn't not watch.

Mr. Leets shoved Lucy's sundress up around her waist. He stood between her legs. He unbuckled, unzipped. He looked quickly at the closed garage door. Then he looked up again at the big fluorescent light as he let his pants drop.

When it was over I must have run, or not so much run but pushed myself out from under there. I remember being swollen inside my pants as I stood up from the crib, and then I turned, I took a deep breath and pushed off, my head brushing the canvas tarp, my mouth filling with spider webs. I needed air, I needed out. My legs were working fast but they seemed a long ways away, and it must have only been a few steps before the world turned to scrap iron—I could feel my face pushed against it—and my body went out from under me. I remember falling . . . .

For a few seconds I couldn't see anything; I didn't have eyes yet. I had no arms, no legs, no muscles. My head was a huge empty room. But there was something spreading over me, something warm, I could feel it, and it felt like a hand on my head.

Far away, my mother broke open a tray of ice cubes. My father scraped steaks off a grill. It got a little quieter as each steak got scraped off.

I found an arm underneath me. I rolled to one side, worked the arm out, touched at my face. It was warm and wet. My face was wet but my mouth tasted of iron and dirt. One eye opened a little, and I lifted myself up.

The sky now was a deep blue, through the trees was a sunset the color of blood.

My mother and father and Lucy were already sitting at the picnic table, eating their steaks by the light of tiki torches. Lucy was looking at a fashion magazine.

Mr. Leets was gone.

My mother looked up at me and said, "Oh my God! He's been in a *fight!*" and my father looked as if he'd just been accused of something.

Lucy set down the fashion magazine and said, "How dis*gusting*. You look like a monster movie."

I looked down at my shirt, at my hands, and it felt as if every wrong thing I had ever done in my life—every small lie and stolen coin, every weakness of heart—all of it was printed on my body, inked in my blood. And Lucy, I knew, could read this best.

My mother and my father, I could tell, were getting ready to attack—not me, but each other: how three or five years ago he or she should have done that, and now look at this, I told you so, don't talk to me like that, and so on.

Lucy must have seen it coming too. She stood up, took me by the hand, and led me into the house.

In the bathroom she ran the hot water, unrolled the gauze, opened the peroxide and mercurochrome. I watched her with my one eye for some kind of sign, some hint of something different. When she picked up the scissors to cut the gauze, I was ready to let her stab me in the heart.

Lucy very tenderly wiped away the blood. "You know, you shouldn't get in fights," she said.

I nodded. I could feel my heartbeat in her hands.

And then I said, "A fight?"

Lucy turned my head to one side to clean some of the rust and dirt from my face, and there in the bathroom mirror I got my first look at myself: the battered eye, darkening already, and above it, on my forehead, a neat cut like a quarter moon, one that looked much too small for so much blood.

I was beginning to understand. *A fight*. A fight could mean that Lucy didn't know what I had seen. A fight could mean that what I saw never happened.

"The girls won't like you if you always get in fights," Lucy said.

I nodded.

"You want the girls to like you, don't you?"

I nodded.

My mother and father stopped talking when Lucy and I got back out to the picnic table. They both kept watching me as I ate. The steak was burnt and cold and tasted of charcoal starter. It was hard to chew. Finally my father cleared his throat and said, "So, you're starting junior high, huh?"

I nodded.

"And Lucy's starting high school," my mother put in.

I kept eating, and waited for my father to say something else. Our father maybe once every hundred years would start a conversation—just start it, but never finish it. Lucy was sitting beside me on the bench, and with my one eye I sneaked a look at her, but Lucy wouldn' t look back at me; if we looked at each other, we would have to laugh.

"Well, you shouldn't get in fights," my father said, but there was in his voice something that sounded almost proud. Then he looked at my mother, which was another thing he did maybe once every hundred years, and said, "They'll be off and married before we know it." Then he smiled, and put his hand on top of hers, and they just looked at each other like that, smiling.

It was as if we suddenly weren't there, Lucy and I. Our mother and father cleared the picnic table, helping each other with the plates, helping each other with the screen door, saying thank you and excuse me, and calling each other by their first names, Willie and Donna, which was something unless they were angry that they almost never did.

Lucy and I stayed outside. We didn't talk. Lucy seemed lost deep inside of herself, and I was lost in there with her.

We heard music from inside the house. Then, through the window of the living room, we could see them—not our father and our mother, but Willie and Donna, moving slow to the music, moving together, holding each other close. As they turned, you could see that they were in pain from their sunburns. But they didn't let go, they kept dancing, and holding each other like that, as if even with the pain, it was worth it.

I watched Lucy watching them. It looked as if watching them like that was beginning to make her itch: She tried to reach behind her back, first with one hand, then with the other, but she couldn't seem to reach where she needed. "I think I'm starting to peel," she said, and turned her back toward me, and lowered a strap on her sundress.

Even by the light of the tiki torch I could see where she meant, where the skin had been roughed up from a corner of a piano bench, and from fingers dug in deep.

Willie and Donna moved in the window like something from a movie.

I told her that I couldn't see, that it was too dark, that it would be better to wait, that it wasn't ready to peel yet anyway, that it would just hurt worse, but Lucy didn't say anything, just stayed there, staring at the window, and I knew that I was going to have to do it.

Lucy's back rippled as I touched her skin. I peeled away a small strip.

"Just think," she said, "next week you'll be in junior high."

Lucy' s skin was warm and smooth—I had never touched anything so smooth—and I peeled away another strip.

"And you'll be in high school," I said. "And have a boyfriend."

"A boyfriend?" Lucy said, and laughed. She pulled the strap of her sundress up, turned, and put her arms around me. "No," she said, and smiled. "*You're* the only boyfriend for me." Lucy turned me around, put her arms around me from behind, the way she used to do with her dolls, the way she used to do with me when I was little.

My head didn't hurt much, yet. The pain would come later. And with Lucy's arms around me, the stinging of my sunburn felt almost good. Because I was beginning to believe it myself—not that I had watched Mr. Leets do that to my sister, not that it shouldn't have happened and I could have stopped it, and not that the wound to my head was from nothing but running scared. No. I was beginning to believe that there had been a fight, a big fight, a heroic fight, and that I had been in it. I was beginning to believe that I had won.

———————

J. D. Dolan was born and raised in Montebello, California, and has since lived in New Orleans, New York City, and Atlanta, Idaho. In addition to *The Antioch Review*, his work has appeared in the *Mississippi Review*, *Shenandoah*, and *The Nation*. He is a recipient of the Jeanne Charpiot Goodheart Prize for Fiction, a Fellowship in Literature from the Idaho Commission on the Arts, and several residencies at the Virginia Center for the Creative Arts. He presently holds a University Fellowship in the Creative Writing Program at Syracuse University, where he is at work on a memoir.

A friend of mine once told me she'd seen her mother kiss every man on a fishing boat. With that image in mind, I wrote a story about a family on vacation in the Gulf. Instead of fun and sun, their vacation was filled with a sexual tension that tended toward violence; by the end, they were all worn down to raw nerves.

This story sprung from that one. I wanted to look at what might have brought these people to such extremes, at how they were changed by that event, and in what ways they would somehow limp forward in their lives.

I happened to write the first draft of this story in a room with a piano, a big window and a fluorescent light.

Ellen Douglas

GRANT

(from *Story*)

T his is a story that may have been waiting for me until I was old enough to tell it. Not that I had forgotten. How could I forget what had happened in my house, under my nose, to me? I even thought from time to time about telling one of the stories that lay next to it, so to speak. There were the bees the night he died. There was Rosalie, who sat by him every day when he was dying, beautiful Rosalie, who had five children and sometimes came to work with a cut lip, a battered nose, a bruised temple. There were the day walks, the night walks. But I didn't want to tell those stories. Nothing came of thinking about them.

My husband's uncle came to live with us during the last year of his life. He was eighty-two. His wife had died several years earlier and he had no children. He had cancer.

He could have gone to a veterans hospital—he was an Annapolis graduate, a retired naval officer. And there were other possibilities. Once he was too feeble to look after himself, he could have hired live-in help or gone into a nursing home. But we invited, insisted, and he came.

I knew Grant as one knows uncles-in-law who live in the same town—as a genial enough fellow who brought his fiddle to family Thanksgiving gatherings and played badly to my husband's piano accompaniment. I can see him now on those occasions, fiddle tucked under his chin, standing over the piano, stooping to read the music, an expression of deep but clearly ironic concentration on his face, his head bent, light bouncing off the balding scalp. They'd play easy pieces from a collection of violin and piano duets: "None but the Lonely Heart," "Humoresque," a Schubert serenade. After they finished a piece he'd sit down, lay the violin across his lap, and smile. "I always have trouble with the triplets in that one," he might say. And his mother, nearly ninety then and nodding in her wheelchair: "Grant plays so well. It's a pity his violin squeaks."

That was a family joke.

So. . . . Why did we invite him in? Well, again, family—he was family. One couldn't send him off to a veterans hospital or put him in a home, could one? But I'm mis-stating the case. No one could send him anywhere. He was perfectly capable of sending himself anywhere he wished, or of staying where he was, in the house his wife had left to her own niece and nephew.

Now there's another story. His wife Kathleen, who was fifteen years younger than he was, had died suddenly of a stroke. She'd doubtless always believed he would die first (he'd been retired early from the navy after a coronary) and had consequently left him nothing. The house and what other modest property they had was in her name. His name was not even mentioned in her will.

Grant could have contested it, of course: In our state you can't leave all your property away from a spouse. But he would never have done such a dishonorable thing. In her will she had said what she wanted. It would be done.

In their dealings with him, the niece and nephew were correct, but they were a cold pair to my way of thinking. Or maybe it's just that they were like me, had other things to think about besides aged uncles-in-law. They gave him permission to live in the house for the rest of his life. So that there could be no confusion about the title, they paid the taxes and he reimbursed them. They didn't charge him any rent. He paid repairs and upkeep.

Now I ask you, no matter how much younger you were than

your husband, no matter if he'd had a coronary, would you leave everything away from him? Wouldn't you think he might by chance survive you? You might get run over by a truck or stung to death by hornets or drown or get trapped in a burning house, or God knows what. Surely you would mention in your will the name of your husband of forty years.

The only light he shed on this story came when he moved in with us and was clearing out of her house the things that belonged to him. He brought with him his clothes, a couple of canvas-covered wicker trunks from his tour in the Philippines before the first World War, a beautiful Japanese tea set, some brass trays from India, a huge piece of tapa cloth, his easy chair. Everything else: the furniture, his wedding silver, china, linens, even the lovely carved cherry bed he'd had made for them by a local cabinetmaker, "All that stuff," he said, "I got it for her. It was hers. She left everything to them. So. . . ."

He brought his navy dress uniform and his cocked hat, circa 1911. They're still in a closet somewhere in our house, the uniform in a mothproof bag, the hat stored in its leather case.

His sword he had given some years earlier to one of our sons. His violin he gave to my husband.

I think of one ray of light his wife shed on their marriage, although, I don't know, it may be misleading.

She was one of those large, soft-looking women, fair-haired and blue-eyed, who, statistical studies indicate, are most vulnerable in middle age to gallbladder attacks and diverticulitis. And indeed she did have the latter, although not for long, since she died when she was sixty.

In any case, what she said surprised me. She'd always seemed an easygoing, lively lady, ready for a good time, and I would have thought her tolerant of other people's foibles and failures and moral lapses. Not so, or not everybody's. We were talking of a man in the county who had left his wife for a woman who was widely known to have had in the course of her life a number of open love affairs—not so common among the small-town gentry of a couple of generations ago. I mean, people had *clandestine* affairs, of course, but not open ones. "She's filth," Grant's wife said to me when I commented once on this lady's charm and wit. "Filth. That's what they both are." She shivered and looked straight at me. (This was when I was quite a young woman, still focused almost to the exclusion of everything else on those lovely nights in bed.) "Men," she said. "There's only one thing men want and she gives it to them."

So, as you see, there's the story of their marriage, if one could dredge it up. And then. . . . There's Rosalie.

But I think, instead, of the day Grant gave his sword to our second son. This was after his wife's death, but long before he came to live with us. As I've said, he had no sons of his own and my husband was the only child of his brother. There were no children of his blood except ours. He came walking slowly up the driveway the afternoon of our son's tenth birthday, bearing the sword in its leather scabbard with the gold tassel attached at the hilt. He didn't have a particularly soldierly bearing, looked more like a slightly seedy, gentle-mannered farmer than a potential admiral. Ross, our son, and three or four of his friends were sitting around a trestle table eating ice cream. Ross had been alerted ahead of time that his great-uncle intended to give him his sword and we had explained that this was a significant gift and he should feel honored. He stood up very straight and looked solemn and said, "Thank you," but it was clear to me he was unimpressed—didn't quite know what use this sword, almost as tall as he was, would be to him. He and his friends were organizing a war with another neighborhood gang for the next day. Mudballs and BB guns would be their weapons of choice. We invited Grant in and he sat and had a drink with us. He was always convivial, happy to join you in a drink, never at a loss for words, often the butt of his own jokes.

So he came to live with us the last year of his life. He had refused treatment for the cancer. "I'm too old to let somebody cut on me," he'd said. "It's out of the question." He knew that he probably had less than a year to live.

The first few months he used to take a long walk every morning through the humming, buzzing, late-spring world, bees swarming around the honeysuckle vines on the back fence, towhees calling, flickers drilling for bugs in the bark of the pecan tree, squirrels chasing each other up and down the trunk. He'd walk slowly, head a little forward, determined to go as far as he could; and then he'd return even more slowly, going to his room by the side door into the wing. He'd stop there sometimes and watch the squirrels. One day he pointed out to me that a wren had built her nest in the potted fern by the side door.

I never joined him on these walks. I didn't have time.

In the afternoon one of his friends or his brother might come to sit with him for a while; at night he and our youngest son sometimes played bridge with my husband and me. Grant was a good bridge player—indifferent, though, whether he won or lost. Or, some nights, he'd go back to his room and watch TV.

Later, as he grew weaker, he walked up and down our front sidewalk every day, too feeble to risk getting far from the house. Then he began to walk at night, up and down the long hall that led from the main part of our house past the two bedrooms where our sons were asleep, to his room and bath at the very back of the wing.

I still slept lightly, a habit most women keep after the years when the least sound from a child's room will wake you, and of course I heard Grant tramping up and down the hall. The first time, I got up and went back to see what was the matter. He was in his bathrobe, his sparse gray hair disheveled, his face drawn. For the first time I noticed how thin he'd gotten.

"What's the matter, Grant?" I asked.

"I'm getting a little exercise," he said. He gave me the same look of ironic concentration I'd seen on his face when he was playing the violin, as if to say: I don't expect you to think I'm good, but I'll give it a try. This time it was: I don't expect you to believe me, but act as if you do.

Or was that what his look said? Might there have been a ques-

tion in his eyes? An invitation to join him? Or was it deep knowledge of my fears, my self-absorption?

I knew he was in pain. He wasn't walking up and down the hall
for exercise. I said to myself that I didn't want to invade his pri-
vacy and went back to bed. Next day I called the doctor and told
him Grant needed something stronger, morphine or Dilaudid; and
he called in a new prescription. For some weeks Grant continued
to walk every night. I would hear him and put my pillow over my
head.

It was during this period or a few weeks later that Grant hired
Rosalie. She had worked for him and his wife a couple of days a
week for several years, and then, after his wife died, had cooked
for him. She was a splendid cook and the kind of woman who
could take charge of a household—intelligent and aggressive. She
could have been an office manager or a clothes buyer in a department store (had a flair for style) or perhaps a lawyer (she knew
how to get what she wanted from almost anyone). Unfortunately
none of these careers had been open to her. She was an illiterate
black woman and the year was 1964.

When Grant had moved in with us, he'd given Rosalie a month's
severance and a bonus and recommended her to several friends.
She'd had no trouble getting another job. Then, when he began to
weaken, could no longer trust himself alone in the bathroom,
needed help with dressing, he arranged with the family for whom
she worked to share her time. She came every morning for a couple of hours, helped him with his bath, made his bed, and, if he
wished, fixed a cold supper and left it for him in the refrigerator.

Sometimes she would stay for a while after he was bathed and
dressed and comfortable. She was a talker, loved to visit—and so
did he. He may already have been talking to her about dying. Or
maybe she began it. She was a devout Christian, offered up a mar-
velous strong soprano voice to God every week at church, and was
president of the choir.

In any case during those morning visits he began to teach her to
read, using the Bible as his text. Oh, how deeply Rosalie wanted to

learn to read the Bible—more, I think, than wanting the changes that reading might make in her life. It was reading the Bible, I'm sure of it, that she was focused on. She needed it, needed the support of religion, I mean. She was trapped in her life, not just because she couldn't read, but because she had five children and an abusive husband who she couldn't leave as long as he paid the rent and made a contribution to the household expenses.

And Grant was bored, of course.

So he occupied himself teaching her. Some days I'd go back and find them sitting side by side, him in his easy chair, Rosalie with a straight-backed desk chair drawn close to his. Together they leaned over his battered King James Bible, turned the onionskin pages. It must have been easier for her to begin to pick out words because she knew so much of it by heart. He'd move his finger along a line: " 'I sink in deep mire where there is no standing I–am–come–into–deep–waters–where–the floods–overflow–me.' " Or: " 'Bless the Lord, oh my soul; and all that is within me, bless his holy name.' " She could read that easily or pretend to, moving her finger from word to word once he started her with "Bless." "Look at every word," he'd say, and they'd do it again. " 'B-b-bless–Bless the Lord–oh–my–soul.' "

One day, putting away clothes in my son's room I heard him laughing and then Rosalie, raising her voice, "Now you know that ain't it, Mr. Grant." I stopped to listen.

"But there it is," he said, "and you ought to like it. 'I am black but comely, O ye daughters of Jerusalem,' and 'I am the rose of Sharon, the lily of the valleys.' And how about this: 'Stay me with flagons. Comfort me with apples: For I am sick of love.' That's the bride talking."

"Oh, Mr. Grant," she said, "that's talking about Jesus and the church. The church is the bride of Jesus. That's not about what you're talking about."

He laughed again. "Anyhow," he said. "It's poetry. It's beautiful poetry."

"It's the Word of God," Rosalie said.

I tiptoed away.

I don't want to wander here. I want to stick with the long, agonizing last months of Grant's illness. Still, I have to tell you before I go on how beautiful Rosalie was. It would be commonplace to compare her profile to Nefertiti's and, remembering her—the full lips, the heavy-lidded eyes, and slightly flattened nose—I think she's more like those elegant attendant ladies on the wall of one of the Rameses' tombs. But there was nothing stiff or narrow or Egyptian about her body. You admired her face when she walked in, and then, when she swung a strong, round hip against the kitchen door to bump it shut, you'd begin to wish your waist was as supple, your legs as shapely, your breasts as softly ample as hers. What a pleasure to have such a person to look at every day.

But one day she would come to work sullen, turning her face away, an eyelid darkened, not with kohl but with the greenish purple stain of a bruise, her sensuous lips cut where her husband's fist had crushed them against her teeth. She'd threaten to leave him or to swear out a restraining order against him and for a while everything would be quiet.

As the weeks passed, it became more and more difficult for me to walk down the long back hall in our house, to raise my hand and knock on Grant's door, to hear his breathy voice saying, "Come in," to listen to his labored breathing, look into his gaunt face.

There he was, a huge presence in our house, and he was family; but I didn't want to see him or to think about him. Every day, morning and afternoon, I forced myself to go back to his room and stay for at least ten minutes. I felt the weight of my watch on my wrist and willed myself not to look at it, but I knew to the minute when I could leave.

During this period several of his friends abandoned him. At first their visits would be less frequent—once a week, once every two weeks. Then they stopped coming altogether. If I saw one of them in the grocery store or in the post office picking up mail, he'd inquire for Grant and say, "I've been out of town." Or, "He's so weak, I don't want to disturb him. But give him our love."

"Yes," I'd say. "All right. I will."

His brother, my father-in-law, still, and to the end, came every day.

There can be only one reason why I hated so deeply the ordeal of going back to visit with this lovely old man. He was dying. His dying was a terrible disgrace, an embarrassment not to be endured. That's the story I could not tell. I abandoned him too.

In the middle of it, I didn't know I was abandoning him, did I? I was busy. I had three children. I had my own work to do, my obligations. And I needed to go fishing, to see my parents, to go out with my friends, to lie beside my husband in our warm bed.

The town where we lived was on a cutoff bend of the Mississippi River, a man-made lake, long and still on windless summer days between its confining levees, fringed with willows and cypress and cottonwood trees, jumping with bream and bass and crappie and catfish. When they were younger, the children and I had picnicked and fished and skied and swum its waters. Now that the eldest was in college and the two younger in high school, they were not interested in picnics with Mama, but I still needed, as I always had, to be out on the water, to hear waves lapping the green sides of my fishing boat, to lie on the sandbar with my friends and watch the sun go down behind the cottonwood trees. I was busy, caught up in my life.

It sometimes seemed to me in those days, as I told a friend when we were out on the lake together, as if our house were panting, the walls swelling and shrinking—as if it were breathing sex. I'd hear the boys come in on weekend nights, would pretend not to hear the soft voices of the girls they sometimes brought with them. In the kitchen, in the morning, I would hear Rosalie teasing them about their girlfriends, asking about this one or that one. And at night, when they came in from a party, from skinny-dipping off the sandbar, from lying on the levee with the radio on. . . . What can I say to tell you how alive that household was?

One night, Ross came in at two or three in the morning, disheveled and half-buttoned, lipstick smeared across his cheek, and found Grant sitting on the floor in the hall, conscious, but unable to get up. Half-asleep, I heard them talking to each other and tiptoed out to see what was the matter. Ross was buttoning his shirt. "Well . . . ," he was saying.

And Grant was laughing. "I was waiting for you," he said. "I knew you'd get here eventually. But look at you!" And then, "Don't try to pick me up. Don't pull on me. I might come apart."

I stood appalled. Ross should not have to face this.

But he stooped without a word—strong as a stevedore he was in those days—and slipped one arm under Grant's shoulders, the other under his knees, lifted him, as it appeared, without effort, and carried him back to his room. I heard them laughing together, waited a minute, then pretended I had just gotten up, walked back to Grant's room, stuck my head in, and asked if I could help.

"No, no," Grant said. "We're okay."

It was shortly after this that he said he needed someone with him at night and from then on he had round-the-clock sitters, Rosalie in the morning and two other women who came in from three until eleven and eleven until seven.

One morning during those last weeks, not so long before he lapsed into a coma, just as I raised my hand to knock at his door, I heard him say to Rosalie in a measured, thoughtful way, "Yes. Yes." A pause, and then, "I do. I do. I don't try to know what it'll be like, but I know I'll see Kathleen."

Rosalie said, "Amen."

"But what will *see* mean?" he said. "I don't know. Somehow she and I will be. . . ." Again a thoughtful pause. ". . . She will be there with me."

"Yes, Lord," Rosalie said. "Amen, Mr. Grant."

He did not speak of those things with me.

There is one more thing about Rosalie and Grant. I had thought I could leave it out, but I find that I can't. It happened after he was entirely bedridden, after everything had to be done for him.

I realize now it's usually the case that one hires men to take care of male patients, but curiously enough I didn't think about that at the time and apparently neither did Grant. We'd started with Rosalie and it seemed natural to keep on with her, and then to find two other women, one a cousin of hers who came with a string of recommendations, the other a trained LPN.

In any case, I came into the kitchen one morning from the car, bringing bags of groceries and found Rosalie standing, her back to me, at the sink.

"Morning, Rosalie," I said and turned to go out for another load.

"I got to leave," she said. "I can't nurse him anymore."

"What?" I stood in the doorway staring at her. "What's the matter?"

"He wants me to touch him," she said.

"Rosalie!"

"He wants me to touch him."

Grant was already at the stage where he spent much of the day dozing, drifting in and out of sleep. Last time the doctor had come to see him, I'd gone back to his room and stood by to make sure we were doing everything we should. The doctor had touched his arm, raised it and lowered it, helped him sit up, pressed the soles of his feet, tapped his knees. Afterwards, as we walked to the car, he'd said, "It's in his brain now. I don't think it will be long. I'm increasing the morphine. We don't want him to suffer."

"He wants me to touch him," Rosalie said. "I can't see after him anymore."

"Oh, Rosalie, Rosalie."

She was weeping. I put my arms around her, patted her shoulder distractedly. "It's in his brain," I said. "The cancer. And the pain medicine. He doesn't know what he's saying."

"I'm scared of him," she said. "I don't want no part of that."

"Rosalie, he's so weak, he couldn't possibly hurt you," I said.

"He says, 'Come on, help me. Let's see if I can get it up.' And then he laughed. I got to go," she said.

But of course she didn't. She stayed to the end.

And I was going to leave out the bees too. The bees seemed, to begin with, no more than a bizarre detail of what happened the night Grant died.

It was toward four o'clock in the morning when the night nurse came to our bedroom door and roused my husband and me. "Mr. Grant has passed," she said.

We got up, put on bathrobes, tiptoed, so as not to wake the boys, down the long hall to his room. He had been unconscious for many days. His body, under the sheet and light blanket, was barely an outline, thin to emaciation, his cheeks sunken. But he seemed now no less alive than when I'd looked in on him the day before. He was still himself, the lines that his life had made vivid in his flesh, his dignity untouched. I even seemed to see that ironic half-smile on his face: *Well, I'll give it a try then.*

I laid my hand on his chest, feeling for a heartbeat, thinking the sitter must be mistaken, put my fingers on his lips to catch a breath. But Grant was dead—as she knew quite well. She had already cleaned him up after the sphincter relaxed; had changed his pajamas before she called us; had opened the curtains and the windows to air out the room and turned on all the lights in the hall. She had even opened the outside door to the mild spring night. She knew her job.

Now she said that she had done all she needed to do and, if we were agreeable, she would go on home.

"All right," my husband said. "Certainly." And he walked with her to the door, thanking her, saying he'd call her in the morning, put her check in the mail, let her know about funeral arrangements. She'd told us that she was a nurse who always attended her patients' funerals. "I show respect," she'd said.

It was at the door, when she couldn't go out, that we saw the bees.

The bees, part of the colony that lived in a high hollow of the pecan tree in the side yard, were swarming. How could such a thing be? Swarming in the middle of the night? But there they were, a heaving mass of them clustered on the screen door, sheets of them clinging to the window screens in the long hall. My husband saw the nurse out through the front door and came back. What should we do?

"If we turn off the lights," he said, "maybe they'll decide to move. They can't start a new hive on a screen door."

So we turned them off, groped our way to our bedroom, sat down, stared at each other. What do you do at four o'clock in the morning with your dead uncle cooling toward rigor in his bed and a swarm of bees on the door?

After a while my husband said, "I should call Daddy."

"It's too early," I said. "Let's wait until six o'clock. He's usually up by six."

"The doctor," he said. "The death certificate. We forgot. And maybe we should call the funeral home to come and get him. I mean, before the boys wake up."

"Yes," I said. "I think we should."

"But what about the bees? How will they get him out the door?"

We went back to check. The bees were still there.

And then we found ourselves outside with burning spills of newspaper flaring in the darkness. We would smoke them into docility and then brush them away so the undertaker could come in with his gurney. But the bees clung and buzzed and crawled over each other and stayed.

We called the doctor and then the funeral home. Of course they managed well enough, rolling the gurney out the long way, down the hall, across the living room, negotiating the sharp turn into the entrance hall, and out the front door.

He was gone.

By then it was almost six and we called my husband's father. The sun was up. The wren was calling from the fern by Grant's door where she'd made her nest. While we were in the kitchen making coffee, talking about arrangements, about who we needed to call, who would be pallbearers, the bees must have decided to leave. They were gone when we went back to the wing to wake the boys.

It was Rosalie who told us why they'd swarmed.

"That fool should've known," she said, talking about the night nurse. "Any fool ought to know. You got to tell the bees immediately when somebody dies." But then she thought better of what she'd said. "Maybe she didn't know there were bees up in that tree," she said. "I saw them, but there wasn't any reason for her to have noticed. She don't come on 'til eleven. How she's going to see bees going in and out in the middle of the night?"

"But what do you mean, Rosalie?" I said. "Why do you have to tell the bees when somebody dies?"

"I forget y'all are not from the country," she said. "In the country they say you got to tell the bees or they'll swarm, they'll leave the hive. I don't s'pose it makes no difference whether it's a hive or a tree. You got to go out right away and say, 'The master is dead,' and then, maybe, something like, 'I'm the new master,' so they'll know somebody is in charge or. . . . I don't know."

I sat down at the kitchen table and put my head in my hands and she sat down across from me. We looked at each other and wept.

About Rosalie. Soon after Grant's death she began to go to night school, leaving her fifteen year old to look after the younger kids. She got her high school equivalency diploma; and then she got a much better job and she left her wicked husband for a while, although I've heard that every now and then she went back to him. At least she was freer, able to leave him if she liked.

And, as it turns out, the will, Rosalie, the bees, all those tales, are a part of the story I didn't tell when Grant died. Now, twenty-odd years later, I can tell that story. Death has become, so to speak, family.

Sometimes, in the morning, when the bees are just beginning to stir (I wake early these days, as old people so often do), I fill my coffee cup and stand listening in the kitchen. The boys are long gone now on their separate ways; the house is still, no longer breathing and swelling with their energy. I take my cup then and go out into the yard and listen to the raucous cries of the jays, the flicker's jackhammer drill, the *tchk tchk* of the squirrels chasing each other through the high branches of the pecan tree. The wind lifts the leaves and there at a fork I see the dark hole where years ago a limb was torn away in a storm and where now the bees still make their home. They've filled the hole with comb, and comb hangs down against the tree trunk. Singly, the bees drift out, circle, drop downward, and begin to draw nectar from the daffodils, to pollinate the clover on the ditchbank, to tumble like drunken bawds in the deep, intoxicating magnolia cups. I lay my hand against the bark and tell the bees that I, too, will die. I admonish them not to swarm, not to leave us, but to stay in their hollow in the pecan tree, to keep making for us all their golden, fragrant, dark, sweet honey.

Ellen Douglas lives in Jackson, Mississippi. She grew up in small towns in Louisiana, Arkansas, and Mississsppi. She has received two NEA fellowships and an award from the Fellowship of Southern Writers for the body of her work. Her most recent novel, *Can't Quit You, Baby*, was published by Atheneum and is presently available in paperback from Penguin. Earlier novels, *The Rock Cried Out*, *A Lifetime Burning*, and *A Family's Affairs*, have been reissued by LSU Press. The University Press of Mississippi has reissued *Apostles of Light* and *Black Cloud, White Cloud*.

I am presently at work on a group of short stories, of which "Grant" is one. The stories are about remembering and forgetting, lying and truth-telling. I think of a quotation from Robert Stone's The Reason for Stories—*"We are forever cleaning up our act"—as an epigraph for "Grant," which is about how we learn to live with our knowledge not only of our failures but of our mortality.*

APPENDIX

A list of the magazines currently consulted for *New Stories from the South: The Year's Best, 1996,* with addresses, subscription rates, and editors.

Agni
Boston Writing Program University
236 Bay State Road
Boston, MA 02215
Semiannually, $14.95
Askold Melnyczak

Alabama Literary Review
253 Smith Hall
Troy State University
Troy, AL 36082
Annually, $5
Theron Montgomery, Editor-in-
   Chief

American Short Fiction
Parlin 14
Department of English
University of Austin
Austin, TX 78712-1164
Quarterly, $24
Laura Furman

The American Voice
Kentucky Foundation for
   Women, Inc.
332 W. Broadway, Suite 1215
Louisville, KY 40202
Triannually, $15
Frederick Smock, Editor
Sallie Bingham, Publisher

Antietam Review
7 W. Franklin
Hagerstown, MD 21740
Once or twice a year, $5.25 each
Susanne Kass

The Antioch Review
P.O. Box 148
Yellow Springs, OH 45387
Quarterly, $35
Robert S. Fogarty

Apalachee Quarterly
P.O. Box 10469
Tallahassee, FL 32302
Triannually, $15
Barbara Hamby

The Atlantic Monthly
745 Boylston Street
Boston, MA 02116
Monthly, $17.94
C. Michael Curtis

Black Warrior Review
University of Alabama
P.O. Box 2936
Tuscaloosa, AL 35486-2936
Semiannually, $11
Leigh Ann Sackrider

Boulevard
P.O. Box 30386

Philadelphia, PA 19103
Triquarterly, $12
Richard Burgin

Carolina Quarterly
Greenlaw Hall CB# 3520
University of North Carolina
Chapel Hill, NC 27599-3520
Triannually, $10
Fiction Editor

The Chariton Review
Northeast Missouri State University
Kirksville, MO 63501
Semiannually, $9
Jim Barnes

The Chattahoochee Review
DeKalb College
2101 Womack Road
Dunwoody, GA 30338-4497
Quarterly, $16
Lamar York, Editor

Cimarron Review
205 Morrill Hall
Oklahoma State University
Stillwater, OK 74078-0135
Quarterly, $12
Gordon Weaver

Columbia
404 Dodge Hall
Columbia University
New York, NY 10027
Semiannually, $13
Nick Schaffzin

Concho River Review
c/o English Department
Angelo State University
San Angelo, TX 76909
Semiannually, $12
Terence A. Dalrymple

Crazyhorse
Department of English
University of Arkansas at Little Rock
2801 South University
Little Rock, AR 72204
Semiannually, $10
Judy Troy, Fiction Editor

The Crescent Review
P.O. Box 15069
Chevy Chase, MD 20825-5069
Triannually, $21
J. Timothy Holland

Crucible
Barton College
College Station
Wilson, NC 27893
Semiannually, $12
Terrence L. Grimes

CutBank
Department of English
University of Montana
Missoula, MT 59812
Semiannually, $12
Jeffery Smith

Double Dealer Redux
632 Pirate's Alley
New Orleans, LA 70116
Quarterly, $25
Rosemary James

DoubleTake Magazine
Center for Documentary Studies
1317 W. Pettigrew Street
Durham, NC 27705
Quarterly, $24
Robert Coles and Alex Harris

Epoch
251 Goldwin Smith Hall
Cornell University
Ithaca, NY 14853-3201

Triannually, $11
Michael Koch

Fiction
c/o English Department
City College of New York
New York, NY 10031
Triannually, $20
Mark J. Mirsky

The Florida Review
Department of English
University of Central Florida
Orlando, FL 32816
Semiannually, $7
Russ Kesler

The Georgia Review
University of Georgia
Athens, GA 30602
Quarterly, $18
Stanley W. Lindberg

The Gettysburg Review
Gettysburg College
Gettysburg, PA 17325-1491
Quarterly, $18
Peter Stitt

Glimmer Train
812 SW Washington Street, Suite 1205
Portland, OR 97205-3216
Quarterly, $29
Susan Burmeister-Brown and Linda
    Davis

GQ
Condé Nast Publications, Inc.
350 Madison Avenue
New York, NY 10017
Monthly, $20
Thomas Mallon

Granta
250 W. 57th Street

Suite 1316
New York, NY 10017
Quarterly, $32
Ian Jack

The Greensboro Review
Department of English
University of North Carolina
Greensboro, NC 27412
Semiannually, $8
Jim Clark

Gulf Coast
Department of English
University of Houston
4800 Calhoun Road
Houston, TX 77204-3012
Semiannually, $12
Glenn Blake

Gulf Stream
English Department
Florida International University
North Miami Campus
North Miami, FL 33181
Semiannually, $8
Lynne Barrett

Harper's Magazine
666 Broadway
New York, NY 10012
Monthly, $18
Lewis H. Lapham

Habersham Review
Piedmont College
Demorest, GA 30535-0010
Semiannually, $12
David L. Greene

High Plains Literary Review
180 Adams Street, Suite 250
Denver, CO 80206
Triannually, $20
Robert O. Greer, Jr.

Image
3100 McCormick Avenue
Wichita, KS 67213
Quarterly, $30
Gregory Wolfe

Indiana Review
316 N. Jordan Avenue
Bloomington, IN 47405
Semiannually, $12
Cara Diaconoff

The Iowa Review
308 EPB
University of Iowa
Iowa City, IA 52242-1492
Triannually, $18
David Hamilton

Iris
P.O. Box 7263
Atlanta, GA 30357
Quarterly, $12
Dennis Adams

The Journal
Ohio State University
Department of English
164 W. 17th Avenue
Columbus, OH 43210
Semiannually, $8
Michelle Herman and Kathy Fagan

Kalliope
Florida Community College
3939 Roosevelt Blvd.
Jacksonville, FL 32205
Triannually, $12.50
Mary Sue Koeppel

The Kenyon Review
Kenyon College
Gambier, OH 43022
Quarterly, $22
Fiction Editor

The Literary Review
Fairleigh Dickinson University
285 Madison Avenue
Madison, NJ 07940
Quarterly, $18
Walter Cummins

The Long Story
18 Eaton Street
Lawrence, MA 01843
Annually, $5
R. P. Burnham

Louisiana Literature
P.O. Box 792
Southeastern Louisiana University
Hammond, LA 70402
Semiannually, $10
David Hanson

Mangrove
University of Miami
Department of English
P.O. Box 248145
Coral Gables, FL 33124-4632
Semiannually, $14
Annabella Paiz

Mid-American Review
106 Hanna Hall
Department of English
Bowling Green State University
Bowling Green, OH 43403
Semiannually, $12
Robert Early, Senior Editor

Mississippi Quarterly
Box 5272
Mississippi State, MS 39762
Quarterly, $12
Robert L. Phillips, Jr.

Mississippi Review
Center for Writers
University of Southern Mississippi

Box 5144
Hattiesburg, MS 39406-5144
Semiannually, $15
Frederick Barthelme

The Missouri Review
1507 Hillcrest Hall
University of Missouri
Columbia, MO 65211
Triannually, $15
Speer Morgan

The Nebraska Review
Writers Workshop
Fine Arts Building 212
University of Nebraska
   at Omaha
Omaha, NE 68182
Semiannually, $9.50
Art Homer

Negative Capability
62 Ridgelawn Drive East
Mobile, AL 36608
Triannually, $15
Sue Walker

New Delta Review
English Department
Louisiana State University
Baton Rouge, LA 70803
Semiannually, $7
Catherine Williamson and Nicola
   Mason

New England Review
Middlebury College
Middlebury, VT 05753
Quarterly, $23
David Huddle

New Texas
Center for Texas Studies
P.O. Box 13016
Denton, TX 76203-3016

Annually
Kathryn S. McGuire

The New Yorker
20 W. 43rd Street
New York, NY 10036
Weekly, $36
Bill Buford, Fiction Editor

Nimrod
2010 Utica Square
Suite 707
Tulsa, OK 74114-1635
Semiannually, $15
Francine Ringold, Editor

The North American Review
University of Northern Iowa
Cedar Falls, IA 50614
Six times a year, $18
Robley Wilson

North Carolina Literary Review
English Department
East Carolina University
Greenville, NC 27858-4353
Annually, $15
Alex Albright

Northwest Review
369 PLC
University of Oregon
Eugene, OR 97403
Triannually, $14
John Witte

Ohioana Quarterly
Ohioana Library Association
1105 Ohio Departments
   Building
65 South Front Street
Columbus, OH 43215
Quarterly, $20
Barbara Maslekoff

The Ohio Review
290-C Ellis Hall
Ohio University
Athens, OH 45701-2979
Semiannually, $16
Wayne Dodd

Old Hickory Review
P.O. Box 1178
Jackson, TN 38302
Semiannually, $12
Dorothy Stanfill and Bill Nance

Ontario Review
9 Honey Brook Drive
Princeton, NJ 08540
Semiannually, $12
Raymond J. Smith and Joyce Carol
   Oates

Other Voices
University of Illinois at Chicago
Department of English
   (M/C 162)
601 S. Morgan Street
Chicago, IL 60607-7120
Semiannually
Dolores Weinberg

Oxford American
P.O. Drawer 1156
Oxford, MS 38655
Bimonthly, $24
Marc Smirnoff

The Paris Review
Box S
541 E. 72nd Street
New York, NY 10021
Quarterly, $34
George Plimpton

Parting Gifts
March Street Press
3413 Wilshire Drive
Greensboro, NC 27408

Semiannually, $8
Robert Bixby

Pembroke Magazine
Box 60
Pembroke State University
Pembroke, NC 28372
Annually, $5
Shelby Stephenson, Editor

Pfeiffer Review
Pfeiffer College
Box 3010
Misenheimer, NC 28109
D. Gregg Cowan

Playboy
680 N. Lake Shore Drive
Chicago, IL 60611
Monthly, $29
Alice K. Turner, Fiction Editor

Ploughshares
Emerson College
100 Beacon Street
Boston, MA 02116-1596
Triannually, $19
Don Lee, Editor

Prairie Schooner
201 Andrews Hall
University of Nebraska
Lincoln, NE 68588-0334
Quarterly, $20
Hilda Raz

Puerto del Sol
Box 3001, Department 3E
New Mexico State University
Las Cruces, NM 88003
Semiannually, $10
Kevin McIlvoy

Quarterly West
317 Olpin Union Hall
University of Utah

Salt Lake City, UT 84112
Semiannually, $11
M. L. Williams

Reckon
Center for the Study of Southern
  Culture
University of Mississippi
University, MS 38677
Quarterly, $21.95
Ann Abadie and Lynn McKnight

River Styx
3207 Washington Avenue
St. Louis, MO 63103
Triannually, $20
Lee Fournier

Santa Monica Review
Santa Monica College
1900 Pico Boulevard
Santa Monica, CA 90405
Semiannually, $12
Jim Krusoe

Shenandoah
Washington and Lee University
Troubadore Theater
2nd Floor
Lexington, VA 24450
Quarterly, $11
R. T. Smith

Snake Nation Review
110 #2 W. Force Street
Valdosta, GA 31601
Triannually, $20
Roberta George

The South Carolina Review
Department of English
Strode Tower Box 341503
Clemson University
Clemson, SC 29634-1503
Semiannually, $10
Richard J. Calhoun

South Dakota Review
Box 111
University of South Dakota
Vermillion, SD 57069
Quarterly, $15
Brian Bedard

Southern Exposure
P.O. Box 531
Durham, NC 27702
Quarterly, $24
Pat Arnow, Editor

Southern Humanities Review
9088 Haley Center
Auburn University
Auburn, AL 36849
Quarterly, $15
Dan R. Latimer

The Southern Review
43 Allen Hall
Louisiana State University
Baton Rouge, LA 70803-5005
Quarterly, $20
James Olney

Sou'wester
Southern Illinois University at
  Edwardsville
Edwardsville, IL 62026-1438
Semiannually, $10
Fred W. Robbins

Southwest Review
6410 Airline Road
Southern Methodist University
Dallas, TX 75275
Quarterly, $20
Willard Spiegelman

Story
1507 Dana Avenue
Cincinnati, OH 45207
Quarterly, $22
Lois Rosenthal

StoryQuarterly
P.O. Box 1416
Northbrook, IL 60065
Quarterly, $14
Anne Brashler, Diane Williams, and
    Margaret Barrett

Tampa Review
Box 19F
University of Tampa Press
401 W. Kennedy Boulevard
Tampa, FL 33606-1490
Semiannually, $10
Richard Mathews, Editor

The Threepenny Review
P.O. Box 9131
Berkeley, CA 94709
Quarterly, $16
Wendy Lesser

TriQuarterly
Northwestern University
2020 Ridge Avenue
Evanston, IL 60208
Triannually, $24
Reginald Gibbons

Turnstile
Suite 2348
175 Fifth Avenue
New York, NY 10010
Semiannually, $12
Editors

The Virginia Quarterly Review
One West Range
Charlottesville, VA 22903
Quarterly, $15
Staige D. Blackford

Voice Literary Supplement
VV Publishing Corp.
36 Cooper Square

New York, NY 10003
Monthly, except the combined
    issues of Dec./Jan. and
    July/Aug., $17
Lee Smith

Weber Studies
Weber State College
Ogden, UT 84408-1214
Triannually, $10
Neila C. Seshachari

West Branch
Bucknell Hall
Bucknell University
Lewisburg, PA 17837
Semiannually, $7
Robert Love Taylor

Whetstone
Barrington Area Arts Council
P.O. Box 1266
Barrington, IL 60011
Annually, $6
Sandra Berris

Wind Magazine
P.O. Box 24548
Lexington, KY 40524
Semiannually, $10
Steven R. Cope and Charlie G.
    Hughes

Window
7005 Westmoreland Drive
Takoma Park, MD 20912
Paul Deblinger

ZYZZYVA
41 Sutter Street
Suite 1400
San Francisco, CA 94104
Quarterly, $28
Howard Junker

PREVIOUS VOLUMES

Copies of previous volumes of *New Stories from the South* can be ordered through your local bookstore or by calling the Sales Department at Algonquin Books of Chapel Hill. Multiple copies for classroom adoptions are available at a special discount. For information, please call 919-967-0108.

NEW STORIES FROM THE SOUTH: THE YEAR'S BEST, 1986

Max Apple, BRIDGING

Madison Smartt Bell, TRIPTYCH 2

Mary Ward Brown, TONGUES OF FLAME

Suzanne Brown, COMMUNION

James Lee Burke, THE CONVICT

Ron Carlson, AIR

Doug Crowell, SAYS VELMA

Leon V. Driskell, MARTHA JEAN

Elizabeth Harris, THE WORLD RECORD HOLDER

Mary Hood, SOMETHING GOOD FOR GINNIE

David Huddle, SUMMER OF THE MAGIC SHOW

Gloria Norris, HOLDING ON

Kurt Rheinheimer, UMPIRE

W. A. Smith, DELIVERY

Wallace Whatley, SOMETHING TO LOSE

Luke Whisnant, WALLWORK

Sylvia Wilkinson, CHICKEN SIMON

NEW STORIES FROM THE SOUTH: THE YEAR'S BEST, 1987

James Gordon Bennett, DEPENDENTS

Robert Boswell, EDWARD AND JILL

Rosanne Coggeshall, PETER THE ROCK

John William Corrington, HEROIC MEASURES/VITAL SIGNS

Vicki Covington, MAGNOLIA

Andre Dubus, DRESSED LIKE SUMMER LEAVES

Mary Hood, AFTER MOORE

Trudy Lewis, VINCRISTINE

Lewis Nordan, SUGAR, THE EUNUCHS, AND BIG G.B.

Peggy Payne, THE PURE IN HEART

Bob Shacochis, WHERE PELHAM FELL

Lee Smith, LIFE ON THE MOON

Marly Swick, HEART

Robert Love Taylor, LADY OF SPAIN

Luke Whisnant, ACROSS FROM THE MOTOHEADS

NEW STORIES FROM THE SOUTH: THE YEAR'S BEST, 1988

Ellen Akins, GEORGE BAILEY FISHING

Rick Bass, THE WATCH

Richard Bausch, THE MAN WHO KNEW BELLE STAR

Larry Brown, FACING THE MUSIC

Pam Durban, BELONGING

John Rolfe Gardiner, GAME FARM

Jim Hall, GAS

Charlotte Holmes, METROPOLITAN

Nanci Kincaid, LIKE THE OLD WOLF IN ALL THOSE WOLF STORIES

Barbara Kingsolver, ROSE-JOHNNY

Trudy Lewis, HALF MEASURES

Jill McCorkle, FIRST UNION BLUES

Mark Richard, HAPPINESS OF THE GARDEN VARIETY

Sunny Rogers, THE CRUMB

Annette Sanford, LIMITED ACCESS

Eve Shelnutt, VOICE

NEW STORIES FROM THE SOUTH: THE YEAR'S BEST, 1989

Rick Bass, WILD HORSES

Madison Smartt Bell, CUSTOMS OF THE COUNTRY

James Gordon Bennett, PACIFIC THEATER

Larry Brown, SAMARITANS

Mary Ward Brown, IT WASN'T ALL DANCING

Kelly Cherry, WHERE SHE WAS

David Huddle, PLAYING

Sandy Huss, COUPON FOR BLOOD

Frank Manley, THE RAIN OF TERROR

Bobbie Ann Mason, WISH

Lewis Nordan, A HANK OF HAIR, A PIECE OF BONE

Kurt Rheinheimer, HOMES

Mark Richard, STRAYS

Annette Sanford, SIX WHITE HORSES

Paula Sharp, HOT SPRINGS

NEW STORIES FROM THE SOUTH: THE YEAR'S BEST, 1990

Tom Bailey, CROW MAN

Rick Bass, THE HISTORY OF RODNEY

Richard Bausch, LETTER TO THE LADY OF THE HOUSE

Larry Brown, SLEEP

Moira Crone, JUST OUTSIDE THE B.T.

Clyde Edgerton, CHANGING NAMES

Greg Johnson, THE BOARDER

Nanci Kincaid, SPITTIN' IMAGE OF A BAPTIST BOY

Reginald McKnight, THE KIND OF LIGHT THAT SHINES ON TEXAS

Lewis Nordan, THE CELLAR OF RUNT CONROY

Lance Olsen, FAMILY

Mark Richard, FEAST OF THE EARTH, RANSOM OF THE CLAY

Ron Robinson, WHERE WE LAND

Bob Shacochis, LES FEMMES CREOLES

Molly Best Tinsley, ZOE

Donna Trussell, FISHBONE

NEW STORIES FROM THE SOUTH: THE YEAR'S BEST, 1991

Rick Bass, IN THE LOYAL MOUNTAINS

Thomas Phillips Brewer, BLACK CAT BONE

Larry Brown, BIG BAD LOVE

Robert Olen Butler, RELIC

Barbara Hudson, THE ARABESQUE

Elizabeth Hunnewell, A LIFE OR DEATH MATTER

Hilding Johnson, SOUTH OF KITTATINNY

Nanci Kincaid, THIS IS NOT THE PICTURE SHOW

NEW STORIES FROM THE SOUTH: THE YEAR'S BEST, 1992

New Stories from the South: The Year's Best, 1993

Richard Bausch, EVENING

Pinckney Benedict, BOUNTY

Wendell Berry, A JONQUIL FOR MARY PENN

Robert Olen Butler, PREPARATION

Lee Merrill Byrd, MAJOR SIX POCKETS

Kevin Calder, NAME ME THIS RIVER

Tony Earley, CHARLOTTE

Paula K. Gover, WHITE BOYS AND RIVER GIRLS

David Huddle, TROUBLE AT THE HOME OFFICE

Barbara Hudson, SELLING WHISKERS

Elizabeth Hunnewell, FAMILY PLANNING

Dennis Loy Johnson, RESCUING ED

Edward P. Jones, MARIE

Wayne Karlin, PRISONERS

Dan Leone, SPINACH

Jill McCorkle, MAN WATCHER

Annette Sanford, HELENS AND ROSES

Peter Taylor, THE WAITING ROOM

New Stories from the South: The Year's Best, 1994

Frederick Barthelme, RETREAT

Richard Bausch, AREN'T YOU HAPPY FOR ME?

Ethan Canin, THE PALACE THIEF

Kathleen Cushman, LUXURY

Tony Earley, THE PROPHET FROM JUPITER

Pamela Erbe, SWEET TOOTH

Barry Hannah, NICODEMUS BLUFF

Nanci Kincaid, PRETENDING THE BED WAS A RAFT

Nancy Krusoe, LANDSCAPE AND DREAM

Robert Morgan, DARK CORNER

Reynolds Price, DEEDS OF LIGHT

Leon Rooke, THE HEART MUST FROM ITS BREAKING

John Sayles, PEELING

George Singleton, OUTLAW HEAD & TAIL

Melanie Sumner, MY OTHER LIFE

Robert Love Taylor, MY MOTHER'S SHOES

NEW STORIES FROM THE SOUTH: THE YEAR'S BEST, 1995

R. Sebastian Bennett, RIDING WITH THE DOCTOR

Wendy Brenner, I AM THE BEAR

James Lee Burke, WATER PEOPLE

Robert Olen Butler, BOY BORN WITH TATTOO OF ELVIS

Ken Craven, PAYING ATTENTION

Tim Gautreaux, THE BUG MAN

Ellen Gilchrist, THE STUCCO HOUSE

Scott Gould, BASES

Barry Hannah, DRUMMER DOWN

MMM Hayes, FIXING LU

Hillary Hebert, LADIES OF THE MARBLE HEARTH

Jesse Lee Kercheval, GRAVITY

Caroline A. Langston, IN THE DISTANCE

Lynn Marie, TEAMS

Susan Perabo, GRAVITY

Dale Ray Phillips, EVERYTHING QUIET LIKE CHURCH

Elizabeth Spencer, THE RUNAWAYS

THE BEST

Shannon Ravenel has read over 10,000 stories in her 10 years as editor of the annual anthology, **New Stories from the South.** She chose only 163 stories for inclusion in the series, which each year offers the year's best contemporary Southern short fiction.

THE BEST OF THE BEST

Now, bestselling fiction writer and short story fan Anne Tyler goes one step further. From Ravenel's 163 selections she has chosen her 20 favorites for the celebratory anniversary anthology, **Best of the South.**

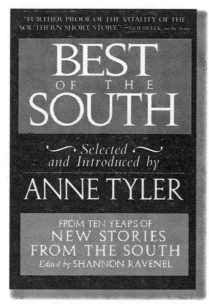

A delectable treasury of contemporary Southern literature.

Available now at bookstores everywhere.
$15.95 paper
ISBN 1-56512-128-7

RICK BASS

RICHARD BAUSCH

MADISON SMARTT BELL

JAMES LEE BURKE

LEON V. DRISKELL

TONY EARLEY

BARRY HANNAH

MARY HOOD

EDWARD P. JONES

NANCI KINCAID

PATRICIA LEAR

FRANK MANLEY

REGINALD MCKNIGHT

LEWIS NORDAN

PADGETT POWELL

MARK RICHARD

BOB SHACOCHIS

LEE SMITH

MELANIE SUMNER

MARLY SWICK